SUPERNATURAL DETECTIVES

3

SUPERNATURAL DETECTIVES

3

THE EXPERIENCES OF FLAXMAN LOW

E. and H. Heron

SOME EXPERIENCES OF LORD SYFRET

Arabella Kenealy

COACHWHIP PUBLICATIONS

Landisville, Pennsylvania

Supernatural Detectives 3: Flaxman Low / Lord Syfret
Copyright © 2011 Coachwhip Publications
No claims made on public domain material.

The Flaxman Low stories were written by E. and H. Heron, and first published from 1898-1899 in *Pearson's Magazine*, then collected in *Ghosts: Being the Experiences of Flaxman Low*. E. and H. Heron were the pseudonyms of Hesketh (1876-1922) Hesketh-Prichard and his mother, Kate Prichard (1851-1935).
The Lord Syfret stories were written by Arabella Kenealy (1859-1938), and first published 1896 in *The Ludgate Magazine*.

ISBN 1-61646-099-7
ISBN-13 978-1-61646-099-0

Front cover: Solar Eclipse © Thomas Tuchan

CoachwhipBooks.com

The Experiences of Flaxman Low

Some Experiences of Lord Syfret

THE EXPERIENCES OF
FLAXMAN LOW

INTRODUCTION

Have ghosts any existence outside our own fancy and emotions? This is the question with which the end of the century concerns itself more and more, for, though a vast amount of evidence with regard to occult phenomena already exists, the ultimate answer has yet to be supplied. In this connection it may not generally be known that, as one of the first steps towards reducing Psychology to the lines of an exact science, an attempt has been made to classify spirits and ghosts, with the result that some very bizarre and terrible theories have been put forward—things undreamt of outside the circle of the select few.

With a view to meeting the widespread interest in these matters, the following series of ghost stories is laid before the public. They have been gathered out of a large number of supernatural experiences with which Mr. Flaxman Low—under the thin disguise of which name many are sure to recognise one of the leading scientists of the day, with whose works on Psychology and kindred subjects they are familiar—has been more or less connected. He is, moreover, the first student in this field of inquiry who has had the boldness and originality to break free from old and conventional methods, and to approach the elucidation of so-called supernatural problems on the lines of natural law.

The details of these stories have been supplied by the narratives of those most concerned, supplemented by the clear and ample notes which Mr. Flaxman Low has had the courtesy to place in our hands.

For obvious reasons, the exact localities where these events are said to have happened are in every case merely indicated.

Lieutenant Roderick Houston, of H.M.S. *Sphinx*, had practically nothing beyond his pay, and he was beginning to be very tired of the West African station, when he received the pleasant intelligence that a relative had left him a legacy. This consisted of a satisfactory sum in ready money and a house in Hammersmith, which was rated at over £200 a year, and was said in addition to be comfortably furnished. Houston, therefore, counted on its rental to bring his income up to a fairly desirable figure. Further information from home, however, showed him that he had been rather premature in his expectations, whereupon, being a man of action, he applied for two months' leave, and came home to look after his affairs himself.

When he had been a week in London he arrived at the conclusion that he could not possibly hope single-handed to tackle the difficulties which presented themselves. He accordingly wrote the following letter to his friend, Flaxman Low:

"The Spaniards, Hammersmith,

23-3-1892.

"Dear Low,—Since we parted some three years ago, I have heard very little of you. It was only yesterday that I met our mutual friend, Sammy Smith ('Silkworm' of our schooldays) who told me that your studies have developed in a new direction, and that you are now a good deal interested in psychical subjects. If this be so, I hope to induce you to come and stay with me here for a few days by promising to introduce you to a problem in your own line. I am just now living at 'The Spaniards,' a house that has lately been left to me, and which in the first instance was built by an old fellow named Van Nuysen, who married a great-aunt of mine. It is a good house, but there is said to be 'something wrong' with it. It lets easily, but unluckily the tenants cannot be persuaded to remain above a week or two. They complain that the place is haunted by something— presumably a ghost—because its vagaries bear just that brand of inconsequence which stamps the common run of manifestations.

"It occurs to me that you may care to investigate the matter with me. If so, send me a wire when to expect you.   Yours ever,

"Roderick Houston."

Houston waited in some anxiety for an answer. Low was the sort of man one could rely on in almost any emergency. Sammy Smith had told him a characteristic anecdote of Low's career at Oxford, where, although his intellectual triumphs may be forgotten, he will always be remembered by the story that when Sands, of Queen's, fell ill on the day before the 'Varsity sports, a telegram was sent to Low's rooms: "Sands ill. You must do the hammer for us." Low's reply was pithy: "I'll be there." Thereupon he finished the treatise upon which he was engaged, and next day his strong, lean figure was to be seen swinging the hammer amidst vociferous cheering, for that was the occasion on which he not only won the event, but beat the record.

On the fifth day Low's answer came from Vienna. As he read it, Houston recalled the high forehead, long neck—with its accompanying low collar—and thin moustache of his scholarly, athletic friend, and smiled. There was so much more in Flaxman Low than anyone gave him credit for.

"My Dear Houston,—Very glad to hear of you again. In response to your kind invitation, I thank you for the opportunity of meeting the ghost, and still more for the pleasure of your companionship. I came here to inquire into a somewhat similar affair. I hope, however, to be able to leave to-morrow, and will be with you some time on Friday evening.

"Very sincerely yours,

"Flaxman Low."

"P.S.—By the way, will it be convenient to give your servants a holiday during the term of my visit, as, if my investigations are to be of any value, not a grain of dust must be disturbed in your house, excepting by ourselves?—F.L."

The Spaniards was within some fifteen minutes' walk of Hammersmith Bridge. Set in the midst of a fairly respectable neighbourhood, it presented an odd contrast to the commonplace dullness of the narrow streets crowded about it. As Flaxman Low drove up in the evening light, he reflected that the house might have come from the back of beyond—it gave an impression of something old-world and something exotic.

It was surrounded by a ten-foot wall, above which the upper storey was visible, and Low decided that this intensely English house still gave some curious suggestion of the tropics. The interior of the house carried out the same idea, with its sense of space and air, cool tints and wide, matted passages.

"So you have seen something yourself since you came?" Low said, as they sat at dinner, for Houston had arranged that meals should be sent in for them from an hotel.

"I've heard tapping up and down the passage upstairs. It is an uncarpeted landing which runs the whole length of the house. One night, when I was quicker than usual, I saw what looked like a bladder disappear into one of the bedrooms—your room it is to be, by the way—and the door closed behind it," replied Houston discontentedly. "The usual meaningless antics of a ghost."

"What had the tenants who lived here to say about it?" went on Low.

"Most of the people saw and heard just what I have told you, and promptly went away. The only one who stood out for a little while was old Filderg—you know the man? Twenty years ago he made an effort to cross the Australian deserts—he stopped for eight weeks. When he left he saw the house-agent, and said he was afraid he had done a little shooting practice in the upper passage, and he hoped it wouldn't count against him in the bill, as it was done in defence of his life. He said something had jumped on to the bed and tried to strangle him. He described it as cold and glutinous, and he pursued it down the passage, firing at it. He advised the owner to have the house pulled down; but, of course, my cousin did nothing of the kind. It's a very good house, and he did not see the sense of spoiling his property."

"That's very true," replied Flaxman Low, looking round. "Mr. Van Nuysen had been in the West Indies, and kept his liking for spacious rooms."

"Where did you hear anything about him?" asked Houston in surprise.

"I have heard nothing beyond what you told me in your letter; but I see a couple of bottles of Gulf weed and a lace-plant ornament, such as people used to bring from the West Indies in former days."

"Perhaps I should tell you the history of the old man," said Houston doubtfully; "but we aren't proud of it!"

Flaxman Low considered a moment.

"When was the ghost seen for the first time?"

"When the first tenant took the house. It was let after old Van Nuysen's time."

"Then it may clear the way if you will tell me something of him."

"He owned sugar plantations in Trinidad, where he passed the greater part of his life, while his wife mostly remained in England— incompatibility of temper it was said. When he came home for good and built this house they still lived apart, my aunt declaring that nothing on earth would persuade her to return to him. In course of time he became a confirmed invalid, and he then insisted on my aunt joining him. She lived here for perhaps a year, when she was found dead in bed one morning—in your room."

"What caused her death?"

"She had been in the habit of taking narcotics, and it was supposed that she smothered herself while under their influence."

"That doesn't sound very satisfactory," remarked Flaxman Low.

"Her husband was satisfied with it anyhow, and it was no one else's business. The family were only too glad to have the affair hushed up."

"And what became of Mr. Van Nuysen?"

"That I can't tell you. He disappeared a short time after. Search was made for him in the usual way, but nobody knows to this day what became of him."

"Ah, that was strange, as he was such an invalid," said Low, and straightway fell into a long fit of abstraction, from which he was roused by hearing Houston curse the incurable foolishness and imbecility of ghostly behaviour. Flaxman woke up at this. He broke a walnut thoughtfully and began in a gentle voice:

"My dear fellow, we are apt to be hasty in our condemnation of the general behaviour of ghosts. It may appear incalculably foolish in our eyes, and I admit there often seems to be a total absence of any apparent object or intelligent action. But remember that what appears to us to be foolishness may be wisdom in the spirit world, since our unready senses can only catch broken glimpses of what is, I have not the slightest doubt, a coherent whole, if we could trace the connection."

"There may be something in that," replied Houston indifferently. "People naturally say that this ghost is the ghost of old Van Nuysen. But what connection can possibly exist between what I have told you of him and the manifestations—a tapping up and down the passage and the drawing about of a bladder like a child at play? It sounds idiotic!"

"Certainly. Yet it need not necessarily be so. There are isolated facts, we must look for the links which lie between. Suppose a saddle and a horse-shoe were to be shown to a man who had never seen a horse, I doubt whether he, however intelligent, could evolve the connecting idea! The ways of spirits are strange to us simply because we need further data to help us to interpret them."

"It's a new point of view," returned Houston, "but upon my word, you know, Low, I think you're wasting your time!"

Flaxman Low smiled slowly; his grave, melancholy face brightened.

"I have," said he, "gone somewhat deeply into the subject. In other sciences one reasons by analogy. Psychology is unfortunately a science with a future but without a past, or more probably it is a lost science of the ancients. However that may be, we stand to-day on the frontier of an unknown world, and progress is the result of individual effort; each solution of difficult phenomena forms a step towards the solution of the next problem. In this case, for example, the bladder-like object may be the key to the mystery."

Houston yawned.

"It all seems pretty senseless, but perhaps you may be able to read reason into it. If it were anything tangible, anything a man could meet with his fists, it would be easier."

"I entirely agree with you. But suppose we deal with this affair as it stands, on similar lines, I mean on prosaic, rational lines, as we should deal with a purely human mystery."

"My dear fellow," returned Houston, pushing his chair back from the table wearily, "you shall do just as you like, only get rid of the ghost!"

For some time after Low's arrival nothing very special happened. The tappings continued, and more than once Low had been in time to see the bladder disappear into the closing door of his bedroom, though, unluckily, he never chanced to be inside the room on these occasions, and however quickly he followed the bladder, he never succeeded in seeing anything further. He made a thorough examination of the house, and left no space unaccounted for in his careful measurement. There were no cellars, and the foundation of the house consisted of a thick layer of concrete.

At length, on the sixth night, an event took place, which, as Flaxman Low remarked, came very near to putting an end to the investigations as far as he was concerned. For the preceding two nights he and Houston had kept watch in the hope of getting a glimpse of the person or thing which tapped so persistently up and down the passage. But they were disappointed, for there were no manifestations. On the third evening, therefore, Low went off to his room a little earlier than usual, and fell asleep almost immediately.

He says he was awakened by feeling a heavy weight upon his feet, something that seemed inert and motionless. He recollected that he had left the gas burning, but the room was now in darkness.

Next he was aware that the thing on the bed had slowly shifted, and was gradually travelling up towards his chest. How it came on the bed he had no idea. Had it leaped or climbed? The sensation he experienced as it moved was of some ponderous, pulpy body, not crawling or creeping, but spreading! It was horrible! He tried to move his lower limbs, but could not because of the deadening weight. A feeling of drowsiness began to overpower him, and a deadly cold, such as he said he had before felt at sea when in the neighbourhood of icebergs, chilled upon the air.

With a violent struggle he managed to free his arms, but the thing grew more irresistible as it spread upwards. Then he became conscious of a pair of glassy eyes, with livid, everted lids, looking into his own. Whether they were human eyes or beast eyes, he could not tell, but they were watery, like the eyes of a dead fish, and gleamed with a pale, internal lustre.

Then he owns he grew afraid. But he was still cool enough to notice one peculiarity about this ghastly visitant—although the head was within a few inches of his own, he could detect no breathing. It dawned on him that he was about to be suffocated, for, by the same method of extension, the thing was now coming over his face! It felt cold and clammy, like a mass of mucilage or a monstrous snail. And every instant the weight became greater. He is a powerful man, and he struck with his fists again and again at the head. Some substance yielded under the blows with a sickening sensation of bruised flesh.

With a lucky twist he raised himself in the bed and battered away with all the force he was capable of in his cramped position. The only effect was an occasional shudder or quake that ran through the mass as his half-arm blows rained upon it. At last, by chance, his hand knocked against the candle beside him. In a moment he recollected the matches. He seized the box, and struck a light.

As he did so, the lump slid to the floor. He sprang out of bed, and lit the candle. He felt a cold touch upon his leg, but when he looked down there was nothing to be seen. The door, which he had locked overnight, was now open, and he rushed out into the passage. All was still and silent with the throbbing vacancy of night time.

After searching round, he returned to his room. The bed still gave ample proof of the struggle that had taken place, and by his watch he saw the hour to be between two and three.

As there seemed nothing more to be done, he put on his dressing-gown, lit his pipe, and sat down to write an account of the experience he had just passed through for the Psychical Research Society—from which paper the above is an abstract.

He is a man of strong nerves, but he could not disguise from himself that he had been at handgrips with some grotesque form of death. What might be the nature of his assailant he could not determine, but his experience was supported by the attack which had been made on Filderg, and also—it was impossible to avoid the conclusion—by the manner of Mrs. Van Nuysen's death.

He thought the whole situation over carefully in connection with the tapping and the disappearing bladder, but, turn these events how he would, he could make nothing of them. They were entirely incongruous. A little later he went and made a shakedown in Houston's room.

"What was the thing?" asked Houston, when Low had ended his story of the encounter.

Low shrugged his shoulders.

"At least it proves that Filderg did not dream," he said.

"But this is monstrous! We are more in the dark than ever. There's nothing for it but to have the house pulled down. Let us leave to-day."

"Don't be in a hurry, my dear fellow. You would rob me of a very great pleasure; besides, we may be on the verge of some valuable discovery. This series of manifestations is even more interesting than the Vienna mystery I was telling you of."

"Discovery or not," replied the other, "I don't like it."

The first thing next morning Low went out for a quarter of an hour. Before breakfast a man with a barrowful of sand came into the garden. Low looked up from his paper, leant out of the window, and gave some order.

When Houston came down a few minutes later he saw the yellowish heap on the lawn with some surprise.

"Hullo! What's this?" he asked.

"I ordered it," replied Low.

"All right. What's it for?"

"To help us in our investigations. Our visitor is capable of being felt, and he or it left a very distinct impression on the bed. Hence I gather it can also leave an impression on sand. It would be an immense advance if we could arrive at any correct notion of what sort of feet the ghost walks on. I propose to spread a layer of this sand in the upper passage, and the result should be footmarks if the tapping comes to-night."

That evening the two men made a fire in Houston's bedroom, and sat there smoking and talking, to leave the ghost "a free run for once," as Houston phrased it. The tapping was heard at the usual hour, and presently the accustomed pause at the other end of the passage and the quiet closing of the door.

Low heaved a long sigh of satisfaction as he listened.

"That's my bedroom door," he said; "I know the sound of it perfectly. In the morning, and with the help of daylight, we shall see what we shall see."

As soon as there was light enough for the purpose of examining the footprints, Low roused Houston.

Houston was full of excitement as a boy, but his spirits fell by the time he had passed from end to end of the passage.

"There are marks," he said, "but they are as perplexing as everything else about this haunting brute, whatever it is. I suppose you think this is the print left by the thing which attacked you the night before last?"

"I fancy it is," said Low, who was still bending over the floor eagerly. "What do you make of it, Houston?"

"The brute has only one leg, to start with," replied Houston, "and that leaves the mark of a large, clawless pad! It's some animal—some ghoulish monster!"

"On the contrary," said Low, "I think we have now every reason to conclude that it is a man."

"A man? What man ever left footmarks like these?"

"Look at these hollows and streaks at the sides; they are the traces of the sticks we have heard tapping."

"You don't convince me," returned Hodgson doggedly.

"Let us wait another twenty-four hours, and to-morrow night, if nothing further occurs, I will give you my conclusions. Think it over. The tapping, the bladder, and the fact that Mr. Van Nuysen had lived in Trinidad. Add to these things this single pad-like print. Does nothing strike you by way of a solution?"

Houston shook his head.

"Nothing. And I fail to connect any of these things with what happened both to you and Filderg."

"Ah! now," said Flaxman Low, his face clouding a little, "I confess you lead me into a somewhat different region, though to me the connection is perfect."

Houston raised his eyebrows and laughed.

"If you can unravel this tangle of hints and events and diagnose the ghost, I shall be extremely astonished," he said. "What can you make of the footless impression?"

"Something, I hope. In fact, that mark may be a clue—an outrageous one, perhaps, but still a clue."

That evening the weather broke, and by night the storm had risen to a gale, accompanied by sharp bursts of rain.

"It's a noisy night," remarked Houston; "I don't suppose we'll hear the ghost, supposing it does turn up."

This was after dinner, as they were about to go into the smoking-room. Houston, finding the gas low in the hall, stopped to run it higher; at the same time asking Low to see if the jet on the upper landing was also alight.

Flaxman Low glanced up and uttered a slight exclamation, which brought Houston to his side.

Looking down at them from over the banisters was a face—a blotched, yellowish face, flanked by two swollen, protruding ears, the whole aspect being strangely leonine. It was but a glimpse, a clash of meeting glances, as it were, a glare of defiance, and the face was quickly withdrawn as the two men literally leapt up the stairs.

"There's nothing here," exclaimed Houston, after a search had been carried out through every room above.

"I didn't suppose we'd find anything," returned Low.

"This fairly knots up the thread," said Houston. "You can't pretend to unravel it now."

"Come down," said Low briefly; "I'm ready to give you my opinion, such as it is."

Once in the smoking-room, Houston busied himself in turning on all the light he could procure, then he saw to securing the windows, and piled up an immense fire, while Flaxman Low, who, as usual, had a cigarette in his mouth, sat on the edge of the table and watched him with some amusement.

"You saw that abominable face?" cried Houston, as he threw himself into a chair. "It was as material as yours or mine. But where did he go to? He must be somewhere about."

"We saw him clearly. That is sufficient for our purpose."

"You are very good at enumerating points, Low. Now just listen to my list. The difficulties grow with every fresh discovery. We're at a deadlock now, I take it? The sticks and the tapping point to an old man, the playing with a bladder to a child; the footmark might be the pad of a tiger minus claws, yet the thing that attacked you at night was cold and pulpy. And, lastly, by way of a wind-up, we see a lion-like, human face! If you can make all these items square with each other, I'll be happy to hear what you have got to say."

"You must first allow me to ask you a question. I understood you to say that no blood relationship existed between you and old Mr. Van Nuysen?"

"Certainly not. He was quite an outsider," answered Houston brusquely.

"In that case you are welcome to my conclusions. All the things you have mentioned point to one explanation. This house is haunted by the ghost of Mr. Van Nuysen, and he was a leper."

Houston stood up and stared at his companion.

"What a horrible notion! I must say I fail to see how you have arrived at such a conclusion."

"Take the chain of evidence in rather different order," said Low. "Why should a man tap with a stick?"

"Generally because he's blind."

"In cases of blindness, one stick is used for guidance. Here we have two for support."

"A man who has lost the use of his feet."

"Exactly; a man who has from some cause partially lost the use of his feet."

"But the bladder and the lion-like face?" went on Houston.

"The bladder, or what seemed to us to resemble a bladder, was one of his feet, contorted by the disease and probably swathed in linen, which foot he dragged rather than used; consequently, in passing through a door, for example, he would in the habit of drawing it in after him. Now, as regards the single footmark we saw. In one form of leprosy, the smaller bones of the extremities frequently fall away. The pad-like impression was, as I believe, the mark of the other foot—a toeless foot which he used, because in a more advanced stage of the disease the maimed hand or foot heals and becomes callous."

"Go on," said Houston; "it sounds as if it might be true. And the lion-like face I can account for myself. I have been in China, and have seen it before in lepers."

"Mr. Van Nuysen had been in Trinidad for many years, as we know, and while there he probably contracted the disease."

"I suppose so. After his return," added Houston, "he shut himself up almost entirely, and gave out that he was a martyr to rheumatic gout, this awful thing being the true explanation."

"It also accounts for Mrs. Van Nuysen's determination not to return to her husband."

Houston appeared much disturbed.

"We can't drop it here, Low," he said, in a constrained voice. "There is a good deal more to be cleared up yet. Can you tell me more?"

"From this point I find myself on less certain ground," replied Low unwillingly. "I merely offer a suggestion, remember—I don't ask you to accept it. I believe Mrs. Van Nuysen was murdered!"

"What?" exclaimed Houston. "By her husband?"

"Indications tend that way."

"But, my good fellow—"

"He suffocated her and then made away with himself. It is a pity that his body was not recovered. The condition of the remains would be the only really satisfactory test of my theory. If the skeleton could even now be found, the fact that he was a leper would be finally settled."

There was a prolonged pause until Houston put another question.

"Wait a minute, Low," he said. "Ghosts are admittedly immaterial. In this instance our spook has an extremely palpable body. Surely this is rather unusual? You have made everything else more or less plain. Can you tell me why this dead leper should have tried to murder you and old Filderg? And also how he came to have the actual physical power to do so?"

Low removed his cigarette to look thoughtfully at the end of it. "Now I lapse into the purely theoretical," he answered. "Cases have been known where the assumption of diabolical agency is apparently justifiable."

"Diabolical agency?—I don't follow you."

"I will try to make myself clear, though the subject is still in a stage of vagueness and immaturity. Van Nuysen committed a murder of exceptional atrocity, and afterwards killed himself. Now, bodies of suicides are known to be peculiarly susceptible to spiritual influences, even to the point of arrested corruption. Add to this our knowledge that the highest aim of an evil spirit is to gain possession of a material body. If I carried out my theory to its logical conclusion, I should say that Van Nuysen's body is hidden somewhere on these premises—that this body is intermittently animated by some spirit, which at certain points is forced to re-enact the gruesome tragedy of the Van Nuysens. Should any living person chance to occupy the position of the first victim, so much the worse for him!"

For some minutes Houston made no remark on this singular expression of opinion.

"But have you ever met with anything of the sort before?" he said at last.

"I can recall," replied Flaxman Low thoughtfully, "quite a number of cases which would seem to bear out this hypothesis. Among them a curious problem of haunting exhaustively examined by Busner in the early part of 1888, at which I was myself lucky enough to assist. Indeed, I may add that the affair which I have recently engaged upon in Vienna offers some rather similar features. There, however, we had to stop short of excavation, by which alone any specific results might have been attained."

"Then you are of the opinion," said Houston, "that pulling the house to pieces might cast some further light upon this affair?"

"I cannot see any better course," said Mr. Low.

Then Houston closed the discussion by a very definite declaration.

"This house shall come down!"

So The Spaniards was pulled down.

Such is the story of The Spaniards, Hammersmith, and it has been given the first place in this series because, although it may not be of so strange a nature as some that will follow it, yet it seems to us to embody in a high degree the peculiar methods by which Mr. Flaxman Low is wont to approach these cases.

The work of demolition, begun at the earliest possible moment, did not occupy very long, and during its early stages, under the boarding at an angle of the landing was found a skeleton. Several of the phalanges were missing, and other indications also established beyond a doubt the fact that the remains were the remains of a leper.

The skeleton is now in the museum of one of our city hospitals. It bears a scientific ticket, and is the only evidence extant of the correctness of Mr. Flaxman Low's methods and the possible truth of his extraordinary theories.

THE STORY OF MEDHANS LEA

The following story has been put together from the account of
the affair given by Nare-Jones, sometime house-surgeon at Bart's,
of his strange terror and experiences both in Medhans Lea and the
pallid avenue between the beeches; of the narrative of Savelsan, of
what he saw and heard in the billiard-room and afterwards; of the
silent and indisputable witness of big, bullnecked Harland himself;
and, lastly, of the conversation which subsequently took place
between these three men and Mr. Flaxman Low, the noted psychologist.

It was by the merest chance that Harland and his two guests
spent that memorable evening of the 18th of January, 1889, in the
house of Medhans Lea. The house stands on the slope of a partially
wooded ridge in one of the Midland Counties. It faces south, and
overlooks a wide valley bounded by the blue outlines of the Bredon
hills. The place is secluded, the nearest dwelling being a small
public-house at the cross roads some mile and a half from the lodge
gates.

Medhans Lea is famous for its long straight avenue of beeches,
and for other things. Harland, when he signed the lease, was
thinking of the avenue of beeches; not of the other things, of which
he knew nothing until later.

Harland made his money by running tea plantations in Assam,
and he owned all the virtues and faults of a man who has spent
most of his life abroad. The first time he visited the house he
weighed seventeen stone and ended most of his sentences with

"don't yer know?" His ideas could hardly be said to travel on the higher planes of thought, and his chief aim in life was to keep himself down to the seventeen stone. He had a red neck and a blue eye, and was a muscular, inoffensive, good-natured man, with courage to spare, and an excellent voice for accompanying the banjo.

After signing the lease, he found that Medhans Lea needed an immense amount of putting in order and decorating. While this was being done, he came backwards and forwards to the nearest provincial town, where he stopped at a hotel, driving out almost daily to superintend the arrangements of his new habitation. Thus he had been away for the Christmas and New Year, but about the 15th January he returned to The Red Lion, accompanied by his friends Nare-Jones and Savelsan, who proposed to move with him into his new house during the course of the ensuing week.

The immediate cause of their visit to Medhans Lea on the evening of the 18th inst. was the fact that the billiard table at The Red Lion was not fit, as Harland remarked, to play shinty on, while there was an excellent table just put in at Medhans Lea, where the big billiard-room in the left wing had a wide window with a view down a portion of the beech avenue.

"Hang it!" said Harland, "I wish they would hurry up with the house. The painters aren't out of it yet, and the people don't come to the Lodge till Monday."

"It's a pity, too," remarked Savelsan regretfully, "when you think of that table."

Savelsan was an enthusiast in billiards, who spent all the time he could spare from his business, which happened to be tea-broking, at the game. He was the more sorry for the delay, since Harland was one of the few men he knew to whom it was not necessary to give points.

"It's a ripping table," returned Harland. "Tell you what," he added, struck by a happy idea, "I'll send out Thoms to make things straight for us tomorrow, and we'll put a case of syphons and a bottle of whisky under the seat of the trap, and drive over for a game after dinner."

The other two agreed to this arrangement, but in the morning Nare-Jones found himself obliged to run up to London to see about securing a berth as ship's doctor. It was settled, however, that on his return he was to follow Harland and Savelsan to Medhans Lea.

He got back by the 8.30, entirely delighted, because he had booked a steamer bound for the Persian Gulf and Karachi, and had gained the cheering intelligence that a virulent type of cholera was lying in wait for the advent of the Mecca pilgrims in at any rate two of the chief ports of call, which would give him precisely the experience he desired.

Having dined, and the night being fine, he ordered a dogcart to take him out to Medhans Lea. The moon had just risen by the time he reached the entrance to the avenue, and as he was beginning to feel cold he pulled up, intending to walk to the house. Then he dismissed the boy and cart, a carriage having been ordered to come for the whole party after midnight. Nare-Jones stopped to light a cigar before entering the avenue, then he walked past the empty lodge. He moved briskly in the best possible temper with himself and all the world. The night was still, and his collar up, his feet fell silently on the dry carriage road, while his mind was away on blue water forecasting his voyage on the S.S. *Sumatra*.

He says he was quite halfway up the avenue before he became conscious of anything unusual. Looking up at the sky, he noticed what a bright, clear night it was, and how well defined the outline of the beeches stood out against the vault of heaven. The moon was yet low, and threw netted shadows of bare twigs and branches on the road which ran between black lines of trees in an almost straight vista up to the dead grey face of the house now barely two hundred yards away. Altogether it struck him as forming a pallid picture, etched in like a steel engraving in black, and grey, and white.

He was thinking of this when he was aware of words spoken rapidly in his ear, and he turned half expecting to see someone behind him. No one was visible. He had not caught the words, nor could he define the voice; but a vague conviction of some horrible meaning fixed itself in his consciousness.

The night was very still, ahead of him the house glimmered grey and shuttered in the moonlight. He shook himself, and walked on oppressed by a novel sensation compounded of disgust and childish fear; and still, from behind his shoulder, came the evil, voiceless murmuring.

He admits that he passed the end of the avenue at an amble, and was abreast of a semi-circle of shrubbery, when a small object was thrust out from the shadow of the bushes, and lay in the open light. Though the night was peculiarly still, it fluttered and balanced a moment, as if windblown, then came in skimming flights to his feet. He picked it up and made for the door, which yielded to his hand, and he flung it to and bolted it behind him.

Once in the warmly lit hall his senses returned, and he waited to recover breath and composure before facing the two men whose voices and laughter came from a room on his right. But the door of the room was thrown open, and the burly figure of Harland in his shirt sleeves appeared on the threshold.

"Hullo, Jones, that you? Come along!" he said genially.

"Bless me!" exclaimed Nare-Jones irritably, "there's not a light in any of the windows. It might be a house of the dead!"

Harland stared at him, but all he said was: "Have a whisky-and-soda?"

Savelsan, who was leaning over the billiard table, trying side-strokes with his back to Nare-Jones, added:

"Did you expect us to illuminate the place for you? There's not a soul in the house but ourselves."

"Say when," said Harland, poising the bottle over a glass. Nare-Jones laid down what he held in his hand on the corner of the billiard table, and took up his glass.

"What in creation's this?" asked Savelsan.

"I don't know; the wind blew it to my feet just outside," replied Nare-Jones, between two long pulls at the whisky-and-soda.

"Blown to your feet?" repeated Savelsan, taking up the thing and weighing it in his hand. "It must be blowing a hurricane then."

"It isn't blowing at all," returned Nare-Jones blankly. "The night is dead calm."

For the object that had fluttered and rolled so lightly across the turf and gravel was a small, battered, metal calf, made of some heavy brass amalgam.

Savelsan looked incredulously into Nare-Jones's face, and laughed.

"What's wrong with you? You look queer."

Nare-Jones laughed too; he was already ashamed of the last ten minutes.

Harland was meantime examining the metal calf.

"It's a Bengali idol," he said. "It's been knocked about a good bit, by Jove! You say it blew out of the shrubbery?"

"Like a bit of paper, I give you my word, though there was not a breath of wind going," admitted Nare-Jones.

"Seems odd, don't yer know?" remarked Harland carelessly. "Now you two fellows had better begin; I'll mark."

Nare-Jones happened to be in form that night, and Savelsan became absorbed in the delightful difficulty of giving him a sound thrashing.

Suddenly Savelsan paused in his stroke.

"What the sin's that?" he asked.

They stood listening. A thin, broken crying could be heard. "Sounds like green plover," remarked Nare-Jones, chalking his cue.

"It's a kitten they've shut up somewhere," said Harland.

"That's a child, and in the deuce of a fright, too," said Savelsan. "You'd better go and tuck it up in its little bed, Harland," he added, with a laugh.

Harland opened the door. There could no longer be any doubt about the sounds; the stifled shrieks and thin whimpering told of a child in the extremity of pain or fear.

"It's upstairs," said Harland. "I'm going to see."

Nare-Jones picked up a lamp and followed him.

"I stay here," said Savelsan, sitting down by the fire.

In the hall the two men stopped and listened again. It is hard to locate a noise, but this seemed to come from the upper landing.

"Poor little beggar!" exclaimed Harland, as he bounded up the staircase. The bedroom doors opening on the square central landing above were all locked, the keys being on the outside. But the crying led them into a side passage which ended in a single room.

"It's in here, and the door's locked," said Nare-Jones. "Call out and see who's there."

But Harland was set on business. He flung his weight against the panel, and the door burst open, the lock ricochetting noisily into a corner. As they passed in, the crying ceased abruptly.

Harland stood in the centre of the room, while Nare-Jones held up the light to look round.

"The dickens!" exclaimed Harland exhaustively.

The room was entirely empty.

Not so much as a cupboard broke the smooth surface of the walls, only the two low windows and the door by which they had entered.

"This is the room above the billiard-room, isn't it?" said Nare-Jones at last.

"Yes. This is the only one I have not had furnished yet. I thought I might—"

He stopped short, for behind them burst out a peal of harsh, mocking laughter, that rang and echoed between the bare walls.

Both men swung round simultaneously, and both caught a glimpse of a tall, thin figure in black, rocking with laughter in the doorway, but when they turned it was gone. They dashed out into the passage and landing. No one was to be seen. The doors were locked as before, and the staircase and hall were vacant.

After making a prolonged search through every corner of the house, they went back to Savelsan in the billiard-room.

"What were you laughing about? What is it anyway?" began Savelson at once.

"It's nothing. And we didn't laugh," replied Nare-Jones definitely.

"But I heard you," insisted Savelsan. "And where's the child?"

"I wish you'd go up and find it," returned Harland grimly. "We heard the laughing and saw, or thought we saw, a man in black—"

"Something like a priest in a cassock," put in Nare-Jones.

"Yes, like a priest," assented Harland, "but as we turned he disappeared."

Savelsan sat down and gazed from one to the other of his companions.

"The house behaves as if it was haunted," he remarked; "only there is no such thing as an authenticated ghost outside the experiences of the Psychical Research Society. I'd ask the Society down if I were you, Harland. You never can tell what you may find in these old houses."

"It's not an old house," replied Harland. "It was built somewhere about '40. I certainly saw that man; and, look to it, Savelsan, I'll find out who or what he is. That I swear! The English law makes no allowance for ghosts—nor will I."

"You'll have your hands full, or I'm mistaken," exclaimed Savelsan, grinning. "A ghost that laughs and cries in a breath, and rolls battered idols about your front door, is not to be trifled with. The night is young yet—not much past eleven. I vote for a peg all round and then I'll finish off Jones."

Harland, sunk in a fit of sullen abstraction, sat on a settee, and watched them. On a sudden he said:

"It's turned beastly cold."

"There's a beastly smell, you mean," corrected Savelsan crossly, as he went round the table. He had made a break of forty and did not want to be interrupted. "The draught is from the window."

"I've not noticed it before this evening," said Harland, as he opened the shutters to make sure.

As he did so the night air rushed in heavy with the smell as of an old well that has not been uncovered for years, a smell of slime and unwholesome wetness. The lower part of the window was wide open and Harland banged it down.

"It's abominable!" he said, with an angry sniff. "Enough to give us all typhoid."

"Only dead leaves," remarked Nare-Jones. "There are the rotten leaves of twenty winters under the trees and outside this window. I noticed them when we came over on Tuesday."

"I'll have them cleared away tomorrow. I wonder how Thoms came to leave this window open," grumbled Harland, as he closed and bolted the shutter. "What do you say—forty-five?" and he went over to mark it up.

The game went on for some time, and Nare-Jones was lying across the table with the cue poised, when he heard a slight sound behind him. Looking round, he saw Harland, his face flushed and angry, passing softly—wonderfully softly for so big a man, Nare-Jones remembers thinking—along the angle of the wall towards the window.

All three men unite in declaring that they were watching the shutter, which opened inwards as if thrust by some furtive hand from outside. At the moment Nare-Jones and Savelsan were standing directly opposite to it on the further side of the table, while Harland crouched behind the shutter intent on giving the intruder a lesson.

As the shutter unfolded to its utmost the two men opposite saw a face pressed against the glass, a furrowed evil face, with a wide laugh perched upon its sinister features.

There was a second of absolute stillness, and Nare-Jones's eyes met those other eyes with the fascinated horror of a mutual understanding, as all the foul fancies that had pursued him in the avenue poured back into his mind.

With an uncontrollable impulse of resentment, he snatched a billiard ball from the table and flung it with all his strength at the face. The ball crashed through the glass and through—the face beyond it! The glass fell shattered, but the face remained for an instant peering and grinning at the aperture, then as Harland sprang forward it was gone.

"The ball went clean through it!" said Savelsan with a gasp.

They crowded to the window, and throwing up the sash, leant out. The dank smell clung about the air, a boat-shaped moon glimmered between the bare branches, and on the white drive beyond the shrubbery the billiard ball could be seen a shining spot under the moon. Nothing more.

"What was it?" asked Harland.

"'Only a face at the window,'" quoted Savelsan with an awkward attempt at making light of his own scare. "Devilish queer face too, eh, Jones?"

"I wish I'd got him!" returned Harland, frowning. "I'm not going to put up with any tricks about the place, don't yer know?"

"You'd bottle any tramp loafing round," said Nare-Jones.

Harland looked down at his immense arms outlined in his shirt-sleeves.

"I could that," he answered. "But this chap—did you hit him?"

"Clean through the face! or, at any rate, it looked like it," replied Savelsan, as Nare-Jones stood silent.

Harland shut the shutter and poked up the fire.

"It's a cursed creepy affair!" he said, "I hope the servants won't get hold of this nonsense. Ghosts play the very mischief with a house. Though I don't believe in them myself, don't yer know?" he concluded.

Then Savelsan broke out in an unexpected place.

"Nor do I—as a rule," he said slowly. "Still you know it is a sickening idea to think of a spirit condemned to haunt the scene of its crime waiting for the world to die."

Harland and Nare-Jones looked at him.

"Have a whisky neat," suggested Harland soothingly. "I never knew you taken that way before."

Nare-Jones laughed out. He says he does not know why he laughed nor why he said what follows.

"It's this way," he said. "The moment of foul satisfaction is gone for ever, yet for all time the guilty spirit must perpetuate its sin— the sin that brought no lasting reward, only a momentary reward experienced, it may be, centuries ago, but to which still clings the punishment of eternally rehearsing in loneliness, and cold, and gloom, the sin of other days. No punishment can be conceived more horrible. Savelsan is right."

"I think we've had enough about ghosts," said Harland cheerfully, "let's go on. Hurry up, Savelsan."

"There's the billiard ball," said Nare-Jones. "Who'll go fetch?"

"Not I," replied Savelsan promptly. "When that—was at the window, I felt sick."

Nare-Jones nodded. "And I wanted to bolt!" he said emphatically.

Harland faced about from the fire.

"And I, though I saw nothing but the shutter, I—hang it!—don't yer know—so did I! There was panic in the air for a minute. But I'm shot if I'm afraid now," he concluded doggedly, "I'll go."

His heavy animal face was lit with courage and resolution. "I've spent close upon five thousand pounds over this blessed house first and last, and I'm not going to be done out of it by any infernal spiritualism!" he added, as he took down his coat and pulled it on.

"It's all in view from the window except those few yards through the shrubbery," said Savelsan. "Take a stick and go. Though, on second thoughts, I bet you a flyer you don't."

"I don't want a stick," answered Harland. "I'm not afraid—not now—and I'd meet most men with my hands."

Nare-Jones opened the shutters again; the sash was low, and he pushed the window up and leant far out.

"It's not much of a drop," he said, and slung his legs out over the lintel; but the night was full of the smell, and something else. He leapt back into the room. "Don't go, Harland!"

Harland gave him a look that set his blood burning.

"What is there, after all, to be afraid of in a ghost?" he asked heavily.

Nare-Jones, sick with the sense of his own newly-born cowardice, yet entirely unable to master it, answered feebly:

"I can't say, but don't go."

The words seemed inevitable, though he could have kicked himself for hanging back.

There was a forced laugh from Savelsan.

"Give it up and stop at home, little man," he said.

Harland merely snorted in reply, and laid his great leg over the window ledge. The other two watched his big, tweed-clad figure as it crossed the grass and disappeared into the shrubbery.

"You and I are in a preposterous funk," said Savelsan, with unpleasant explicitness, as Harland, whistling loudly, passed into the shadow.

But this was a point on which Nare-Jones could not bring himself to speak at that moment. Then they sat on the sill and waited. The moon shone out clearly above the avenue, which now lay white and undimmed between its crowding trees.

"And he's whistling because he's afraid," continued Savelsan. "He's not often afraid," replied Nare-Jones shortly; "beside, he's doing what neither of us were very keen on."

The whistling stopped suddenly. Savelsan said afterwards that he fancied he saw Harland's huge, grey-clad shoulders, with uplifted arms, rise for a second above the bushes.

Then out of the silence came peal upon peal of that infernal laughter, and, following it, the thin, pitiful crying of the child. That too ceased, and an absolute stillness seemed to fall upon the place.

They leant out and listened intently. The minutes passed slowly. In the middle of the avenue the billiard ball glinted on the gravel, but there was no sign of Harland emerging from the shrubbery path.

"He should be there by now," said Nare-Jones anxiously.

They listened again; everything was quiet. The ticking of Harland's big watch on the mantelpiece was distinctly audible.

"This is too much," said Nare-Jones. "I'm going to see where he is."

He swung himself out on the grass, and Savelsan called to him to wait, as he was coming also. While Nare-Jones stood waiting, there was a sound as of a pig grunting and rooting among the dead leaves in the shrubbery.

They ran forward into the darkness, and found the shrubbery path. A minute later they came upon something that tossed and snorted and rolled under the shrubs.

"Great Heavens!" cried Nare-Jones, "it's Harland!"

"He's breaking somebody's neck," added Savelsan, peering into the gloom.

Nare-Jones was himself again. The powerful instinct of his profession—the help-giving instinct, possessed him to the exclusion of every other feeling.

"He's in a fit—just a fit," he said in matter of fact tones, as he bent over the struggling form, "that's all."

With the assistance of Savelsan, he managed to carry Harland out into the open drive. Harland's eyes were fearful, and froth hung about his blue puffing lips as they laid him down upon the ground. He rolled over, and lay still, while from the shadows broke another shout of laughter.

"It's apoplexy. We must get him away from here," said Nare-Jones. "But, first, I'm going to see what is in those bushes."

He dashed through the shrubbery, backwards and forwards. He seemed to feel the strength of ten men as he wrenched and tore and trampled the branches, letting in the light of the moon to its darkness. At last he paused, exhausted.

"Of course, there's nothing," said Savelsan wearily. "What did you expect after the incident of the billiard ball?"

Together, with awful toil, they bore the big man down the narrow avenue, and at the lodge gates they met the carriage.

Some time later the subject of their common experiences at Medhans Lea was discussed amongst the three men. Indeed, for many weeks Harland had not been in a state to discuss any subject at all, but as soon as he was allowed to do so, he invited Nare-Jones and Savelsan to meet Mr. Flaxman Low, the scientist, whose works on psychology and kindred matters are so well-known, at the Métropole to thresh out the matter.

Flaxman Low listened with his usual air of gentle abstraction, from time to time making notes on the back of an envelope. He looked at each narrator in turn as he took up the thread of the story. He understood perfectly that the man who stood furthest from the mystery must inevitably have been the self-centred Savelsan; next in order came Nare-Jones, with sympathetic possibilities, but a crowded brain; closest of all would be big, kindly Harland, with more than one strong animal instinct about him, and whose bulk of matter was evidently permeated by a receptive spirit.

When they had ended, Savelsan turned to Flaxman Low.

"There you have the events, Mr. Low. Now, the question is how to deal with them."

"Classify them," replied Flaxman Low.

"The crying would seem to indicate a child," began Savelsan, ticking off the list on his fingers; "the black figure, the face at the window, and the laughter are naturally connected. So far I can go alone. I conclude that we saw the apparition of a man, possibly a priest, who had during his lifetime ill-treated a child, and whose punishment it is to haunt the scene of his crime."

"Precisely—the punishment being worked out under conditions which admit of human observation," returned Flaxman Low. "As for the child the sound of crying was merely part of the *mis-en-scène*. The child was not there."

"But that explanation stops short of several points. How about the suggestive thoughts experienced by my friend, Nare-Jones; what brought on the fit in the case of Mr. Harland, who assures us that he was not suffering from fright or other violent emotion; and what connection can be traced between all these things and the Bengali idol?" Savelsan ended.

"Let us take the Bengali idol first," said Low. "It is just one of those discrepant particulars which, at first sight, seem wholly irreconcilable with the rest of the phenomena, yet these often form a test point, by which our theories are proved or otherwise." Flaxman Low took up the metal calf from the table as he spoke. "I should be inclined to connect this with the child. Observe it. It has not been roughly used; it is rubbed and dinted as a plaything usually is. I should say the child may have had Anglo-Indian relations."

At this, Nare-Jones bent forward, and in his turn examined the idol, while Savelsan smiled his thin, incredulous smile.

"These are ingenious theories," he said; "but we are really no nearer to facts, I am afraid."

"The only proof would be an inquiry into the former history of Medhans Lea; if events had happened there which would go to support this theory, why, then— But I cannot supply that information since I never heard of Medhans Lea or the ghost until I entered this room."

"I know something of Medhans Lea," put in Nare-Jones. "I found out a good deal about it before I left the place. And I must congratulate Mr. Low on his methods, for his theory tallies in a wonderful manner with the facts of the case. The house was long known to be haunted. It seems that many years ago a lady, the widow of an Indian officer, lived there with her only child, a boy, for whom she engaged a tutor, a dark-looking man, who wore a long black coat like a cassock, and was called 'the Jesuit' by the country people.

"One evening the man took the boy out into the shrubbery. Screams were heard, and when the child was brought in he was found to have lost his reason. He used to cry and shriek incessantly, but was never able to tell what had been done to him as long as he lived. As for this idol, the mother probably brought it with her from India, and the child used it as a toy, perhaps, because he was allowed no others. Hullo!" In handling the calf, Nare-Jones had touched some hidden spring, the head opened, disclosing a small cavity, from which dropped a little ring of blue beads, such as children make. He held it up. "This affords good proof."

"Yes," admitted Savelsan grudgingly. "But how about your sensations and Harland's seizure? You must know what was done to the child, Harland—what did you see in the shrubbery?"

Harland's florid face assumed a queer pallor.

"I saw something," replied he hesitatingly, "but I can't recall what it was. I only remember being possessed by a blind terror, and then nothing more until I recovered consciousness at the hotel next day."

"Can you account for this, Mr. Low?" asked Nare-Jones, "and there was also my strange notion of the whispering in the avenue."

"I think so," replied Flaxman Low. "I believe that the theory of atmospheric influences, which includes the power of environment to reproduce certain scenes and also thoughts, would throw light upon your sensations as well as Mr. Harland's. Such influences play a far larger part in our everyday experience than we have as yet any idea of."

There was a silence of a few moments; then Harland spoke:

"I fancy that we have said all that there is to be said upon the matter. We are much obliged to you, Mr. Low. I don't know how it strikes you other fellows, but, speaking for myself, I have seen enough of ghosts to last me for a very long time.

"And now," ended Harland wearily, "if you have no objection, we will pass on to pleasanter subjects."

THE STORY OF THE MOOR ROAD

"The medical profession must always have its own peculiar off-shoots," said Mr. Flaxman Low, "some are trades, some mere hobbies, others, again, are allied subjects of a serious and profound nature. Now, as a student of psychical phenomena, I account myself only two degrees removed from the ordinary general practitioner."

"How do you make that out?" returned Colonel Daimley, pushing the decanter of old port invitingly across the table.

"The nerve and brain specialist is the link between myself and the man you would send for if you had a touch of lumbago," replied Low with a slight smile. "Each division is but a higher grade of the same ladder—a step upwards into the unknown. I consider that I stand just one step above the specialist who makes a study of brain disease and insanity; he is at work on the disorders of the embodied spirit, while I deal with abnormal conditions of the free and detached spirit."

Colonel Daimley laughed aloud.

"That won't do, Low! No, no! First prove that your ghosts are sick."

"Certainly," replied Low gravely. "A very small proportion of spirits return as apparitions after the death of the body. Hence we may conclude that a ghost is a spirit in an abnormal condition. Abnormal conditions of the body usually indicate disease; why not of the spirit also?"

"That sounds fair enough," observed Lane Chaddam, the third man present. "Has the Colonel told you of our spook?"

The Colonel shook his handsome grey head in some irritation.

"You haven't convinced me yet, Lane, that it is a spook," he said drily. "Human nature is at the bottom of most things in this world according to my opinion."

"What spook is this?" asked Flaxman Low. "I heard nothing of it when I was down with you last year."

"It's a recent acquisition," replied Lane Chaddam. "I wish we were rid of it for my part."

"Have you seen it?" asked Low as he relit his long German pipe.

"Yes, and felt it!"

"What is it?"

"That's for you to say. He nearly broke my neck for me—that's all I can swear to."

Low knew Chaddam well. He was a long-limbed, athletic young fellow, with a good show of cups in his rooms, and was one of the various short-distance runners mentioned in the *Badminton* as having done the hundred in level time, and not the sort of man whose neck is easy to break.

"How did it happen?" asked Flaxman Low.

"About a fortnight ago," replied Chaddam. "I was flight-shooting near the burn where the hounds killed the otter last year. When the light began to fail, I thought I would come home by the old quarry, and pot anything that showed itself. As I walked along the far bank of the burn, I saw a man on the near side standing on the patch of sand below the reeds and watching me. As I came nearer I heard him coughing; it sounded like a sick cow. He stood still as if waiting for me. I thought it odd, because amongst the meres and water-meadows down there one never meets a stranger."

"Could you see him pretty clearly?"

"I saw his outline clearly, but not his face, because his back was toward the west. He was tall and jerry-built, so to speak, and had a little head no bigger than a child's, and he wore a fur cap with queer upstanding ears. When I came close, he suddenly slipped away; he jumped behind a big dyke, and I lost sight of him.

But I didn't pay much attention; I had my gun, and I concluded it was a tramp."

"Tramps don't follow men of your size," observed Low with a smile.

"This fellow did, at any rate. When I got across to the spot where he had been standing—the sand is soft there—I looked for his tracks. I knew he was bound to have a big foot of his own considering his height. But there were no footprints!"

"No footprints? You mean it was too dark for you to see them?" broke in Colonel Daimley.

"I am sure I should have seen them had there been any," persisted Chaddam quietly. "Besides, a man can't take a leap as he did without leaving a good hole behind him. The sand was perfectly smooth, because there had been a strong east wind all day. After looking about and seeing no marks, I went on to the top of the knoll above the quarry. After a bit I felt I was followed, though I couldn't see anyone. You remember the thorn bush that overhangs the quarry pool? I stopped there and bent over the edge of the cliff to see if there was anything in the pool. As I stooped I felt a point like a steel puncheon catch me in the small of the back. I kicked off from the quarry wall as well as I could, so as to avoid the broken rocks below, and I just managed to clear them, but I fell into the water with a flop that knocked the wind out of me. However, I held on to the gun, and, after a minute, I climbed to a ledge under the cliff and waited to see what my friend on top would do next. He waited, too. I couldn't see him, but I heard him—he coughed up there in the dusk, the most ghastly noise I ever heard. The Colonel laughs at me, but it was about as nasty a half-hour as I care to have. In the end, I swam out across the pool and got home."

"I laugh at Lane," said the Colonel, "but all the same, it's a bad spot for a fall."

"You say he struck you in the back?" asked Flaxman Low, turning to Chaddam.

"Yes, and his finger was like a steel punch."

"What does Mrs. Daimley say to this affair?" went on Low presently.

"Not a word to my wife or Olivia, my dear Low!" exclaimed Colonel Daimley. "It would frighten them needlessly; besides, there would be an infernal fuss if we wanted to go flighting or anything after dark. I only fear for them, as they often drive into Nerbury by the Moor Road, which passes close by the quarry."

"Do they go in for their letters every evening as they used to do?"

"Just the same. And they won't take Stubbs with them, in spite of advice." The Colonel looked disconsolately at Low. "Women are angels, bless them! But they are the dickens to deal with because they always want to know why?"

"And now, Low, what have you to say about it?" asked Chaddam.

"Have you told me all?"

"Yes. The only other thing is that Livy says she hears someone coughing in the spinney most nights."

"If all is as you say, Chaddam—pardon me, but in cases like this imagination is apt to play an unsuspected part—I should think that you have come upon a unique experience. What you have told me is not to be explained upon the lines of any ordinary theory."

After this they followed the ladies into the drawing-room, where they found Mrs. Daimley immersed in a novel as usual, and Livy looking pretty enough to account for the frequent presence of Lane Chaddam at Low Riddings. He was a distant cousin of the Colonel, and took advantage of his relationship to pay protracted visits to Northumberland.

Some years previous to the date of the above events, Colonel Daimley had bought and enlarged a substantial farmhouse which stood in a dip south of a lonely sweep of Northumbrian moors. It was a land of pale blue skies and far off fringes of black and ragged pine trees.

From the house a lane led over the wind-swept shoulder of the upland down to a hollow spanned by a railway bridge, then up again across the high levels of the moors until at length it lost itself in the outskirts of the little town of Nerbury. This Moor Road was peculiarly lonely; it approached but one cottage the whole way, and ran very nearly over the doorstep of that one—a deserted-looking slip of a place between the railway bridge and the quarry. Beyond the quarry stretched acres of marshland, meadows and reedy meres, all of which had been manipulated with such ability by the Colonel, that the duck shooting on his land was the envy of the neighbourhood.

In spite of its loneliness the Moor Road was much frequented by the Daimleys, who preferred it to the high road, which was un-interesting and much longer. Mrs. Daimley and Olivia drove in of an evening to fetch their letters—being people with nothing on earth to do, they were naturally always in a hurry to get their let-ters—and they perpetually had parcels waiting for them at the sta-tion which required to be called for at all sorts of hours. Thus it will be seen that the fact of the quarry being haunted by Lane Chaddam's assailant, formed a very real danger to the inhabitants of Low Riddings.

At breakfast next day Livy said the tramp had been coughing in the spinney half the night.

"In what direction?" asked Flaxman Low.

Livy pointed to the window which looked on to the gate and the thick boundary hedge, the last still full of crisp ruddy leaves.

"You feel an interest in your tramp, Miss Daimley?"

"Of course, poor creature! I wanted to go out to look for him the other night, but they would not allow me."

"That was before we knew he was so interesting," said Chaddam. "I promise we'll catch him for you next time he comes."

And this was in fact the programme they tried to carry out, but although the coughing was heard in the spinney, no one even caught a glimpse of any living thing moving or hiding among the trees.

The next stage of the affair happened to be an experience of Livy. In some excitement she told the assembled family at dinner that she had had just seen the coughing tramp.

Lane Chaddam changed colour. "You don't mean to say, Livy, that you went to search for him alone?" he exclaimed half-angrily.

Flaxman Low and the Colonel wisely went on eating oyster pat-ties without taking any apparent notice of the girl's news.

"Why shouldn't I?" asked Livy quickly, "but as it happens I saw him in Scully's cottage by the quarry this evening."

"What?" exclaimed Colonel Daimley, "in Scully's cottage. I'll see to that."

"Why? Are you all so prejudiced against my poor tramp?"

"On the contrary," replied Flaxman Low, "we all want to know what he's like."

"So odd-looking! I was driving home alone from the post when, as I passed the quarry cottage, I heard the cough. You know it is quite unmistakable; I looked up at the window and there he was. I have never seen anybody in the least like him. His face is ghastly pale and perfectly hairless, and he has such a little head. He stared at me so threateningly that I whipped up Lorelie."

"Were you frightened, then?"

"Not exactly, but he had such a wicked face that I drove away as fast as I could."

"I understood that you had arranged to send Stubbs for the letters?" said Colonel Daimley with some annoyance. "Why can't girls say what they mean?"

Livy made no reply, and after a pause Chaddam put a question.

"You must have passed along the Moor Road about seven o'clock?"

"Yes, it was after six when I left the Post-Office," replied Livy. "Why?"

"It was quite dark—how did you see the hairless man so plainly? I was round on the marshes all the evening, and I am quite certain there was no light at any time in Scully's cottage."

"I don't remember whether there was any light behind him in the room," returned Livy after a moment's consideration; "I only know that I saw his head and face quite plainly."

There was no more said on the subject at the time, though the Colonel forbade Livy to run any further risks by going alone on the Moor Road. After this, the three men paraded the lane and lay in wait for the hairless tramp or ghost. On the second evening their watch was rewarded, when Chaddam came hurriedly into the smoking-room to say that the coughing could at that instant be heard in the hedge by the dining-room. It was still early, although the evening had closed in with clouds, and all outside was dark.

"I'll deal with him this time effectually!" exclaimed the Colonel. "I'll slip out the back way, and lie in the hedge down the road by the field gate. You two must chivy him out to me, and when he comes along, I'll have him against the sky-line and give him a charge of No. 4 if he shows fight."

The Colonel stole down the lane while the others beat the spinney and hedge, Flaxman Low very much chagrined at being forced to deal with an interesting problem in this rough and ready fashion. However, he saw that on this occasion at least it would be useless to oppose the Colonel's notions. When he and Chaddam met after beating the hedge they saw a tall figure shamble away rapidly down the lane towards the Colonel's hiding-place.

They stood still and waited for developments, but the minutes followed each other in intense stillness. Then they went to find the Colonel.

"Hullo, Colonel, anything wrong?" asked Chaddam on nearing the field gate.

The Colonel straightened himself with the help of Chaddam's arm.

"Did you see him?" he whispered.

"We thought so. Why did you not fire?"

"Because," said the Colonel in a husky voice, "I had no gun!"

"But you took it with you?"

"Yes."

Flaxman Low opened the lantern he carried, and, as the light swept round in a wide circle, something glinted on the grass. It was the stock of the Colonel's gun. A little further off they came upon the Damascus barrels bent and twisted into a ball like so much fine wire. Presently the Colonel explained.

"I saw him coming and meant to meet him, but I seemed dazed—I couldn't move! The gun was snatched from me, and I made no resistance—I don't know why." He took the gunbarrels and examined them slowly, "I give in. Low, no human hand did that."

"During dinner Flaxman Low said abruptly: "I suspect you have lately had an earthquake down here."

"How did you know?" asked Livy. "Have you been to the quarry?"

Low said he had not.

"It was such a poor little earthquake that even the papers did not think it worth while to mention it!" went on Livy. "We didn't feel any shock, and, in fact, knew nothing about it until Dr. Petterped told us."

"You had a landslip though?" went on Low.

Livy opened her pretty eyes.

"But you know all about it," she said. "Yes, the landslip was just by the old quarry."

"I should like to see the place to-morrow," observed Low.

Next day, therefore, when the Colonel went off to the coverts with a couple of neighbours, whom he had invited to join him, Flaxman Low accompanied Chaddam to examine the scene of the landslip.

From the edge of the upland, looking across the hollow crowded with reedy pools, they could see in the torn, reddish flank of the opposite slope the sharp tilt of the broken strata. To the right of this lay the old quarry, and about a hundred yards to the left the lonely house and the curving road.

Low descended into the hollow and spent a long time in the spongy ground between the back of the quarry and the lower edge of the newly-uncovered strata, using his little hammer freely, especially about one narrow black fissure, round which he sniffed and pottered in absorbed silence. Presently he called to Chaddam.

"There has been a slight explosion of gas—a rare gas, here," he said. "I hardly hoped to find traces of it, but it is unmistakeable."

"Very unmistakeable," agreed Chaddam, with a laugh. "You'd have said so had you been here when it happened."

"Ah, very satisfactory indeed. And that was a fortnight ago, you say?"

"Rather more now. It took place a couple of days before my fall into the quarry pool."

"Anyone ill near by—at that cottage for instance?" asked Low, as he joined Chaddam.

"Why? Was that gas poisonous? There's a man in the Colonel's employ named Scully in that cottage, who has had pneumonia, but he was on the mend when the landslip occurred. Since then he has grown steadily worse."

"Is there anyone with him?"

"Yes, the Daimleys sent for a woman to look after him. Scully's a very decent man. I often go in to see him."

"And so does the hairless man apparently," added Low.

"No, that's the queer part of it. Neither he nor the woman in charge have ever seen such a person as Livy described. I don't know what to think."

"The first thing to be done is to get the man from here at once," said Low decidedly. "Let's go in and see him."

They found Scully low and drowsy. The nurse shook her head at the two visitors in a despondent way.

"He grows weaker day by day," she said.

"Get him away from here at once," repeated Low, as they went out.

"We might have him up at Low Riddings, but he seems almost too weak to be moved," replied Chaddam doubtfully.

"My dear fellow, it's his only chance of life."

The Daimleys made arrangements for the reception of Scully, provided Dr. Thomson of Nerbury gave his consent to the removal. In the afternoon, therefore, Chaddam bicycled into Nerbury to see the doctor on the subject. "If were you, Chaddam," said Low before he started, "I'd be back by daylight."

Unfortunately Dr. Thomson was on his rounds, and did not return until after dark, by which time it was too late to remove Scully that evening. After leaving the doctor's house Chaddam went to the station to inquire about a box from Mudie's. The books having arrived, he took out a couple of volumes for Mrs. Daimley's present consumption, and was strapping them on in front of his bicycle, when it struck him that unless he went home by the Moor Road he would be late for dinner.

Accordingly he branched off into the bare track which led over the moors. The twilight had deepened into a fine, cold night, and a moon was swinging up into a pale, clear sky. The spread of heather, purple in the daytime, appeared jet black by moonlight, and across it he could see the white ribbon of road stretching ahead into the distance. The scents of the night were fresh in his nostrils, as he ran easily along the level with the breeze behind him.

He soon reached the incline past Scully's cottage. Well away to the left lay the quarry pool like a blotch of ink under its shadowing cliff. There was no light in the cottage, and it seemed even more deserted-looking than usual.

As Chaddam flashed under the bridge, he heard a cough, and glanced back over his shoulder.

A tall, loose-jointed form he had seen once before, was rearing itself up upon the railway bridge. There was something curiously unhuman about the lank outlines and the cant of the small head with its prick-eared cap showing out so clearly against the lighter sky behind.

When Chaddam looked again, he saw the thing on the bridge fling up its long arms and leap down on to the road some thirty feet below.

Then Chaddam rode. He began to think he had been a fool to come, and he counted that he was a good mile from home. At first he fancied he heard footfalls, then he fancied there were none. The hard road flew under him, all thoughts of economising his strength were lost, his single aim was to make the pace.

Suddenly his bicycle jerked violently, and he was shot over into the road. As he fell, he turned his head and was conscious of a little, bleached, bestial face, wet with fury, not ten yards behind!

He sprang to his feet, and ran up the road as he had never run before. He ran wonderfully, but he might as well have tried to race a cheetah. It was not a question of speed, the game was in the hands of this thing with the limbs of a starved Hercules, whose bony knees seemed to leap into its ghastly face at every stride. Chaddam topped the slope with a sickening sense of his own powerlessness. Already he saw Low Riddings in the distance, and a dim light came creeping along the road towards him. Another frantic spurt, and he had almost reached the light, when a hand closed like a vice on his shoulder, and seemed to fasten on the flesh. He rushed blindly on towards the house. He saw the door-handle gleam, and in another second he had pitched head foremost on to the knotted matting in the hall.

When he recovered his senses, his first question was: "Where is Low?"

"Didn't you meet him?" asked Livy, "I—that is, we were anxious about you as you were so late, and I was just going to meet you when Mr. Low came downstairs and insisted on going instead."

Chaddam stood up.

"I must follow him."

But as he spoke the front door opened, and Flaxman Low entered, and looked up at the clock.

"Eight-twenty," he said, "You're late, Chaddam."

Afterwards in the smoking-room he gave an account of what he had seen.

"I saw Chaddam racing up the road with a tall figure behind him. It stretched out its hand and grasped his shoulder. The next instant it stopped short as if it had been shot. It seemed to reel back and collapse, and then limped off into the hedge like a disappointed dog."

Chaddam stood up and began to take off his coat.

"Whatever the thing is, it is something out of the common. Look here!" he said, turning up his shirtsleeve over the point of his shoulder, where three singular marks were visible, irregularly placed as the fingers of a hand might fall. They were oblong in shape, about the size of a bean, and swollen in purple lumps well above the surface of the skin.

"Looks as if someone had been using a small cupping glass on you," remarked the Colonel uneasily. "What do you say to it, Low?"

"I say that since Chaddam has escaped with his life, I have only to congratulate him on what, in Europe certainly, is a unique adventure."

The Colonel threw his cigar into the fire.

"Such adventures are too dangerous for my taste," he said. "This creature has on two occasions murderously attacked Lane

Chaddam, and it would, no doubt, have attacked Livy if it had had the chance. We must leave this place at once, or we shall be murdered in our beds!"

"I don't think, Colonel, that you will be troubled with this mysterious visitant again," replied Flaxman Low.

"Why not? Who or what is this horrible thing?"

"I believe it to be an Elemental Earth Spirit," returned Low. "No other solution fits the facts of the case."

"What is an Elemental?" resumed the Colonel irritably. "Remember, Low, I expect you to prove your theories so that a plain man may understand, if I am to stay on at Low Riddings."

"Eastern occultists describe wandering tribes of earth spirits, evil intelligences, possessing spirit as distinct from soul—all inimical to man."

"But how do you know that the thing on the Moor Road is an Elemental?"

"Because the points of resemblance are curiously remarkable. The occultists say that when these spirits materialize, they appear in grotesque and uncouth forms; secondly, that they are invariably bloodless and hairless; thirdly, they move with extraordinary rapidity, and leave no footprints; and, lastly, their agility and strength is superhuman. All these peculiarities have been observed in connection with the figure on the Moor Road."

"I admit that no man I have ever met with," commented Colonel Daimley, "could jump uninjured from a height of 30ft., race a bicycle, and twist up gunbarrels like so much soft paper. So perhaps you're right. But can you tell me why or how it came here?"

"My conclusions," began Low, "may seem to you far-fetched and ridiculous, but you must give them the benefit of the fact that they precisely account for the otherwise unaccountable features which mark this affair. I connect this appearance with the earthquake and the sick man."

"What? Scully in league with the devil?" exclaimed the Colonel bluntly. "Why the man is too weak to leave his bed; besides, he is a short, thick-set fellow, entirely unlike our haunting friend."

"You mistake me, Colonel," said Low, in his quiet tones. "These Elementals cannot take form without drawing upon the resources of the living. They absorb the vitality of any ailing person until it is exhausted, and the person dies."

"Then they begin operations upon a fresh victim? A pleasant look-out to know we keep a well-attested vampire in the neighbour-hood!"

"Vampires are a distinct race, with different methods; one being that the Elemental is a wanderer, and goes far afield to search for a new victim."

"But why should it want to kill me?" put in Chaddam.

"As I have told you, they are animated solely by a blind malignity to the human race, and you happened to be handy."

"But the earthquake, Low; where is the connection there?" demanded the Colonel, with the air of a man who intends to corner his opponent.

Flaxman Low lit one cigar at the end of another before he replied.

"At this point," he said, "my own theories and observations and those of the old occultists overlap. The occultists held that some of these spirits are imprisoned in the interior of the earth, but may be set free in consequence of those shiftings and disturbances which take place during an earthquake. This in more modern language simply means that Elementals are in some manner connected with certain of the primary strata. Now, my own researches have led me to conclude that atmospheric influences are intimately associated with spiritual phenomena. Some gases appear to be productive of such phenomena. One of these is generated when certain of the primary formations are newly exposed to the common air."

"This is almost beyond belief—I don't understand you," said the Colonel.

"I am sorry that I cannot give you all the links in my own chain of reasoning," returned Low. "Much is still obscure, but the evidence is sufficiently strong to convince me that in such a case of earthquake and landslip as has lately taken place here the phenomenon of an embodied Elemental might possibly be expected to follow, given the one necessary adjunct of a sick person in the near neighbourhood of the disturbance."

"But when this brute got hold of me, why didn't it finish me off?" asked Chaddam. "Or was it your coming that prevented it?"

Flaxman Low considered.

"No, I don't think I can flatter myself that my coming had anything to do with your escape. It was a near thing—how near you will understand when we hear further news of Scully in the morning."

A servant entered the room at this moment.

"The woman has come up from the cottage, sir, to say that Scully is dead."

"At what hour did he die?" asked Low.

"About ten minutes past eight, sir, she says."

"The hour agrees exactly," commented Low, when the man had left the room. "The figure stopped and collapsed so suddenly that I believed something of this kind must have happened."

"But surely this is a very unprecedented occurrence?"

"It is," said Flaxman Low. "But I can assure you that if you take the trouble to glance through the pages of the psychical periodicals you will find many statements at least as wonderful."

"But are they true?"

"At any rate," said he, "we know this is."

The Daimleys have spent many pleasant days at Low Riddings since then, but Chaddam—who has acquired a right to control Miss Livy's actions more or less—persists in his objection to any solitary expeditions to Nerbury along the Moor Road. For, although the figure has never been seen about Low Riddings since, some strange stories have lately appeared in the papers of a similar mysterious figure which has been met with more than once in the lonelier spots about North London. If it be true that this nameless wandering spirit, with the strength and activity of twenty men, still haunts our lonely roads, the sooner Mr. Flaxman Low exorcises it the better.

THE STORY OF BAELBROW

It is a matter for regret that so many of Mr. Flaxman Low's reminiscences should deal with the darker episodes of his experiences. Yet this is almost unavoidable, as the more purely scientific and less strongly marked cases would not, perhaps, contain the same elements of interest for the general public, however valuable and instructive they might be to the expert student. It has also been considered better to choose the completer cases, those that ended in something like satisfactory proof, rather than the many instances where the thread broke off abruptly amongst surmisings, which it was never possible to subject to convincing tests.

North of a low-lying strip of country on the East Anglian coast, the promontory of Bael Ness thrusts out a blunt nose into the sea. On the Ness, backed by pinewoods, stands a square, comfortable stone mansion, known to the countryside as Baelbrow. It has faced the east winds for close upon three hundred years, and during the whole period has been the home of the Swaffam family, who were never in anywise put out of conceit of their ancestral dwelling by the fact that it had always been haunted. Indeed, the Swaffams were proud of the Baelbrow Ghost, which enjoyed a wide notoriety, and no one dreamt of complaining of its behaviour until Professor Jungvort, of Nuremburg, laid information against it, and sent an urgent appeal for help to Mr. Flaxman Low.

The Professor, who was well acquainted with Mr. Low, detailed the circumstances of his tenancy of Baelbrow, and the unpleasant events that had followed thereupon.

It appeared that Mr. Swaffam, senior, who spent a large portion of his time abroad, had offered to lend his house to the Professor for the summer season. When the Jungvorts arrived at Baelbrow, they were charmed with the place. The prospect, though not very varied, was at least extensive, and the air exhilarating. Also the Professor's daughter enjoyed frequent visits from her betrothed—Harold Swaffam—and the Professor was delightfully employed in overhauling the Swaffam library.

The Jungvorts had been duly told of the ghost, which lent distinction to the old house, but never in any way interfered with the comfort of the inmates. For some time they found this description to be strictly true, but with the beginning of October came a change. Up to this time and as far back as the Swaffam annals reached, the ghost had been a shadow, a rustle, a passing sigh—nothing definite or troublesome. But early in October strange things began to occur, and the terror culminated when a housemaid was found dead in a corridor three weeks later. Upon this the Professor felt that it was time to send for Flaxman Low.

Mr. Low arrived upon a chilly evening when the house was already beginning to blur in the purple twilight, and the resinous scent of the pines came sweetly on the land breeze. Jungvort welcomed him in the spacious, fire-lit hall. He was a stout man with a quantity of white hair, round eyes emphasised by spectacles, and a kindly, dreamy face. His life-study was philology, and his two relaxations chess and the smoking of a big bowled meerschaum.

"Now, Professor," said Mr. Low when they had settled themselves in the smoking-room, "how did it all begin?"

"I will tell you," replied Jungvort, thrusting out his chin, and tapping his broad chest, and speaking as if an unwarrantable liberty had been taken with him. "First of all, it has shown itself to me!" Mr. Flaxman Low smiled and assured him that nothing could be more satisfactory.

"But not at all satisfactory!" exclaimed the Professor. "I was sitting here alone, it might have been midnight—when I hear something come creeping like a little dog with its nails, tick-tick, upon the oak flooring of the hall. I whistle, for I think it is the little 'Rags' of my daughter, and afterwards opened the door, and I saw"—he hesitated and looked hard at Low through his spectacles, "something that was just disappearing into the passage which connects the two wings of the house. It was a figure, not unlike the human figure, but narrow and straight. I fancied I saw a bunch of black hair, and a flutter of something detached, which may have been a handkerchief. I was overcome by a feeling of repulsion. I heard a few clicking steps, then it stopped, as I thought, at the museum door. Come, I will show you the spot."

The Professor conducted Mr. Low into the hall. The main staircase, dark and massive, yawned above them, and directly behind it ran the passage referred to by the Professor. It was over twenty feet long, and about midway led past a deep arch containing a door reached by two steps.

Jungvort explained that this door formed the entrance to a large room called the Museum, in which Mr. Swaffam, senior, who was something of a dilettante, stored the various curios he picked up during his excursions abroad. The Professor went on to say that he immediately followed the figure, which he believed had gone into the museum, but he found nothing there except the cases containing Swaffam's treasures.

"I mentioned my experience to no one. I concluded that I had seen the ghost. But two days after, one of the female servants coming through the passage, in the dark, declared that a man leapt out at her from the embrasure of the Museum door, but she released herself and ran screaming into the servants' hall. We at once made a search but found nothing to substantiate her story.

"I took no notice of this, though it coincided pretty well with my own experience. The week after, my daughter Lena came down late one night for a book. As she was about to cross the hall, something leapt upon her from behind. Women are of little use in serious investigations—she fainted! Since then she has been ill and the doctor says 'run down.'" Here the Professor spread out his hands. "So she leaves for a change tomorrow. Since then other members of the household have been attacked in much the same manner, with always the same result, they faint and are weak and useless when they recover.

"But, last Wednesday, the affair became a tragedy. By that time the servants had refused to come through the passage except in a crowd of three or four,—most of them preferring to go round by the terrace to reach this part of the house. But one maid, named Eliza Freeman, said she was not afraid of the Baelbrow Ghost, and undertook to put out the lights in the hall one night.

"When she had done so, and was returning through the passage past the Museum door, she appears to have been attacked, or at any rate frightened. In the grey of the morning they found her lying beside the steps dead. There was a little blood upon her sleeve but no mark upon her body except a small raised pustule under the ear. The doctor said the girl was extraordinarily anæmic, and that she probably died from fright, her heart being weak. I was surprised at this, for she had always seemed to be a particularly strong and active young woman."

"Can I see Miss Jungvort to-morrow before she goes?" asked Low, as the Professor signified he had nothing more to tell.

The Professor was rather unwilling that his daughter should be questioned, but he at last gave his permission, and next morning Low had a short talk with the girl before she left the house. He found her a very pretty girl, though listless and startlingly pale, and with a frightened stare in her light brown eyes. Mr. Low asked if she could describe her assailant. "No," she answered. "I could not see him for he was behind me. I only saw a dark, bony hand, with shining nails, and a bandaged arm pass just under my eyes before I fainted."

"Bandaged arm? I have heard nothing of this."

"Tut—tut, mere fancy!" put in the Professor impatiently.

"I saw the bandages on the arm," repeated the girl, turning her head wearily away, "and I smelt the antiseptics it was dressed with."

"You have hurt your neck," remarked Mr. Low, who noticed a small circular patch of pink under her ear.

She flushed and paled, raising her hand to her neck with a nervous jerk, as she said in a low voice: "It has almost killed me. Before he touched me, I knew he was there! I felt it!"

When they left her the Professor apologised for the unreliability of her evidence, and pointed out the discrepancy between her statement and his own.

"She says she sees nothing but an arm, yet I tell you it had no arms! Preposterous! Conceive a wounded man entering this house to frighten the young women! I do not know what to make of it! Is it a man, or is it the Baelbrow Ghost?"

During the afternoon when Mr. Low and the Professor returned from a stroll on the shore, they found a dark-browed young man with a bull neck, and strongly marked features, standing sullenly before the hall fire. The Professor presented him to Mr. Low as Harold Swaffam.

Swaffam seemed to be about thirty, but was already known as a far-seeing and successful member of the Stock Exchange.

"I am pleased to meet you, Mr. Low," he began, with a keen glance, "though you don't look sufficiently high-strung for one of your profession."

Mr. Low merely bowed.

"Come, you don't defend your craft against my insinuations?" went on Swaffam. "And so you have come to rout out our poor old ghost from Baelbrow? You forget that he is an heirloom, a family possession! What's this about his having turned rabid, eh, Professor?" he ended, wheeling round upon Jungvort in his brusque way.

The Professor told the story over again. It was plain that he stood rather in awe of his prospective son-in-law.

"I heard much the same from Lena, whom I met at the station," said Swaffam. "It is my opinion that the women in this house are suffering from an epidemic of hysteria. You agree with me, Mr. Low?"

"Possibly. Though hysteria could hardly account for Freeman's death."

"I can't say as to that until I have looked further into the particulars. I have not been idle since I arrived. I have examined the

Museum. No one has entered it from the outside, and there is no other way of entrance except through the passage. The flooring is laid, I happen to know, on a thick layer of concrete. And there the case for the ghost stands at present." After a few moments of dogged reflection, he swung round on Mr. Low, in a manner that seemed peculiar to him when about to address any person. "What do you say to this plan, Mr. Low? I propose to drive the Professor over to Ferryvale, to stop there for a day or two at the hotel, and I will also dispose of the servants who still remain in the house for, say, forty-eight hours. Meanwhile you and I can try to go further into the secret of the ghost's new pranks?"

Flaxman Low replied that this scheme exactly met his views, but the Professor protested against being sent away. Harold Swaffam, however, was a man who liked to arrange things in his own fashion, and within forty-five minutes he and Jungvort departed in the dogcart. The evening was lowering, and Baelbrow, like all houses built in exposed situations, was extremely susceptible to the changes of the weather. Therefore, before many hours were over, the place was full of creaking noises as the screaming gale battered at the shuttered windows, and the tree-branches tapped and groaned against the walls.

Harold Swaffam on his way back was caught in the storm and drenched to the skin. It was, therefore, settled that after he had changed his clothes he should have a couple of hours' rest on the smoking-room sofa, while Mr. Low kept watch in the hall.

The early part of the night passed over uneventfully. A light burned faintly in the great wainscotted hall, but the passage was dark. There was nothing to be heard but the wild moan and whistle of the wind coming in from the sea, and the squalls of rain dashing against the windows.

As the hours advanced, Mr. Low lit a lantern that lay at hand, and, carrying it along the passage tried the Museum door. It yielded, and the wind came muttering through to meet him. He looked round at the shutters and behind the big cases which held Mr. Swaffam's treasures, to make sure that the room contained no living occupant but himself.

Suddenly he fancied he heard a scraping noise behind him, and turned round, but discovered nothing to account for it. Finally, he laid the lantern on a bench so that its light should fall through the door into the passage, and returned again to the hall, where he put out the lamp, and then once more took up his station by the closed door of the smoking-room.

A long hour passed, during which the wind continued to roar down the wide hall chimney, and the old boards creaked as if furtive footsteps were gathering from every corner of the house. But Flaxman Low heeded none of these; he was awaiting for a certain sound.

After a while, he heard it—the cautious scraping of wood on wood. He leant forward to watch the Museum door. Click, click, came the curious dog-like tread upon the tiled floor of the Museum, till the thing, whatever it was, paused and listened behind the open door. The wind lulled at the moment, and Low listened also, but no further sound was to be heard, only slowly across the broad ray of light falling through the door grew a stealthy shadow.

Again the wind rose, and blew in heavy gusts about the house, till even the flame in the lantern flickered; but when it steadied once more, Flaxman Low saw that the silent form had passed through the door, and was now on the steps outside. He could just make out a dim shadow in the dark angle of the embrasure.

Presently, from the shapeless shadow came a sound Mr. Low was not prepared to hear. The thing sniffed the air with the strong, audible inspiration of a bear, or some large animal. At the same moment, carried on the draughts of the hall, a faint, unfamiliar odour reached his nostrils.

Lena Jungvort's words flashed back upon him—this, then, was the creature with the bandaged arm!

Again, as the storm shrieked and shook the windows, a darkness passed across the light. The thing had sprung out from the angle of the door, and Flaxman Low knew that it was making its way towards him through the illusive blackness of the hall. He hesitated for a second; then he opened the smoking-room door.

Harold Swaffam sat up on the sofa, dazed with sleep. "What has happened? Has it come?"

Low told him what he had just seen. Swaffam listened half-smilingly.

"What do you make of it now?" he said.

"I must ask you to defer that question for a little," replied Low.

"Then you mean me to suppose that you have a theory to fit all these incongruous items?"

"I have a theory, which may be modified by further knowledge," said Low. "Meantime, am I right in concluding from the name of this house that it was built on a barrow or burying-place?"

"You are right, though that has nothing to do with the latest freaks of our ghost," returned Swaffam decidedly.

"I also gather that Mr. Swaffam has lately sent home one of the many cases now lying in the Museum?" went on Mr. Low.

"He sent one, certainly, last September."

"And you have opened it," asserted Low.

"Yes; though I flattered myself I had left no trace of my handiwork."

"I have not examined the cases," said Low. "I inferred that you had done so from other facts."

"Now, one thing more," went on Swaffam, still smiling. "Do you imagine there is any danger—I mean to men like ourselves? Hysterical women cannot be taken into serious account."

"Certainly; the gravest danger to any person who moves about this part of the house alone after dark," replied Low.

Harold Swaffam leant back and crossed his legs.

"To go back to the beginning of our conversation, Mr. Low, may I remind you of the various conflicting particulars you will have to reconcile before you can present any decent theory to the world?"

"I am quite aware of that."

"First of all, our original ghost was a mere misty presence, rather guessed at from vague sounds and shadows—now we have a something that is tangible, and that can, as we have proof, kill with fright. Next Jungvort declares the thing was a narrow, long and distinctly armless object, while Miss Jungvort has not only seen the arm and hand of a human being, but saw them clearly enough to tell us that the nails were gleaming and the arm bandaged. She also felt its strength. Jungvort, on the other hand, maintained that it clicked along like a dog—you bear out this description with the additional information that it sniffs like a wild beast. Now what can this thing be? It is capable of being seen, smelt, and felt, yet it hides itself, successfully in a room where there is no cavity or space sufficient to afford covert to a cat! You still tell me that you believe that you can explain?"

"Most certainly," replied Flaxman Low with conviction.

"I have not the slightest intention or desire to be rude, but as a mere matter of common sense, I must express my opinion plainly. I believe the whole thing to be the result of excited imaginations, and I am about to prove it. Do you think there is any further danger to-night?"

"Very great danger to-night," replied Low.

"Very well; as I said, I am going to prove it. I will ask you to allow me to lock you up in one of the distant rooms, where I can get no help from you, and I will pass the remainder of the night walking about the passage and hall in the dark. That should give proof one way or the other."

"You can do so if you wish, but I must at least beg to be allowed to look on. I will leave the house and watch what goes on from the window in the passage, which I saw opposite the Museum door. You cannot, in any fairness, refuse to let me be a witness."

"I cannot, of course," returned Swaffam. "Still, the night is too bad to turn a dog out into, and I warn you that I shall lock you out."

"That will not matter. Lend me a macintosh, and leave the lantern lit in the Museum, where I placed it."

Swaffam agreed to this. Mr. Low gives a graphic account of what followed. He left the house and was duly locked out, and, after groping his way round the house, found himself at length outside the window of the passage, which was almost opposite to the door of the Museum. The door was still ajar and a thin band of light cut out into the gloom. Further down the hall gaped black and void. Low, sheltering himself as well as he could from the rain, waited for Swaffam's appearance. Was the terrible yellow watcher balancing itself upon its lean legs in the dim corner opposite, ready to spring out with its deadly strength upon the passer-by? Presently Low heard a door bang inside the house, and the next moment Swaffam appeared with a candle in his hand, an isolated spread of weak rays against the vast darkness behind. He advanced steadily down the passage, his dark face grim and set, and as he came Mr. Low experienced that tingling sensation, which is so often the forerunner of some strange experience.

Swaffam passed on towards the other end of the passage. There was a quick vibration of the Museum door as a lean shape with a shrunken head leapt out into the passage after him. Then all together came a hoarse shout, the noise of a fall and utter darkness.

In an instant, Mr. Low had broken the glass, opened the window, and swung himself into the passage. There he lit a match and as it flared he saw by its dim light a picture painted for a second upon the obscurity beyond.

Swaffam's big figure lay with outstretched arms, face downwards, and as Low looked a crouching shape extricated itself from the fallen man, raising a narrow vicious head from his shoulder.

The match spluttered feebly and went out, and Low heard a flying step click on the boards, before he could find the candle Swaffam had dropped. Lighting it, he stooped over Swaffam and turned him on his back. The man's strong colour had gone, and the wax-white face looked whiter still against the blackness of hair and brows, and upon his neck under the ear was a little raised pustule, from which a thin line of blood was streaked up to the angle of his cheekbone.

Some instinctive feeling prompted Low to glance up at this moment. Half extended from the Museum doorway were a face and bony neck—a high-nosed, dull-eyed, malignant face, the eye-sockets hollow, and the darkened teeth showing. Low plunged his hand into his pocket, and a shot rang out in the echoing passage-way and hall. The wind sighed through the broken panes, a ribbon of stuff fluttered along the polished flooring, and that was all, as Flaxman Low half dragged, half carried Swaffam into the smoking-room.

It was some time before Swaffam recovered consciousness. He listened to Low's story of how he had found him with a red angry gleam in his sombre eyes.

"The ghost has scored off me," he said, with an odd, sullen laugh, "but now I fancy it's my turn! But before we adjourn to the Museum to examine the place, I will ask you to let me hear your notion of things. You have been right in saying there was real danger. For myself I can only tell you that I felt something spring upon me, and I knew no more. Had this not happened I am afraid I should never have asked you a second time what your idea of the matter might be," he added with a sort of sulky frankness.

"There are two main indications," replied Low. "This strip of yellow bandage, which I have just now picked up from the passage floor, and the mark on your neck."

"What's that you say?" Swaffam rose quickly and examined his neck in a small glass beside the mantelshelf.

"Connect those two, and I think I can leave you to work it out for yourself," said Low.

"Pray let us have your theory in full," requested Swaffam shortly.

"Very well," answered Low good-humouredly—he thought Swaffam's annoyance natural in the circumstances— "The long, narrow figure which seemed to the Professor to be armless is developed on the next occasion. For Miss Jungvort sees a bandaged arm and a dark hand with gleaming—which means, of course, gilded—nails. The clicking sound of the footsteps coincides with these particulars, for we know that sandals made of strips of leather are not uncommon in company with gilt nails and bandages. Old and dry leather would naturally click upon your polished floor."

"Bravo, Mr. Low! So you mean to say that this house is haunted by a mummy!"

"That is my idea, and all I have seen confirms me in my opinion."

"To do you justice, you held this theory before to-night—before, in fact, you had seen anything for yourself. You gathered that my father had sent home a mummy, and you went on to conclude that I had opened the case?"

"Yes. I imagine you took off most of, or rather all, the outer bandages, thus leaving the limbs free, wrapped only in the inner bandages which were swathed round each separate limb. I fancy this mummy was preserved on the Theban method with aromatic spices, which left the skin olive-coloured, dry and flexible, like tanned leather, the features remaining distinct, and the hair, teeth, and eyebrows perfect."

"So far, good," said Swaffam. "But now, how about the intermittent vitality? The pustule on the neck of those whom it attacks? And where is our old Baelbrow ghost to come in?"

Swaffam tried to speak in a rallying tone, but his excitement and lowering temper were visible enough, in spite of the attempts he made to suppress them.

"To begin at the beginning," said Flaxman Low, "everybody who, in a rational and honest manner, investigates the phenomena of spiritism will, sooner or later, meet in them some perplexing element, which is not to be explained by any of the ordinary theories. For reasons into which I need not now enter, this present case appears to me to be one of these. I am led to believe that the ghost which has for so many years given dim and vague manifestations of its existence in this house is a vampire."

Swaffam threw back his head with an incredulous gesture.

"We no longer live in the middle ages, Mr. Low! And besides, how could a vampire come here?" he said scoffingly.

"It is held by some authorities on these subjects that under certain conditions a vampire may be self-created. You tell me that this house is built upon an ancient barrow, in fact, on a spot where we might naturally expect to find such an elemental psychic germ. In those dead human systems were contained all the seeds for good and evil. The power which causes these psychic seeds or germs to grow is thought, and from being long dwelt on and indulged, a thought might finally gain a mysterious vitality, which could go on increasing more and more by attracting to itself suitable and appropriate elements from its environment. For a long period this germ remained a helpless intelligence, awaiting the opportunity to assume some material form, by means of which to carry out its desires. The invisible is the real; the material only subserves its manifestation. The impalpable reality already existed, when you provided for it a physical medium for action by unwrapping the mummy's form. Now, we can only judge of the nature of the germ by its manifestation through matter. Here we have every indication of a vampire intelligence touching into life and energy the dead human frame. Hence the mark on the neck of its victims, and their bloodless and anæmic condition. For a vampire, as you know, sucks blood."

Swaffam rose, and took up the lamp.

"Now, for proof," he said bluntly. "Wait a second, Mr. Low. You say you fired at this appearance?" And he took up the pistol which Low had laid down on the table.

"Yes, I aimed at a small portion of its foot which I saw on the step."

Without more words, and with the pistol still in his hand, Swaffam led the way to the Museum. The wind howled round the house, and the darkness, which precedes the dawn, lay upon the world, when the two men looked upon one of the strangest sights it has ever been given to men to shudder at.

Half in and half out of an oblong wooden box in a corner of the great room, lay a lean shape in its rotten yellow bandages, the scraggy neck surmounted by a mop of frizzled hair. The toe strap of a sandal and a portion of the right foot had been shot away.

Swaffam, with a working face, gazed down at it, then seizing it by its tearing bandages, he flung it into the box, where it fell into a life-like posture, its wide, moist-lipped mouth gaping up at them.

For a moment Swaffam stood over the thing; then with a curse he raised the revolver and shot into the grinning face again and again with a deliberate vindictiveness. Finally he rammed the thing down into the box, and, clubbing the weapon, smashed the head into fragments with a vicious energy that coloured the whole horrible scene with a suggestion of murder done.

Then, turning to Low, he said: "Help me to fasten the cover on it."

"Are you going to bury it?"

"No, we must rid the earth of it," he answered savagely. "I'll put it into the old canoe and burn it."

The rain had ceased when in the daybreak they carried the old canoe down to the shore. In it they placed the mummy case with its ghastly occupant, and piled faggots about it. The sail was raised and the pile lighted, and Low and Swaffam watched it creep out on the ebb-tide, at first a twinkling spark, then a flare and waving fire, until far out to sea the history of that dead thing ended 3000 years after the priests of Armen had laid it to rest in its appointed pyramid.

THE STORY OF THE GREY HOUSE

Mr. Flaxman Low declares that only on one occasion has he undertaken, unasked, the solving of a psychical mystery. To that case he always refers as the "affair of the Grey House." The house bears a different name in the annals of more than one scientific society, and much controversy has raged over the strange details of a story that seems to open up a new province of fantastic horror. Papers and treatises have been written about it in almost every European language, and many dismaying facts of a somewhat analogous nature have thus been brought to light. There was some hesitation at first about laying this matter—backed as it is by an explanation, which, though terrible, is not altogether unsupported—before the public, but it has finally been decided to incorporate it in the present series.

During the dry summer of 1893 Mr. Low happened to be staying in a lonely village on the coast of Devon. He was deeply immersed in some antiquarian work connected with the old Norse calendars, and therefore limited his acquaintance in the neighbourhood to one individual, a Dr. Fremantle, who, beside being a medical man, was a botanist of some note.

One afternoon, when driving together, Mr. Low and Dr. Fremantle passed through a valley which nestled cup-like in the higher ground a few miles inland. As they passed along a deep, steep lane with overhanging hedges they caught a glimpse, through a break in the leaves, of a grey gable peeping out between the horizontal branches of a cedar.

Flaxman Low pointed it out to his companion.

"That's young Montesson's house," answered Fremantle, "and it bears a very sinister reputation. Nothing in your line, though," with a smile. "Indeed, no ghost would lend the same hideous associations to the place it now possesses as the result of a succession of mysterious murders that have occurred there."

"The grounds seem neglected. I don't remember to have seen such rank growth anywhere."

"Certainly not inside the British Isles," returned Fremantle. "The estate is left to take care of itself, partly because Montesson won't live there, partly because it is impossible to find labourers to work near the house. Our warm, damp climate and this sheltered position give rise to extraordinary luxuriance of growth. A stream runs along the bottom, and I expect all the low-lying land, where you see that belt of yellow African grass, is little better than a morass now."

Fremantle drew up as they gained the top of the slope. From there they could overlook the tangle of vegetation, dimmed by a rising mist, which surrounded and almost hid the roof of the Grey House.

"Yes," said Fremantle, in answer to an observation of Mr. Low, "Montesson's guardian, who lived here and looked after the property for him, turned the place into a subtropical garden. It used to be one of my chief pleasures to wander about here, but since my marriage my wife objects to my doing so, on account of the tales she has heard."

"What is the danger?"

"Death!" replied Fremantle shortly.

"What form of death? Malaria?"

"No disease at all, my dear fellow. The persons who die at the Grey House are hanged by the neck until they are dead!"

"Hanged?" repeated Flaxman Low in surprise.

"Yes, hanged. Not only strangled but suspended, as the marks on the necks show. If there were any hint of a ghost in it you might investigate—Montesson would be only too grateful if you could fathom the mystery."

"Tell me something more definite."

"I'll tell you what has happened in my own knowledge. Montesson's father died some fifteen years ago and left him to the guardianship of a cousin named Lampurt, who, as I told you, was a horticulturist, and planted the place with a wonderful variety of foreign shrubs and flowers. Lampurt had a bad name in the county, and his appearance was certainly against him—a squint-eyed, pig-faced fellow, who sidled along like a crab, and could not look you in the face. He died first."

"Was he hanged? Or did he hang himself?"

"Neither, in this case. He dropped in a kind of fit, right up in front of the house, while he was engaged in planting some new acquisition. Had it not been for the evidence of the persons who were present at the time, I should have said his death resulted from some tremendous mental shock. But the gardener and his relation, Mrs. Montesson, agreed in saying that he was not exerting himself unduly, and that he had had no disturbing news. He was a healthy man and I could see no sufficient reason for his death. He was simply gardening, and had apparently pricked himself with a nail for he had a spot of blood upon his forefinger.

"After that all went well for a couple of years, when, during the summer holidays, the trouble began. Montesson must have been about sixteen at the time, and had a tutor with him. His mother and sister—a pretty girl rather older than himself—were also here. One morning the girl was found lying on the gravel under her window, quite dead. I was sent for, and, upon examination, discovered the extraordinary fact that she had been hanged!"

"Murder?"

"Of course, though we could find no trace of the murderer. The girl had been taken from her bedroom and hanged. Then the rope was removed and she was thrown in a heap under her window. The crime caused a tremendous sensation in the neighbourhood, and the police were busy for a long time, but nothing came of their inquiries.

"About a fortnight later, Platt, the tutor, sat up smoking at the open study window. In the morning he was found lying out over the sill. There could be no mistake as to how he met his death, for in addition to the deep line round his throat, his neck was broken as neatly as they could have done it at Newgate! As in the other case, there was nothing to show how he came by his death, no rope, no trace of footsteps or any struggle to lead one to suspect the presence of another person or persons. Yet from the facts it could not have been suicide."

"I see you had some suspicion of your own," said Flaxman Low.

"Well, yes, I had. But time has passed, and I now think I must have been mistaken. I must explain that the branches of the cedar you saw jut to within a few feet of the windows of the rooms occupied by Miss Montesson and Platt respectively at the time of death. I told you there were no traces of anyone having approached the house. It therefore struck me that some active person might have leaped from the cedar into the open windows and escaped in the same way, for the windows open vertically, and when both leaves are thrown back, there is a large aperture. But the murders were so purposeless and disconnected that they suggested irresponsible agency. I recollected Poe's story of the Rue Morgue, where, you remember, the crimes were committed by an ourang-outang. It seemed to me possible that Lampurt, who was of a morose and strange temper, might, among other things, have secretly imported an ape and turned it loose in the woods. I had a thorough search made in the park and grounds, but we found nothing, and I have long ago abandoned the theory."

Low thought silently over the story for some time, then he asked for the dates of the three deaths. Fremantle answered categorically, and it appeared that all had taken place about the same season of the year—during summer, in fact. Upon this Mr. Low made an offer to investigate the affair on psychical lines, if Montesson made no objection. In answer to this message Montesson took the next train down to Devon, and begged to be allowed to accompany Mr. Low in his inquiries.

Flaxman Low quickly saw that Montesson might prove a very useful companion. He was a blond, heavily built man, and plainly possessed of a strong will and temper. Low put aside his books and went off at once with Montesson to have a closer look at the Grey House while the daylight lasted.

It is difficult to give any adequate impression of the teeming exuberance of wild and tangled growth through which they had to cut their way. Young, lush, sappy leafage overlay and half disguised the dank rottenness of the older vegetation beneath. After wading more than breast-high through the matted reeds, below which the spreading stream was fast reducing the land to a swamp, they emerged into a fairly open space that had once been the lawn round the house.

Here brambles and lusty weeds now grew abundantly under the untended trees. Curious shrubs and plants flourished here and there. As they came up a stoat sneaked away by a narrow footpath, nettle-grown and caked with damp, which led past blackened bushes round the house. Otherwise the place was deserted, not a leaf seemed to move in the windless heat of the afternoon. The squat, grey face of the house was scarred across by a dark-leaved creeper, hung with orchid-like blossoms, a little to the left of which Low noticed the cedar mentioned by Dr. Fremantle.

Low drew up at the weed-twisted, sunken little gate that gave upon the lawns and spoke for the first time.

"Tell me about it," and he nodded towards the house.

Montesson repeated the story already told, but added further details. "From here," went on Montesson, "you can see the exact spot where all these things took place. The upper of these two windows surrounded by the creeper and under the shadow of the cedar, belonged to my sister's room; the lower is that of the study where Platt died. The gravel path below ran the whole length of the house, but it is now over-grown— Has Fremantle told you of Lawrence?"

Low shook his head.

"I hate the very sight of the place!" said Montesson hoarsely; "the mystery and the horror of it all seem in my blood. I can't forget! My mother left on the day of Platt's death, and has never been here since. But when I came of age I resolved to make another attempt to live here, meaning to sift the past if I got the chance of doing so. I had the grounds cleared about the house, and after leaving Oxford, came down with a man of my own year, called Lawrence. We spent the Easter vacation here reading, and all went right enough. Meanwhile I had the house examined, thinking there might be a secret entrance or room, but nothing of the kind exists. This house is not haunted. Nothing has ever been seen or heard of a supernatural character—nothing but the same awful repetition of blind murder!"

After a few seconds he resumed.

"During the following summer Lawrence came down with me again. One hot evening we were smoking as we walked up and down the gravel under the windows. It was bright moonlight, and I remember the heavy scent of those red flowers—" Montesson glanced round him strangely.

"I went in to fetch a cigar. It took me some minutes to find the box I wanted, and to light the cigar. When I came out, Lawrence lay crumpled up as if he had fallen from a height, and he was dead. Round his neck was the same bluish line I had seen in the two other cases. You can understand what it was to leave the man not five minutes before, in health and strength, and to come back to find him dead—hanged—to judge from appearances! But as usual, no trace of rope or struggle or murderer!"

After some further talk, Mr. Low proposed to go into the house. It had evidently been deserted in haste. In the room once occupied by Miss Montesson, her girlish treasures still lay about, dusty, moth-eaten, and discoloured. Montesson paused on the threshold.

"Poor little Fan! It's just as she left it!" he said hurriedly.

The cedar outside threw a gloomy shade into the room, and the fantastic red blossoms drooped motionless in the stagnant air.

"Was the window open when your sister was found?" inquired Low after he had examined the room.

"Yes, it was hot weather—early in August. This room has not been occupied since. After Platt's affair, I have always avoided this side of the house, so that it was only by chance Lawrence and I came round to this part of the lawn to smoke."

"Then we may suppose that the danger, whatever it is, exists on this side of the house only?"

"So it seems," replied Montesson.

"Your sister was last seen alive in this room? Platt in the room directly below? and your friend—what of him?"

"Lawrence was lying on the gravel path just under the study window. All of them have died under the shadow of the cedar. Did Fremantle give you his idea? Poor Lawrence's death disposed of that theory. No big ape could live in England all those five years in the open, and in any case it must have been seen sometime in the interval."

"I think so," replied Low abstractedly. "Now as to what we must do to try and get at the meaning of all this. Do you feel equal, considering all you have gone through in this house, do you feel equal to remaining here with me for a night or two?"

Montesson again glanced over his shoulder nervously.

"Yes," he said. "I know my nerves are not as stiff and steady as they should be, but I'll stand by you—especially as you would not find another man about here willing to run the risk. You see it is not a ghost or any fanciful trouble, it means a real danger. Think over it, Mr. Low, before you undertake so hazardous an attempt."

Low looked into the blue eyes Montesson had fixed upon him. They were weary, anxious eyes, and, taken in combination with his compressed lips and square chin, told Low of the struggle this man constantly endured between his shaken nervous system and the strong will that mastered it.

"If you'll stand by me, I'll try to get to the bottom of it," said Low.

"I wonder if I should allow you to risk your life in this way?" returned Montesson, passing his hand over his prematurely lined forehead.

"Why not? Besides it is my own wish. As for risking our lives—it is for the good of mankind."

"I can't say I see it in that light," said Montesson in surprise.

"If we lose our lives it will be in the effort to make another spot of earth clean and wholesome and safe for men to live on. Our duty to the public requires us to run a murderer to earth. Here we have a murderous power of some subtle kind; is it not quite as much our duty to destroy it if we can, even at risk to ourselves?"

The result of this conversation was an arrangement to pass the night at the Grey House. About ten o'clock they set out, intending to follow the path they had more or less successfully cleared for themselves in the afternoon. By Flaxman Low's advice, Montesson carried a long knife. The night was unusually hot and still, and lit only by a thin moon as they made their way along, stumbling over matted weeds and roots and literally feeling for the path, until they came to the little gate by the lawn. There they stopped a moment to look at the house, standing out among its strange sea of over-growth, the dim moon low on the horizon, glinting palely upon the windows and over the deserted countryside. As they waited a night-bird hooted and flapped its way across the open.

At any moment they might be at handgrips with the mysteri-ous power of death which haunted the place. The warm lush-scented air and the sinister shadows seemed charged with some ominous influence. As they drew near the house Low perceived a sweet, heavy odour.

"What is it?" he asked.

"It comes from those scarlet flowers. It's unbearable! Lampurt imported the thing," replied Montesson irritably.

"Which room will you spend the night in?" asked Low as they gained the hall.

Montesson hesitated. "Have you ever heard the expression 'grey with fear'?" he said, laughing in the dark; "I'm that!"

Low did not like the laugh, it was only one remove, and that a very little one, from hysteria.

"We won't find out much unless we each remain alone, and with open windows as they did," said Low.

Montesson shook himself.

"No, I suppose not. *They* were each alone when—good night, I'll call if anything happens, and you must do the same for me. For Heaven's sake, don't go to sleep!"

"And remember," added Low, "with your knife to cut at any-thing that touches you." Then he stood at the study door and listened to Montesson's heavy steps as they passed up the stairs, for he had elected to pass the night in his sister's room. Low heard him walk across the floor above and throw wide the window.

When Mr. Low turned into the study and tried to open the window there, he found it impossible to do so: the creeper outside had fastened upon the woodwork, binding the sashes together. There was but one thing left for him to do, he must go outside and stand where Lawrence had stood on the fatal night. He let himself out softly and went round to the south side of the house.

There he paced up and down in the shadow for perhaps an hour.

In the deceptive, iridescent moonlight a pallid head seemed to wag at him from the gloom below the cedar, but, moving towards it, he grasped only the yellow bunched blossom of a giant ragwort. Then he stood still and looked up into the branches above; the gnarled black branches with their fringes of black sticky leaves. Fremantle's theory of the ape passing stealthily among them to spring upon his victims found a sudden horror of possibility in Low's mind. He imagined the girl awaking in the brute's cruel hands—

Out upon the quiet brooding of the night broke a scream—or rather a roar, a harsh, jagged, pulsating roar, that ceased as abruptly as it had begun.

Without a moment's consideration, Mr. Low seized the branch nearest to him and, swinging himself up into the tree, he climbed with a frantic effort towards the window of Montesson's room, from which he was almost sure the sound had come. Being an unusually active and athletic man he leaped from the branch towards the open window, and fell headlong in upon the floor. As he did so, something seemed to pass him, something swift and sinuous that might have been a snake, and disappear out of the window!

Remembering a candle on the toilet table, he lit it when he regained his feet and looked about him.

Montesson lay on the floor "crumpled up" as he had himself described Lawrence's position. Low recalled this with misgiving as he hurried to his side. A dark smear like blood was on Montesson's cheek, but though unconscious, he was still alive. Low lifted him on to the bed and did what he could to rouse him, but without success. He lay rigid, breathing the slow almost imperceptible respiration of deep stupor.

Low was about to go to the window, when the candle suddenly went out, and he was left in the increasing darkness, to all intents alone, to face an unknown though tangible assailant.

Silence had again fallen upon the house—that is, the silence of night, and woodlands, and many-folded leafage, and the things that go by night. He stood by the window and listened. His senses were acute and throbbing; he felt as if he could hear for miles. The scent of the scarlet blossoms rose like deadening fumes into his brain, and he drew away from the window, and, feeling strangely spent, threw himself upon a couch. Then he drew out the knife at his belt, and strung himself up to watchfulness with an effort.

He knew that the attack he had to expect would be likely to come from the direction of the window. He saw the faint, swimming moonlight that fell through the leaves and tendrils of the creeper fade slowly away. Probably clouds were coming up over the sky, for the steamy heat was even more oppressive.

The low window-sill was scarcely more than a foot above the floor, and presently he fancied something was moving along the carpet among the entangling shadows of the leaves, but the darkness was now intensified, and he could not be sure. Montesson's breathing had become quieter. It was the dead hour of the night; hardly a sound was to be heard.

Suddenly Low felt a soft touch upon his knee. His whole consciousness had been so absorbed in the act of listening that this unexpected appeal to another sense startled him. Here and there, rapid, soft, and light, the touches passed over his body. It might have been some animal nosing about him in the dark. Then a smooth, cold touch fell upon his cheek.

Low sprang up, and slashed about him in the darkness with his knife.

In that instant the thing closed with him—a flexuous, snaky thing that flung its coils about his limbs and body in one swift spring like a curling whiplash!

Flaxman Low was all but helpless in the winding grasp of what?—the tentacles of some strange creature? or was it some great snake, this sentient thing that was feeling for his throat? There was not an instant to lose. The knife was pressed against his body; with a violent effort he drew it sharply, edge outwards, against the tightening coils. A spurt of clammy fluid fell upon his hand, and the thing loosed and fell away from him into the stifling gloom.

In the morning Montesson came to himself in one of the lower rooms at the other side of the house. Fremantle was beside him.

"What's the matter?" he asked. "Ah, I remember now. There's Low. It has beaten us again, Fremantle! It is hopeless. I don't know what happened—I was not asleep, when I found myself seized, lifted up, drawn towards the window, and strangled by living ropes. Look at Low!" he went on harshly, raising himself. "Why, man, you're all over blood!"

Flaxman Low glanced down at his hands.

"Looks like it," he said.

"It has beaten even you, Low!" went on Montesson. "There is something much more terrible and tangible than a ghost in this cursed house! See here!"

He pulled down his collar. A faint bluish circle with suffused dots was drawn round his throat.

"It is some deadly species of snake," exclaimed Fremantle.

Low sat down astride a chair thoughtfully.

"I'm sorry to disagree with both of you. But I am inclined to think it is not a snake, and on the other hand I fancy it has a great deal to do with what we may roughly call a ghost. The whole evidence points in only one direction."

"You mustn't let your prejudice in favour of psychical problems run away with your reason," said Fremantle drily. "Has a ghost actual, palpable power?—to go further, has it blood?"

Montesson, who had been looking at his neck in the glass, turned quickly. "It's some horrible thing in nature! Something between a snake and an octopus! What do you say to it, Low?"

Low looked up gravely.

"In spite of Fremantle's objections the steps from beginning to end are very clear."

Fremantle and Montesson exchanged a glance of incredulity.

"My dear fellow, much learning has warped your mind," said Fremantle with an embarrassed laugh.

"First of all," continued Low, "we know where all the deaths have occurred."

"To speak precisely, they have all occurred in different places," interposed Fremantle.

"True; but within a strictly limited area. The slight differences have been of material help to me. In all cases they have occurred in the vicinity of one thing."

"The cedar!" cried Montesson, with some excitement.

"That was my first idea—now I refer to the wall. Will you tell me the probable weight of Lawrence and Platt at the date of death?"

"Platt was a small man—perhaps under nine stone. Lawrence, though much taller, was thin, and could not have weighed more than eleven. As for poor little Fan, she was only a slip of a girl."

"Three people have been killed—one has escaped. In what way do you differ from the others, Montesson?" asked Low.

"If you mean I'm heavier, I certainly am. I scale something like fifteen. But what has that to do with it?"

"Everything. The coils have evidently not sufficient compressive power to destroy life by strangulation simply—there must be suspension as well. You were simply too heavy for them to tackle."

"Coils of what?"

"Of this." Low held up a tapering, reddish-brown tendon or line, which had red curved triangular teeth set on it at intervals.

The two other men stared at this object, and then Montesson burst out: "The creeper on the wall!" he said, in a tone of disappointment. "It couldn't be! Besides, has a plant blood?"

"Let us go and look at it," said Low. "This creeper has never been cut because it withers away every winter to the ground and grows again in the spring. Look here!" He took out his knife and cut a leathery shoot. A crimson stain spurted out on his cuff. "The only person, as far as I can gather, who cut this plant was Mr. Lampurt in nailing it to the wall. He died of shock when he saw the red stain on his finger, as he knew something of its deadly properties. But though stupefying—as your condition last night proved, Montesson—they are not fatal. Even to stupefy they must get into the blood. Now the deaths have all occurred within reach of the tendrils of this plant. And all have happened at the same season of the year, that is to say, at the time when it attains its full annual strength and growth. Another point in favour of Montesson's escape was the dryness of the season. The growth is not quite so good as usual this summer, is it?"

"No, the tendrils are thinner—a good deal thinner and smaller."

"Just so. Therefore your weight saved you, though you were stupefied by the punctures of the thorns. I feared that, and warned you to use your knife."

"But the brain of the thing?" cried Fremantle. "Why, man, has a plant will and knowledge and malevolence?"

"Not of itself, as I believe," answered Low. "Perhaps you will prefer to attribute much to the long arm of coincidence, but the explanation I can offer is one that has long been held by occultists in other countries. Pythagoras and others have taught that the forms of incarnation change as the soul raises or debases itself during each spell of Life. Connect with this the belief of the Brahmins, and I may add of various African tribes, that an earth-bound spirit, at the moment of a premature or sudden death, may pass into plants or trees of certain species, by virtue of an inherent attraction possessed by these plants for such entities. To go further, it is said that these degraded souls have intervals during which they have power of voluntary action to do good or evil, and such action has influence on their future incarnations."

"What do you mean? What do you intend us to believe?" Montesson said, and stopped.

"It is hard to put it into words in these latter days of unbelief," said Low, "but the evidence goes to show that a man—presumably not a good man—dies a sudden death near this plant, even

innoculated with its sap. Fremantle knows this plant to be a Ma-
layan creeper, belonging to a family that possesses strange powers
and properties. I may recall the old story of the upas tree, and more
lately still the murder tree discovered near Kolwe, in East Africa,
by Herr Boltze. There are also other instances."

"It is incredible!" said Fremantle almost angrily.

"I don't ask you to believe it," said Flaxman Low quietly, "I only
tell you such beliefs exist. Montesson can do something towards
proving my theory. Let him have the plant destroyed, and judge by
results."

The tendril of the creeper severed by Mr. Low in his struggle
was presented by him to the authorities at Kew.

Mr. Montesson has acted upon Mr. Flaxman Low's suggestions.
The Grey House is now occupied and safe, and it is a strange fact
that no plant, not even the hardy ivy, will live where the red-blos-
somed creeper once grew.

THE STORY OF YAND MANOR HOUSE

Looking through the notes of Mr. Flaxman Low, one sometimes catches through the steel-blue hardness of facts, the pink flush of romance, or more often the black corner of a horror unnameable. The following story may serve as an instance of the latter. Mr. Low not only unravelled the mystery at Yand, but at the same time justified his life-work to M. Thierry, the well-known French critic and philosopher.

At the end of a long conversation, M. Thierry, arguing from his own standpoint as a materialist, had said:

"The factor in the human economy which you call 'soul' cannot be placed."

"I admit that," replied Low. "Yet, when a man dies, is there not one factor unaccounted for in the change that comes upon him? Yes! For though his body still exists, it rapidly falls to pieces, which proves that that has gone which held it together."

The Frenchman laughed, and shifted his ground.

"Well, for my part, I don't believe in ghosts! Spirit manifestations, occult phenomena—is not this the ashbin into which a certain clique shoot everything they cannot understand, or for which they fail to account?"

"Then what should you say to me, Monsieur, if I told you that I have passed a good portion of my life in investigating this particular ashbin, and have been lucky enough to sort a small part of its contents with tolerable success?" replied Flaxman Low.

"The subject is doubtless interesting—but I should like to have some personal experience in the matter," said Thierry dubiously.

"I am at present investigating a most singular case," said Low. "Have you a day or two to spare?"

Thierry thought for a minute or more.

"I am grateful," he replied. "But, forgive me, is it a convincing ghost?"

"Come with me to Yand and see. I have been there once already, and came away for the purpose of procuring information from MSS. to which I have the privilege of access, for I confess that the phenomena at Yand lie altogether outside any former experience of mine."

Low sank back into his chair with his hands clasped behind his head—a favourite position of his—and the smoke of his long pipe curled up lazily into the golden face of an Isis, which stood behind him on a bracket. Thierry, glancing across, was struck by the strange likeness between the faces of the Egyptian goddess and this scientist of the nineteenth century. On both rested the calm, mysterious abstraction of some unfathomable thought. As he looked, he decided.

"I have three days to place at your disposal."

"I thank you heartily," replied Low. "To be associated with so brilliant a logician as yourself in an inquiry of this nature is more than I could have hoped for! The material with which I have to deal is so elusive, the whole subject is wrapped in such obscurity and hampered by so much prejudice, that I can find few really qualified persons who care to approach these investigations seriously. I go down to Yand this evening, and hope not to leave without clearing up the mystery."

"You will accompany me?"

"Most certainly. Meanwhile pray tell me something of the affair."

"Briefly the story is as follows. Some weeks ago I went to Yand Manor House at the request of the owner, Sir George Blackburton, to see what I could make of the events which took place there. All they complain of is the impossibility of remaining in one room—the dining-room."

"What then is he like, this M. le Spook?" asked the Frenchman, laughing.

"No one has ever seen him, or for that matter heard him."

"Then how—"

"You can't see him, nor hear him, nor smell him," went on Low, "but you can feel him and—taste him!"

"*Mon Dieu!* But this is singular! Is he then of so bad a flavour?"

"You shall taste for yourself," answered Flaxman Low smiling. "After a certain hour no one can remain in the room, they are simply crowded out."

"But who crowds them out?" asked Thierry.

"That is just what I hope we may discover to-night or tomorrow."

The last train that night dropped Mr. Flaxman Low and his companion at a little station near Yand. It was late, but a trap in waiting soon carried them to the Manor House. The big bulk of the building stood up in absolute blackness before them.

"Blackburton was to have met us, but I suppose he has not yet arrived," said Low. "Hullo! the door is open," he added as he stepped into the hall.

Beyond a dividing curtain they now perceived a light. Passing behind this curtain they found themselves at the end of the long hall, the wide staircase opening up in front of them.

"But who is this?" exclaimed Thierry.

Swaying and stumbling at every step, there tottered slowly down the stairs the figure of a man.

He looked as if he had been drinking, his face was livid, and his eyes sunk into his head.

"Thank Heaven you've come! I heard you outside," he said in a weak voice.

"It's Sir George Blackburton," said Low, as the man lurched forward and pitched into his arms.

They laid him down on the rugs and tried to restore consciousness.

"He has the air of being drunk, but it is not so," remarked Thierry. "Monsieur has had a bad shock of the nerves. See the pulses drumming in his throat."

In a few minutes Blackburton opened his eyes and staggered to his feet.

"Come. I could not remain there alone. Come quickly."

They went rapidly across the hall, Blackburton leading the way down a wide passage to a double-leaved door, which, after a perceptible pause, he threw open, and they all entered together.

On the great table in the centre stood an extinguished lamp, some scattered food, and a big, lighted candle. But the eyes of all three men passed at once to a dark recess beside the heavy, carved chimneypiece, where a rigid shape sat perched on the back of a huge, oak chair.

Flaxman Low snatched up the candle and crossed the room towards it.

On the top of the chair, with his feet upon the arms, sat a powerfully-built young man huddled up. His mouth was open, and his eyes twisted upwards. Nothing further could be seen from below but the ghastly pallor of cheek and throat.

"Who is this?" cried Low. Then he laid his hand gently on the man's knee.

At the touch the figure collapsed in a heap upon the floor, the gaping, set, terrified face turned up to theirs.

"He's dead!" said Low after a hasty examination. "I should say he's been dead some hours."

"Oh, Lord! Poor Batty!" groaned Sir George, who was entirely unnerved. "I'm glad you've come."

"Who is he?" said Thierry, "and what was he doing here?"

"He's a gamekeeper of mine. He was always anxious to try conclusions with the ghost, and last night he begged me to lock him in here with food for twenty-four hours. I refused at first, but then I thought if anything happened while he was in here alone, it would interest you. Who could imagine it would end like this?"

"When did you find him?" asked Low.

"I only got here from my mother's half an hour ago. I turned on the light in the hall and came in here with a candle. As I entered the room, the candle went out, and—and—I think I must be going mad."

"Tell us everything you saw," urged Low.

"You will think I am beside myself; but as the light went out and I sank almost paralysed into an armchair, I saw two barred eyes looking at me!"

"Barred eyes? What do you mean?"

"Eyes that looked at me through thin vertical bars, like the bars of a cage. What's that?"

With a smothered yell Sir George sprang back. He had approached the dead man and declared something had brushed his face.

"You were standing on this spot under the overmantel. I will remain here. Meantime, my dear Thierry, I feel sure you will help Sir George to carry this poor fellow to some more suitable place," said Flaxman Low.

When the dead body of the young gamekeeper had been carried out, Low passed slowly round and about the room. At length he stood under the old carved overmantel, which reached to the ceiling and projected bodily forward in quaint heads of satyrs and animals. One of these on the side nearest the recess represented a griffin with a flanged mouth. Sir George had been standing directly below this at the moment when he felt the touch on his face. Now alone in the dim, wide room, Flaxman Low stood on the same spot and waited. The candle threw its dull yellow rays on the shadows which seemed to gather closer and wait also. Presently a distant door banged, and Low, leaning forward to listen, distinctly felt something on the back of his neck!

He swung round. There was nothing! He searched carefully on all sides, then put his hand up to the griffin's head. Again came the same soft touch, this time upon his hand, as if something had floated past on the air.

This was definite. The griffin's head located it. Taking the candle to examine more closely, Low found four long black hairs depending from the jagged fangs. He was detaching them when Thierry reappeared.

"We must get Sir George away as soon as possible," he said.

"Yes, we must take him away, I fear," agreed Low. "Our investigation must be put off till to-morrow."

On the following day they returned to Yand. It was a large country-house, pretty and old-fashioned, with lattice windows and deep gables, that looked out between tall shrubs and across lawns set with beaupots, where peacocks sunned themselves on the velvet turf. The church spire peered over the trees on one side; and an old wall covered with ivy and creeping plants, and pierced at intervals with arches, alone separated the gardens from the churchyard.

The haunted room lay at the back of the house. It was square and handsome, and furnished in the style of the last century. The oak overmantel reached to the ceiling, and a wide window, which almost filled one side of the room, gave a view of the west door of the church.

Low stood for a moment at the open window looking out at the level sunlight which flooded the lawns and parterres.

"See that door sunk in the church wall to the left?" said Sir George's voice at his elbow. "That is the door of the family vault. Cheerful outlook, isn't it?"

"I should like to walk across there presently," remarked Low.

"What! Into the vault?" asked Sir George, with a harsh laugh. "I'll take you if you like. Anything else I can show you or tell you?"

"Yes. Last night I found this hanging from the griffin's head," said Low, producing the thin wisp of black hair. "It must have touched your cheek as you stood below. Do you know to whom it can belong?"

"It's a woman's hair! No, the only woman who has been in this room to my knowledge for months is an old servant with grey hair, who cleans it," returned Blackburton. "I'm sure it was not here when I locked Batty in."

"It is human hair, exceedingly coarse and long uncut," said Low; "but it is not necessarily a woman's."

"It is not mine at any rate, for I'm sandy; and poor Batty was fair. Good-night; I'll come round for you in the morning."

Presently, when the night closed in, Thierry and Low settled down in the haunted room to await developments. They smoked and talked deep into the night. A big lamp burned brightly on the table, and the surroundings looked homely and desirable.

Thierry made a remark to that effect, adding that perhaps the ghost might see fit to omit his usual visit.

"Experience goes to prove that ghosts have a cunning habit of choosing persons either credulous or excitable to experiment upon," he added.

To M. Thierry's surprise, Flaxman Low agreed with him.

"They certainly choose suitable persons," he said, "that is, not credulous persons, but those whose senses are sufficiently keen to detect the presence of a spirit. In my own investigations, I try to eliminate what you would call the supernatural element. I deal with these mysterious affairs as far as possible on material lines."

"Then what do you say of Batty's death? He died of fright—simply."

"I hardly think so. The manner of his death agrees in a peculiar manner with what we know of the terrible history of this room. He died of fright and pressure combined. Did you hear the doctor's remark? It was significant. He said: 'The indications are precisely those I have observed in persons who have been crushed and killed in a crowd!'"

"That is sufficiently curious, I allow. I see that it is already past two o'clock. I am thirsty; I will have a little seltzer." Thierry rose from his chair, and, going to the side-board, drew a tumblerful from the syphon. "Pah! What an abominable taste!"

"What? The seltzer?"

"Not at all?" returned the Frenchman irritably. "I have not touched it yet. Some horrible fly has flown into my mouth, I suppose. Pah! Disgusting!"

"What is it like?" asked Flaxman Low, who was at the moment wiping his own mouth with his handkerchief.

"Like? As if some repulsive fungus had burst in the mouth."

"Exactly. I perceive it also. I hope you are about to be convinced."

"What?" exclaimed Thierry, turning his big figure round and staring at Low. "You don't mean—"

As he spoke the lamp suddenly went out.

"Why, then, have you put the lamp out at such a moment?" cried Thierry.

"I have not put it out. Light the candle beside you on the table."

Low heard the Frenchman's grunt of satisfaction as he found the candle, then the scratch of a match. It sputtered and went out. Another match and another behaved in the same manner, while Thierry swore freely under his breath.

"Let me have your matches, Monsieur Flaxman; mine are, no doubt, damp," he said at last.

Low rose to feel his way across the room. The darkness was dense.

"It is the darkness of Egypt—it may be felt. Where then are you, my dear friend?" he heard Thierry saying, but the voice seemed a long way off.

"I am coming," he answered, "but it's so hard to get along."

After Low had spoken the words, their meaning struck him. He paused and tried to realise in what part of the room he was. The silence was profound, and the growing sense of oppression seemed like a nightmare. Thierry's voice sounded again, faint and receding.

"I am suffocating, Monsieur Flaxman, where are you? I am near the door. Ach!"

A strangling bellow of pain and fear followed, that scarcely reached Low through the thickening atmosphere.

"Thierry, what is the matter with you?" he shouted. "Open the door."

But there was no answer. What had become of Thierry in that hideous, clogging gloom! Was he also dead, crushed in some ghastly fashion against the wall? What was this? The air had become palpable to the touch, heavy, repulsive, with the sensation of cold humid flesh!

Low pushed out his hands with a mad longing to touch a table, a chair, anything but this clammy, swelling softness that thrust itself upon him from every side, baffling him and filling his grasp.

He knew now that he was absolutely alone—struggling against what? His feet were slipping in his wild efforts to feel the floor— the dank flesh was creeping upon his neck, his cheek—his breath came short and labouring as the pressure swung him gently to and fro, helpless, nauseated!

The clammy flesh crowded upon him like the bulk of some fat, horrible creature; then came a stinging pain on the cheek. Low clutched at something—there was a crash and a rush of air—

The next sensation of which Mr. Flaxman Low was conscious was one of deathly sickness. He was lying on wet grass, the wind blowing over him, and all the clean, wholesome smells of the open air in his nostrils.

He sat up and looked about him. Dawn was breaking windily in the east, and by its light he saw that he was on the lawn of Yand Manor House. The latticed window of the haunted room above him was open. He tried to remember what had happened. He took stock of himself, in fact, and slowly felt that he still held something clutched in his right hand—something dark-coloured, slender, and twisted. It might have been a long shred of bark or the cast skin of an adder—it was impossible to see in the dim light.

After an interval the recollection of Thierry recurred to him. Scrambling to his feet, he raised himself to the window-sill and looked in. Contrary to his expectation, there was no upsetting of furniture; everything remained in position as when the lamp went out. His own chair and the one Thierry had occupied were just as when they had arisen from them. But there was no sign of Thierry.

Low jumped in by the window. There was the tumbler full of seltzer, and the litter of matches about it. He took up Thierry's box of matches and struck a light. It flared, and he lit the candle with ease. In fact, everything about the room was perfectly normal; all the horrible conditions prevailing but a couple of hours ago had disappeared.

But where was Thierry? Carrying the lighted candle, he passed out of the door, and searched in the adjoining rooms. In one of them, to his relief, he found the Frenchman sleeping profoundly in an armchair.

Low touched his arm. Thierry leapt to his feet, fending off an imaginary blow with his arm.

Then he turned his scared face on Low.

"What! You, Monsieur Flaxman! How have you escaped?"

"I should rather ask you how you escaped," said Low, smiling at the havoc the night's experiences had worked on his friend's looks and spirits.

"I was crowded out of the room against the door. That infernal thing—what was it?—with its damp, swelling flesh, inclosed me!" A shudder of disgust stopped him. "I was a fly in an aspic. I could not move. I sank into the stifling pulp. The air grew thick. I called to you, but your answers became inaudible. Then I was suddenly thrust against the door by a huge hand—it felt like one, at least. I had a struggle for my life, I was all but crushed, and then, I do not know how, I found myself outside the door. I shouted to you in vain. Therefore, as I could not help you, I came here, and—I will confess it, my dear friend—I locked and bolted the door. After some time I went again into the hall and listened; but, as I heard nothing, I resolved to wait until daylight and the return of Sir George."

"That's all right," said Low. "It was an experience worth having."

"But, no! Not for me! I do not envy you your researches into mysteries of this abominable description. I now comprehend perfectly that Sir George has lost his nerve if he has had to do with this horror. Besides, it is entirely impossible to explain these things."

At this moment they heard Sir George's arrival, and went out to meet him.

"I could not sleep all night for thinking of you!" exclaimed Blackburton on seeing them; "and I came along as soon as it was light. Something has happened."

"But certainly something has happened," cried M. Thierry shaking his head solemnly; "something of the most bizarre, of the most horrible! Monsieur Flaxman, you shall tell Sir George this story. You have been in that accursed room all night, and remain alive to tell the tale!"

As Low came to the conclusion of the story Sir George suddenly exclaimed:

"You have met with some injury to your face, Mr. Low."

Low turned to the mirror. In the now strong light three parallel weals from eye to mouth could be seen.

"I remember a stinging pain like a lash on my cheek. What would you say these marks were caused by, Thierry?" asked Low.

Thierry looked at them and shook his head.

"No one in their senses would venture to offer any explanation of the occurrences of last night," he replied.

"Something of this sort, do you think?" asked Low again, putting down the object he held in his hand on the table.

Thierry took it up and described it aloud.

"A long and thin object of a brown and yellow colour and twisted like a sabre-bladed corkscrew," then he started slightly and glanced at Low.

"It's a human nail, I imagine," suggested Low.

"But no human being has talons of this kind—except, perhaps, a Chinaman of high rank."

"There are no Chinamen about here, nor ever have been, to my knowledge," said Blackburton shortly. "I'm very much afraid that, in spite of all you have so bravely faced, we are no nearer to any rational explanation."

"On the contrary, I fancy I begin to see my way. I believe, after all, that I may be able to convert you, Thierry," said Flaxman Low.

"Convert me?"

"To a belief in the definite aim of my work. But you shall judge for yourself. What do you make of it so far? I claim that you know as much of the matter as I do."

"My dear good friend, I make nothing of it," returned Thierry, shrugging his shoulders and spreading out his hands. "Here we have a tissue of unprecedented incidents that can be explained on no theory whatever."

"But this is definite," and Flaxman Low held up the blackened nail.

"And how do you propose to connect that nail with the black hairs—with the eyes that looked through the bars of a cage—the fate of Batty, with its symptoms of death by pressure and suffocation—our experience of swelling flesh, that something which filled and filled the room to the exclusion of all else? How are you going to account for these things by any kind of connected hypothesis?" asked Thierry, with a shade of irony.

"I mean to try," replied Low.

At lunch time Thierry inquired how the theory was getting on.

"It progresses," answered Low. "By the way, Sir George, who lived in this house for some time prior to, say, 1840? He was a man—it may have been a woman, but, from the nature of his studies, I am inclined to think it was a man—who was deeply read in ancient necromancy, Eastern magic, mesmerism, and subjects of a kindred nature. And was he not buried in the vault you pointed out?"

"Do you know anything more about him?" asked Sir George in surprise.

"He was, I imagine," went on Flaxman Low reflectively, "hirsute and swarthy, probably a recluse, and suffered from a morbid and extravagant fear of death."

"How do you know all this?"

"I only asked about it. Am I right?"

"You have described my cousin, Sir Gilbert Blackburton, in every particular. I can show you his portrait in another room."

As they stood looking at the painting of Sir Gilbert Blackburton, with his long, melancholy, olive face and thick, black beard, Sir George went on. "My grandfather succeeded him at Yand. I have often heard my father speak of Sir Gilbert, and his strange studies and extraordinary fear of death. Oddly enough, in the end he died rather suddenly, while he was still hale and strong. He predicted his own approaching death, and had a doctor in attendance for a week or two before he died. He was placed in a coffin he had had made on some plan of his own and buried in the vault. His death occurred in 1842 or 1843. If you care to see them I can show you some of his papers, which may interest you."

Mr. Flaxman Low spent the afternoon over the papers. When evening came, he rose from his work with a sigh of content, stretched himself, and joined Thierry and Sir George in the garden.

They dined at Lady Blackburton's, and it was late before Sir George found himself alone with Mr. Flaxman Low and his friend.

"Have you formed any opinion about the thing which haunts the Manor House?" he asked anxiously.

Thierry elaborated a cigarette, crossed his legs, and added: "If you have in truth come to any definite conclusion, pray let us hear it, my dear Monsieur Flaxman."

"I have reached a very definite and satisfactory conclusion," replied Low. "The Manor House is haunted by Sir Gilbert Blackburton, who died, or, rather, who seemed to die, on the 15th of August, 1842."

"Nonsense! The nail fifteen inches long at the least—how do you connect it with Sir Gilbert?" asked Blackburton testily.

"I am convinced that it belonged to Sir Gilbert," Low answered.

"But the long black hair like a woman's?"

"Dissolution in the case of Sir Gilbert was not complete—not consummated, so to speak—as I hope to show you later. Even in the case of dead persons the hair and nails have been known to grow. By a rough calculation as to the growth of nails in such cases, I was enabled to indicate approximately the date of Sir Gilbert's death. The hair too grew on his head."

"But the barred eyes? I saw them myself!" exclaimed the young man.

"The eyelashes grow also. You follow me?"

"You have, I presume, some theory in connection with this?" observed Thierry. "It must be a very curious one."

"Sir Gilbert in his fear of death appears to have mastered and elaborated a strange and ancient formula by which the grosser factors of the body being eliminated, the more ethereal portions continue to retain the spirit, and the body is thus preserved from absolute disintegration. In this manner true death may be indefinitely deferred. Secure from the ordinary chances and changes of existence, this spiritualised body could retain a modified life practically for ever."

"This is a most extraordinary idea, my dear fellow," remarked Thierry.

"But why should Sir Gilbert haunt the Manor House, and one special room?"

"The tendency of spirits to return to the old haunts of bodily life is almost universal. We cannot yet explain the reason of this attraction of environment."

"But the expansion—the crowding substance which we ourselves felt? You cannot meet that difficulty," said Thierry persistently.

"Not as fully as I could wish, perhaps. But the power of expanding and contracting to a degree far beyond our comprehension is a well-known attribute of spiritualised matter."

"Wait one little moment, my dear Monsieur Flaxman," broke in Thierry's voice after an interval; "this is very clever and ingenious indeed. As a theory I give it my sincere admiration. But proof—proof is what we now demand."

Flaxman Low looked steadily at the two incredulous faces.

"This," he said slowly, "is the hair of Sir Gilbert Blackburton, and this nail is from the little finger of his left hand. You can prove my assertion by opening the coffin."

Sir George, who was pacing up and down the room impatiently, drew up.

"I don't like it at all, Mr. Low, I tell you frankly. I don't like it at all. I see no object in violating the coffin. I am not concerned to verify this unpleasant theory of yours. I have only one desire; I want to get rid of this haunting presence, whatever it is."

"If I am right," replied Low, "the opening of the coffin and exposure of the remains to strong sunshine for a short time will free you for ever from this presence."

In the early morning, when the summer sun struck warmly on the lawns of Yand, the three men carried the coffin from the vault to a quiet spot among the shrubs where, secure from observation, they raised the lid.

Within the coffin lay the semblance of Gilbert Blackburton, maned to the ears with long and coarse black hair. Matted eyelashes swept the fallen cheeks, and beside the body stretched the bony hands, each with its dependent sheaf of switch-like nails. Low bent over and raised the left hand gingerly.

The little finger was without a nail!

Two hours later they came back and looked again. The sun had in the meantime done its work; nothing remained but a fleshless skeleton and a few half-rotten shreds of clothing.

The ghost of Yand Manor House has never since been heard of. When Thierry bade Flaxman Low good-bye, he said:

"In time, my dear Monsieur Flaxman, you will add another to our sciences. You establish your facts too well for my peace of mind."

THE STORY OF SEVENS HALL

"It may be quite true," said Yarkindale gloomily; "all that I can answer is that we always die the same way. Some of us choose, or are driven, to one form of suicide, and some to another, but the result is alike. For three generations every man of my family has died by his own hand. I have not come to you hoping for help, Mr. Low, I merely want to tell the facts to a man who may possibly believe that we are not insane, that heredity and madness have nothing to do with our leaving the world; but that we are forced out of it by some external power acting upon us, I do not know how. If we inherit anything it is clear-headedness and strength of will, but this curse of ours is stronger. That is all."

Flaxman Low kicked the fire into a blaze. It shown on the silver and china of the breakfast service, and on the sallow, despairing face of the man in the arm-chair opposite. He was still young, but already the cloud that rested upon his life had carved deep lines upon his forehead in addition to the long tell-tale groove from mouth to nostril.

"I conclude death does not occur without some premonition. Tell me something more. What precedes death?" inquired Flaxman Low.

"A regular and well-marked series of events—I insist upon calling them events," replied Yarkindale. "This is not a disease with a series of symptoms. Whatever it is it comes from the outside. First we fall into an indescribable depression, causeless except as being the beginning of the end, for we are all healthy men, fairly rich, and even lucky in the other affairs of life—and of love. Next comes the ghost or apparition or whatever you like to call it. Lastly we die by our own hands." Yarkindale brought down a sinewy brown hand upon the arm of his chair. "And because we have been powers in the land, and there must be as little scandal as possible, the doctors and the coroner's jury bring it in 'Temporary insanity.'"

"How long does this depression last before the end?" Flaxman Low's voice broke in upon the other's moody thinking.

"That varies, but the conclusion never. I am the last of the lot, and though I am full of life and health and resolve today, I don't give myself a week to live. It is ghastly! To kill oneself is bad enough, but to know that one is being driven to do it, to know that no power on earth can save us, is an outlook of which words can't give the colour."

"But you have not yet seen the apparition—which is the second stage."

"It will come to-day or to-morrow—as soon as I go back to Sevens Hall. I have watched two others of my family go through the same mill. This irresistible depression always comes first. I tell you, in two weeks I shall be dead. And the thought is maddening me!

"I have a wife and child," he went on after an interval; "and to think of the poor little beggar growing up only to suffer this!"

"Where are they?" asked Low.

"I left them in Florence. I hope the truth can be kept from my wife; but that also is too much to hope. 'Another suicide at Sevens Hall.' I can see the headlines. Those rags of newspapers would sell their mothers for half-a-crown!"

"Then the other deaths took place at Sevens Hall?"

"All of them." He stopped and looked hard at Mr. Low.

"Tell me about your brothers," said Low.

Yarkindale burst into laughter.

"Well done, Mr. Low! Why didn't you advise me not to go back to Sevens Hall? That is the admirable counsel which the two brain specialists, whom I have seen since I came up to town, have given me. Go back to the Hall? Of course I shouldn't—if I could help it.

That's the difficulty—I can't help it! I must go. They thought me mad!"

"I hardly wonder," said Low calmly, "if you exhibited the same excitement. Now, hear me. If, as you wish me to suppose, you are fighting against supernatural powers, the very first point is to keep a firm and calm control of your feelings and thoughts. It is possible that you and I together may be able to meet this trouble of yours in some new and possibly successful way. Tell me all you can remember with regard to the deaths of your brothers."

"You are right," said Yarkindale sadly enough. "I am behaving like a maniac, and yet I'm sane, Heaven knows!—To begin with, there were three of us, and we made up our minds long ago when we were kids to see each other through to the last, and we determined not to yield to the influence without a good fight for it. Five years ago my eldest brother went to Somaliland on a shooting trip. He was big, vigorous, self-willed man, and I was not anxious about him. My second brother, Jack, was an R.E., a clever, sensitive, quiet fellow, more likely to be affected by the tradition of the family. While he was out in Gib., Vane suddenly returned from Africa. I found him changed. He had become gloomy and abstracted, and kept saying that the curse was coming upon him. He insisted upon going down to Sevens Hall. I was savage with him. I thought he should have resisted the inclination; I know more about it now. One night he rushed into my bedroom, crying out: 'He's come; he's come!'"

"Did he ever describe what he had seen?" asked Low.

"Never. None of us know definitely what shape the cursed thing takes. No one of us has ever seen it; or, at any rate, in time to describe it. But once it comes—and this is the horrible part—it never leaves us. Step by step it dogs us, till—" Yarkindale stopped, and in a minute or two resumed. "For two nights I sat up with him. He said very little, for Vane never talked much; but I saw the agony in his face, the fear, the loathing, the growing horror—he, who I believe, had never before feared anything in his life.

"The third night I fell asleep. I was worn out, though I don't offer that as an excuse. I am a light sleeper, yet while I slept Vane killed himself within six feet of me! At the inquest it was proved he had bought a silken waist-rope at Cairo, and it was contended that he must have concealed it from me, as I had never seen it. I found him with his head nearly twisted off, and a red rubbed weal across his face. He was lying in a heap upon the floor, for the rope was frayed and broken by his struggles. The theory was that he had hanged himself, and then repented of it, and in his efforts to get free had wrenched his head around, and scarred his face."

Yarkindale stopped and shuddered violently.

"I tried to hush the matter up as well as I could, but of course the news of it reached Jack. Then a couple of years passed, and he went from Gib. to India, and wrote in splendid spirits, for he had met a girl he liked out there, and he had told me that there was never so happy a man on earth before. So you can fancy how I felt when I had a wire from the Hall imploring me to go down at once for Jack had arrived. It is very hard to tell you what he suffered." Yarkindale broke off and wiped his forehead. "For I have been through it all within the last two weeks myself. He cared for that girl beyond anything on earth; yet within a couple of days of their marriage, he had felt himself impelled to rush home to England without so much as bidding her good-bye, though he knew that at the end of his journey death was waiting for him. We talked it over rationally, Mr. Low, and we determined to combine against the power, whatever it was, that was driving him out of the world. We are not monomaniacs. We want to live; we have all that makes life worth living; and yet I am going the same way, and not any effort or desire or resolution on my part can save me!"

"It is a pity you make up your mind to that," said Flaxman Low. "One will pitted against another will has at least a chance of success. And a second point I beg you will bear in mind. Good is always inherently stronger than evil. If, for instance, health were not, broadly speaking, stronger than disease, the poisonous germs floating about the world would kill off the human race inside twelve months."

"Yes," said Yarkindale; "but where two of us failed before, it is not likely that I alone will succeed."

"You need not be alone," said Flaxman Low; "for if you have no objection, I should be glad to accompany you to Sevens Hall, and to give you any aid that may be in my power."

It is not necessary to record what Yarkindale had to say in answer to this offer. Presently he resumed his story:

"Jack was dispirited, and unlike Vane, desperately afraid of his fate. He hardly dare to fall asleep. He recalled all he knew of our father's death, and tried to draw me on to describe Vane's, but I knew better than that. Still, with all my care, he went the same way! I did not trust my own watchfulness a second time; I had a man in the house who was a trained attendant. He sat outside Jack's door of nights. One morning early—it was summer-time, and he must have dropped into a doze—he was shoved over, chair and all, and before he could pick himself up, Jack had flung himself from the balcony outside one of the gallery windows."

Sevens Hall is a large Elizabethan mansion hidden away among acres of rich pasture lands, where wild flowers bloom abundantly in their seasons and rooks build and caw in the great elms. But none of the natural beauties of the country were visible when Mr. Low arrived late on a November evening with Yarkindale. The interior of the house, however, made up for the bleakness outside. Fires and lights blazed in the hall and in the principal rooms. During dinner, Yarkindale seemed to have relapsed into his most dejected mood. He scarcely opened his lips, and his face looked black, not only with depression, but anger. For he was by no means ready to give up life; he rebelled against his fate with the strenuous fury of a man whose pride and strength of will and nearest desires are baffled by an antagonist he cannot evade.

During the evening they played billiards, for Low was aware that the less his companion thought over his own position, the better.

Flaxman Low arranged to occupy a room opposite Yarkindale's. So far the latter was in the same state as on the day when he first saw Mr. Low. He was conscious of the same deep and causeless depression, and the wish to return to Sevens Hall had grown beyond his power to resist. But the second of the fatal signs, the following footsteps, had not yet been heard.

During the next forenoon, to Yarkindale's surprise, Flaxman Low, instead of avoiding the subject, threshed out the details of the former deaths at Sevens Hall, especially those of which Yarkindale could give the fullest particulars. He examined the balcony from which Jack Yarkindale had thrown himself. The iron-work was wrenched and broken in one part.

"When did this happen?" asked Low, pointing to it.

"On the night that Jack died," was the reply. "I have been very little at home since, and I did not care at the time to bother about having it put right."

"It looks," said Flaxman Low, "as if he had a struggle for his life, and clung to the upper bar here where it is bent outwards. He had wounds on his hands, had he not?" he continued looking at a dull long splash of rust upon the iron.

"Yes, his hands were bleeding."

"Please try to recollect exactly. Were they cut or bruised upon the palm? Or was it on the back?"

"Now I come to think of it, his hands were a good deal injured, especially on the knuckles—one wrist was broken—by the fall no doubt."

Flaxman Low made no remark.

Next they went into the spacious bedroom where Vane and more of one of those who went before him had died, and which Yarkindale now occupied. His companion asked to see the rope with which Vane had hanged himself. Most unwillingly Yarkindale brought it out. The two pieces, with their broken strands and brown stains, appeared to be of great interest to Low. He next saw the exact spot on the great bedstead from which it had been suspended, and searching along the back, he discovered the jagged edge of the wood against which Vane in his last agony had endeavoured to free himself by fraying the rope.

"We suppose the rope gave after he was dead, and that was because of his great weight," said Yarkindale. "This is the room in which most of the tragedies have taken place. You will probably witness the last one."

"That will depend on yourself," answered Flaxman Low. "I am inclined to think there will be no tragedy if you will stiffen your back, and hold out. Did either of your brothers on waking complain of dreams?"

Yarkindale looked suspiciously at him under drawn brows. "Yes," he said harshly, "they both spoke of tormenting dreams, which they could not recall after walking, but that was also taken as a symptom of brain disease by the experts. And now that you have learned about the matter, you, too, begin upon the old, worn theory."

"On the contrary, my theory has nothing to do with insanity, though the phenomena connected with the deaths of your brothers seem to be closely associated with sleep. You tell me that your brother Jack was afraid to sleep. Your other brother awoke to find his death somehow. Therefore, we may be certain that at a certain stage of these series of events, as you call them, sleep becomes both a dread and a danger."

Yarkindale shivered and glanced nervously over his shoulder.

"This room is growing very cold. Let us go down to the hall. As to sleep, I have been afraid of it for a long time."

All the day Low noticed that his companion continued to look excessively pale and nervous. Every now and then he would turn his face round as if listening. In the evening they again played billiards late into the night. The house was full of silence before they went upstairs. A long strip of polished flooring led from the billiard-room door to the hall. Yarkindale motioned to Low to stand still while he walked slowly to the foot of the staircase. In the stillness Flaxman Low distinctly heard mingled steps, a softer tread following upon Yarkindale's purposely loud footfalls. The hall was in darkness with the exception of a gas jet at the staircase. Yarkindale stopped, leant heavily against the pillar of the balustrade, and with a ghastly face waited for Low to join him. Then he gripped Low by the arm and pointed downwards. Beside his shadow, a second dim, hooded, formless shadow showed faintly on the floor.

"Stage two," said Yarkindale. "You can see it is no fancy of our unhealthy brains."

Mr. Low has placed it upon record that the following week contained one of the most painful experiences through which it has been his lot to pass. Yarkindale fought doggedly for his life. He thrust aside his dejection. He followed the advice given him with marvellous courage. But still the ominous days dragged on, seeming at times too slow, at times too rapid in their passage. Yarkindale's physical strength began to fail—a mental battle is the most exhausting of all struggles.

"The next point in which you can help," said Low on the eighth night, "is to try to recollect what you have been dreaming of immediately before waking."

Yarkindale shook his head despondently.

"I have tried over and over again, and though I wake in a cold sweat of terror, I cannot gather my senses quickly enough to seize the remembrance of the thing that has spoiled my sleep," he answered with a pallid smile. "You think the psychological moment with us is undoubtedly the first waking moment?"

Low admitted that he thought it was so.

"I understand now why you have emptied this room of everything except the two couches on which we lie. You are afraid I shall lay hands upon myself! I feel the danger and yet I have no suicidal desire. I want to live—Heaven, how I long to live! To be happy, and prosperous, and light-hearted as I was once was!"

Yarkindale lay back upon the couch.

"I wish I could give you the faintest notion of the desperate misery in my mind to-night! I could almost ask to die to escape from it!" he went on; "the burden only appears to grow heavier and more unbearable every day—I sometimes feel I can no longer endure it."

"Think, on the contrary, how much you have to live for. For your own self it matters less than for your boy. Your victory may mean his."

"How? Tell me how?"

"It is rather a long explanation, and I think we had better defer it until I can form some definite ideas on the subject."

"Very well." Yarkindale turned his face from the light. "I will try to sleep and forget all this wretchedness if I can. You will not leave me?"

Through the long winter night, Flaxman Low watched beside him. He felt he dared not leave him for one moment. The room was almost dark, for Yarkindale could not sleep otherwise. The flickering firelight died down, until nothing was left of the last layer of glowing wood ashes. The night lamp in a distant corner threw long shadows across the empty floor, that wavered now and then as if a wind touched the flame.

Outside the night was still and black; not a sound disturbed the silence except those strange unaccountable creakings and groanings which seem like inarticulate voices in an old house.

Yarkindale was sleeping heavily, and as the night deepened Low got up and walked about the room in circles, always keeping his face towards the sleeper. The air had grown very cold, and when he sat down again he drew a rug about him, and lit a cigar. The change in the atmosphere was sudden and peculiar, and he softly pulled his couch close to Yarkindale's and waited.

Creakings and groanings floated up and down the gaunt old corridors, the mystery and loneliness of night became oppressive. The shadow from the night lamp swayed and fluttered as if a door had been opened. Mr. Low glanced at both doors. He had locked both, and both were closed, yet the flame bent and flickered until Low put his hand across his companion's chest, so that he might detect any waking movement, for the light had now become too dim to see by.

To his intense surprise he found his hand at once in the chill of a cold draught blowing on it from above. But Flaxman Low had no time to think about it, for a terrible feeling of cold and numbness was stealing upwards through his feet, and a sense of weighty and deadly chill seemed pressing in upon his shoulders and back. The back of his neck ached, his outstretched hand began to stiffen.

Yarkindale still slept heavily.

New sensations were borne in slowly upon Low. The chill around him was the repulsive clammy chill of a thing long dead.

Desperate desires awoke in his mind; something that could almost be felt was beating down his will.

Then Yarkindale moved slightly in his sleep.

Low was conscious of a supreme struggle, whether of mind or body he does not know, but to him it appeared to extend to the ultimate effort a man can make. A hideous temptation rushed wildly across his thoughts to murder Yarkindale! A dreadful longing to feel the man's strong throat yielding and crushing under his own sinewy strangling fingers, was forced into his mind.

Suddenly, Low became aware that, although the couch and part of Yarkindale's figure were visible, his head and the upper part of his body were blotted out as if by some black intervening object. But there was no outline of the interposed form, nothing but a vague thick blackness.

He sprang to his feet as he heard an ominous choking gasp from Yarkindale, and with his swift hands he felt over the body through the darkness. Yarkindale lay tense and stiff.

"Yarkindale!" shouted Low, as his fingers felt the angle of an elbow, then hands upon Yarkindale's throat, hands that clutched savagely with fingers of iron.

"Wake man!" shouted Low again, trying to loosen the desperate clutch. Then he knew that the hands were Yarkindale's hands, and that the man was apparently strangling himself.

The ghastly struggle, that in the darkness, seemed half a dream and half reality, ceased abruptly when Yarkindale moved and his hands fell limp and slack into Low's as the darkness between them cleared away.

"Are you awake?" Low called again.

"Yes. What is it? I feel as if I had been fighting for my life. Or have I been very ill?"

"Both, in a sense. You have passed the crisis, and you are still living. Hold on, the lamp's gone out."

But, as he spoke, the light resumed its steady glimmer, and, when a couple of candles added their brightness, the room was shown bare and empty, and as securely closed as ever. The only change to be noted was that the temperature had risen.

A frosty sun was shining into the library windows next morning when Flaxman Low talked out the matter of the haunting presence which had exerted so sinister an influence upon generations of the Yarkindale family.

"Before you say anything, I wish to admit, Mr. Low, that I, and no doubt those who have gone before me, have certainly suffered from a transient touch of suicidal mania," began Yarkindale gloomily.

"And I am very sure you make a mistake," replied Low. "In suicidal mania the idea is not transient, but persistent, often extending over months, during which time the patient watches for an opportunity to make away with himself. In your case, when I woke you last night, you were aware of a desire to strangle yourself, but directly you became thoroughly awake, the idea left you?"

"That is so. Still—"

"You know that often when dreaming one imagines oneself to do many things which in the waking state would be entirely impossible, yet one continues subject to the idea for a moment or so during the intermittent stage between waking and sleeping. If one has a nightmare, one continues to feel a beating of the heart and a sensation of fright even for some interval after waking. Yours was an analogous condition."

"But look here, Mr. Low. How do you account for it that I, who at this moment have not the slightest desire to make away with myself, should, at the moment of awaking from sleep, be driven to doing that which I detest and wish to avoid?"

"In every particular," said Flaxman Low, "your brothers' cases were similar. Each of them attempted his life in that transient moment while the will and reason were still passive, and action was still subject to an abnormally vivid idea which had evidently been impressed upon the consciousness during sleep. We have clear proof of this, I say, in the struggles of each to save himself when actually *in extremis*. Contemporary psychology has arrived at the conclusion that every man possesses a subconscious as well as a conscious self," added Low, after a pause. "This second or submerged self appears to be infinitely more susceptible of spiritual influences than the conscious personality. Such influences work most strongly when the normal self is in abeyance during sleep, dreaming, or the hypnotic condition. In your own family you have an excellent example of the idea of self-destruction being suggested during sleep, and carried into action during the first confused, unmastered moments of waking."

"But how do you account for the following footsteps? Whose wishes or suggestions do we obey?"

"I believe them to be different manifestations of the same evil intelligence. Ghosts sometimes, as possibly you are aware, pursue a purpose, and your family has been held in subjection by a malicious spirit that has goaded them on to destroy themselves. I could bring forward a number of other examples; there is the Black Friar of the Sinclairs and the Fox of the Oxenholms. To come back to your own case—do you remember of what you dreamed before I woke you?"

Yarkindale looked troubled.

"I have a dim recollection, but it eludes me. I cannot fix it." He glanced round the room, as if searching for a reminder. Suddenly he sprang up and approached a picture on the wall— "Here it is!" he shouted. "I remember now. A dark figure stood over me; I saw the long face and the sinister eyes—Jules Cevaine!"

"You have not spoken of Cevaine before. Who was he?"

"He was the last of the old Cevaines. You know this house is called Sevens Hall—a popular corruption of the Norman name Cevaine. We Yarkindales were distant cousins, and inherited this place after the death of Jules Cevaine, about a hundred years ago. He was said to have taken a prominent part—under another name— in the Reign of Terror. However that may be—he resented our inheriting the Hall."

"He died here?" asked Flaxman Low.

"Yes."

"His purpose in haunting you," said Low, "was doubtless the extermination of your family. His spirit lingers about this spot where the final intense passion of terror, pain, and hatred was felt. And you yourselves have unknowingly fostered his power by dwelling upon and dreading his influence, thus opening the way to spirit communication, until from time to time his disembodied will has superimposed itself upon your wills during the bewildered moment of waking, and the several successive tragedies of which you told me have been the result."

"Then how can we ever escape?"

"You have already won one and your most important victory; for the rest, think of him as seldom as may be. Destroy this painting and any other articles that may have belonged to him; and if you take my advice you will travel for a while."

In pursuance of Mr. Flaxman Low's advice, Yarkindale went for the cold weather to India. He has had no recurrence of the old trouble, but he loathes Sevens Hall, and he is only waiting for his son to be old enough to break the entail, when the property will be placed on the market.

THE STORY OF SADDLER'S CROFT

Although Flaxman Low has devoted his life to the study of psychical phenomena, he has always been most earnest in warning persons who feel inclined to dabble in spiritualism, without any serious motive for doing so, of the mischief and danger accruing to the rash experimenter. Extremely few persons are sufficiently masters of themselves to permit of their calling in the vast unknown forces outside ordinary human knowledge for mere purposes of amusement.

In support of this warning the following extraordinary story is laid before our readers.

Deep in the forest land of Sussex, close by an unfrequented road, stands a low half-timbered house, that is only separated from the roadway by a rough stone wall and a few flower borders.

The front is covered with ivy, and looks out between two conical trees upon the passers-by. The windows are many of them diamond-paned, and an unpretentious white gate leads up to the front door. It is a quaint, quiet spot, with an old-world suggestion about it which appealed strongly to pretty Sadie Corcoran as she drove with her husband along the lane. The Corcorans were Americans, and had to the full the American liking for things ancient. Saddler's Croft struck them both as ideal, and when they found out that it was much more roomy and comfortable than it looked from the road, and also that it had large lawns and grounds attached to it, they decided at once on taking it for a year or two.

When they mentioned the project to Phil Strewd, their host, and an old friend of Corcoran, he did not favour it. Much as he should have liked to have them for neighbours, he thought that Saddler's Croft had too many unpleasant traditions connected with it. Besides, it had lain empty for three years, as the last occupants were spiritualists of some sort, and the place was said to be haunted. But Mrs. Corcoran was not to be put off, and declared that a flavour of ghostliness was all that Saddler's Croft required to make it absolutely the most attractive residence in Europe.

The Corcorans moved in about October, but it was not till the following July that Flaxman Low met Mr. Strewd on the Victoria platform.

"I'm glad you're coming down to Andy Corcoran's," Strewd began. "You must remember him? I introduced you to him at the club a couple of years ago. He's an awfully decent fellow, and an old friend of mine. He once went with an Arctic expedition, and has crossed Greenland or San Josef's Land on snowshoes or something. I've got the book about it at home. So you can size him up for yourself. He's now married to a very pretty woman, and they have taken a house in my part of the world.

"I didn't want them to rent Saddler's Croft, for it had a bad name some years ago. Some of your psychical folk used to live there. They made a sort of Greek temple at the back, where they used to have queer goings on, so I'm told. A Greek was living with them called Agapoulos, who was the arch-priest of their sect, or whatever it was. Ultimately Agapoulos died on a moonlight night in the temple, in the middle of their rites. After that his friends left, but, of course, people said he haunted the place. I never saw anything myself, but a young sailor, home on leave about that time, swore he'd catch the ghost, and he was found next morning on the temple steps. He was past telling us what had happened, or what he had seen, for he was dead. I'll never forget his face. It was horrible!"

"And since then?"

"After that the place would not let, although the talk of the ghost being seen died away until quite lately. I suppose the old caretaker went to bed early, and avoided trouble that way. But during the last few months Corcoran has seen it repeatedly himself, and—in fact, things seem to be going on very strangely. What with Mrs. Corcoran wild on studying psychology, as she calls it—"

"So Mrs. Corcoran has a turn that way?"

"Yes, since young Sinclair came home from Ceylon about five months ago. I must tell you he was very thick with Agapoulos in former times, and people said he used to join in all the ruffianism at Saddler's Croft. You'll see the rest for yourself. You are asked down ostensibly to please Mrs. Corcoran, but Andy hopes you may help him to clear up the mystery."

Flaxman Low found Corcoran a tall, thin, nervy American of the best type; while his wife was as pretty and as charming as we have grown accustomed to expect an American girl to be.

"I suppose," Corcoran began, "that Phil has been giving you all the gossip about this house? I was entirely sceptical once; but now—do you believe in midsummer madness?"

"I believe there often is a deep truth hidden in common beliefs and superstitions. But let me hear more."

"I'll tell you what happened not twenty-four hours ago. Everything has been working up to it for the last three months, but it came to a head last night, and I immediately wired for you. I had been sitting in my smoking-room rather late reading. I put out the lamp and was just about to go to bed when the brilliance of the moonlight struck me, and I put my head through the window to look over the lawn. Directly I heard chanting of a most unusual character from the direction of the temple, which lies at the back of that plantation. Then one voice, a beautiful tenor, detached itself from the rest, and seemed to approach the house. As it came nearer I saw my wife cross the grass to the plantation with a wavering, uncertain gait. I ran after her, for I believed she was walking in her sleep; but before I could reach her a man came out of the grass alley at the other side of the lawn.

"I saw them go away together down the alley towards the temple, but I could not stir, the moonbeams seemed to be penetrating my brain, my feet were chained, the wildest and most hideous thoughts seemed rocking—I can use no other term—in my head. I made an effort, and ran round by another way, and met them on the temple steps. I had strength left to grasp at the man—remember I saw him plainly, with his dark, Greek face—but he turned aside and leapt into the underwood, leaving in my hand only the button from the back of his coat.

"Now comes the incomprehensible part. Sadie, without seeing me, or so it appeared, glided away again towards the house; but I was determined to find the man who had eluded me. The moonlight poured upon my head; I felt it like an absolute touch. The chanting grew louder, and drowned every other recollection. I forgot Sadie, I forgot all but the delicious sounds, and I—I, a nineteenth-century, hard-headed Yankee—hammered at those accursed doors to be allowed to enter. Then, like a dream, the singing was behind me and around me—some one came, or so I thought, and pushed me gently in. The moon was pouring through the end window; there were many people. In the morning I found myself lying on the floor of the temple, and all about me the dust was undisturbed but for the mark of my own single footstep and the spot where I had fallen. You may say it was all a dream, Low, but I tell you some infernal power hangs about that building."

"From what you tell me," said Flaxman Low, "I can almost undertake to say that Mrs. Corcoran is at present nearly, if not quite, ignorant of the horrible experience you remember. In her case the emotions of wonder and curiosity have probably alone been worked upon as in a dream."

"I believe in her absolutely," exclaimed Corcoran, "but this power swamps all resistance. I have another strange circumstance to add. On coming to myself I found the button still in my hand. I have since had the opportunity of fitting it to its right position in the coat of a man who is a pretty constant visitor here," the American's lips tightened, "a young Sinclair, who does tea-planting in Ceylon when he has the health for it, but is just now at home to recruit. He is the son of a neighbouring squire, and in every particular of face and figure unlike the handsome Greek I saw that night."

"Have you spoken to him on the subject?"

"Yes; I showed him the button, and told him I had found it near the temple. He took the news very curiously. He did not look confused or guilty, but simply scared out of his senses. He offered no explanation, but made a hasty excuse, and left us. My wife looked on with the most perfect indifference, and offered no remark."

"Has Mrs. Corcoran appeared to be very languid of late?" asked Low.

"Yes, I have noticed that."

"Judging from the effect produced by the chanting upon you, I should say that you were something of a musician?" said Low irrelevantly.

"Yes," replied the other, astonished.

"Then, this evening, when I am talking with Mrs. Corcoran, will you reproduce the melody you heard on that night?"

Corcoran agreed, and the conversation ended with a request on the part of Mr. Low to be permitted to make the acquaintance of Mrs. Corcoran, and further, to be given the opportunity of talking to her alone.

Sadie Corcoran received him with effusion.

"O Mr. Low, I'm just perfectly delighted to see you! I'm looking forward to the most lovely spiritual talks. It's such fun! You know I was in quite a psychical set before I married, but afterwards I dropped it, because Andy has some effete old prejudices."

Flaxman Low inquired how it happened that her interest had revived.

"It is the air of this dear old place," she replied, with a more serious expression. "I always found the subject very attractive, and lately we have made the acquaintance of a Mr. Sinclair, who is a—" she checked herself with an odd look, "who knows all about it."

"How does he advise you to experiment?" asked Mr. Low. "Have you ever tried sleeping with the moonlight on your face?"

She flushed, and looked startled.

"Yes, Mr. Sinclair told me that the spiritualists who formerly lived in this house believed that by doing so you could put yourself into communication with—other intelligences. It makes one dream," she added, "such strange dreams."

"Are they pleasant dreams?" asked Flaxman Low gravely.

"Not now, but by and by he assures me that they will be."

"But you must think of your dreams all day long, or the moonlight will not affect you so readily on the next occasion, and you are obliged to repeat a certain formula? Is it not so?"

She admitted it was, and added: "But Mr. Sinclair says that if I persevere I shall soon pass through the zone of the bad spirits and enter the circle of the good. So I choose to go on. It is all so wonderful and exciting. Oh, here is Mr. Sinclair! I'm sure you will find many interesting things to talk over."

The drawing-room lay at the back of the house, and overlooked a strip of lawn shut in on the further side by a thick plantation of larches. Directly opposite to the French window, where they were seated, a grass alley which had been cut through the plantation gave a glimpse of turf and forest land beyond. From this alley now emerged a young man in riding-breeches, who walked moodily across the lawn with his eyes on the ground. In a few minutes Flaxman Low understood that young Sinclair had a pronounced admiration for his hostess, the reckless, headstrong admiration with which a weak-willed man of strong emotions often deceives himself and the woman he loves. He was manifestly in wretched health and equally wretched spirits, a combination that greatly impaired the very ordinary type of English good-looks which he represented.

While the three had tea together Mrs. Corcoran made some attempt to lead up to the subject of spiritualism, but Sinclair avoided it, and soon Mrs. Corcoran lost her vivacity, which gave place to a well-marked languor, a condition that Low shortly grew to connect with Sinclair's presence.

Presently she left them, and the two men went outside and walked up and down smoking for a while till Flaxman Low turned down the path between the larches. Sinclair hung back.

"You'll find it stuffy down there," he said, with curved nostrils.

"I rather wanted to see what building that roof over the trees belongs to," replied Low.

With manifest reluctance Sinclair went on beside him. Another turn at right angles brought them into the path leading up to the little temple, which Low found was solidly built of stone. In shape it was oblong, with a pillared Ionic façade. The trees stood closely round it, and it contained only one window, now void of glass, set high in the further end of the building. Low asked a question.

"It was a summer-house made by the people who lived here formerly," replied Sinclair, with brusqueness. "Let's get away. It's beastly damp."

"It is an odd kind of summer-house. It looks more like—" Low checked himself. "Can we go inside?" He went up the low steps and tried the door, which yielded readily, and he entered to look round.

The walls had once been ornamented with designs in black and some glittering pigment, while at the upper end a daïs nearly four feet high stood under the arched window, the whole giving the vague impression of a church. One or two peculiarities of structure and decoration struck Low.

He turned sharply on Sinclair.

"What was this place used for?"

But Sinclair was staring round with a white, working face; his glance seemed to trace out the half-obliterated devices upon the walls, and then rested on the daïs. A sort of convulsion passed over his features, as his head was jerked forward, rather as if pushed by some unseen force than by his own will, while, at the same time, he brought his hand to his mouth, and kissed it. Then with a strange, prolonged cry he rushed headlong out of the temple, and appeared no more at Saddler's Croft that day.

The afternoon was still and warm with brooding thunderstorm, but at night the sky cleared. Now it happened that Andy Corcoran was, amongst many other good things, an accomplished musician, and, while Flaxman Low and Mrs. Corcoran talked at intervals by the open French window, he sat down at the piano and played a weird melody. Mrs. Corcoran broke off in the middle of a sentence, and soon she began swaying gently to the rhythm of the music, and presently she was singing. Suddenly, Corcoran dropped his hand on the notes with a crash. His wife sprang from her chair.

"Andy! Where are you? Where are you?" And in a moment she had thrown herself, sobbing hysterically, into his arms, while he begged her to tell him what troubled her.

"It was that music. Oh, don't play it any more! I liked it at first, and then all at once it seemed to terrify me!" He led her back towards the light.

"Where did you learn that song, Sadie? Tell me."

She lifted her clear eyes to his.

"I don't know! I can't remember, but it is like a dreadful memory! Never play it again! Promise me!"

"Of course not, darling."

By midnight the moon sailed broad and bright above the house. Flaxman Low and the American were together in the smoking-room. The room was in darkness. Low sat in the shadow of the open window, while Corcoran waited behind him in the gloom. The shade of the larches lay in a black line along the grass, the air was still and heavy, not a leaf moved. From his position, Low could see the dark masses of the forest stretching away into the dimness over the undulating country. The scene was very lovely, very lonely, and very sad.

A little trill of bells within the room rang the half-hour after midnight, and scarcely had the sound ceased when from outside came another—a long cadenced wailing chant of voices in unison that rose and fell faint and far off but with one distinct note, the same that Low had heard in Sinclair's beast-like cry earlier in the day.

After the chanting died away, there followed a long sullen interval, broken at last by a sound of singing, but so vague and dim that it might have been some elusive air throbbing within the brain. Slowly it grew louder and nearer. It was the melody Sadie had begged never to hear again, and it was sung by a tenor voice, vibrating and beautiful.

Low felt Corcoran's hand grip his shoulder, when out upon the grass Sadie, a slim figure in trailing white, appeared advancing with uncertain steps towards the alley of the larches. The next moment the singer came forward from the shadows to meet her. It was not Sinclair, but a much more remarkable-looking personage. He stopped and raised his face to the moon, a face of an extraordinary perfection of beauty such as Flaxman Low had never seen before. But the great dark eyes, the full powerfully moulded features, had one attribute in common with Sinclair's face, they wore the same look of a profound and infinite unhappiness.

"Come." Corcoran gripped Flaxman Low's shoulder. "She is sleep-walking. We will see who it is this time."

When they reached the lawn the couple had disappeared. Corcoran leading, the two men ran along under the shadow of the house, and so by another path to the back of the temple.

The empty window glowed in the light of the moon, and the hum of a subdued chanting floated out amongst the silent trees. The sound seized upon the brain like a whiff of opium, and a thousand unbidden thoughts ran through Flaxman Low's mind. But his mental condition was as much under his control as his bodily movements. Pulling himself together he ran on. Sadie Corcoran and her companion were mounting the steps under the pillars. The girl held back, as if drawn forward against her will; her eyes were blank and open, and she moved slowly.

Then Corcoran dashed out of the shadow.

What occurred next Mr. Low does not know, for he hurried Mrs. Corcoran away towards the house, holding her arm gently. She yielded to his touch, and went silently beside him to the drawing-room, where he guided her to a couch. She lay down upon it like a tired child, and closed her eyes without a word.

After a while Flaxman Low went out again to look for Corcoran. The temple was dark and silent, and there was no one to be seen. He groped his way through the long grass towards the back of the building. He had not gone far when he stumbled over something soft that moved and groaned. Low lit a match, for it was impossible to see anything in the gloom under the trees. To his horror he found the American at his feet, beaten and battered almost beyond recognition.

The first thing next morning Mr. Strewd received a note from
Flaxman Low asking him to come over at once. He arrived in the
course of the forenoon, and listened to an account of Corcoran's
adventures during the night, with an air of dismay.

"So it's come at last!" he remarked, "I'd no idea Sinclair was
such a bruiser."

"Sinclair? What do you suppose Sinclair had to do with it?"

"Oh, come now, Low, what's the good of that? Why, my man
told me this morning when I was shaving that Sinclair went home
some time last night all covered in blood. I'd half a guess at what
had happened then."

"But I tell you I saw the man with whom Corcoran fought. He
was an extraordinarily handsome man with a Greek face."

Strewd whistled.

"By George, Low, you let your imagination run away with you,"
he said, shaking his head. "That's all nonsense, you know."

"We must try to find out if it is," said Low. "Will you come over
to-night and stay with me? There will be a full moon."

"Yes, and it has affected all your brains! Here's Mrs. Corcoran
full of surprise over her husband's condition! You don't suppose
that's genuine?"

"I know it is genuine," replied Low quietly. "Bring your Kodak
with you when you come, will you?"

The day was long, languorous, and heavy; the thunderstorm had
not yet broken, but once again the night rose cloudless. Flaxman Low
decided to watch alone near the temple while Strewd remained on the
alert in the house, ready to give his help if it should be needed.

The hush of the night, the smell of the dewy larches, the sil-
very light with its bewildering beauty creeping from point to point
as the moon rose, all the pure influences of nature, seemed to Low
more powerful, more effective, than he had ever before felt them
to be. Forcing his mind to dwell on ordinary subjects, he waited.
Midnight passed, and then began indistinct sounds, shuffling footsteps, murmurings, and laughter, but all faint and evasive. Gradually the tumultuous thoughts he had experienced on the previous
evening began to run riot in his brain.

When the singing began he does not know. It was only by an immense effort of will that he was able to throw off the trance that was stealing over him, holding him prisoner—how nearly a willing prisoner he shudders to remember. But habits of self-control have been Low's only shield in many a dangerous hour. They came to his aid now. He moved out in front of the temple just in time to see Sadie pass within the temple door. Waiting only a moment to make quite sure of his senses, and concentrating his will on the single desire of saving her, he followed. He says he was conscious of a crowd of persons at either side; he knew without looking that the pictures on the wall glowed and lived again.

Through the high window opposite him a broad white shaft of light fell, and immediately under it, on the daïs, stood the man whom Mr. Low in his heart now called Agapoulos. Supreme in its beauty and its sadness that beautiful face looked across the bowed heads of those present into the eyes of Mr. Flaxman Low. Slowly, very slowly, as a narrow lane opened up before him amongst the figures of the crowd, Low advanced towards the daïs. The man's smile seemed to draw him on; he stretched out his hand as Flaxman Low approached. And Low was conscious of a longing to clasp it even though that might mean perdition.

At the last moment, when it seemed to him he could resist no longer, he became aware of the white-clad figure of Sadie beside him. She also was looking up at the beautiful face with a wild gaze. Low hesitated no longer. He was now within two feet of the daïs. He swung back his left hand and dealt a smashing half-arm blow at the figure. The man staggered with a very human groan, and then fell face forward on the daïs. A whirlwind of dust seemed to rise and obscure the moonlight; there was a wild sense of motion and flight, a subdued sibilant murmur like the noise of a swarm of bats in commotion, and then Flaxman Low heard Phil Strewd's loud voice at the door, and he shouted to him to come.

"What has happened?" said Strewd, as he helped to raise the fallen man. "Why, whom have we got here? Good heavens, Low, it is Agapoulos! I remember him well!"

"Leave him there in the moonlight. Take Mrs. Corcoran away and hurry back with the Kodak. There is no time to lose before the moon leaves this window."

The moonlight was full and strong, the exposure prolonged and steady, so that when afterwards Flaxman Low came to develop the film—but we are anticipating, for the night and its revelations were not over yet. The two men waited through the dark hour that precedes the dawn, intending when daylight came to remove their prisoner elsewhere. They sat on the edge of the daïs side by side, Strewd at Low's request holding the hand of the unconscious man, and talked till the light came.

"I think it's about time to move him now," suggested Strewd, looking round at the wounded man behind him. As he did so, he sprang to his feet with a shout.

"What's this, Low? I've gone mad, I think! Look here!"

Flaxman Low bent over the pale, unconscious face. It bore no longer the impress of that exquisite Greek beauty they had seen an hour earlier; it only showed to their astonished gaze the haggard outlines of young Sinclair.

Some days later Strewd rubbed the back of his head energetically with a broad hand, and surmised aloud.

"This is a strange world, my masters," and he looked across the cool shady bedroom at Andy Corcoran's bandaged head.

"And the other world's stranger, I guess," put in the American drily, "if we may judge by the sample of the supernatural we have lately had.

"You know I hold that there is no such thing as the supernatural; all is natural," said Flaxman Low. "We need more light, more knowledge. As there is a well-defined break in the notes of the human voice, so there is a break between what we call natural and supernatural. But the notes of the upper register correspond with those in the lower scale; in like manner, by drawing upon our experience of things we know and see, we should be able to form accurate hypotheses with regard to things which, while clearly pertaining to us, have so far been regarded as mysteries."

"I doubt if any theory will touch this mystery," Strewd objected. "I have questioned Sinclair, and noted down his answers as you asked me, Low. Here they are."

"No, thank you. Will you compare my theory with what he has told you? In the first place, Agapoulos was, I fancy, one of a clique calling themselves Dianists, who desired to revive the ancient worship of the moon. That I easily gathered from the symbol of the moon in front of the temple and from the half-defaced devices on the walls inside. Then I perceived that Sinclair, when we were standing before the daïs, almost unconsciously used the gesture of the moon worshippers. The chant we heard was the lament for Adonis. I could multiply evidences, but there is no need to do so. The fact also tells that the place is haunted on moonlight nights only."

"Sinclair's confession corroborates all this," said Strewd at this point.

Corcoran turned irritably on his couch.

"Moon-worship was not exactly the nicest form of idolatry," he said in a weary tone; "but I can't see how that accounts for the awkward fact that a man who not only looks like Agapoulos, but was caught, and even photographed as Agapoulos, turns out at the end of an hour or so, during which there was no chance of substituting one for the other, to be another person of an entirely different appearance. Add to this that Agapoulos is dead and Sinclair is living, and we have an array of facts that drive one to suspect that common-sense and reason are delusions. Go on, Low."

"The substitution, as you call it, of Agapoulos for Sinclair is one of the most marked and best attested cases of obsession with which I have personally come into contact," answered Flaxman Low. "You will notice that during Sinclair's absence in Ceylon nothing was seen of the ghost—on his return it again appeared."

"What is obsession? I know what it is supposed to be, but—" Corcoran stopped.

"I should call it in this case as nearly as possible an instance of spiritual hypnotism. We know there is such a thing as human hypnotism; why should not a disembodied spirit have similar powers?

Sinclair has been obsessed by the spirit of Agapoulos; he not only yielded to his influence in the man's lifetime, but sought it again after his death. I don't profess to claim any great knowledge of the subject, but I do know that terrible results have come about from similar practices. Sinclair, for his own reasons, invited the control of a spirit, and, having no inherent powers of resistance, he became its slave. Agapoulos must have possessed extraordinary willforce; his soul actually dominated Sinclair's. Thus not only the mental attributes of Sinclair but even his bodily appearance became modified to the likeness of the Greek. Sinclair himself probably looked upon his experiences as a series of vivid dreams induced by dwelling on certain thoughts and using certain formulae, until this morning when his condition proved to him that they were real enough."

"That is perhaps all very well so far as it goes," put in Strewd, "but I fail to understand how a seedy, weakly chap like Sinclair could punish my friend Andy here, as we must suppose he has done, if we accept your ideas, Low."

"You are aware that under abnormal conditions, such as may be observed in the insane, a quite extraordinary reserve of latent strength is frequently called out from apparently weak persons. So Sinclair's usual powers were largely reinforced by abnormal influences."

"I have another question to ask, Low," said Corcoran. "Can you explain the strange attraction and influence the temple possessed over all of us, and especially over my wife?"

"I think so. Mrs. Corcoran, through a desire for amusement and excitement, placed herself in a degree of communication with the spiritual world during sleep. Remember, the Greek lived here, and the thoughts and emotions of individuals remain in the *aura* of places closely associated with them. Personally, I do not doubt that Agapoulos is a strong and living intelligence, and those persons who frequent the vicinity of the temple are readily placed in rapport with his wandering spirit by means of this *aura*. To use common words, evil influences haunt the temple."

"But this is intolerable. What can we do?"

"Leave Saddler's Croft, and persuade Mrs. Corcoran to have no more to do with spiritism. As for Sinclair, I will see him. He has opened what may be called the doors of life. It will be a hard task to close them again, and to become his own master. But it may be done."

THE STORY OF NO. 1 KARMA CRESCENT

The following story is the first full relation of the extraordinary features of the case connected with the house in South London, that at one time occupied so large a portion of the public attention. It may be remembered that several mysterious deaths took place within a few months of each other in a certain new suburb. In each instance the same unaccountable symptoms were present, and the successive inquests gave rise to a quite remarkable amount of discussion in the Press as the evidence furnished points of peculiar interest for the Psychical Societies.

It is a recognised fact that the public will die patiently, and to a large percentage, of any known and preventable epidemic before they trouble to make a stir about it, but they resent instantly and bitterly the removal of half-a-dozen individuals, provided these die from some unknown and, therefore, unpreventable cause. Thus the fate of the victims at No. 1 Karma Crescent, raised a storm of comment, conjecture, and vague accusation; in time this died away, however, and the whole business was forgotten, or only recalled to serve as an example of the many dark and sinister mysteries London carries in her unfathomed heart.

As many people may not be able to recall the details to mind, a brief *résumé* of the chief incidents is given below, together with additional information supplied later by Flaxman Low, the well-known psychical investigator.

Karma Crescent is one of several similar terraces planned and partially built upon a newly opened estate in an outlying suburb of

London. The locality is good, though not fashionable, hence the houses, though of fair size, are offered at moderate rentals. Karma Crescent has never been completed. It consists of six or seven houses, most of which were let when Colonel Simpson B. Hendriks and his son walked over from the railway station to inspect No. 1. This was a detached corner house, overlooking an untidy spread of building land, beyond which railway sheds and a network of lines on a rather high level rose against the sky. To the right of the house an old country lane, deeply rutted, led away between ragged hedges to a congeries of small houses about half a mile distant. These houses form the outer crust of a poor district, of which no more need be said than that it provides a certain amount of dock labour.

The Americans were, however, not deterred by the dreary surroundings; they had come to London on business, and since No. 1 was cheap, commodious, and well-furnished, they closed with the agent who showed them over. It was only when the lease was signed, and they had begun to inquire for servants, that the distinctive characteristics of the abode they had chosen was borne in upon them. Upon making inquiry they gathered that the house had been occupied by three successive sets of tenants, all of whom complained that it was haunted by a dark, evil, whispering face, that lurked in dusky corners, met them in lonely rooms, or hung over the beds, terrifying the awakened sleepers.

This silent, flitting presence foretold death, for each family had left hurriedly and in deep distress upon the loss of one of its members, but as the drains and the roof were sound, and it has been definitely decided that the English law can take no account of ghosts, the Hendrikses were obliged to stick to their bargain. Finally, the Colonel, who was a widower, secured the services of a gaunt Scotch housekeeper, professing herself well acquainted with the habits of ghosts, and took up his residence with his son at No. 1, being fully persuaded that a free use of shooting-irons was likely to prove as good a preventive against hauntings as against any other form of annoyance.

Three days later, on the 5th February, the first symptoms of disturbance set in. The Hendrikses had been out very late, and on

their return in the small hours, found their housekeeper scared
and shaking, and with a circumstantial story to tell of the apparition. She said she had been awakened from sleep by the touch of a
death-cold hand. Opening her eyes, she saw a fearsome, whispering face hanging over her; she could not catch the meaning of the
words it said, but was persuaded that they were threatening.

A faint light flickered about the face, "like I've seen brandy on
a dish of raisins," continued Miss Anderson, "and I could see it
was wrapped up in its winding-sheet, gone yellow wi' age and lying
by. At last the light went out wi' a flash, and I lay trembling in the
dairk till I heard the latch-keys in the door, for I was fair frechtened
at yon ghaist." One further detail she added, to the effect that on
going to bed she had locked the door and put the key under her
pillow, where she found it safe after the visit of the apparition,
although the door was still fast locked when she tried to leave the
room an hour later.

After this experience the Americans had all the bolts and locks
of the house examined and strengthened, also one or other of them
remained at home every evening.

It was in the course of the following week that young Lamartine
Hendriks went out to a theatre, leaving his father at home. He was
absent something over three hours and a half. When he returned
between eleven and twelve o'clock, he found Colonel Hendriks sitting at a table in the dining-room, his body swollen to an enor-
mous size, his face of a livid indigo, and quite dead. Calling down
the housekeeper, the young man went for a doctor. He recollected
having seen a doctor's plate on the door of a house in a shabby
street close by. Dr. Mulroon was at home, a big powerful Irishman,
rather the worse for liquor, but with the deep eye and square jaw
that indicate ability. Hendriks hurried him round to Karma Crescent. On the way Mulroon asked no questions, he walked silently
into the dining-room and looked steadily to the Colonel. Then he
shook his head.

"Bedad! It's just what I expected!" he said.

"What?" asked Hendriks sharply.

Mulroon was sober enough by this time.

"It's the old story," he replied with a strong brogue. "This makes the fourth case of this kind I've been called in to see in this house during the last eighteen months."

"In this neighbourhood?"

"In this house, faith, and nowhere else! Didn't ye know it was haunted? Haven't you heard of the 'Strange Deaths in South London'? The papers had them in capitals an inch long."

Hendriks leant against the table and spoke hoarsely.

"We have just come from America, and I can recall something of what you mention, but I did not connect them with this house. As you have attended similar cases, tell me what is the cause of death?"

"The Public Analyst himself couldn't do that! Not in the way you want to hear it. I made an examination in each case as well as he, and maybe I'm as capable as he, perhaps more so! For I swept off every medal and honour that came in my way at Dublin, and—but what's the use of talking? No man living can tell you more than this. The blue colour of the tissues and the swelling are produced by a change in the condition of the blood, though the most exhaustive examination has failed to discover any reason or cause for such a change. The result is death, that is the only certainty about it."

A long silence ensued, and then Hendriks said quietly: "If it takes me to the last day of my life, I'll get at this business from the inside. I'll never give it up until I know everything!"

"Well, now, look here, Mr. Hendriks, will you take my advice? The police and the doctors have done their living best over this business, and they're just where they were at the beginning. There's only one man in Europe can help you—Flaxman Low, the psychologist."

But Hendriks demurred on the ground of having seen enough of such gentry in the States,

"Low is not like any of them. He is as sensible and as practical a man as you or I. I know what he can do and how he sets about it, for I was in practice in the country four or five years ago, and he came down there and cleared up a mystery that had bothered the neighbourhood for above ten years. Leave this room exactly as it is. Wire for him first—you can get the police in after."

The upshot of this conversation was that Mr. Low arrived at Karma Crescent soon after it became light, having been fetched by Mulroon in person.

The dining-room was a square room opening on to the garden by a French window. It was richly furnished, everything was in order, there was no sign of a struggle. At the table about ten feet from the glass doors sat the dead man—a disfigured and horrible spectacle. The body was inclined to the left side, the head dropped rather forward on the left shoulder, the left arm hanging straight down at his side, and the left trouser leg slightly turned up. Low bent over him and looked at the puffed blue lips.

"Does the attitude suggest anything to you?" asked Flaxman Low after some time.

"He was bending forward to get his breath," returned Mulroon.

"On the contrary he had been stooping forward and to the left, but leant back for relief when the final spasm seized him," said Low. "Whatever may have been the cause of death, its action was rapid. Now can you give me the details of the former deaths which have taken place here?"

"I can do that same." Mulroon drew out a pocket-book. "Here you are."

"The first tenant of this house was Dr. Philipson Vines (D.D., you understand). On the 16th November, 1889, he was found dead sitting in that same chair by the servants at 6.30 a.m. A fine edition of Froissart was open on the table before him. He had evidently been dead for several hours. His age was fifty-three, the body was well nourished, and all the organs healthy.

"Next, Richard Stephen Holding, a retired linen draper, with a large family, took the house. On the 3rd February, 1890, he was found dead by his wife at 2 a.m. He was also seated at the table, and in the same attitude as you have noticed in Colonel Hendriks's case. Like the Colonel, he was still warm. His age was sixty-three, and a progressive heart trouble existed—which was not, however, the cause of death.

"Next, the house was taken by a widow lady named Findlater, with one daughter and an invalid son. The son kept to his bedroom during the first fortnight of their stay, but one warm May morning he ventured down here. His sister left him in an armchair at 11.45 in the forenoon, and on returning half-an-hour after to bring him some beef-tea, she found him seated at the table, blue and swollen and dead, just like the others. Findlater was twenty-seven, and must in any case have died shortly from phthisis."

"Can you recollect the attitudes of the bodies when you saw them?"

"Only in the case of Holding. The two others had been laid on the couch before my arrival," answered Mulroon.

"Have you not noticed this left trouser leg?" continued Low.

"Yes; it was the same with Holding's. Probably a convulsive clutch at the last moment, and, no doubt, involuntary."

Some further conversation having taken place, it was eventually arranged that Mr. Low should return in the evening to spend a few days with young Hendriks, and to study the surroundings.

After he had gone notice of the death was given and the usual formalities were carried out. The police examined the whole house, but as far as could be judged by prolonged searching, no one from outside could have got in, yet Colonel Hendriks had been done to death although no wound appeared upon the body.

The evidence of Miss Anderson at the inquest excited much attention. Several persons interested in psychical mysteries were present and made copious notes, besides cross-examining the housekeeper subsequently at great length. But no one, police, doctors, or psychists, had any workable theory to offer. Miss Anderson stated before the coroner that she wished to leave No. 1 Karma Crescent at once, as she was firmly persuaded that the malignant whispering face, which hung over her while she lay in bed, was the face of the "Wicked One."

The jury returned an open verdict, and Hendriks walked back to his house feeling very dejected. His father's unaccountable death weighed upon him. He could not rid himself of the remembrance of the hideously changed aspect of the keen, handsome face that had been so much to him from his boyhood.

He knew that Flaxman Low had been present unofficially at the inquest, and resolved to question him on arrival. But when Low came, he declined to commit himself to any opinion, though he went so far as to say that he hoped some further information might soon be forthcoming. And with this Hendriks had to be satisfied.

"I should like to occupy your late housekeeper's room, where, I understand, several manifestations have taken place," continued Mr. Low, "and if you would allow it to be understood that I am merely a servant, whom you have hired for the time being to attend upon you, I think it might be a wise precaution."

During the next few days Flaxman Low was busy. He had brought with him a number of solid and peculiar bolts, which he fixed on the various doors and windows, it seemed, almost at random. He shut off the basement very securely, and put another bolt on the outside of the shutters inclosing the glass doors leading from the dining-room into the garden. Yet, after all, Hendriks noticed that he went to bed for several nights leaving one or other of these fittings unbolted.

Meanwhile, Low loitered about the garden, and inside and outside the house. He walked over to the railway junction, and lingered in the little lane. He visited the unpleasant colony of houses by the river, and altogether gained a pretty thorough knowledge of the neighbourhood.

"Has that garden door from the lane been much used since you came here?" he asked Hendriks one morning.

"No; my father thought that, under the circumstances, it had better be secured. It was never used. And, as there is no cellarage, I don't see how any persons can enter the house except after the ordinary style of the burglar."

Mulroon dropped in very often to see them, and one night he inquired of Flaxman Low if the apparition had made its appearance. To his astonishment, Mr. Low replied in the affirmative.

"What did you do?" asked Mulroon.

"Nothing," replied Mr. Low. "My plans do not admit of any overt action yet. But I can assure you that Miss Anderson is a good observer, she gave us a very correct description of its appearance."

"Then it was an evil spirit?"

Mr. Flaxman Low smiled a little. "Undoubtedly," he said.

That night Mr. Low securely locked off the basement from the upper floor. He had since his coming insisted that no one but himself should enter the dining-room at any time or for any purpose. He begged that it should be neither ventilated nor aired, but left closed and unopened. Every day he went in and remained for some time, morning and evening. On this occasion he paid the room his usual nightly visit, and Hendriks from the hall could hear him locking the French windows.

"Won't you draw your patent safety bolt outside, too?" he called out. "You've forgotten that every night."

"I think I may leave that for the present," was Low's reply.

"There's nothing to be got out of you, Mr. Low," said Hendriks with some irritation.

"Not yet, but I hope soon to have something to say for myself," Flaxman Low answered.

On the next day Mr. Low did not visit the dining-room until the afternoon. He opened the doors to air the room and lit the fire, after which he locked the French windows, and, shutting the door behind him, went to speak to Hendriks in the next room.

"I am going out for a short time," he said. "Will you be good enough not to enter the dining-room during my absence? Mulroon will probably come round. Please warn him also."

It was already growing dark when Mr. Low left the house. He remained away but a short time, and on his return was much disturbed by hearing Mulroon's big voice arguing with Hendriks in the dining-room. He opened the door. Mulroon was sitting in the same high-backed chair. He was a little tipsy, and, in consequence, annoyingly obstinate.

Mr. Low laid down the basket he held in his hand.

"For Heaven's sake, Mulroon, don't move! If you do, you're a dead man!" he said, approaching him. "Now, keep your legs straight—so, and rise gently."

Mulroon, grumbling a good deal, but partially sobered by Flaxman Low's manifest alarm, did as he was told.

"Now," added Low, "if you will kindly leave me for a few minutes alone, I will join you later."

Mulroon, however, had patients to attend to, and left, so that when Mr. Low followed Hendriks into the drawing-room a quarter of an hour afterwards, he found the American alone.

"There were two questions which I set myself to answer when I came to this house," said Low. "One was—Why did these persons die? There was a peculiar and obscure cause, of which we saw the effects. The second was—By what agency were these persons subjected to the cause of death? I have partially solved one problem tonight. Tomorrow I have some hope of reaching the other. To begin with, I have already satisfied myself as to the precise manner of death. Tomorrow night, if you and Mulroon will meet me here, I will tell you, as far as I can, how the whole mystery may be solved."

All the next day Flaxman Low and Hendriks kept close to the house. After dark Flaxman Low disappeared, and had not returned by eleven o'clock. Mulroon and Hendriks sat waiting for him in the drawing-room, until presently he walked into the room, and threw himself into an armchair.

"I think now," he said, "that I may venture to say that I have something to show you.

"To begin at the beginning, this house was declared by successive tenants to be haunted. Further, the manifestations were said to be connected in some way with the deaths that took place after the apparitions had been seen—in all cases by some member of the household other than the victim. Whether these saw or heard anything prior to death was naturally beyond the power of their relatives to discover. But I fancy I can now answer that question. I have fairly good proof that they did not see any apparition."

"There never was any sign of a struggle or disturbance," put in Mulroon. "And that reminds me of what an old Irish charwoman, who worked here in the Findlaters' time, told me—that many cases had been known in her part of Ireland where the sight of a ghost turned the blood in the veins of the beholder. To be sure, we only smile at such sayings, but if you can give me any better reason why these men died, I'll thank you."

"This is exactly the point I hope to make," replied Low. "But to return to the manifestations. Miss Anderson's account of the ghost tallies with the stories of other residents. It nearly always appeared to the servants, by the way. The thing was evil and whispered, and each was convinced they could have understood what it said had they not been too frightened to do so. Then all agreed in saying it wore its winding-sheet. This added strength to my first conclusion and the further I pushed my inquiries the more I was confirmed in my theory."

"But the deaths. You cannot account for them?" asked Hendriks. "You can't persuade me that any whispering face killed my father. He would have put a bullet through it on sight."

"Pray be patient," said Flaxman Low. "You must remember that I had very little data to go upon. In all cases the post-mortem aspect was the same—the terribly distended bodies, the puffy lips, the bluish skin. Something had brought about this aspect with its concurrent effect—death, but no one could find out anything more. Knowledge stopped at the ultimate fact of death. It appeared to be impossible to get behind that last wall."

Hendriks made a movement of impatience.

"Yes, yes, but where do the ghosts come in?"

"Nowhere," replied Flaxman Low decisively. "At a very early stage of the business I entirely cast aside all thoughts of spiritual phenomena. Two points I noticed in connection with Colonel Hendriks' appearance aided me—the turning up of the left trouser leg and the position of the body in the chair. From these two facts the conclusion was obvious. I then knew why the people had died. There was, of course, no ghost at all. They had simply been murdered!"

"By whom? I shall be glad to meet that man," said Hendriks suddenly.

"But allow me to ask you what you deduced from the winding-sheet and the whisperings?" asked Mulroon.

"Taken in conjunction with the manner of death of the inmates of this house," said Flaxman Low, "I deduced a Chinaman. The winding-sheet meant simply loose garments, which might readily be nothing more than the formless wide-sleeved jacket of dirty yellow worn by the Chinese. Upon this I searched the whole neighbourhood for a yellow skin, and came upon a furtive little colony down by the riverside."

"But we had this house secured in all sorts of ways. How could this fellow have gained an entrance, and what grudge can he bear against us? Then, as you know, there was no struggle."

"The reason of the haunting and the murders are evident. Certain persons wanted to keep this house empty. They have some means of entering from the basement, and they are in possession of duplicate keys for every lock, a matter which reduces the haunting to a very simple process. If you remember one of my very first steps was to fix bolts—which cannot be unlocked—upon some of the doors. I bolted off the basement for two nights after my arrival and consequently I slept in peace. On the third night I left the dividing door locked only, and I was at once favoured with a glimpse of the whispering face lit up by the usual phosphorescent trick. As I expected, the face was of the Malay cast, and it threatened in mumbling pidgin English.

"You told me, Mr. Hendriks, that the garden door had not been opened since your tenancy began—that it was in fact secured. I had reason to think otherwise, and made certain of the correctness by tying a thread across the doorway on the inner side, which was broken more than once. From the garden door to the French window in the dining-room was a natural step in my theory."

"But that bolt you put upon the outside of the wooden shutters?" said Mulroon.

"It suited my plans to put it there; in fact, I hope it is holding well at this moment. Knowing that duplicate keys existed, I presumed that someone would enter the dining-room shortly, for a purpose which I will presently explain. I, therefore, put up my little thread-detective, and it also gave satisfactory evidence. Someone had entered the room, and to make sure of their motive for doing so, I purchased a rat, which I brought back in a basket with me last evening, but Mulroon very nearly saved me the trouble of trying any experiment on my own part by sitting down in the chair which seems to be the fatal one here."

Mulroon turned pale, and laughed in a forced manner.

"Well, well," he said; "the drink makes fools of us all, but my luck stood to me. How did I escape, Mr. Low?"

"You had the luck of long legs, that is all. When you sat in the chair, the backs of your knees did not come against the frame of the seat; if they had, you would have been in your coffin by now."

"Then you have discovered how my father met his death?" exclaimed Hendriks.

"Yes. In examining the chair, I found the legs had been neatly cut, so as to tilt back the chair at a slight angle, and any person sitting in it would naturally sit far back in consequence, thus bringing the back of the knees against the wooden bar in front of the seat. To the left of this bar I found a tiny splinter of steel fixed in, and I tried its effect last night upon a rat, with the result that it died almost immediately, its body being dreadfully swollen in the course of a few minutes. The turned-up trouser on the left leg led me directly to this discovery. To take the case of Colonel Hendriks, he felt the prick on the inner side of the left knee, and was turning up his trouser when the poison took effect, and he died in the act."

"I remember now that at the post-mortem examination you pointed out a hardly visible mark on the Colonel's knee," said Mulroon; "but it seemed too faint and tiny to afford any clue. But as you are in a position to prove that the persons who have died here have died of poison, can you account for the fact that no trace of poison has been discovered in any of the bodies?"

"Other known poisons disappear from the system in a similar manner. In this instance, guided by my supposition that the perpetrators of the murders were Chinese, I naturally set about finding out as much as possible upon the subject of Chinese poisons. I cannot tell you the name, much less the specific nature of the poison used here, but I am prepared to show proofs that similar results have been recorded with regard to the victims of a certain dreaded secret society in China, which owes much of its power and prestige to the fact that it can strike its opponents with the dreaded 'Blue Death.'"

"But we are as far as ever from finding the murderer," objected Hendriks. "To find him and punish him is all that I care for. Nothing else has the slightest interest for me."

"I calculated," began Low, when this outburst was over, "I calculated that as the murderer had not yet accomplished his purpose of driving us out of the house, he would return to his diabolical work sooner or later. Hence I was quite cheered when the ghost visited me. I had identified my man two days ago, but I waited to get an opportunity of bringing his crimes home to him. Will you come with me into the dining-room?"

Hendriks and Mulroon followed Flaxman Low, who carried a candle. For a second he listened at the door of the dining-room, but dead silence reigned. "I bolted the shutters of the windows on the outside after I had seen my man enter to renew the supply of poison on the steel point," said Flaxman Low. "I hope we may find him still here. He will probably make a dash at us. Will you be careful?"

"All right," said Hendriks, showing his revolver.

Low opened the door. Nothing moved inside the room, but sitting at the table was a huddled figure. The hat had fallen off, the head with its coiled pig-tail lay upon the outstretched arms. Another moment made it clear that the man was dead. They lit the candles on the mantelpiece, and proceeded to examine the dead body.

The yellow face was puffed beyond recognition, the whole man was strangely and quiescently horrible. On the table before him lay a small lacquered box containing a scrap of a dark ointment, and in the man's forefinger was found a splinter of steel. Finding himself trapped, he had made away with himself rather than face his captors.

At this stage of the proceedings, Flaxman Low retired from the affair.

The police managed to hush up the business—the death of a Chinaman more or less makes little stir at any time—and they had further investigations of importance to make, which they wished to keep quiet.

It was, indeed, ultimately proved that No. 1 Karma Crescent formed a very convenient headquarters for Chinese and other ruffianism, being situated as it was near a junction, near the river, and near a low part of London. It was found that extensive excavations had been made in communication with the house and a well-built tunnel opened by a cleverly masked entrance into the lane.

Thus by Flaxman Low's efforts a very distinct danger had been warded off, for the society in question were making very alarming headway in London, chiefly by allying themselves with other bands of criminals in this country, to whom they offered a secure place of hiding.

THE STORY OF KONNOR OLD HOUSE

"I hold," Mr. Flaxman Low, the eminent psychologist, was saying, "that there are no other laws in what we term the realm of the supernatural but those which are the projections or extensions of natural laws."

"Very likely that's so," returned Naripse, with suspicious humility. "But, all the same, Konnor Old House presents problems that won't work in with any natural laws I'm acquainted with. I almost hesitate to give voice to them, they sound so impossible and—and absurd."

"Let's judge of them," said Low.

"It is said," said Naripse, standing up with his back to the fire, "it is said that a Shining Man haunts the place. Also a light is frequently seen in the library—I've watched it myself of a night from here—yet the dust there, which happens to lie very thick over the floor and the furniture, has afterwards shown no sign of disturbance."

"Have you satisfactory evidence of the presence of the Shining Man?"

"I think so," replied Naripse shortly. "I saw him myself the night before I wrote asking you to come up to see me. I went into the house after dusk, and was on the stairs when I saw him: the tall figure of a man, absolutely white and shining. His back was towards me, but the sullen, raised shoulders and sidelong head expressed a degree of sinister animosity that exceeded anything I've ever met with. So I left him in possession, for it's a fact that anyone who has tried to leave his card at Konnor Old House has left his wits with it."

"It certainly sounds rather absurd," said Mr. Low, "but I suppose we have not heard all about it yet?"

"No, there is a tragedy connected with the house, but it's quite a commonplace sort of story and in no way accounts for the Shining Man."

Naripse was a young man of means, who spent most of his time abroad, but the above conversation took place at the spot to which he always referred as home—a shooting-lodge connected with his big grouse-moor on the West Coast of Scotland. The lodge was a small new house built in a damp valley, with a trout-stream running just beyond the garden-hedge.

From the high ground above, where the moor stretched out towards the Solway Firth, it was possible on a fine day to see the dark cone of Ailsa Crag rising above the shimmering ripples. But Mr. Low happened to arrive in a spell of bad weather, when nothing was visible about the lodge but a few roods of sodden lowland, and a curve of the yellow tumbling little river, and beyond a murky outline of shouldering hills blurred by the ever-falling rain. It may have been eleven o'clock on a depressing, muggy night, when Naripse began to talk about Konnor Old House as he sat with his guests over a crackling flaming fire of pinewood.

"Konnor Old House stands on a spur of the ridge opposite-one of the finest sites possible, and it belongs to me. Yet I am obliged to live in this damp little boghole, for the man who would pass a night in Konnor is not to be met with in this county!"

Sullivan, the third man present, replied he was, perhaps—with a glance at Low—there were two, which stung Naripse, who turned his words into a deliberate challenge.

"Is it a bet?" asked Sullivan, rising. He was a tallish man, dark, and clean-shaven, whose features were well-known to the public in connection with the emerald green jersey of the Rugby International Football Team of Ireland. "If it is, it's a bet I'm going to win! Good-night. In the morning, Naripse, I'll trouble you for the difference."

"The affair is much more in Low's line than in yours," said Naripse. "But you're not really going?"

"You may take it I am though!"

"Don't be a fool, Jack! Low, tell him not to go, tell him there are things no man ought to meddle with—" he broke off.

"There are things no man can meddle with," replied Sullivan, obstinately fixing his cap on his head, "and my backing out of this bet would stand in as one of them!"

Naripse was strangely urgent.

"Low, speak to him! You know—"

Flaxman Low saw that the big Irishman's one vanity had got upon its legs; he also saw that Naripse was very much in earnest.

"Sullivan's big enough to take care of himself," he said laughing. "At the same time, if he doesn't object, we might as well hear the story before he starts."

Sullivan hesitated, then flung his cap into a corner.

"That's so," he said.

It was a warm night for the time of the year, and they could hear, through the open window, the splashing downpour of the rain.

"There's nothing so lonely as the drip of heavy rain!" began Naripse, "I always associate it with Konnor Old House. The place has stood empty for ten years or more, and this is the story they tell about it. It was last inhabited by a Sir James Mackian, who had been a merchant of sorts in Sierra Leone. When the baronetcy fell to him, he came to England and settled down in this place with a pretty daughter and a lot of servants, including a nigger, named Jake, whose life he was said to have saved in Africa. Everything went on well for nearly two years, when Sir James had occasion to go to Edinburgh for a few days. During his absence his daughter was found dead in her bed, having taken an overdose of some sleeping draught. The shock proved too great for her father. He tried travelling, but, on his return home, he fell into a settled melancholy, and died some months later a dumb imbecile at the asylum."

"Well, I shan't object to meeting the girl as she's so pretty," remarked Sullivan with a laugh. "But there's not much in the story."

"Of course," added Naripse, "countryside gossip adds a good deal of colour to the plain facts of the case. It is said that terrible details connected with Miss Mackian's death were suppressed at the inquest, and people recollected afterwards that for months the girl had worn an unhappy, frightened look. It seemed she disliked the negro, and had been heard to beg her father to send him away, but the old man would not listen to her."

"What became of the negro in the end?" asked Flaxman Low.

"In the end Sir James kicked him out after a violent scene, in the course of which he appears to have accused Jake of having some hand in causing the girl's death. The nigger swore he'd be revenged on him, but, as a matter of fact, he left the place almost immediately, and has never been heard of since—which disposes of the nigger. A short time after the old man went mad; he was found lying on a couch in the library—a hopeless imbecile." Saying this, Naripse went to the window, and looked out into the rainy darkness. "Konnor Old House stands on the ridge opposite, and a part of the building, including the library window, where the light is sometimes seen, is visible through the trees from here. There is no light there tonight, though."

Sullivan laughed his big, full laugh.

"How about your shining man? I hope we may have the luck to meet. I suspect some canny Scots tramp knows where to get a snug roost rent free."

"That may be so," replied Naripse, with a slow patience. "I can only say that after seeing the light of a night, I have more than once gone up in the morning to have a look at the library, and never found the thick dust in the least disturbed."

"Have you noticed if the light appears at regular intervals?" said Low.

"No; it's there on and off. I generally see it in rainy weather."

"What sort of people have gone crazy in Konnor Old House?" asked Sullivan.

"One was a tramp. He must have lived pleasantly in the kitchen for days. Then he took to the library, which didn't agree with him apparently. He was found in a dying state lying upon Sir James's couch, with horrible black patches on his face. He was too far gone to speak, so nothing was gleaned from him."

"He probably had a dirty face, and, having caught cold in the rain, went into Konnor Old House and died quietly there of pneumonia or something of the kind, just as you or I might have done, tucked up in our own little beds at home," commented Sullivan.

"The last man to try his luck with the ghosts," went on Naripse, without noticing this remark, "was a young fellow, called Bowie, a nephew of Sir James. He was a student at Edinburgh University and he wanted to clear up the mystery. I was not at home, but my factor allowed him to pass a night in the house. As he did not appear next day, they went to look for him. He was found lying on the couch—and he has not spoken a rational word since."

"Sheer—mere physical fright, acting on an overwrought brain!" Sullivan summed up the case scornfully. "And now I'm off. The rain has stopped, and I'll get up to the house before midnight. You may expect me at dawn to tell you what I've seen."

"What do you intend to do when you get there?" asked Flaxman Low.

"I'll pass the night on the ghostly couch which I suppose I shall find in the library. Take my word for it, madness is in Sir James's family; father and daughter and nephew all gave proof of it in different ways. The tramp, who was perhaps in there for a couple of days, died a natural death. It only needs a healthy man to run the gauntlet and set all this foolish talk at rest."

Naripse was plainly much disturbed though he made no further objection, but when Sullivan was gone, he moved restlessly about the room looking out of the window from time to time. Suddenly he spoke:

"There it is! The light I mentioned to you."

Mr. Low went to the window. Away on the opposite ridge a faint light glimmered out through the thick gloom. Then he glanced at his watch.

"Rather over an hour since he started," he remarked. "Well, now, Naripse, if you will be so good as to hand me *Human Origins* from the shelf behind you, I think we may settle down to wait for

dawn. Sullivan's just the man to give a good account of himself—
under most circumstances."

"Heaven send there may be no black side to this business!" said
Naripse. "Of course I was a fool to say what I did about the Old
House, but nobody except an ass like Jack would think I meant it.
I wish the night was well over! That light is due to go out in two
hours anyway."

Even to Mr. Low the night seemed unbearably long; but at the
first streak of dawn he tossed his book on to the sofa, stretched
himself, and said: "We may as well be moving; let's go and see what
Sullivan is doing."

The rain began to fall again, and was coming down in close
straight lines as the two men drove up the avenue to Konnor Old
House. As they ascended, the trees grew thicker on the banks of
the cutting which led them in curves to the terrace on which stood
the house. Although it was a modern red-brick building, rather
picturesque with its gables and sharply-pitched overhanging roofs,
it looked desolate and forbidding enough in the grey daybreak. To
the left lay lawns and gardens, to the right the cliff fell away steeply
to where the burn roared in spate some three hundred feet below.
They drove round to the empty stables, and then hurried back
to the house on foot by a path that debouched directly under the
library window. Naripse stopped under it, and shouted: "Hullo!
Jack, where are you?"

But no answer came, and they went on to the hall door. The
gloom of the wet dawning and the heavy smell of stagnant air filled
the big hall as they looked round at its dreary emptiness. The
silence within the house itself was oppressive. Again Naripse
shouted, and the noise echoed harshly through the passages, jar-
ring on the stillness, then he led the way to the library at a run.

As they came in sight of the doorway a wave of some nauseating odour met them, and at the same moment they saw Sullivan
lying just outside the threshold, his body twisted and rigid like a
man in the extremity of pain, his contorted profile ivory-pale
against the dark oak flooring. As they stooped to raise him, Mr.
Low had just time to notice the big gloomy room beyond, with its

heaped and trampled layers of accumulated dust. There was no time for more than a glance, for the indescribable, fetid odour almost overpowered them as they hastened to carry Sullivan into the open air.

"We must get him home as soon as we can," said Mr. Low, "for we have a very sick man on our hands."

This proved to be true. But in a few days, thanks to Mr. Low's treatment and untiring care, the severe physical symptoms became less urgent, and in due time Sullivan's mind cleared.

The following account is taken from the written statement of his experience in Konnor Old House:

"On reaching the house he entered as noiselessly as possible, and made for the library, finding his way by the help of a series of matches to Sir James's couch, upon which he lay down. He was conscious at once of an acrid taste in his mouth, which he accounted for by the clouds of dust he had raised in crossing the room.

"First he began to think about the approaching football match with Scotland, for which he was already in training. He was still in his mood of derisive incredulity. The house seemed vastly empty, and wrapped in an uneasy silence, a silence which made each of his comfortable movements an omen of significance. Presently the sense of a presence in the room was borne in upon him. He sat up, and spoke softly. He almost expected someone to answer him, and so strong did this feeling become that he called out: 'Who's there?' No reply came, and he sat on amidst the oppressive silence. He says the slightest noise would have been a relief. It was the listening in the silence that bred in him so intense a longing to grapple with some solid opponent.

"Fear! He, who had denied the very existence of cause for fear, found himself shivering with an untranslatable terror! This was fear! He realised it with an infinite recoil of anger.

"Presently he became aware that the darkness about him was clearing. A feeble light filtered slowly through it from above. Looking up at the ceiling, he perceived directly above his head an irregular patch of pale phosphorescent luminance, which grew gradually brighter. How long he sat with his head thrown back, staring at the light, he does not know. It seemed years. Then he spoke to himself plainly. With an immense effort, he forced his eyes away from the light and got upon his feet to drag his limbs round the room. The phosphorescence was of a greenish tint, and as strong as moonlight, but the dust rose like vapour at the slightest movement, and somewhat obscured its power. He moved about, but not for long. A clogging weight, such as one feels in nightmare, pressed upon him, and his exhaustion was intensified by the overpowering physical disgust bred in him by the repulsive odour which passed across his face as he staggered back to the couch.

"For a few moments he would not look up. He says he had an impression that someone was watching him through the radiance as through a window. The atmosphere about him was thickening and cloaking the walls with drowsy horror, while his senses revolted and choked at the growing odour. Then followed a state of semi-sleep, for he recollects no more until he found himself staring again at the luminous patch on the ceiling.

"By this time the brightness was beginning to dim; dark smears showed through it here and there, which ran slowly together till out of them grew and protruded a fat, black, evil face. A second later Sullivan was aware that the horrible face was sinking down nearer and nearer to his own, while all about it the light changed to black, dripping fluid, that formed great drops and fell.

"It seemed as if he could not save himself; he could not move! The fighting blood in him had died out. Then fear, mad fear and strong loathing gave him the strength to act. He saw his own hand working savagely, it passed through and through the impending face, yet he swears that he felt a slight impact and that he saw the fat, glazed skin quiver! Then, with a final struggle, he tore it himself from the couch, and, rushing to the door, he wrenched open, and plunged forward into a red vacancy, down—down— After that he remembered no more."

While Sullivan still lay ill and unable to give an account of himself or of what had happened at Konnor Old House, Mr. Flaxman Low expressed his intention of paying a visit to the asylum for the purpose of seeing young Bowie. But on arrival at the asylum, he found that Bowie had died during the previous night. A weary-eyed assistant doctor took Mr. Low to see the body. Bowie had evidently been of a gaunt, but powerful build. The features, though harsh, were noble, the face being somewhat disfigured by a rough, raised discoloration, which extended from the centre of the forehead to behind the right ear.

Mr. Low asked a question.

"Yes, it is a very obscure case," observed the assistant, "but it is the disease he died of. When he was brought here some months ago he had a small dark spot on his forehead, but it spread rapidly, and there are now similar large patches over the whole of his body. I take it to be of a cancerous character, likely to occur in a scrofulous subject after a shock and severe mental strain, such as Bowie chose to subject himself to by passing a night in Konnor Old House. The first result of the shock was the imbecility, an increasing lethargic condition of the body supervened and finally coma."

While the doctor was speaking, Mr. Low bent over the dead man and closely examined the mark upon the face.

"This mark appears to be the result of a fungoid growth, perhaps akin to the Indian disease known as *mycetoma*?" he said at length.

"It may be so. The case is very obscure, but the disease, whatever we may call it, appears to be in Bowie's family, for I believe his uncle, Sir James Mackian, had precisely similar symptoms during his last illness. He also died in this institution, but that was before my time," replied the assistant.

After a further examination of the body Mr. Low took his leave, and during the following day or two was busily engaged in a spare empty room placed at his disposal by Naripse. A deal table and chair were all he required, Mr. Low explained, and to these he added a microscope, an apparatus for producing a moist heat, and the coat worn by Sullivan on the night of his adventure. At the end of the third day, as Sullivan was already on the road to recovery, Mr. Low, accompanied by Naripse, paid a second visit to Konnor Old House, during which Low mentioned some of his conclusions about the strange events which had occurred there. It will be an easy task to compare Mr. Flaxman Low's theory with the experience detailed by Sullivan and with the one or two subsequent discoveries that added something like confirmation to his conclusions.

Mr. Low and his host drove up as on the previous occasion, and stabled the horse as before. The day was dry, but grey, and the time the early afternoon. As they ascended the path leading to the house, Mr. Low remarked, after gazing up for a few seconds at the library window:

"That room has the air of being occupied."

"Why?—What makes you think so?" asked Naripse nervously.

"It is hard to say, but it produces that impression." Naripse shook his head despondently.

"I've always noticed it myself," he returned, "I wish Sullivan were all right again and able to tell us what he saw in there. Whatever it was it has nearly cost him his life. I don't suppose we shall ever know anything more definite about the matter."

"I fancy I can tell you," replied Low, "but let us get on into the library, and see what it looks like before we enter into the subject any further. By the way, I should advise you to tie your handkerchief over your mouth and nose before we go into the room."

Naripse, upon whom the events of the last few days had had a very strong effect, was in a state of scarcely-controllable excitement.

"What do you mean, Low?—you can't have any idea—"

"Yes, I believe the dust in that house to be simply poisonous. Sullivan inhaled any amount of it—hence his condition."

The same suggestion of loneliness and stagnation hung about the house as they passed through the hall and entered the library. They halted at the door and looked in. The amount of greenish dust in the room was extraordinary; it lay in little drifts and mounds over the floor, but most abundantly just about the couch. Immediately above this spot, they perceived on the ceiling a long, discoloured stain. Naripse pointed to it.

"Do you see that? It is a bloodstain, and, I give you my word, it grows larger and larger every year!" He finished the sentence in a low voice, and shuddered.

"Ah, so I should have expected," observed Flaxman Low, who was looking at the stained ceiling with much interest. "That, of course, explains everything."

"Low, tell me what you mean? A bloodstain that grows year by year explains everything?" Naripse broke off and pointed to the couch. "Look there! a cat's been walking over that sofa."

Mr. Low put his hand on his friend's shoulder and smiled.

"My dear fellow! That stain on the ceiling is simply a patch of mould and fungi. Now come in carefully without raising the dust, and let us examine the cat's footsteps, as you call them."

Naripse advanced to the couch and considered the marks gravely.

"They are not the footmarks of any animal, they are something much more unaccountable. They are raindrops. And why should raindrops be here in this perfectly watertight room, and even then only in one small part of it? You can't very well explain that, and you certainly can't have expected it?"

"Look round and follow my points," replied Mr. Low. "When we came to fetch Sullivan, I noticed the dust which far exceeds the ordinary accumulation even in the most neglected places. You may also notice that it is of a greenish colour and of extreme fineness. This dust is of the same nature as the powder you find in a puff-ball, and is composed of minute sporuloid bodies. I found that Sullivan's coat was covered with this fine dust, and also about the collar and upper portion of the sleeve I found one or two gummy drops which correspond to these raindrops, as you call them. I naturally concluded from their position that they had fallen from above. From the dust, or rather spores, which I found on Sullivan's coat, I have since cultivated no fewer than four specimens of fungi, of which three belong to known African species; but the fourth, so far as I know, has never been described, but it approximates most closely to one of the *phalliodei*."

"But how about the raindrops, or whatever they are? I believe they drop from that horrible stain."

"They are drops from the stain, and are caused by the unnamed fungus I have just alluded to. It matures very rapidly, and absolutely decays as it matures, liquefying into a sort of dark mucilage, full of spores, which drips down, and diffuses a most repulsive odour. In time the mucilage dries, leaving the dust of the spores."

"I don't know much about these things myself," replied Naripse dubiously, "and it strikes me you know more than enough. But look here; how about the light? You saw it last night yourself."

"It happens that the three species of African fungi possess well known phosphorescent properties, which are manifested not only during decomposition, but also during the period of growth. The light is only visible from time to time; probably climatic and atmospheric conditions only admit of occasional efflorescence."

"But," object Naripse, "supposing it to be a case of poisoning by fungi as you say, how is it that Sullivan, though exposed to precisely the same sources of danger as the others who have passed a night here, has escaped? He has been very ill, but his mind has already regained its balance, whereas, in the three other cases, the mind was wholly destroyed."

Mr. Low looked very grave.

"My dear fellow, you are such an excitable and superstitious person that I hesitate to put your nerves to any further test."

"Oh, go on!"

"I hesitate for two reasons. The one I have mentioned, and also because in my answer I must speak of curious and unpleasant things, some of which are proved facts, others only more or less well-founded assumptions. It is acknowledged that fungi exert an important influence in certain diseases, a few being directly attributable to fungi as a primary cause. Also it is an historical fact that poisonous fungi have more than once been used to alter the fate of nations. From the evidence before us and the condition of Bowie's body, I can but conclude that the unknown fungus I have alluded to is of a singularly malignant nature, and acts through the skin upon the brain with terrible rapidity afterwards gradually inter-penetrating all the tissues of the body, and eventually causing death. In Sullivan's case, luckily, the falling drops only touched his clothing, not his skin."

"But wait a minute, Low, how did these fungi come here? And how can we rid the house of them? Upon my word, it is enough to make a man go off his head to hear about it. What are you going to do now?"

"In the first place we will go upstairs and examine the flooring just above that stained patch of ceiling."

"You can't do that I'm afraid. The room above this happens to be divided into two portions by a hollow partition between 2ft. and 3ft. thick," said Naripse, "the interior of which may originally have been meant for a cupboard, but I don't think it has ever been used."

"Then let us examine the cupboard; there must be some way of getting into it."

Upon this Naripse led the way upstairs, but, as he gained the top, he leant back, and grasping Mr. Low by the arm thrust him violently forward.

"Look! the light—did you see the light?" he said.

For a second or two it seemed as if a light, like the elusive light thrown by a rotating reflector, quivered on the four walls of the landing, then disappeared almost before one could he certain of having seen it.

"Can you point me out the precise spot where you saw the shining figure you told us of?" asked Low.

Naripse pointed to a dark corner of the landing.

"Just there in front of that panel between the two doors. Now that I come to think of it, I fancy there is some means of opening the upper part of that panel. The idea was to ventilate the cupboard-like space I mentioned just now."

Naripse walked across the landing and felt round the panel, till he found a small metal knob. On turning this, the upper part of the panel fell back like a shutter, disclosing a narrow space of darkness beyond. Naripse thrust his head into the opening and peered into the gloom, but immediately started back with a gasp.

"The shining man!" he cried. "He's there!"

Mr. Flaxman Low, hardly knowing what to expect, looked over his shoulder; then, exerting his strength, pulled away some of the lower boarding. For within, at arm's length, stood a dimly shining figure! A tall man, with his back towards them, leaning against the left of the partition, and shrouded from head to foot in faintly luminous white mould.

The figure remained quite motionless while they stared at it in surprise; then Mr. Flaxman Low pulled on his glove, and, leaning forward, touched the man's head. A portion of the white mass came away in his fingers, the lower surface of which showed a bunch of frizzled negroid hair.

"Good Heavens, Low, what do you make of this?" asked Naripse. "It must be the body of Jake. But what is this shining stuff?"

Low stood under the wide skylight and examined what he held in his fingers.

"Fungus," he said at last. "And it appears to have some property allied to the mouldy fungus which attacks the common housefly. Have you not seen them dead upon window-panes, stiffly fixed upon their legs, and covered with a white mould? Something of the same kind has taken place here."

"But what had Jake to do with the fungus? And how did he come here?"

"All that, of course, we can only surmise," replied Mr. Low. "There is little doubt that secrets of nature hidden from us are well known to the various African tribes. It is possible that the negro possessed some of these deadly spores, but how or why he made use of them are questions that can never be cleared up now."

"But what was he doing here?" asked Naripse.

"As I said before we can only guess the answer to that question, but I should suppose that the negro made use of this cupboard as a place where he could be free from interruption; that he here cultivated the spores is proved by the condition of his body and of the ceiling immediately below. Such an occupation is by no means free from danger, especially in an airless and inclosed space such as this. It is evident that either by design or accident he became infected by the fungus poison, which in time covered his whole body as you now see. The subject of obeah," Flaxman Low went on reflectively, "is one to the study of which I intend to devote myself at some future period. I have, indeed, already made some arrangements for an expedition in connection with the subject into the interior of Africa."

"And how is the horrible thing to be got rid of? Nothing short of burning the place down would be of any radical use," remarked Naripse.

Low, who by this time was deeply engrossed in considering the strange facts with which he had just become acquainted, answered abstractedly: "I suppose not."

Naripse said no more, and the words were only recalled to Mr. Low's mind a day or two later, when he received by post a copy of the *West Coast Advertiser*. It was addressed in the handwriting of Naripse, and the following extract was lightly scored:

"Konnor Old House, the property of Thomas Naripse, Esquire, of Konnor Lodge, was, we regret to say, destroyed by fire last night. We are sorry to add that the loss to the owner will be considerable, as no insurance policy had been effected with regard to the property."

THE STORY OF CROWSEDGE

A fixed aversion to notoriety is one of Mr. Flaxman Low's most marked characteristics. Had this not been so, he would undoubtedly have formed the subject of many an interview in the illustrated magazines. But his manner of life and pursuits set him apart from the common lot, and he stands aloof, a solitary and interesting figure surrounded by his books, his Egyptian treasures, and his grotesque memories, a man who has dived deep into the past and also explored daringly beyond the borders of that vast realm of mystery, of which the public catch but a very slight glimpse through the medium of these stories.

Athlete, Egyptologist, and psychical student, his is a strangely blended existence, at one moment breathing the mental atmosphere of the Sixth Dynasty, the next hour perhaps fighting single-handed some fearless battle against an opponent from whom the bravest need find no shame in accepting defeat. But Flaxman Low is a man, who finds defeat intolerable; with him there is no end to a struggle, he will pursue the interpretation of a tough linguistic problem in exactly the same spirit as he applies himself to the elucidation of the most baffling and dangerous psychical phenomena. Yet this unassuming English gentleman, who combines in his own personality the reckless courage of a Regency blood and the knowledge of a profound scholar, is best known among his friends for his kind smile and the genial help he is ready to offer in every case of need.

The following story differs from those which have gone before it, in that it does not deal solely with the mystery of some haunted spot; it draws across the page another figure, possessing in a high degree the intellectual grasp, the wide knowledge, and the exhaustive will-power which distinguish Mr. Low, but using them for very different purposes.

In the beginning of 1893 Dr. Kalmarkane first rose upon the horizon of Mr. Low's life. Any detailed history of the transactions between them is here impossible, but a slight sketch of one or two of the principal incidents may not be altogether out of place. Up to January 1893, Mr. Low had very little knowledge of Dr. Kalmarkane beyond the fact that he was a man of extraordinary ability, whose researches had led him deeply into those very recesses of knowledge, to the exploration of which Mr. Low has given up his own life. He also knew that it was Kalmarkane's habit to visit town occasionally, to stalk about for a couple of days on the pavements, to drop in upon psychical meetings, where he would listen to the proceedings with a face of sour scorn, and then to plunge back into the obscurity of his lonely life in some remote corner of the Isle of Purbeck.

The more intimate dealings between these great rivals began on a winter night when a thin powdering of snow lay upon the London pavements. For three days banks of swollen yellowish-grey clouds had rolled up slowly before a north wind that cut round every corner. It was already late, and Mr. Flaxman Low was sitting alone in his chambers in Fassifern Court, when a gentleman was shown up, who carried in with him something of the rawness of the night outside.

The visitor, as he threw back his thick ulster, showed a young, slim, and well-formed figure; then he flicked a flake or two of snow from his small, black imperial, and stood in some embarrassment opposite to Mr. Low.

"Do you remember a fresher, who came up to Oxford the year you left, of the name of d'Imiran?" he said.

Mr. Flaxman Low extended his hand.

"You must forgive me," he said. "The hair on your face alters you a good deal. I recollect meeting you very often at your cousin's rooms, and, believe me, I am very heartily glad to see you. Where is Field? Still in China?"

Mr. Low now had time to look at his visitor. He saw that d'Imiran's eyes were restless, and that he seemed worn out for want of sleep.

"Yes, bug-hunting up the Hoang-ho when last I heard of him," replied d'Imiran perfunctorily. Then fixing his dark eyes on Mr. Low, he added: "Mr. Low, I have been driven here tonight by the sheer necessity of sharing a secret with some human soul. Do you happen to know Dr. Kalmarkane? He is a hirsute giant, with a tremendous frame, raw-boned and ungainly. He has a long, strong, fleshy nose, a shock head of dark grey hair, and a ragged beard, which he is in the habit of twisting into spirals as he talks."

"I know something of him."

"You can't know him as I do. I have spent the last six months in his house. I daresay you fail to see why that fact should send me to disturb you at 10.30, but—"

Flaxman Low had in the meantime been attending to the wants of his guest. As d'Imiran paused, he smiled.

"My dear d'Imiran," he said, "I would gladly get up in the middle of my beauty-sleep to offer my sympathy to any man who had spent six months with Kalmarkane. Pray, tell me what I can do for you."

"I have been twenty-seven weeks under his roof," went on d'Imiran, "and I can only tell you that I grew to dislike the man more every day of that time. There are mysteries about him; but you will hear enough of them if you will allow me to tell you my story. I know that I am straining your forbearance in coming to you with this tale; I know I have no right to ask you to listen to me, and I am almost afraid that at the end of it all I shall find you laughing at me. But I thought you were my best chance. There is no other man in London who would hear half-a-dozen sentences without advising me to see a nerve specialist and knock off work. But I assure you there is nothing whatever wrong with me in that way. I have not been overworking, though I admit that for the last six weeks the pressure of what I am about to tell you has bothered me."

"I am entirely at your service, and I promise to give you as fair a hearing as possible," said Low. "Am I right in supposing that you have studied medicine?"

D'Imiran nodded.

"I won the Scully Scholarship, which took me round the European schools of medicine. I have been house-surgeon at St. Mar-tha's, and I have passed various necessary—and unnecessary—exams. About a year ago I felt that I must begin to turn some of the knowledge I had in my head into coin, and a friend of mine, knowing what I wanted, introduced me to Dr. Kalmarkane, who happened to be in need of an assistant with my qualifications to aid him for a time in his researches.

"The terms he offered me were good, so good that I accepted his proposal, and went down in June to Dorset, where he lives in a lonely house, called Crowsedge. It lies between miles of empty heath and miles of sand dunes. There Kalmarkane leads the life of a savage, a half-blind and almost idiotic old crone being the only creature he can get to serve him in the whole countryside, where he bears a most evil reputation; and the sight of his huge figure, swinging a heavy yellow cane he carries, is enough to make people take to the bypaths to avoid him. If I were to repeat the many anecdotes which his self-centred and morose habits have given rise to, I should keep you up into the small hours. But I will hurry on as quickly as I can into the core of my story.

"Kalmarkane is, in fact, a sullen savage, who works eighteen hours out of the twenty-four, and the range of his knowledge is almost incredible. The object of his studies is a secret he keeps in his own brain, and I may say I have never fathomed its precise nature. Once or twice I put out a feeler to discover in what direction our researches were leading us, but I was met with a black look and a monosyllabic reply. At last on one occasion he told me that I was merely a hired servant, and that he did not pay me to pry into his affairs.

"This was in September, just before he started for Jutland to be present at the opening of some tumuli belonging to the Bronze Age. However he smoothed the thing over with a sort of apology, and begged me to remain. After his return Kalmarkane's attitude towards me altered. He allowed me to go further into every investigation, until, in fact, we trenched upon things with which I plainly refused to have anything to do. He towered over me with gripping hands as if he could have killed me, then he conquered himself and laughed: 'I believed you to be a man with a true love of knowledge, and I must remind you of Professor Clifford's words, "that it is wrong, always, everywhere, and for anyone to believe anything upon insufficient evidence,"' he said. 'You and I are merely searching for the truth, Mr. d'Imiran, but I will for the future remember your susceptibilities. I myself think that your prejudice is an almost inconceivable survival of the mediaeval superstition that certain kinds of knowledge are unlawful.' I replied that there were certain methods of acquiring knowledge which were certainly unlawful!"

D'Imiran paused and drew his handkerchief across his white lips.

"We were, and for that matter, are engaged in carrying out various investigations which bear upon an obscure subject. You, of course, know Kalmarkane's work on *Potencies of Etheric Energy*, dealing with the subject from the standpoint that such energies are excited and may be controlled by the mental condition. You can imagine where this might lead one—"

"I am acquainted with the book."

"Now pray consider what I am about to tell you as possible fact," continued d'Imiran, "though I confess that without the evidence of my own senses I could not have been brought to regard the thing in that light. After this conversation I became aware that Kalmarkane had grown to dislike me in a positive and malignant manner, which he nevertheless took pains to hide. Now I come to the point of my story. I have only two separate and not necessarily connected facts to put before you, both of which, however, go to prove that Kalmarkane is possessed of strange powers.

"Crowsedge is built on to a little square tower, which is probably of much older date than the house itself. The upper part of the tower serves Kalmarkane as a study, while the lower portion is a bare, damp, flagged space. The connecting stairs are of stone, very steep and narrow, which lead through a hole cut in the study floor on to a small, partitioned landing. One side of these steps is attached to the wall, the other is unprotected by even a handrail, so that a slip or fall would send you headlong on to the flags below. One evening Kalmarkane, who was in my laboratory, sent me to fetch some papers from the tower. I had never before been allowed to enter the study alone.

"I carried a candle, and must mention that I was wearing a knickerbocker suit, with shoes, not boots. I found the papers at once, and at the same time happened to notice an ancient oblong box, which Kalmarkane had obtained from the tumuli in Jutland. It was lying on the floor, open and empty. When I was returning down the steps an unaccountable incident occurred. I have explained to you the position of that flight of steps. On my right there was the blank wall, on my left an open space, and I was about fourteen feet from the ground.

"I fancied I heard someone moving, and, holding my candle over my head, I bent and looked down into the square, flagged room below. As I did so, a hand suddenly grasped my left ankle, and jerked me off my feet with a violent wrench. I crashed down on to the flags, and by what good luck I escaped having my neck broken I can't say. I put out my hands to save my head and pitched on my shoulder, and so got off with a severe shaking. Now, Mr. Low, I contend that no human arm could have reached me in the position I have described to you!"

"What had Kalmarkane to say about it?" asked Flaxman Low.

"He insisted that I had slipped in some way. I felt it better to seem to accept that explanation. But look here," and d'Imiran pulled down his sock, "I did not show him that!"

Upon the ankle was the distinct mark of a thumb and fingers clearly outlined in bruises.

"Will you note one peculiarity about this?" said d'Imiran. "You perceive that it is the mark of a small hand, the grasp is short, the fingers slender, yet you can judge of its extraordinary strength."

"Now for the other incident," said Mr. Low.

"Next day I was at work as usual, but I could not sleep. I had a perpetual horror of that grasping hand. Then followed a most extraordinary coincidence, if it can never be proved to be anything more. I have told you that I had never entered Kalmarkane's study alone excepting on the one occasion immediately before my fall. One afternoon Kalmarkane had gone out for one of his long rambles over the heath, when I found myself at a standstill while making some notes, for I wished to verify a passage from an old treatise on alchemy, which Kalmarkane had carried off to his study during the morning. For a few minutes I hesitated. It was early in the afternoon, and, recollecting that he had already sent me there, I decided on finding out if the study door were open, and if so to take it as a sign that Kalmarkane would have no objection to my going in.

"I passed along the passage which led to the tower, and went up the steps, and as the handle turned quite easily, I went in. I saw the treatise I had come for at once. It lay on the farther side of the table, just beyond the box I had seen before. I bent across to get the book, and in doing so I perceived something in the box which startled me.

"Inside lay a human hand and part of a forearm. From its size I judged it to be the hand of a woman. It was brown and rough-skinned, and the wrist bore a bronze bracelet. I noticed that the bracelet was a ring open at one side, and decorated by those combinations of straight and curved lines so characteristic of the Bronze Age. Crowsedge, I must tell you, is full of the singular paraphernalia indispensable for studies such as Kalmarkane's, and odds and ends of humanity were not very unusual.

"But there was something in the appearance of this hand lying there, sienna-brown upon the discoloured cloths, that gave a horrible suggestion of life! It was resting back upwards with half-closed fingers, the muscles and flesh rising firmly over the bones. At the point of scission the surface was drawn and dried, so that separation from the body was not of recent date. I give you all these details in full, and I can swear to them. By chance, or, perhaps, out of curiosity, I touched the hand, and—it was warm!

"I declare to you that hand and arm felt in every particular like living flesh! I was still stooping over it, when I heard a sound behind me, and looked up to find Kalmarkane glaring at me with a diabolical expression. 'What are you doing here?' he roared. I answered that I was examining the hand. He shut down the lid of the box with a sharp movement. 'That severed hand has a history,' he said with a sinister laugh. 'It has let out many a man's life, and—who knows?'

"That little incident decided me. I came up to town for a few days, and I felt impelled tonight, before returning to Crowsedge, to come and tell you all about it."

Mr. Low was silent for some time, then he asked:

"It is a very strange story, but I should be sorry to say it was not a true one. Put into plain words, you wish me to understand that Dr. Kalmarkane possesses a hand and arm, presumably from the ornament upon it, belonging to some prehistoric man or woman of the Bronze Age; that this human remnant is endowed with life, and further putting certain facts together, you are inclined to think that Kalmarkane can use this hand for his own purposes?"

D'Imiran heard Low out with his face buried in his hands. After Low had ceased speaking, however, he raised his head and replied:

"Put in that bald and blunt fashion, it sounds nothing more or less than the worst kind of madness!" he said despondently, "yet I am a sane man at this moment. Also I have seen these things. Much as I know of Kalmarkane's studies, I am not acquainted with his occult methods. The man has power of some kind which defies the limits of ordinary knowledge. He knows infinitely more than other men. Besides, who can say nowadays that anything is beyond possibility? Are there not well-known facts, such as hypnotism, suggestion, evidences of submerged personality, and so on, of which it is out of our power to give any adequate explanation in scientific terms?"

"All this is quite true," admitted Flaxman Low. "But just now, to come to the practical side, what do you propose to do?"

D'Imiran got on to his feet, and his dark face looked resolute.

"I am going back there by the midnight train, because I am determined to get to the bottom of this. But I have told you how matters stand, Low, so that you may know what to do in case I don't return. This is Tuesday; if I am not here by Sunday I shall be dead."

"I don't think you are acting wisely in pitting yourself single-handed against such a man as you believe Kalmarkane to be."

"Thank you, but I am resolved to go through with it. I have also to thank you for the patient hearing you have given me, and for even seeming to believe me. I shall feel infinitely more confidence now that I am sure if I lose my life you will in some manner try to bring it home to Kalmarkane. I am convinced his power is the result of occult processes, which for want of a better term may still come under the head of Black Magic." D'Imiran stopped and smiled with a satiricial twist of the lip. "Black Magic! A couple of months ago I should have sent any man expressing my present opinions to a lunatic asylum."

"To conventional ears your story would certainly sound doubtful," said Low. "But, however that may be, the fact remains that Kalmarkane, from whatever source he derives his powers, is dangerous. You are still bent on returning to Crowsedge? Well, goodbye."

Crowsedge is a lonely, plain-looking house built on to a squat square tower of Portland stone. From the high road a rough track leads towards it over some miles of lonely heath; through dips where marsh and sedge encroach upon the footway, and on across wide ups and downs of dense, wiry heather, where each undulation seems to cut one off more and more hopelessly from the outer world. On the seaward edge of this wild land, Kalmarkane's house rose on the horizon like a stranded ship on a desert shore. At least so it appeared to d'Imiran as he walked over the heath towards it on the morning following his visit to Flaxman Low. Behind the tower crowded rugged sand dunes, and beyond them again, as d'Imiran knew, lay miles of pools and shallows.

With a keener sense of loneliness than he had ever before experienced, he turned and looked back in the direction of the high road, as if the very sight of its white windings over the downs, suggestive of human proximity and help, might give him renewed courage to face the unclassified dangers which awaited him. But the road had already sunk out of view behind the low ridges of dry heath. For a moment he stopped. After all, was he not a fool to run again the gauntlet of a danger, from which he had once escaped? But then came back upon him the determination to get at the bottom of the unaccountable and evil things he had experienced and seen. D'Imiran came of a stiff-necked stock—Huguenot blood on the one side and Ulster energy on the other. So he gripped his bag more firmly, and went on.

Kalmarkane received him gruffly as usual, but gave him a prolonged and searching stare from under his tufted brows.

D'Imiran at once intimated his intention of leaving Crowsedge for good on the following Saturday, that being the date on which his original engagement would terminate.

"As you please," replied Kalmarkane, "I have no longer any use for your experiments."

During the Wednesday, Thursday, and Friday, Kalmarkane kept to his study, giving short fierce orders that he was on no account to be disturbed. On the Saturday morning when d'Imiran came down to breakfast, he found on the table a letter, inclosing a handsome cheque for his services, and informing him that Kalmarkane had been obliged to go to London and would probably not return before d'Imiran left. This was a disappointment, for the matter of the severed hand still remained unexplained. However, the only thing to be done was to wait for Kalmarkane's return.

D'Imiran wrote a line to Low, and passed the day in packing and making ready for his departure. Next morning he awoke with an entirely unaccountable feeling of depression weighing upon him, which increased as the day went on. In the late afternoon, he went up to his own room and, lighting a fire, prepared to spend the evening there rather than in the dreary living rooms below. He stood long at his windows; from one he could see the endless moor rising fold behind fold into the distance, from the other dunes and dry sea-grasses, with a far away touch of red and purple lights defining the salt marshes to the south. As the light faded, a fog slid up from the sea, muffling everything from sight, and rolled in waves close against his windows.

At eight o'clock he went down to the dining-room, where he found a cold meal laid out for him, which he knew of old meant that the deaf housekeeper had left Crowsedge for the night on some business of her own. Dinner swallowed, d'Imiran felt impelled to go to the door of Kalmarkane's study, to see if it was fastened. Very carefully he trod the stone stairs, and tried the door. It was fast, and, with something of relief, he came down again and returned to his own room.

He sat drowsily over the fire, dipping into the Lancet, but presently he flung the paper upon the sofa, and sat staring into the dull glow of the coals and trying in vain to reason himself out of his causeless depression. He had furnished his room with a few 'Varsity photographs, and his eyes wandered from one to another as the hand of the clock crept on towards midnight. Presently he heard something like the scrape of a boot on the passage floor outside. He went to the door and peered out, but nothing was to be seen or heard.

Unable to fix his mind on any book, he lay down upon his bed fully dressed as he was, and a sudden sleepiness fell upon him. Judging by subsequent events, he thinks he must have slept for hours, but all through his sleep he seemed to hear a knocking at the door. Again and again, from the depths of a profound weariness, he almost rose to the point of waking—all the while conscious of a vague uneasiness. At length he forced himself awake, and swung from the bed to make up the fire. Then he crouched over it shivering a little, and tried once more to fix his mind on the pages

of a magazine. But it was of no use; the words conveyed no meaning to his brain, and he found himself listening to the little vague
noises of the house.

Then he began to have trouble with his fire, which waned and
smouldered out in spite of his efforts. He took to pacing the room
and revolving in his mind the strange incidents he had determined
to fathom. But all the while fear was growing upon him. At last
with a frantic heartleap he stopped to listen. Someone was softly
trying the handle of the door! D'Imiran sat down on the edge of
the table. In the silence he could hear the slow drip of the gathering moisture from the eaves on to the broad window-sills. And then
came another sound—two stealthy knuckle-knocks on the door.

"Who's there?" called d'Imiran, in a strained voice.

There was no immediate answer; then two other knocks, still
soft, but now grown imperious. The very repetition of the noise
served to quiet d'Imiran's shaken nerves, and he finally rose, a good
deal ashamed of himself, to open the door and see who it was. The
lamp was burning brightly as he stepped swiftly and noiselessly
across the floor, and threw open the door.

Only the hollow darkness of the passage met him. But at the
same instant he received a violent upward blow under the chin,
which sent him reeling back against the wall, choking and dizzy.
His senses whirled, then settled. A throttling grip was on his throat,
pinning him against the wall with an increasing pressure. Blindly
he flung out his hands to thrust away his assailant, but they encountered only the air! Then he knew what it was, and grasped at
his throat in a wild struggle for life.

He was wrenching at those slender fingers that seemed of iron,
his head and chest bursting under the fearful strain of suffocation,
when a laugh, a long, resounding laugh, rang out through the open-
doored emptiness of the house. On a sudden the deadly hand
dropped off like a ferret from a keeper's hand, and d'Imiran, with
an effort that was agony, filled his lungs in a deep breath.

When he came to himself, he saw something lying at his feet. It
was the bronze bracelet, with every curve and line of which he felt

he was familiar. Then he recalled the laughter; Kalmarkane had returned.

D'Imiran fastened himself in, and sitting down at his desk, gave himself to covering sheet after sheet of foolscap. When he had finished, he put the whole into an envelope, and directed it to Flaxman Low, and locked it up in his desk.

It will be well here to give the closing words of this statement, from which the greater part of the foregoing narrative is drawn. After describing minutely the course events had taken since he had parted from Mr. Low, d'Imiran went on to say:

> And now I can only see one course open before me. I owe a certain duty to myself, and, if I may say so, to my fellow men. Perhaps nobody, with the possible exception of yourself, may believe my very inconceivable story. Nevertheless, I know it to be true, and I feel it to be my only course to tax Kalmarkane with the things I have here written down. What answer I may get from him I do not know. I can only reiterate my firm resolve that, in one way or another, I intend to try and put a stop to what I think I am justified in describing as the man's devilish schemes. I need only add that I am deeply indebted to you for all the consideration you have shown me in this affair.
>
> Yours very truly,
>
> G. d'Imiran

Then d'Imiran rose, his eyes searching for a weapon, but nothing presented itself except a heavy geologist's hammer. Snatching it up he ran through the empty rooms, the echo of his footsteps following him until he reached the tower. A light shone from the study above; he mounted the stairs and pushed open the door.

The room was dimly lit, and there, in a high-backed chair, sat the man himself, with a hand in his beard, and the black stump of a cigar clenched between his teeth. D'Imiran turned the key in the door and walked over to the other side of the table, where he stood among a litter of scientific appliances.

"What do you want?" said Kalmarkane slowly, bringing out the words with an effort, and d'Imiran had time to notice that the great hairy face was ghastly pale. "Earlier in the evening I heard you trying the door. I must own that I expected more honourable dealings from so punctilious a gentleman!" he ended with a sneer.

"I thought you were gone to London."

Kalmarkane raised his big eyebrows contemptuously.

"Naturally. But as it happens, I have been at work here all day. Now what do you want?"

"Where is that fiendish hand?" burst out d'Imiran. "Twice you have tried to murder me by its agency, and now you are not going to leave this room until you have destroyed it."

Kalmarkane rose, his great form standing stark and upright.

"Vapouring!" he said. "What could you do? It is true that I have tried to kill you, but it was merely by way of experiment. Now, however, if you will answer one or two questions, I will let you go. As for the hand—you shall see me destroy it, because it is no longer of any use to me."

As he spoke he took the hand from its box and laid it in a metal bath. Then he poured out a white liquid over it. And d'Imiran saw the brown fingers contract and twitch horribly as the flesh curled and smoked under the action of the acid. In a few moments nothing remained but a little darkish slime. This again was subjected to the draught of a blowpipe, the apparatus connected with which was unlike any that d'Imiran had knowledge of. Its action was effectual; a puff of dust rose from the bath, leaving its surface perfectly clear.

"If I wished to do away with you, d'Imiran," said Kalmarkane grimly, "you see that I have means at my disposal. Yesterday, that process was part of my equipment of power. Today, I do not any longer need it. All power resides in the mind of the man who knows how to make his will effectual in the spiritual as in the physical world."

Chilled and shaken as he was, the scientist was still strong in d'Imiran.

"Tell me more," he said. "That hand—"

"Do you ask me to tell you when and how that little hand, full as it was of forgotten treacheries, was hewn off in some prehistoric tragedy? No, d'Imiran, for, though you might believe it to-night, you will doubt the evidence of your own senses tomorrow. Now, go!"

The last d'Imiran saw of Kalmarkane was the hair-framed pallor of his face reflected in a mirror as he closed the door behind him.

"Can you account for his power over the hand?" d'Imiran was saying to Mr. Low during the course of the following afternoon.

"As to that," replied Flaxman Low, "I can do no more than indicate a theory. You are acquainted with the phenomena of moving solid substances which frequently forms a leading feature in spiritual séances. The kind of force which is exerted, and the manner in which it is exerted, is still, as you may know, an unsolved problem. When we come to consider the power of Kalmarkane's brain, the years he has spent upon mastering psychical secrets, and his extensive travels in Thibet and elsewhere, I cannot but think that, starting from some such basis as I have alluded to, he may have gone forward, step by step, until he reached to the extraordinary degree of power of which you were so nearly the victim. The weakness and pallor you mention also go far to support the probability of my surmise."

"It may be so," said d'Imiran. "But why, then, did he destroy the thing?"

"Either," answered Low, "he was influenced by your threats, or it has become, as he said, useless to him, because he has advanced to a still higher point of knowledge."

"Can I do nothing to bring him to account?"

Flaxman Low shook his head. "At present I am afraid not," he said. "Some day, perhaps, we may go a little further into many matters with Dr. Kalmarkane."

THE STORY OF MR. FLAXMAN LOW

The very extraordinary dealings between Mr. Flaxman Low and the late Dr. Kalmarkane have from time to time formed the nucleus of much comment in the press. This is partly the reason for the narration of the present story, which may safely be said to be the first true account of those passages which have provoked so much contention.

It has been urged that Mr. Flaxman Low was vastly to blame as the person upon whom lies the onus of the very remarkable termination to the affair.

That is a matter for the reader to judge of when he has carefully perused the facts which we have endeavoured to set forth in the following pages. We have related in the preceding chapter an account of the one previous occasion on which Flaxman Low was brought face to face with Dr. Kalmarkane's strange influence. This was in the matter of the young doctor, Gerald d'Imiran, at that time assistant to Dr. Kalmarkane, whom Dr. Kalmarkane endeavoured to murder under circumstances which left no doubt in Flaxman Low's mind of the extraordinary powers attained by his great enemy.

It was in the closing days of January that Mr. Flaxman Low, while attending a special meeting of an Anglo-American Society of Psychical Students—on which occasion he read a very remarkable paper on the three-fold aspect of the soul as regarded from the ancient Egyptian standpoint—perceived amongst the audience the massive head with its wild aureole of hair, which distinguished Dr. Kalmarkane.

After the meeting Mr. Flaxman Low drove home to his chambers, where some five minutes later he received Dr. Kalmarkane's card. He was a good deal surprised at the proferred visit, knowing what he did of the morose and solitary habits of his visitor. This interview proved to be the first episode in a strange train of events, which directly connected Mr. Low with that formidable and relentless man. Probably it had early become apparent to Kalmarkane that there was no room for Mr. Low upon his path, and that the interview we are about to relate merely brought matters to a head; however that may be, we must proceed first to hint at an extraordinary offer made by Dr. Kalmarkane to Flaxman Low, and afterwards to describe, as far as it is within the province of words to describe, the singular series of circumstances resultant therefrom.

Kalmarkane strode in hatted and cloaked, his stooping gaunt figure seeming to dwarf the proportions of the room. He nodded slightly to Low, and then his eyes ranged slowly round, as if by the aid of his surroundings, to gain some insight into the character of his host. Meanwhile Low recognised the fidelity of d'Imiran's word-portrait of Kalmarkane. "A hirsute giant with a tremendous frame, raw-boned and ungainly. He has a long, strong, fleshy nose, a shock head of dark grey hair, and a ragged beard, which he is in the habit of twisting into spirals as he talks."

As Kalmarkane turned to speak to Flaxman Low, his big hairy hand went up into his beard.

"I have come," he said, "in order to tell you that I was greatly interested in your paper of this afternoon. You have reached a point attained by very few before you— By the way, how old are you?"

Mr. Low, in some surprise, answered.

"Ah," said Kalmarkane, "I am by fifteen years your senior, and I think I may say quite as many years in advance of you in that special branch of knowledge, to which we have both chosen to devote ourselves. Are you sure that we cannot be overheard? I have a certain proposal to lay before you. Let me advise you to give it your careful consideration."

Mr. Low having replied suitably, Kalmarkane went on.

"I came here intending to warn you to draw the line of your studies at the precise point where you find yourself today."

"May I inquire why?"

"You have an intellect of a very high order, as well as strength and audacity, and these qualities might hold you safely where you now stand. One step further the whole aspect of your position changes."

"I do not pretend to misunderstand you," replied Flaxman Low. "But all knowledge is good, if applied only to legitimate ends."

Kalmarkane broke in stormily. "However we may choose to designate our motives, the final aim of every man is to secure individual power! When you shall have learnt the ultimate secret of power, can you answer for yourself that you will never use that power to secure your own ends? Listen! Give me your word that you will reveal nothing of what I am about to say to you, and—and I have no doubt but that we can work very well together."

Thereupon followed in plain but pregnant words an offer to share with Mr. Low the final and immense result of his lifelong toil on certain conditions. Mr. Low listened as his companion flung out each forcible, trenchant sentence; but when he had heard a part of Kalmarkane's communication, stopped him with a deliberate and definite refusal.

Kalmarkane wrenched at his beard.

"Take time to think; for if you now refuse what I offer, neither heaven nor hell can help you!"

"I have decided," was Low's answer.

"This is d'Imiran's work!" said Kalmarkane furiously. "I warn you—!"

"I do not see," said Low, rising, "that we shall either of us gain much by prolonging this interview, and you may be very sure that you are dealing with a man who does not permit threats. And will you allow me in my turn to warn you? You forget, Dr. Kalmarkane, that though there seems no limit to human knowledge, there will always be—as long as body and soul are interdependent—a close-set limit to mortal power."

Kalmarkane swung towards the door.

"I came here entirely in your interests," he said, "and I now add also in your interests," he ended with a snarl, "that I do not warn twice."

In a day or two Mr. Low had completely forgotten Kalmarkane's strange visit, being engrossed in further abstruse and deeply interesting investigations on the lines suggested by the paper he had read at the meeting before mentioned. In the course of a fortnight, however, he began to recognise that a new and untoward mental condition was gradually becoming habitual with him, even to the extent of interfering in a serious manner with his hours of study.

Whether its source lay in mind or body was difficult to determine. Mr. Flaxman Low says that he first became conscious of something wrong by noticing that the amount of work he usually got through between the hours of ten p.m. and two a.m. was growing perceptibly less and less, and that the notes made by him during that interval were of a comparatively valueless character. For a day or two he fancied that he must have become sleepy in the middle of his reading, and hence the absence of usual results. The next step was to perceive that at all other times, excepting between the hours named, his work, on retrospective examination, was of normal quality and quantity. Thus it was evident that the attacks of mind-vacuity recurred at regular intervals, and he resolved to watch these intervals.

Accordingly, on the night of the 30th January, he placed his books before him as usual, and waited. Almost exactly at midnight he was seized with a feeling of overwhelming despondency, which grew into a condition of resentful frenzy as he brooded helplessly and miserably over some unknown wrong. This phase in its turn passed imperceptibly away, and Flaxman Low found himself reading in his usual manner when the clock struck three, and recalled him to a full consciousness of what his intention had been when he sat down to work. Think as he might, however, a large part of the intervening hours only supplied dim and unsatisfactory memories.

As time went on, these attacks recurred more frequently. The harder he endeavoured to work, the less he seemed to accomplish.

His writing began to lose character, many of the letters were slurred; his faculty for close study deserted him, which he felt the more as he was at the time engaged upon some minute and intricate work in connection with a half-defaced Ptolemaic inscription.

At first he was inclined to believe that his health was perhaps to blame for these strange lapses, but in time it grew clear that his mind was at intervals burdened by alien thoughts superimposed upon his own. In other words he could not concentrate his attention upon his work because he was busy thinking of something else. But what that other subject or subjects could be, he had only a very general notion. His brain was filled with memories which eluded him, memories of some vague and awful unhappiness, a sense of helpless revolt against some crushing fate, but all dim and undefinable.

In the intervals when he possessed himself and could follow out his own train of thought, his position absolutely horrified him, and he resolved time after time to throw off this mysterious ailment by sheer effort of will. For some ten days or more his mental attitude was one of tense resistance, at the end of which time, though physically exhausted, he had in a great measure thrown off his spiritual incubus.

But a further phase of his remarkable sequence of experiences was close upon him. One night, when walking home from his club, he felt that he was being followed. On looking round he saw no one in the deserted street but a policeman at a distant corner. He walked on more rapidly, his pursuer keeping pace with him. He knew those other footsteps fell in exact unison with his own, and that if he could but stop a fraction of a second sooner he must hear them. He hurried on, and shut the door of his chambers behind him with a sigh of relief, which even at the time struck him as ludicrous and unnecessary. Merely waiting to take off his overcoat, Mr. Low sat down at once to work, refusing to allow himself to think over his latest experience.

He believes he was reading when he found himself glancing quickly back to catch sight of the face that had been peering over his shoulder, but he was too late. This happened more than once.

Soon the permanent impression of a haunting presence grew intolerable. Day and night he was never alone, never free from the consciousness of that other intelligence oppressing his own, and by degrees it usurped his thinking powers, seeming to suck from his brain all independent mentality, and to use it solely for its own weird and elusive ponderings.

He knows that he struggled continuously but feebly to rid himself of the tyranny of the thoughts, which were not his thoughts, but those of that hateful personality that dogged him. He always knew that had he looked up, or back, or turned, or stopped a fraction of a second sooner, he must have seen, or heard, or felt his tracker; but he was always by that same fraction of a second too late. On retrospection he now recognises that time after time his intangible companion drove him into situations where by a hair's breadth only he escaped death. If the reader will for a moment place himself in Flaxman Low's position and imagine himself possessed by an intelligence determined to wreck him body and mind, he will readily perceive how terrible was a life of which the most ordinary conditions teemed with danger.

Through the long February nights he struggled and waited, set in his resolve to defeat this mysterious influence by sheer, solid effort of will.

At this period there happened to be a sudden burst of bright weather, and Mr. Flaxman Low made up his mind to go over to Paris for a week for a change of air and scene, for he was still inclined, during moments of sunshine and activity, to put down his experiences to some physical origin. In Paris he felt better, and often forgot his late troubles. He went out a good deal and saw many friends, M. Thierry amongst others; and, altogether, returned to London feeling fit to face most difficulties that could present themselves.

He attacked his neglected work with fresh vigour, and a delightful sense of recovered power. One night he placed his books and papers in order, and made the one other arrangement which always accompanied a long spell of tough work. It is Flaxman Low's habit to fill and place in readiness a succession of pipes in the rack above his head. He apportions them to the amount of work he intends to do, and while his mind is delving in the lore of Egypt, his fingers lay pipe after pipe aside until as many as ten yawn black or ashy from the tray. On this occasion he worked and smoked as usual.

It was long past midnight, and the empty streets lay silent but for the passing of some stray hansom at long intervals. All at once the silence seemed ghastly to Flaxman Low as he stood and looked heavily out of his window. Why he had risen from his chair he could not recall, and the hours since his return from the club had been full, not of work, but of indistinct, puzzling dreams. He knew also that the haunting presence had returned. Never before had he felt its nearness so acutely, nor with the same degree of shrinking repugnance. Tonight it almost seemed as if his unseen companion were tangible to the touch, and the perplexing sensation of loss of personality grew upon him as the mysterious presence, pressing closer, usurped the active functions of his brain to brood over some blind, far-off, uncomprehended wrong.

He remembers pushing outwards with his arms as a man might make way for himself in a crowd, and returning hurriedly to his desk. There was a sickly smell in the air, which was known to him, but which he failed to specify. He lit another pipe—the sixth as he afterwards had reason to believe—and sat down to his work. After that his recollections became intermittent. He was taking up another pipe, dreams and thoughts beyond all power of description were crowding upon him. He was struggling with drowsiness—then he was leaning back in his chair, and eyes were looking down into his own, dark eyes, full of hatred and despair, that carried with them the meaning and the memory of those long, vague, unhappy thoughts—he found himself considering the strange, conical cap his companion wore; it was of some woollen material, and thickly covered with short, loose threads, every one of which ended in a knot—then the shadowy eyes, full of compelling hatred, again held his gaze—

Late in the afternoon of the next day he woke to find himself staring at the ceiling of his bedroom, which seemed to sink and recede as he looked upwards. A deadly inertia overcame him until presently the clock struck five. Recollection began to flow back upon him; he knew he must have slept for fifteen hours. It all came to him now—the beautiful malignant eyes, and the dark fingers laid upon his brow while his brain swung and reeled into sleep.

By some connection of ideas, Flaxman Low involuntarily looked down at his own hand. Upon his right forefinger was a brown stain. Raising it closer to examine it more thoroughly, he inhaled the same faint, sickly odour that had pervaded his experience of last night. His mind, working sluggishly, hit at length upon the explanation, and the thought sent him reeling from his bed.

Steadying himself by a chair, he looked through a case of drugs which stood beside the door. A bottle of powerful tincture of opium was missing. He staggered into the next room and to the table at which he was in the habit of working. The missing bottle stood uncorked among his papers, half empty.

A horrible suspicion flashed across his mind. One of his pipes still remained unsmoked, and it reeked of opium. Others—the sixth and seventh in order upon the tray—were full of ashes, but the tell-tale odour hung about them still. Mr. Low took up the bottle, and for a moment wonder held him—wonder at the rare strength of constitution that had carried him safely through an ordeal under which most men must have sunk. To a wiry constitution, a clean life, and regular and wholesome habits, he owed the privilege of standing there alive.

After throwing the windows wide, he began to pace the room. He understood now the unaccountable mental lapses of the last few weeks. Some intelligence, other than his own, possessed him at intervals, and, taking advantage of the routine of his life and his ordinary habits, had used his own hands to compass his death. He detailed to himself the many escapes he had lately had, and the commonplace events which had led up to them. This brought him to the most important question of all. Who could be the author of so subtle a plot? It is worthy of remark that the possibility of Kalmarkane being connected with it did not at once strike him.

It was at this juncture that Flaxman Low at length acknowledged the absolute need of some human cooperation and assistance.

The experience of last night might recur at any time, and the idea that the thing was not possible but probable sent him once more striding rapidly up and down the floor. He ran over the list of his friends and acquaintances, and he began to be sorry there was so little faith left in the world.

D'Imiran had said something similar. Ah, d'Imiran! The name opened up a new vista of thought. Kalmarkane! In a moment the whole affair became clear to him. Turning to the books he had been using on the previous evening, he examined the marginal notes last written. The few broken sentences bore no connection whatever with the text, but they seemed the echo of those dreams of despair and wrong which had of late worked beneath and independent of his objective consciousness. We may add that these remarkable sentences formed the basis of much subsequent investigation on the part of Mr. Low.

In a very few minutes Flaxman Low had decided on his course of action. First he must see d'Imiran, since d'Imiran was the only man who would believe such strange experiences possible, and was also the only man in a position to give him much necessary information, and perhaps combine with him in the effort he was about to make to shake off for ever the yoke which Dr. Kalmarkane's incredible powers had forced upon him. He looked up the address d'Imiran had given him, and in an hour was hastening thither in a hansom. D'Imiran was in town, but chanced to be out, and Mr. Low left a note for him.

> My Dear d'Imiran—If you can possibly manage it, I should like to see you tonight. If you could come over between seven and eight, we might dine together.
>
> Yours very truly,
> Flaxman Low

He walked back to his rooms across the park, and several men who met him on the way remarked that he was looking very seedy.

Once at home, he had nothing to do but to wait for d'Imiran. During the whole of this time he was slowly coming to a conclusion.

"I should have been to see you before had I not had a very strong reason for staying away," were d'Imiran's first words. "But now that you have sent for me I am very glad to have the opportunity of meeting you again."

"Ah, Kalmarkane, I suppose?"

"Yes, Kalmarkane."

"He objected to our meeting? For what reason?"

"He appeared to have strong ones," replied d'Imiran with manifest hesitation; "and it seemed to me that it might be well, both for your sake and my own, to do as he wished."

"I don't know what you may think about that when you have heard my story," said Low. "I had an interview with Kalmarkane about a month ago, and on that occasion he threatened me, and you will, I fancy, agree with me that he has fully carried out his words."

Thereupon Mr. Low narrated his experiences, adding:

"And now you will perceive there is no time to be lost. Tonight I go to Crowsedge. I do not know whether you will feel equal to accompanying me."

D'Imiran kicked the fender savagely.

"How do you connect Kalmarkane with all this? He is capable of anything, as I have good reason to believe, but—"

"I am quite willing to tell you what I suspect," replied Mr. Low. "I have told you of the visit he paid me; during that visit he offered to share his secret with me on the condition that I cooperated with him in his horrible schemes. From that time I date my troubles. Let us take the events: my loss of brain power, my strange periods of possession, and finally my incomprehensible lapse of last night. I believe that Kalmarkane is using some parasite intelligence to prey upon and wreck my mind and body. I have no doubt that if I do not act at once his next attack will be fatal."

"If you knew as much as I do, I think you would hesitate to go to Crowsedge. What do you intend to do there?"

"My dear d'Imiran, you will understand that there are matters between myself and Dr. Kalmarkane which must be settled once and for all!— On second thoughts, it may be rash to ask you to accompany me."

Flaxman Low rose and slipped a revolver from a drawer into his pocket. D'Imiran, still kicking at the fender, watched the significant action.

"Yes," said Low, in reply to d'Imiran's glance. "It may come to that. At any rate, I am resolved that the settlement between us to-night shall be in one way or another a final one."

D'Imiran's answer was to get his hat. Mr. Low put out his hand. "I'm going too," said d'Imiran. "I have also, as you know, one or two questions to settle with Dr. Kalmarkane."

The night mail landed the two men at a station not more than six miles from Crowsedge. D'Imiran, who knew the country well, started along the dark road seawards. The salt wind blew in their faces as they walked on rapidly through the starless, windy night. After a time, they left the high road and struck into a stony track across the heath. Now and then as they topped a rise, they could see a flash-light far out at sea, but on the land all was black and lonely, and nothing was to be heard but the dry rustling of the heather as the strong gusts swept over it.

Presently, d'Imiran pointed to a distant light.

"Crowsedge," he said.

They stumbled on in silence till the thunder of the ground-swell on the coast could be distinctly heard. They were now approaching the house, and d'Imiran remarked that the light was burning in Kalmarkane's study.

They felt their way in the pitchy darkness round to the house-door, which they found unlocked. Then, passing through halls and rooms, they emerged into the lower portion of the tower, where above them at the head of the flight of stone steps, a slip of light showed about the door-frame of Kalmarkane's study.

"What do you intend to do?" asked d'Imiran in a low voice.

"Give him a choice," replied Low, as he mounted the steps.

Kalmarkane was seated at his desk, and looked up with a flare of angry surprise visible in his eyes.

"What has brought you here?" he said. "Have you come to tell me that you have reconsidered my proposal?"

"On the contrary," replied Flaxman Low, "I have come to discuss very thoroughly those other matters that are open between us."

"I have shown you that my boasting was not altogether vain," returned Kalmarkane derisively. "You taunted me with the limits set for mortal men. I have effectually answered you! It is by a mere chance that you are alive at this moment. I am still only learning my powers, but I promise you not to fail a second time! Man, think what you have refused! I have grasped the supreme secret, which has been sought so eagerly but not found; the secret of the mother-force of nature—cosmic ether! All other forces—electricity, magnetism, heat—are but secondary. I assert that as men have found means to make these secondary forces subserve their purposes, so have I discovered how to control the primal force, for the human Will is above all.

"I have sufficiently demonstrated that I have power, and I can prove that all force is Will-force, acting by and through the vibrations of ether. What are thoughts and emotions but etheric vibrations? And since man can control thought, the conclusion is perfectly logical that he can control the ether. This makes him absolute master not only of the material world, but of those other influences lying beyond its borders!"

"And yet you are only a man," said Low, covering Kalmarkane as he spoke with his revolver. "And as man to man we must deal with each other."

Kalmarkane smiled.

"I give you a choice," went on Low, "I will either shoot you as you sit there or—"

"Shooting means the gallows for my murderer."

"Possibly, but as the law cannot help me, I must take its functions into my own hands. As an alternative, I suggest that you make a little journey with me abroad, where we can even up our differences as men. This was, I believe, the course adopted by Busner and Wolff, as you probably remember, some three years ago."

D'Imiran has given a graphic description of that scene. Low no longer was the scholar and the man of science, he was the elemental man, ready to abide by the law of the stronger hand. Kalmarkane sat silent, the drops gathering on his furrowed forehead, as he glared savagely at the pistol barrel, which gave Flaxman Low the right to dictate to him.

"You have just sixty seconds to decide in," said Low.

"You have given yourself a great deal of unnecessary trouble," answered Kalmarkane at last. "I will be glad to shoot you when and where you will!"

"That is well; the sooner we start then the better, for we don't part, Dr. Kalmarkane, until this affair is finished. D'Imiran will act for me. Pray let me know what are your wishes."

Kalmarkane scowled heavily.

"I have a friend, a Count Julowski, who understands matters of this sort extremely well. He is now at Calais. There is a little cove down the coast there, which will suit our purpose admirably," he replied shortly.

There is no need to give here any description of the journey and crossing to Calais, nor of the many precautions taken by Mr. Low. Suffice it is to say that the duel was arranged under severe and even murderous conditions, at the express instance of the two principals. The distance was to be twelve paces and the shots alternate.

On the way to the spot arranged for the meeting, d'Imiran could not control his desire to ask Flaxman Low one or two questions.

"You were able to put forward a very plausible theory in the case of the Brown Hand," he said. "What do you make out of your own experience?"

"There are one or two possible explanations," returned Flaxman Low, "but the one which most satisfactorily coincides with the events is that which I fancy I have mentioned to you already. Kalmarkane appears to have obtained power over some disembodied spirit whose intelligence he uses to further his own purposes.

If you consider the chain of events—my unaccountable depression, the intervals of half-suspended consciousness during which my annotatory writings bore the same stamp of vague desperation, and, lastly, my attempt to make away with myself by adding opium to my pipes—I say if you consider all these things, they certainly point to the probability that a parasite intelligence was acting upon and usurping my mental and physical faculties. This theory covers all the facts."

"But how came Kalmarkane to have influence over a spirit?"

"I am driven to believe that he has discovered not only the secret of etheric energy, but also how to make that energy subservient to the directed will. Did he not boast to you that all power resides in the mind of the man who knows how to make his will effectual in the spiritual as in the physical world? Because I believe in that power and Kalmarkane's unscrupulous use of it, I am here today."

"If you were aware that he had so much dangerous power," said d'Imiran, "why did you allow him the chance of fighting? I should have shot him down on sight. By your action you are submitting tremendous issues to the lottery of a duel. I cannot think you are well advised."

"One does not readily bring oneself to shoot an unarmed man, and as to his escaping, I hope, my dear d'Imiran, to render that impossible by the stringency of the conditions under which I had resolved the matter should be decided. He may, and most probably will, succeed in revenging himself but I can assure you that we will go together, and I do not think that either here or hereafter the death of Dr. Kalmarkane is likely to weigh too heavily upon my conscience."

Such was the conversation between d'Imiran and Flaxman Low as they drove to the appointed place of meeting.

The affair came off in the little cove already alluded to. The gusty breeze had risen to a gale when the combatants stood up between wind and sea. We cannot give any prolonged account of how luck favoured Kalmarkane, who, securing the first shot, brought Mr. Low to the ground, nor of how Flaxman Low, with his bleeding shoulder and right arm dangling useless, fired from the ground, his bullet entering Kalmarkane's brain; nor of how Kalmarkane's great form stood upright for a moment, his finger twitching on the trigger, till he plunged forward shoulder-first into the sand.

That ten minutes upon the Calais coast has been widely discussed in the papers, and we can only hope that this story will clear Mr. Low from the accusations of savagery that have from time to time been forced upon him. His action in this matter, as in all others, was, we venture to contend, dictated by that high-mindedness which has always formed one of his most prominent characteristics.

It is a somewhat significant fact that at the sale of Dr. Kalmarkane's effects d'Imiran purchased an ancient oblong box, which was found to contain a bronze bracelet (of which d'Imiran already possessed the fellow), and also a conical woollen cap furred on the outside with little knotted threads.

Of the strange series of experiences in which Dr. Gerald d'Imiran and Mr. Flaxman Low were participators, it is difficult to determine how much may have been due to hypnotic or kindred influences, and how much was naked fact.

Of the secrets possessed by Dr. Kalmarkane, Mr. Flaxman Low can still do no more than indicate the drift. Whether the scientific formula will ever come to light is another matter; at any rate, for the present, the knowledge rests with Dr. Kalmarkane in his grave.

In these stories we are afraid it has only been possible to give a very slight and cursory account of the pursuits and character of Flaxman Low. Some day, perhaps, they may be resumed, for who shall say how far his hand shall reach into a science, amongst the exponents of which we are certainly justified in calling his the first great name.

SOME EXPERIENCES OF
LORD SYFRET

INTRODUCTION

At forty I had exhausted the resources of civilized life. I had health, wealth, and position, yet I knew that unless I could devise some new expedient for passing time suicide would be my last sensation. As to whether suicide were justifiable or not I did not concern myself. I was bored, and I did not propose to continue being bored. Exploring my mental reserves I lighted upon a vein which, suitably worked, might profit me. I set about working it. So far I have done this successfully. Once more life is tolerable, occasionally exhilarating.

The vein is an insatiable and absorbing interest—curiosity—call it what you will—in other people's lives. Fiction has no charm for me. I am always conscious that its personages are but printer's ink. And I like my pages of story wet with the ink of life. I meet a man or a woman whose appearance or conditions stir me. By the expenditure of a little ingenuity, some trouble, and more or less hard cash, that person's story lies to my hand. Aided by a staff of well-drilled agents, whose duty I make it to shadow in one capacity, or another the fortunes of such persons as have roused my curiosity—I am enabled to read their stories like a book. And, I can answer for it, few romances approach in interest some of the realities I have thus been able to trace. My right to peer into my fellows' lives may be denied. I myself have never questioned it. To do so amuses me. That is sanction enough for my morality.

It has occurred to me to record a few of the stories whereon I have chanced. That thus set down they will interest others as they interested me who watched them welding in the forge of life I do not pretend. Yet may they serve for entertainment. As already stated, my concern is purely psychological, or, if you prefer a simpler term, impertinent curiosity. With the right or wrong of things I do not meddle.

STRONHEIM'S EXTREMITY

I had called on my friend the Keeper of Coins and Medals at the British Museum. We had been College churns and did not stand on ceremony.

"I shall be busy for an hour," he said, as we shook hands. He pointed to a batch of medals, marred and defaced to bewilderment. "I am getting to the end of them. If you can come back again I shall be delighted. We will lunch together. Or if you care to remain here till I have finished, I can give you a rare old folio to dip into."

"I will remain," I replied. "I enjoy this musty odour of antiquity."

The Keeper smiled.

"If you were fated to endure so much of it as I do," he returned, "you would probably prefer oxygen."

Five minutes later an attendant entered.

"A gentleman to see you, sir."

The Keeper glanced up through his spectacles displeased. He read the card before him.

"Did you tell him I am busy?"

"I told him, sir. He says it is urgent. It has to do with the Hierator coin."

"Ah!"

The Keeper laid down his magnifying glasses. If there were a tender spot in his heart the Hierator coin had found it. It was a superb specimen recently added to the collection under his charge. Its history was sufficiently recondite to have taxed without baffling his skill in the matter of classification, yet was it so well preserved, the classic obverse so exquisite and clear, that even a tyro in the numismatic art, like myself, could not have failed to admire it. Apart from its beautiful workmanship, its value was determined by the fact that it belonged to a period whereof but few evidences remained. Moreover, it was an unique specimen, no other of its kind being known to exist. It had had a whole column of the *Times* devoted to it, a column which was a very monument of lore. Its value in specie was variously estimated at from £50 to £2000. It was probably worth £1000, but the authorities of the Museum into whose possession it had come, entertained not the remotest intention of parting with it. To them it was priceless, for it completed a series long incomplete.

The Keeper looked anxious. The source of the coin had not been altogether satisfactory, and he had suffered, he told me, not a few waking nightmares lest somebody should turn up to establish a claim upon it.

"I will see the gentleman," he said.

He swept the mouldering bronze and silver heap before him into a drawer, which he carefully locked. Then he changed his glasses, and leaned back in his chair, his eyes on the door, an anxious fold between his brows.

"I wish I could feel secure about that Hierator," he remarked.

The attendant appeared presently ushering in a tall, thin, shabbily-dressed man. The man bowed squarely, and ceremoniously. He was obviously a foreigner.

"Herr Stronheim," the Keeper read, consulting the card and returning the bow, "what can I do for you, sir?

It may have been prejudice in the interests of the Hierator, but I thought he did not like the look of the man. His face was sharp and thin and his glances travelled nervously—almost furtively—about the room.

"Sir, I am obliged to you," the stranger rejoined, with only a slight German accent, and in a pleasant enough voice. "I have a letter to you from Professor Von Brau, of Berlin. I take the liberty of presenting it in person."

"Von Brau, Von Brau?" the Keeper echoed dubiously, "do I know him?"

Stronheim seemed taken aback.

"I understood him to be a friend—a friend of many years. Is it Doctor Keith Bernard I have the honour of addressing?"

"Yes, I am Dr. Bernard. With your permission I will read the letter. Please sit down."

The visitor sat down. His face was agitated. His glance still travelled furtively about the room. The Keeper reading the note observed him from time to time above his spectacles. It was briefly, I learned later, a letter of introduction. Professor Von Brau, dating from a medical college in Berlin, recalled himself to the recollection of Dr. Keith Bernard, whom he had met some years earlier at an Antiquarian Congress. He begged to be allowed to present to Dr. Keith Bernard, Herr Stronheim, a gentleman with whom he himself was but slightly acquainted, though he came to him warmly commended by friends. There was some small matter wherein he should regard it as an honour to himself and a personal kindness if Dr. Keith Bernard would assist Herr Stronheim.

"You now remember the Professor?" Stronheim queried.

The Keeper shook his head.

"One meets so many gentlemen at conferences—I fear I cannot for the moment recall your friend." The German leaned forward in his chair.

"May I, nevertheless, hope—" he began, hurriedly.

He stopped short. The Keeper noticed that his hand on the rail of his chair was trembling. It occurred to him, as it did to me, that the man had had no breakfast.

"I made the journey on purpose—" Stronheim began again. His pinched face suggested at what cost.

"I shall be glad," my friend responded kindly, "if I call help you in anyway. I am afraid if it should be a position you are seeking—"

Stronheim shook his head.

"It is not that," he said. "You are very good. It is not that, but the matter is of much moment to me."

The Keeper implied by a gesture that he awaited Herr Stronheim's pleasure.

"You have here a coin—"

"The Hierator," Bernard interjected.

"The Hierator. May I be permitted to see it?" The Keeper kept his eyes fixed on the other. Plainly this was a claimant.

"The Hierator is on public view in Coin Room No. III., in the centre case, facing the window," he said briefly, adding, "If you wish it I will send a man to point it out to you."

"Sir, you are good; but I wish more. I ask for the privilege to examine it closely—to take it in my hands."

The request was unusual. Bernard scanned him. Certainly, his credentials did not warrant the placing of much trust in him. He was shabby and ill at ease, and his boots, though decently blacked, were broken. In England we are apt to think lightly of men with broken boots, especially if we have reason for doubting that they have breakfasted. Moreover, I could see my friend was jealous for his Hierator.

"The request is unusual," he demurred, "may I inquire the object?"

Stronheim evaded the question.

"I but wish to take it in my hands one moment."

"You will surely explain your purpose."

"Pardon me, I must beg of you to permit me to reserve that."

Bernard hardened. Obviously no good was intended to his treasure.

"I fear, sir," he said, civilly, but firmly, "I fear, then, I cannot comply with your request."

The German made a gesture of protest.

"Sir," he exclaimed, "you surely do not suspect me—of what can you suspect me?"

"Your request is unusual, and you give me no reason."

Stronheim put a hand to his throat and turned away. The fingers of the other hand grappled convulsively with the chair-rail. After a minute he faced round.

"I cannot tell you the importance of this matter to me," he faltered. "My future—the future of others—depends upon it."

My friend had warm spots in his heart beside that occupied by the Hierator. I saw him weaken.

"Bless me," he said cordially, "if you are so anxious you shall see it."

"I, too?" I motioned with my lips. He assented, smiling.

He took up his velvet skull-cap, and cutting short the Teuton's effusive and guttural gratitude, with a British and kindly "Not at all, not at all," preceded us across a lobby and up sundry steps to Room No III. of Coins and Medals.

The great room, its walls lined with shelved glass cases, its space pervaded by them, only narrow intersections being left for the passage of visitors, was apparently empty; but a moment later a custodian, bearing his wand of office, respectfully joined us.

We went quickly down the narrow passages, the cases filled with green and mouldy-looking treasures seeming to engulf us in a tomb-like silence. Nobody was there, but few persons taking interest in coins.

The Keeper stood before a case—he could have found his way there in the dark, I believe—where in the centre, on the velvet bosom of a handsome casket, rested the Hierator. An inscription beneath recorded its date, and briefly a portion of its history.

Bernard, for the moment mindless of the stranger's possible designs upon his treasure, pointed it out with pride.

"There he is," he said, smiling, "there he is—the finest coin in our collection."

The German gazed with greedy eyes. He pressed his features close against the glass, examining it absorbedly. There was a strange light on his face.

The Keeper watched him, as did I. What was his motive? His eyes fastened on it as upon some long-loved prize.

He thrust a pale, long-fingered hand toward it. "Let me examine it," he broke out hoarsely.

I thought Bernard regretted his concession. But he was a man of his word. He fitted a key to the door. The custodian, wand in hand, stood by. He maintained a vigilant scrutiny of the stranger. Obviously he did not like his looks. Possibly he, too, suspected that the shabby foreigner had had no breakfast.

Bernard took the leather casket from the case, and held it a moment in his hand. He looked with pleasure and affection on its occupant. Then he passed it over to the German.

Stronheim bowed as he stretched his trembling fingers for it. His eyes devoured its every curve and marking. He bent above it with an ashen face. Soon he lost consciousness of everything beside. He did not see the respectful, half-questioning glance of the custodian upon the Keeper, nor the Keeper's fixed scrutiny upon himself. He put a finger on the coin with a suggestion of lifting it from its casket.

"May I be permitted?" he inquired.

Bernard nodded. His face was grave. Certainly one might have suspected that this was the Hierator's lawful owner. Only one in whose possession it had been could love it as this man plainly did. The German removed it, setting the empty casket on a neighbouring case.

At that moment a man entering the room at the further end suddenly stumbled, and with three clattering steps to recover his balance, and a loud guttural cry, measured his length on the floor. We all instinctively turned. There was a sound as of metal striking wood and ringing sharply, a muttered exclamation, and the German was down on hands and knees feeling and searching with his long blanched fingers.

"I started and dropped it," he explained tremulously.

We had turned our heads but for a second. As my glance swung back from the prostrate man at the end of the room, I thought I saw something fall and disappear. In a moment Bernard was on his knees. A few swift looks and sweeps of his hand sufficed to show him that the coin had vanished. If it were there at all it would take time to find. He turned his eyes from Stronheim's face, bent white and anxious on the floor, instinctively towards the figure of the man who, now erect, was leaving the room. Something in the latter's threadbare aspect, linked with the recollection of his guttural cry, seemed to impress him. He whispered the custodian. A moment later the latter's steps were echoing loud and hollow down the room. He followed the stranger out through the lower doorway.

Bernard furtively turned up a coat sleeve, mentally measuring his strength against that of his adversary. He glanced at me with a grim expression.

"Sir, how can I express my regret," the German apologised, still searching with agitated eye and hand. "It was unpardonably awkward. But I am not well to-day. The man falling unnerved me. I let the Hierator drop. It must have rolled far."

There was a strange exultation in his voice. Under cover of his stooping posture he smiled secretly. He searched with care, but the anxiety of some minutes earlier had died out of his face.

"You can laugh as you like, my man," the Keeper muttered in a savage aside, "but your troubles are only beginning. Englishmen are not so easily fooled."

The custodian now came back. He nodded to his superior's questioning eye. Then he, too, went on hands and knees, apparently searching, but his gaze made significantly for one after another of the shabby German's pockets, as though he were speculating as to which at that moment concealed the Hierator.

Stronheim grew anxious. He began to search feverishly, and with a degree of wild aimlessness. He swept his glances near and far. His features worked. Then he put a curb on himself and fell to more methodically. He took a knife from his pocket. We kept our eyes on him. He opened a blade and proceeded to slip it carefully some six or eight feet's length along the cracks between the boards. He probed thus every crack of the passage in which we stood. This failing, "Mein Gott!" he said, in hollow tones, straightening himself for a moment to get the ache out of his back. With a haggard face he started further down and worked slowly up the floor, dragging the knife-blade vigilantly in the crevices, his ear inclined, his fingers a-search for the clink of metal as though his life depended on it. He carried this manœuvre several yards further in either direction up the room.

As one after another the cracks failed him, his hands trembled visibly. The Keeper and the custodian had risen to their feet. They viewed him with disapproving faces, faces that spoke of rising exasperation at this which seemed to them a farce.

The German, absorbed in his efforts, paid them no heed. Bernard turned, closed the door of the case whence the Hierator had been taken, and locked it.

A party of children entering and detecting the group—one man on hands and knees—clattered hurriedly up the room, the small feet of the younger members of the party multiplying the footsteps of those bigger by hollow two-to-ones as they scrambled along, keeping pace with their elders. The custodian motioned them. They remained at a distance, disappointed but breathlessly whispering and watching with widely-opened eyes.

"Mein Gott!" the German exclaimed again, as he came to the end of the longer span of cracks without finding anything. The sweat stood thick on his face. He looked up to where we stood regarding him.

"I have never seen such a thing," he cried. "It dropped. I saw it strike the floor and roll, and then it disappeared. I could swear it rolled no further than this."

He indicated a spot with a broken boot.

The Keeper and the custodian regarded the boot.

A clock clanged twelve. Stronheim started up.

"If you permit it," he addressed Bernard, "I will return in an hour, and search till it is found. Lock up the room and I will go carefully over every inch. I have at a quarter past twelve an appointment with the Consul; but I will return at once."

The custodian laughed outright.

The Keeper regarded him sternly.

"Monstrous!" he said. "Do you suppose I shall allow you to leave this place until the coin is found? Is it of any use to continue this farce?"

Stronheim stood staring at him. Then:

"Himmel!" he protested, "do you suspect me of stealing it?

Bernard made a movement of impatience.

"The coin must be found before you leave," he rejoined shortly.

"Must I lose my appointment with the Consul, sir?"

"Undoubtedly."

The German wiped his brow helplessly.

"What an unfortunate I am," he muttered, "and just as I hoped everything. Sir, I swear to you—sir, I am a man of birth and education. I assure you—"

Bernard cut him short.

"I have made no accusation, I only demand the coin. A few minutes since it was in your possession; where is it now?"

"On the floor, sir, assuredly somewhere on the floor. It must be to be found."

"Assuredly," my friend returned, "it must be to be found."

The German went again on hands and knees.

The children from their distance watched him breathlessly. They also ran their sharp eyes over the floor. To them the scene was absorbingly interesting. What was the man on the floor so anxiously hunting? And would he find it? And if he did not find it what would happen? It was a thousand times more diverting than old pennies and mouldy things in glass cases. The German rose to his feet again.

"I have failed," he admitted, spreading his hands out with a fatalistic gesture. He glanced toward the fog-darkened windows. "The light is little," he deprecated.

"It will be my unpleasant duty to have you searched," the Keeper said, "unless the coin be at once produced. I have wasted time enough."

Yet he seemed sorry for the man, as I was. He was obviously a person of cultivation, despite his poor condition.

Stronheim started as though he had been struck. "Searched?" he echoed, in a hollow voice.

"Searched" he repeated overwhelmed. He steadied himself against the corner of a cabinet. He panted as though he had run a race. The Keeper observed him. Why should he dread being searched if he had not the coin? If he were innocent he would surely court inquiry. There was but one inference to be drawn.

"It is our routine practice," he said shortly.

The German was taken with convulsive shuddering. The custodian eyed him contemptuously. He glanced impatiently at his superior. What was the good of this fuss? Why did he not straightway hand him over to the police? He attracted Bernard's attention. His lips formed a voiceless word. Bernard shook his head. Give the poor devil a chance, he indicated compassionately. Only—his face hardened—the Hierator must be found.

The German composed himself.

"I refuse to be searched," he cried. He wiped the sweat-crop from his brow. "I refuse to be searched," he repeated.

"Why should you mind if you are innocent?"

"Why should I mind? I mind much. It is—it is—" he was manifestly seeking excuse— "it is an insult. You suspect me of theft. I come to you as one gentleman to another, sir. I bring a letter of introduction from Professor Von Brau—"

"I have no alternative," the Keeper answered. He had now not a doubt as to the other's guilt. This dread of being searched convicted him out of hand.

"I will look again," Stronheim said desperately, sweeping a swift instinctive glance toward the door. But the custodian forestalled him, moving a few paces between it and the suspect. Stronheim understanding glared upon him. He made a gesture of despair. Then he took out a pencil, and marking off an area still larger than that he had already gone over, and using his handkerchief duster-wise, swept every inch of the floor. He found nothing.

He shook his head muttering:

"I will never be searched."

He took a box of matches from a pocket, and striking half a dozen, he scanned the boards minutely. Still he found nothing.

"Gott im Himmel!" he muttered again, "they shall never search me."

He started slipping his knife along the cracks again, taking the wider area. But nothing came of it. He went over the ground once more: with no result. He sat up, and covering his face with his hands moaned under his breath.

"I give it up," he wailed brokenly. "Fate is against me. Some devil is in it."

"You will submit to be searched?"

He threw out his palms. His eyes seemed to start from his head.

"Then I am a lost man," he exclaimed.

"You had better give the coin up," Bernard remarked quietly.

"I have it not." Yet his hand went instinctively to an inner pocket.

"If you do not give it up I must send for the police." Stronheim stared stupidly before him.

"I am a lost man," he mumbled. Then he suddenly swayed, and fell forward on his face. In the excitement ensuing the children drew nearer. They thought he was dead. It was a rare morning's entertainment indeed—to see a man die.

"Shall I take it from him, sir?" the custodian queried, his hand on the German's coat.

The Keeper shook his head.

"It's here in his breast pocket," the man urged. "I can feel it through the cloth."

"Let it be," the other said. "Undo his collar, and open the window."

Stronheim had just unclosed his lids, and was blinking the misery awaiting him into his consciousness, when suddenly a commotion rose among the children.

"It's mine." "No 'taint, I seed it furst." "Oh! you little liar, I seed it." "I picked it up anyways." "Give it me!" "Give it *me!*" "Yes, giv' it 'im, he's my bruvver."

The cries waxed to a hubbub. The custodian bore down upon the disputants. Two were on the point of blows. The man rapped their heads with his wand.

"Now then, clear out, you youngsters. Make yourselves scarce, I say."

The boys sobered. They eyed one another, muttering fiercely. One whimpered.

"Now then, clear out, or the police will have you," the custodian threatened.

"He's got my penny," the whimpering boy protested.

"Taint yours, and 'taint a penny," the other retorted.

The chorus began again. "You're a liar, I seed it first." "Giv' it 'im, he's my bruvver."

The custodian rapped heads and knuckles indiscriminately.

"Police!" he called in a loud whisper.

As the boys scuffled, something fell to the ground. A girl darted toward it. But the custodian was before her. He had it in his hand. He examined it amazedly. It was the Hierator!

"Where did you find it?" he demanded.

"I picked it up," the boy exclaimed. "I seed it lying be'ind the leg of a taible, and I picked it up. It's mine, not Bill's."

"It isn't either of yours," the custodian said. "It belongs here. Now then, be off with you."

He was considerably crestfallen. He had been so confident of the German's guilt.

Bernard strode toward him.

"God bless me!" he said, taking the Hierator tenderly. "Who would have thought it? Here, children," he called to the departing and depressed youngsters, "here is a shilling between you. Two-pence a piece, big and little."

The German smiled faintly when they laid it before him.

"I told you," he murmured. "I am no thief. But, mein Gott, what a fright I have had!"

"Why in the name of all that is inexplicable did you refuse to be searched?" the Keeper asked some minutes later, when the still faint Stronheim reclined in his room, imbibing strength from brandy and water. The other German, whom they had taken for an accomplice, and had placed under detention, was released, and the Hierator safely locked into its case again.

The German smiled. Then he sat up and looked at us one after the other.

He put a hand into his breast pocket, and with an air of mystery, drew out a small object. Still smiling he held it toward Bernard.

"Good Heavens!—the Hierator. I thought I had—"

"So you did, sir. This is not your Hierator, though a Hierator. I picked it up in an old iron shop in Vienna. Till I chanced upon the article in your *Times* I had no notion that the coin was worth money. I brought it over to compare with yours. I had been unfortunate. An illness robbed me of a good position. My money was gone. My family was starving. Just then a good opening offered, but it needed some £500 capital. I read your *Times*. I spent my remaining funds in coming to England. You kindly permitted me to examine the coin. I found it identical with mine. It was my last hope. If I had failed, Heaven knows what would have become of us!"

There was a moment's silence. He resumed.

"You ask me why I refused to be searched. I ask you and this gentleman"—he bowed toward me— "what chance should I have had with a Hierator, a coin understood to be unique, in my pocket. Would anybody have troubled to look further? I should have been convicted of theft—ruined. Now—"

He spread out his hands with his former fatalistic gesture. But this time he expressed that destiny left nothing to be desired. My friend looked gloomy for the space of a minute. The uniqueness of the Hierator had been such a feather in the cap of his collection. Then the man got the better of the numismatist.

He stepped forward and shook the German's trembling hand.

"I congratulate you, sir," he said heartily. "Any museum of consequence, or a private collector, will give you at least £1000 for it."

"In the meantime," I suggested, "if you and this gentleman," indicating Stronheim, "will give me the pleasure of your company, we will go and get some lunch."

THE WOLF AND THE STORK

I

I detest hotels. I have in them always a sense of being in a menagerie. Whether it be that persons in a crowd revert to primitive conditions, or whether it be that their collective atmosphere betrays the lower origin, I cannot say. I only know that individuals who at home would be refined enough and decent members of society, when massed together in hotel suggest a zoo. As will doubtless become apparent, I am no amiable person, nor do I think I can be suspected of loving, no matter what scientific interest it pleases me to take in my fellowman. Therefore, I avoid a crowd: therefore I am no frequenter of hotels.

Chance took me, however, one summer to a holiday resort in Scotland, a place where men pursue the sport of golf and women prosecute the sport of man. It was but a moderate-sized hotel, and, having been fortunate enough to secure a pleasant suite of rooms, I could retreat into my lair whensoever the gambollings or growlings of my fellow-brutes threatened to disturb my composure.

Saturday being the day of my arrival, the next day was Sunday and unconscionably dull. To relieve the tedium somewhat I dined with the menagerie. At the table next to mine there sat a girl who reminded me of nothing so much as a little white rabbit—she was so blonde of colouring, so mentally and physically fluffy. With her was her mother—a person of sagacious, stork-like aspect, whose bland eye and beaky profile surveyed the scene from the height of a neck characteristically long and adroit of movement. That eye detecting me seated lonely at my bachelor table, she by a deft manœuvre changed places with her daughter, so that Miss Bunny of the dimpling cheek and downy hair faced me in all her charm.

"Why am I to sit this side, mother?" I heard her whisper. She glanced sidelong from beneath her lashes toward a neighbouring table.

"There is such a draught, my darling," Mrs. Stork returned, responding to her daughter's question. Then answering her glance, "Sir Alfred left this morning."

Miss Bunny sent one little sigh in the train of the departed Alfred, then apparently dismissed him. A moment later she had lifted a demure engaging glance at me from out the folds of her serviette.

My vanity was little flattered to discover this inspection followed by a disappointed droop at the corners of her mouth. Plainly I was no welcome substitute for the absent Alfred. Possibly I was twice as old.

Two evenings later, Miss Bunny sat again in the draught. For Sir Alfred's table was once more occupied. A young, good-looking man sat there—a stranger, apparently, for the Storks made no show of recognising him. I had thought the evening chilly, but Mrs. Stork to all appearance thought otherwise, for she leaned forward and loosened a pink lace scarf the girl wore round her shoulders—loosened it till her soft little throat and shoulders were bared.

"You look so heated, dear Dolly," she exclaimed tenderly.

"Yes, mother darling," the girl responded with a shiver.

The eye of Mrs. Stork, suffused by the gentlest solicitude, sought mine. I noticed then that my long-necked neighbour was exceptionally smart; and she wore a new and very fine cap. It occurred to me that Mr. Stork had, in all probability, been gathered to his feathered fathers.

At times I am subject to strange impressions. Dinner was over, and I was engaged on my filberts, when suddenly my surface chilled as though a wind passed over it. My hair lifted. The phenomenon known as goose-skin shivered through me. At the same time I was

conscious of an eerie, high-pitched wailing. I looked round quickly.
All the doors were closed. There was no opened window whence
draught or sound might enter. All that had happened was that the
young man at the next table had left his place and was just about
to make his exit by the swinging door. He must have passed behind me at the moment of that wailing.

I observed him later in the smoke-room. There was nothing
about him to warrant the uncanny or unwonted. He was a well-
grown, fresh-faced youngster of about twenty-four. He had the
manner and bearing of a youth of breeding. He sat apart with a
somewhat reserved air, smoking and watching a game of billiards.
It was a close game, and most of the men in the room were following it with interest. A few bets even were exchanged.

Once I observed the young man, at a moment when all eyes
were bent on a crucial stroke, suddenly sweep a swift glance round
the room, and discovering no eye upon him, fling up his head and
break into a short, rough laugh. I was sitting near, and it struck on
my ear with a jar of savagery. An instant later his face was composed, his looks were on the game, his lips set about his cigarette.
One or two persons turned round sharply in his direction, as though
they also had heard and wondered. He met their eyes coolly, and
with his air of reserve. "That young man, for all his fresh-facedness,
is meditating a mischief," I decided. My impression returned. I felt
uncomfortable, for if ever a laugh threatened murder that laugh of
his did.

In the course of the evening I addressed some commonplace to
him. Was he a golfer? He answered pleasantly. He had an agree-
able voice; his eyes were of an engaging blue; his well-cut features
lightened when he talked. I thought his adversary, whosoever he
might be, must have treated him badly indeed to rouse such rancour
in a youth so well-favoured. Some love affair, possibly.

Yet was he not inconsolable, for by ten o'clock next day he had
succumbed to the charms of Miss Bunny. I met him with his case
of clubs as I went up the hotel steps. "Bitten with the fever?" I
interrogated.

"Not badly, sir," he answered. "Only, lady sitting at table next me—lady with long neck—dropped her knitting. Awfully civil when I picked it up. Asked me to show her girl how to make a tee."

A soft little voice at my side insinuated sibilantly—

"I am ready now, Mr. Carvill. Mother has bought me a new driver. Don't you think it sweetly pretty with that band of blue leather on it."

He turned and looked down at the narrow little face with its prominent pink lips and white teeth. He ran a cool eye over her features and smartly-clad form. His slight moustache lifted as though he smiled. He turned and went down the steps. At the foot he dropped a pace behind, his eyes appraising her the while he adjusted a strap of his clubs. Then he glanced round with that same look I had seen the previous evening. Nobody being at hand he lifted up his head—and laughed. The jar of it came grating on the air. My skin rose in pinpoints. I heard a muffled wailing.

Then they disappeared round the corner, a couple of comely young persons chattering in the sunlight.

I passed into the house and into the drawing-room. At a window, half-concealed behind a curtain, Mrs. Stork craned her long neck. Every line of her betokened exultation. Complacent satisfaction played about her beak. Hearing me, she turned. She made two steps in my direction. I fled precipitately.

II

That night young Carvill sat at the Stork table.

Little Miss Bunny dimpled and frisked, lifting shy, silly glances to him from beneath her pale lashes. She wore no scarf at all that evening, and she shivered in her sleeveless frock. Mrs. Stork's cap was supernaturally fine.

Carvill accepted their attentions with a kind of absent nonchalance. He seemed out of sorts, being pale and self-absorbed. But I noticed his glances linger with a curious stare on the undulant curve of the girl's white throat. Once meeting his look she blushed and fluttered, shielding her eyes with her pale-fringed lids. I thought the youth forgetful of his breeding. Mrs. Stork's blandishments were not improving—as they were not calculated to improve—his manners. I noticed that he drank a good deal of wine.

In the smoke-room later he was hilarious, not to say uproarious. I thought if little Miss Bunny could have heard him talk, his fresh, young, handsome face would have lost some of its charm for her. I wondered whether, had she heard certain views of his, Mrs. Stork would have trusted poor little Bunny of the brain of thistledown so much in his company. But nobody made it his business to acquaint either mother or daughter with the creed of this avowed young prodigal.

Miss Bunny started early next morning to complete her education in that matter of a tee. Mrs. Stork stood in the hotel portico, her be-ribboned and rosetted cranium bobbing with a fatuous contentment on her long neck.

"Such a very nice young man," I heard her remark to an acquaintance. The acquaintance nodded.

"Who is he?" she inquired.

I caught complacent whisperings.

"Very good connections—wealthy squire—eldest son."

The lady nodded again, interested. Then she glanced somewhat wistfully in the direction of a daughter of her own—a person hopelessly plain of face, who stood brandishing her clubs and talking boisterously of some phenomenal stroke she had made.

"Do you think so much golf-playing improves girls' looks?" she questioned anxiously.

"My girl Dolly doesn't play much," Mrs. Stork returned, with that air of condescension adopted by the mother of beauty to the mother whose ducklings are but plain. "In fact she hasn't got farther than learning to make a tee—whatever a tee may be."

"I think it's that waggly way they swing their sticks before they knock the ball. That's either a tee or a bunker. They do give such queer names in golf. But really I don't fancy modern girls have the complexions girls had when they worked samplers."

I was on the point of rising. It was impossible to appreciate Chamberlain's discomfiture at the hands of wily old Kruger during this sort of thing. But at that moment Mrs. Stork spread her wings and swooped down upon me.

"Pardon, my lord," she began, with the lofty air inseparable from her long neck, "but may I borrow your *Times* a moment? I am solicitous about my friend Sir Alfred Baxendale, who is yachting in the Mediterranean. I will return it to you immediately."

I delivered it to her.

"Pray do not trouble to return it, madam," I said "I provide myself with it solely for the pleasure of presenting it to the first person who does me the honour of asking for it."

I bowed and rose. Then I repaired to my room and raged. I had read two lines of an exciting despatch, and these were merely prefatory. It would be hours before a paper would be available in the reading-room. Not twenty minutes later a note on scented crocodile paper, my *Times*, and a popular novel were brought to me. The note ran thus: "Mrs. (I forget the name, but I fancy it was not Stork) presents her compliments to Lord Syfret, and thanks him exceedingly for the *Times*. She begs at the same time to lend him a copy of *East Lynne*, which he may not have read, and which may serve to amuse him in this very dull hotel."

I returned the volume with thanks, assuring Mrs. Stork that I never read novels. I gave orders that should any lady under whatsoever pretext attempt to make her way into my rooms she was to be inexorably repulsed. Then I breathed once more and dined that evening by myself.

Later I strolled in the gardens. There was a bench whence I could hear the sea break while I smoked. The night was dark, and I had sat some minutes before I perceived the red glow of another cigar a few yards from me. In the dark I distinguished an undefined mass. Then a silly little voice exclaimed:

"I like a man to be awfully good-looking, Mr. Carvill."

Mr. Carvill took two puffs at his cigar. Then he said, indifferently: "Ah!"

After a pause the silly voice remarked:

"Don't you like good-looking girls, Mr. Carvill?"

"I prefer 'em decent-looking," Carvill admitted without enthusiasm.

"I suppose you like dark girls best?"

"Oh, I like 'em all colours. It's a change, you know."

There was a longer pause. Then the voice, this time depressed, was heard again:

"That's a good-looking girl who sits at the table in the left-hand window, don't you think—the girl with rather a red nose?"

"Is her nose red? Good figure. Wears white hats."

"Well, they were once white. But the sea does spoil things so dreadfully. You would never think I've only worn that blue hat I wore this morning once before, now would you?"

Perhaps Mr. Carvill was not listening. Anyhow he answered "No," which was certainly not the answer poor little Bunny was seeking. She was silent for quite an appreciable time.

Then she started bravely again:

"I did so like that heather coat you wore this morning."

Mr. Carvill took out his cigar and yawned. Then he lifted up his head—and laughed. The bench gave a sudden lurch. There was a flutter of skirts as though she had started up, and a smothered little cry.

"Oh, you said you'd never do it again," she panted. "You know—Oh, you know how it frightens me. Let me go. Oh, let me go."

He smothered an imprecation. Apparently he took her by the shoulders and forced her down on to the bench again.

"I told you," he protested savagely, "it's only a habit. For Heaven's sake don't keep on about it so. I did theatricals once, and had to laugh like that, and caught the trick."

"Let me go. *Let me go*," she insisted. "Mr. Carvill, you are hurting my arm."

His voice changed. A red glow made a hissing curve in the darkness, as he threw his cigar away.

"I'm awfully sorry," he apologised. "Horribly rude of me. I forgot. I get savage when it's noticed."

Plainly Miss Bunny was frightened.

"I want to go in," she whimpered.

"You won't mention it. Promise you won't mention it."

"I promise. No, don't you come. Good-night."

"Good night. I say, mayn't I though—just one? I did last night, you know."

But Bunny's white skirts had rustled away in the darkness.

He resumed his seat and lighted another cigar. He puffed it slowly into condition. Then he lifted up his head—and laughed.

III

From the hotel steps next morning Mrs. Stork watched them start. Little Bunny wore a new frock and a serious air which suited its pink frills and flounces ill. She glanced once with beseeching eyes into her mother's face, and then, with a curious side-long apprehension, at the fresh-coloured profile above her.

The storcine visage smiled with a smile which granite might have envied for its obduracy. Poor little Bunny, seeing it, shuddered, and shouldered her club with the band of blue leather about it. She tripped along beside him, stealing frightened glances up at him so long as they were visible. Then Mrs. Stork turned and ascended the steps, still smiling.

She had gained the doorway when her glance caught me. She coughed, and retraced her way as though seeking something. Finally, with an absent air, she sidled across and sat down at the opposite end of the verandah. I had made up my mind the previous evening. The opportunity presented. I am not wholly devoid of heroism, as my conduct on this occasion shows. I walked over to where she sat. I bowed and extended my *Times*.

"Your friend Sir Alfred Baxendale arrived at Nice last evening," I began. "Perhaps you would like to see for yourself."

She fairly blushed. She lifted and flapped her wings and hopped to her long legs.

"How excessively good of you," she simpered. "Really, how can I thank you."

I sat down as far from her as my powers of vocalisation and the subject at my tongue's end made advisable.

"Your daughter seems fond of golf," I said.

"Devoted," she answered.

"She is a pretty little girl."

Her own and her maternal instincts struggled. Her own had the victory.

"She is not seventeen," she murmured, adding in low tones, "I was myself but a child when I married my late husband."

"Ah!" I answered, abstractedly.

There was a pause, during which the Stork's eyes fathomed mine, seeking avidly an answer to the question as to whether my interest in Dolly were conjugal or step-fatherly.

To keep to the subject of Dolly, for though my intentions were neither the one nor the other, it was of Dolly I desired to speak, "An only child?" I suggested.

Mrs. Stork nodded. That my interest should extend to other members of the family pointed rather step-paternal.

"An only daughter," she assented, evasively.

I concluded that Dolly had possibly some half-dozen brothers. But I concealed my suspicion, while Mrs. Stork stole a plump, complacent hand up and settled her cap ribbons. Then she cast down her eyes and waited.

"You know Mr. Carvill?"

It was not a question she expected. She rearranged her views. An interest in Carvill suggested jealousy on my part, in which case— Mrs. Stork raised her lids and looked directly into my eyes. Once more she was merely maternal.

"Oh yes," she said, less sweetly. "He has been here nearly a week. We have seen a great deal of him. Such a very nice young man we think him."

"Ah!" I said.

She stole a sharp glance toward me. Plainly this was jealousy. I thought the storcine vanity ruffled. But if not mother, why not daughter?

"My Dolly has quite taken to him," she insinuated tentatively.

"You will pardon me," I answered. "He who does not confine himself to his own affairs generally makes a fool of himself; but I should like to say a word about this same young Carvill. Ladies"— here I bowed with my best air— "ladies are proverbially single-minded. But is it altogether wise to allow Miss Dolly to spend so much time in the company of a stranger?"

"It is so good of you to advise me," she murmured. "I need always somebody to advise me," she added in a flutter. The step-paternal theory was working uppermost again.

"I am interested in young people," I asserted distantly.

"It is so good of you," she murmured a second time. "But Mr. Carvill has been so well brought up, Lord Syfret."

"I haven't a doubt of it," I agreed, "I am speaking on general principles. To tell the truth, the boy has a rough way." I was calling to mind the previous evening. "He is a little strange."

"If there were anybody else," she said, "Dolly feels so lonely. She is such a loving child. She must attach herself to somebody. Now if an older man—someone more responsible—someone I could trust implicitly—"

"The girls here are good golfers, and seem friendly with one another," I interposed. Mrs. Stork bridled her long neck. She stared at me somewhat coldly. But she still maintained her smiling front.

"Dolly is timid with girls," she said, "and the girls here are mere hoydens. To tell the truth, Lord Syfret, Dolly—little puss—prefers masculine society. She is so fond of intellectual and progressive thought."

I mentally reviewed poor little Bunny's cranial development. I remembered her loose little lips and prominent teeth.

"Indeed," I responded without a smile.

"Yet she is nothing of a blue," she added, in a hurry.

"I am sure of it," I said.

"Perhaps you play golf?" Mrs. Stork suggested, with a sudden change of front.

"Heaven forbid!"

"Or croquet? Dolly said, yesterday—"

"Nor croquet, madam."

Mrs. Stork became all at once dignified. It began possibly to dawn upon her that my interest was without intention. She made one more effort.

"You are like me," she said, insinuatingly. "You are above the trivialities of life. All that you need to complete your happiness is quiet and congenial companionship—"

"You are right, madam," I assented, "the most quiet and congenial of all companionship—the company of books."

She rose. "Lord Syfret," she said with dignity, and not without acrimony, "I thank you extremely for your kind consideration. My belief in human nature would be greatly strengthened could I but think you had spoken from some other than mere personal motives. However, despite your evident hostility—quite unfounded—against dear Mr. Carvill, I shall be careful not to breathe a word to the poor young man of your unwarranted—may I say unworthy—suspicions. The boy is so sensitive, so generous—he would be cut to the heart, indeed, if he knew what an implacable secret enemy he has. Your *Times*, Lord Syfret, and *Good-morning!*"

I dined that evening in my room alone.

IV

"Mr. Carble says, 'Damn you!' and why didn't you get his knife prop'ly ground?" the waiter inquired of the porter as I crossed the hall next morning.

"Tell Mr. Carble damn him, and his knife can't be ground not any sharper than it is," the porter rejoined, in a tone of suppressed exasperation. "The fuss he's made about that knife of his nobody wouldn't believe. It's been at the cutler's three times already. If he wants it done any better, he'd best set to and do it himself."

"That's what he seems to think. He was sharping away at it on his strop like mad when I come down. He says he'll put a hedge on it to raise Cain."

At this juncture they perceived me. The conversation ceased abruptly.

Carvill passed some minutes later with his clubs. From a glance of his I had met the previous evening, I was aware that Mrs. Stork had faithfully reported my remarks. I reflected that yet again before I should die I had rendered myself ridiculous. For Miss Bunny and Carvill had spent the whole evening together, and had risen early in order to go round the links before breakfast.

This morning he was all smiles. Seeing his fresh young face beaming friendly upon me, I experienced some discomfiture. I never regret, or I might have regretted my lack of discretion.

"Golfing again?" I exclaimed, returning his salute.

"Golfing again," he assented cheerily. He was a youth of contradictions. The night before the smoke-room had fairly resounded with his uproarious and iniquitous doctrine. This morning he was boyish and fresh-skinned.

Mrs. Stork came out as usual to see them off. She bowed to me with an air of majestic forbearance.

"Everybody has gone over to North Berwick to see Balfour play, they tell me," she gurgled, "so you two will have the golf course to yourselves."

"Mother," I heard little Bunny whisper, agitatedly, "why has he got a big knife in his pocket?"

Mrs. Stork laughed and frowned together. She patted the girl's pale cheek.

"Little little mammy's silly," she exclaimed. "Why, the knife of course is to—to cut the tee with."

"Oh, but how stupid. You can't cut tees, mother. Oh! I don't want to go with him."

There was no smile now on Mrs. Stork's face. Granite again might have envied her.

"I shall take you home to-morrow, then," she said, in tones which whipped.

The girl put a faltering face up.

"No, no," she whispered, with a little sob, "not that, mother dear. I will—I will go with him."

She went.

At the corner where the path turned out of sight I saw him pat his pocket. Then he lifted up his head—and laughed.

V

At lunch the coffee-room was empty. There had been an exodus, indeed, to see Mr. Balfour play.

I had just sat down to my table and was grumbling about something or another—in hotels the man who grumbles most loudly is the man best served—when Mrs. Stork entered alone. The triumph in the eye she cast on me was complacent to fatuity. Had she belonged to a different class she would have set her elbows on her hips and hurled a "yah!" at me.

Instead of this she beckoned a waiter and demanded fussily, "Have you seen Miss —" the name scarcely sounded like "Stork"— "and Mr. Carvill?"

"No, ma'am," the answer was, "not since they went out after breakfast."

"Not since they went out after breakfast," Mrs. Stork reiterated for my benefit.

She ordered champagne. Then she set the full-stop of her eye upon me with an eloquence denied to speech. "If this don't mean business, my lord," said that eye of hers, "I'll just thank you to tell me what it does mean."

At the moment I should have been grateful if I could. The conviction that I could not spoilt the flavour of my lobster. My appetite was gone. I thought I would try a stroll across the golf-links.

"Heavens! sir, where are you going in such a hurry?" a rasping voice demanded. I had run full tilt into somebody entering as I left.

I did not waste breath in answering. I picked up the two heaviest-looking sticks the hat-stand held. One I kept for myself, the other I put into the hands of the hall-porter.

"You are to come with me," I said.

"Your lordship," he protested, "it's as much as my place is worth."

"Leave that to me. I have something for you to do."

Perhaps my manner impressed him, for without further ado he grasped the stick and strode after me. He was a powerful fellow I was pleased to note.

"Is it Mr. Carble, your lordship?" he puffed. He was scarcely in condition for the pace we were making.

"I am anxious about a lady who went out with him this morning."

"Not been back since?"

"No."

The man whistled apprehensively.

"Looks bad," he said. "His man was saying only last night he didn't like the looks of him. He's got a brother in an asylum. Can't really get on any faster, my lord."

The links were a desert of sand, with here and there bunkers, and furze clumps, and artificial water-courses, doing duty as "burns." The ground was of the roughest, up hills and down dales of miniature size, with sundry smooth stretches of grass for "putting greens." There was not a soul in sight. But with that irregular formation we might at any moment come upon them in some dip of ground, or behind some sand-hill. We kept our eyes about us, and our weapons out of sight. Our sudden appearance might by some horrible mischance precipitate matters. If indeed— We hurried on.

Had luck not been on our side that mischance would have happened.

We were striding up a furze bank when I heard him laugh. There was no repression in it now. It rasped out terrible and long. It gashed the silent air. He had flung off the mask. God grant we were not too late!

I turned and caught the man behind me by the shoulder. I forced him to his knees. We crept up silently amid the furze. Arrived at the top we came in sight of them. They were some distance below us on a ledge in the sandy side of the slope. It would be impossible for us to approach without being seen. It would be impossible to reach them without giving him some minutes' start, for the ground was rugged and soft, and there was a hollow we must dip into and scale again before we could get to them.

Poor little Bunny sat huddled together facing the point where we crouched and the situation with distended eyes. Carvill stood over her, his profile to us, keeping a furtive and continuous watch about him. One end of a razor strop was between his teeth, the other was in his left hand.

Along its stretched surface he slipped the sharp blade of a murderous-looking knife. I cursed the fate of circumstance. We could not advance a foot without discovering ourselves. And the slightest thing might set that knife at her throat.

"You'll never have a chance now of telling about my laugh," he said.

His speech was hindered by the ring of the strop between his teeth, but the words came clearly enough up the bank.

"No," she assented helplessly, her eyes fixed fascinated on him.

"It's you women who do all the mischief in the world," he went on, argumentatively. "You've got to be got rid of."

She made no other answer than an inarticulate moan.

He turned on her savagely, brandishing his knife. "What did you say?" he demanded.

"I said yes," she cried meekly.

"So, as I said, I'm going to cut your throat the moment I get this damned knife sharp enough." Then, "What did you say?" he demanded again, flourishing the blade.

I measured the distance between us; I rose on my knees. But I feared. The slightest thing might set him on her.

"I said yes," she repeated meekly.

Then, whether from sheer silliness or design, the poor little creature added feebly, "It will spoil my new frock, you know, Mr. Carvill."

I heard the big man beside me draw breath into his chest with a sob like a child's. I put my hand in warning on his shoulder. Carvill stopped sharpening his knife.

"Confound it! I never thought of that," he said. Little Bunny had some sense after all. She saw her advantage, and made capital.

"It's so very light," she continued, looking guilelessly into his face; "it will show every stain."

"Confound it," he broke out violently, "I never thought of that. Why didn't you put on a darker one?"

"I will to-morrow," she assented, eagerly. "We can come again to-morrow. I will wear my old blue serge. That will not matter a bit."

Her voice broke. I could see by her terrible pallor the horror she was striving with.

"No," he objected. "It's going to be done now. You're not to be trusted. And by to-morrow there have got to be a thousand women less in the world. It's they do all the mischief."

But there was an air of discomfiture about him. In the ill-balance of his unhinged mind the thought of the spoiled frock affected him unpleasantly.

He sharpened his knife with an air which, though dogged, had an element of irresolution in it. He muttered to himself. Once he clenched his fist and shook it toward high heaven, the while the pupils of her eyes distended on him till their china-blueness was a blackened horror.

Then he proceeded to strengthen his position by argument.

"You tell lies—all you women do," he blustered. "You deserve anything. You do nothing but deceive and cheat a man."

"But I don't," she pleaded, "I never tell big lies, Mr. Carvill, only little fibs sometimes that don't hurt anybody. Really I never do."

Her voice half broke again.

"It's a lie, it's a lie, it's a lie," he shouted frenziedly. "I'm not going to be talked out of it. If *you* don't, other women do, and you've got to die with the rest. You rob a chap's money and you want diamonds and anything you can get. You're so confounded greedy."

She stretched two trembling palms to him, palms as pink and impotent as flowers.

"I am not really greedy," she appealed. "Really, Mr. Carvill, I am not. I only thought you might not mind me having that golf ball. You have so many. And I didn't really expect you to give me the gloves—not if you don't want to. You're wrong if you think I am greedy."

He stuffed his fingers into his ears.

"I am not listening. I cannot hear a word you say," he said. He shuffled with his feet and hummed. "I'm not going to be talked out of it. I only wish there was edge enough on this confounded blade, and you'd see how little effect your talking has."

"Eve was the first of you," he began again. "She was a woman, and brought all the trouble into the world. You can't deny that."

"No," she said hopelessly, "I can't deny that, because it's in the Bible."

"Well, then," he shouted, "that clinches it, and you've got to be killed."

She took refuge in her former plea.

"It will spoil my new frock," she cried out piteously.

"Well, hang it, why didn't you put on some other," he vociferated.

Suddenly he broke out laughing.

"Why," he cried, "you can take it off. What a little fool you are! Of course you can take it off."

Her face fell dismally. The loose lips twitched with a grievous helplessness. And all the while we lay there afraid almost of breathing, lest we should set him on her.

"Yes, I could take it off," she faltered.

He passed his nail across the knife-edge. He flung the strop away.

"Then damn it, why don't you?" he shouted. "I'm ready now, and a precious lot I've got to do before morning."

The poor thing made one heroic effort. She cast her eyes down shyly. I believe she actually blushed, though how her bloodless cheeks accomplished it Heaven only knows.

"O Mr. Carvill, I should be ashamed to take my frock off with you here," she stammered modestly. Again he was taken aback.

"I never thought of that," he said, nonplussed. "Curse it, why do you make such a fuss. I shall never have done to-night."

Her hand, resting on the sand beside her, flung up a feathery spray to the tremble of her fingers.

"If you were to go up the bank—" she faltered, with a pretty timidity, pointing directly where we lay.

("I thought, from the first, she'd caught sight of us," the porter gulped in my ear, "bless her plucky little heart and spare her.")

"If you were to go up the bank," she repeated, tremulously, "I could—I could—"

She could say no more. Now Heaven grant she do not break down! It must have been fear rather than courage that sustained her, for breath and strength were spent.

I gathered myself for a rush. In any case there could be but one ending. He strode in front of her and stood there glaring. If she had cried out or shown the slightest fear he would have killed her then. But she showed no fear. Her large eyes rested on him vacantly.

"Swear you won't run away?"

Poor little creature. She had no breath to swear. But she nodded.

"And you won't call anyone?"

Her lips motioned "No."

He turned with an impatient oath and came clambering up the bank.

"A chap can't be a beastly cad," he muttered.

A minute later he cried out and fell. The porter's stick and muscles had effected that. We took his knife from him and secured him as well as we were able.

Then I leapt down the slope. Poor little girl! She was sitting wan and pallid, her trembling fingers fumbling at the buttons of her half-unfastened bodice.

"I saw you all the time," she whispered, "but I didn't think it would be any use."

She caught my hand clingingly. "Lord Syfret," she entreated with a little sob, "don't ever tell mother I hadn't time to fasten up my frock."

Then she slipped down from her sitting posture, and lay in a faint amid the sand.

THE VILLA OF SIMPKINS

There is an atmosphere about houses. They who live and joy and grieve in them invest them with a kind of aura. So some houses come to wear a face of gloom, of gaiety, of tragedy or terror. This circumstance, to me so manifest, escapes the notice of many.

One can see that tiles are broken on the roof; another that the window curtains are in need of washing; another that the masonry demands repointing or the woodwork painting; while a fourth condemns the sanitary arrangements. But the more intrinsic fact, the fact of desolation or disaster, to my mind most obvious, they miss; and even when perceived they refer it to some detail of dilapidation or poverty.

That my instinct is infallible I do not claim. On the contrary, it has more than once deceived me; but in cases where it has been rooted and tenacious, even though proofs have not substantiated it, I am satisfied my conviction of mystery or calamity has had its origin in fact; that the sense I have of violence or murder in the midst of a smiling family is an echo, a shadow, a stain on the fabric of life left by some former catastrophe. Sometimes I have been able to justify it by raking up the ashes of the past. Sometimes—and this is singular—the tragedy has happened long after I have sensed it. Of this the following is an example.

Sauntering one day down a road in a suburban town, whither I had gone a-search for adventure, I came upon a house a-building. It was a villa residence much after the style of other villa residences in the neighbourhood, a sixteen or eighteen-roomed house divided from its fellows by an acre of geometrically laid-out garden wherein it stood with a pretentious and pharisaical air of being some Englishman's castle. The structure was completed, and men were painting the woodwork, gravelling the walks and putting in other finishing touches which would for a year or two make its ostentatious freshness a reproach to its less lately smartened neighbours. There was nothing to stir one's interest. It was only another of the housings of opulent vulgarity wherewith the place abounded—housings which smacked of the shop and suggested sleek overfed occupants, in whom wine and good living had produced a kind of mental adiposity to act as buffer between their natures and the higher issues of life, as the flesh of physical plethora obliterated the lines divine of their persons. I passed on unconcerned. At the further entrance to the drive a man was standing, overlooking the hinging of a gate. I took him to be owner or builder.

The man's face arrested me. I stopped short. He glanced up, scowling as though he would have despatched me about my business. Now I was interested. I had seldom seen a face of so much malignity. It struck me that I would not care to occupy a house designed by so evil a fellow. A shock of rough red hair and beard overgrew his cheeks. His nose, slightly awry, was long and flattened at the nostrils, bespeaking both cruelty and sensuality. His lips were thick and protrusive. His hand and wrist extended, directing the men, were shaggy with a coarse red thatch. One eye had a sinister droop. No, I should not care to tenant a house of his building.

"Do you want anything?" he demanded roughly after a minute. He was well-dressed and apparently a person of some education.

I returned his savage glances with a cool stare.

"I want nothing," I said curtly.

He had more than a mind to inquire why then (with qualifications) I filled up the path. But he thought better of it. There is no law to prohibit a man from staring, and my manner proclaimed my determination to stare just so long as it pleased me.

"Damn you, you'll scrape the paint!" he shouted, as one of the workmen stumbled and jammed against the post the gate he was lifting.

The man grumbled something to the effect that the job was more than enough for two.

"Then go and be damned to you," the builder rasped. "Get your wage in the office and march!"

The man mumbled sullenly again, "I'm sick o' bein' swore at from mornin' to night."

"Easy, mate," his comrade counselled. "Now then, stretch yer limbs and in she goes."

With an effort they hoisted the gate and lowered it, dropping the bolts into the sockets with a rush.

"Damn you!" the builder shouted again; "it wasn't your fault you didn't snap the hinges."

The labourers, panting, mopped their faces.

"You have a limited glossary, my friend," I interposed, addressing the red-haired bully. "Take the advice of an older man, and curb your tongue. That 'damn' of yours is not calculated to bring the best out of men."

He swung his evil eye upon me like a lamp. Only the self-control of habit prevented him from striking me. All at once his manner changed. He scanned me closely; then he raised his hat.

"Pardon, my lord," he said obsequiously. "I did not recognise you. Your lordship does not know me perhaps. I have the honour to be your new agent at Rossmore."

"The deuce you have!" I answered. "From your credentials I should have supposed you a different man."

I resolved on the spot that never again, no matter how excellent his testimonials, would I engage a man without an interview.

"Your lordship misjudges me," he submitted plausibly. "I confess to being in bad humour. If you had much to do with this class, you would find there is but one way of dealing with it."

"It will not do at Rossmore," I said sharply. "My people are not used to the treatment of dogs."

"In dealing with your lordship's concerns I shall follow your lordship's wishes," he responded, adding with a spasm of independence: "Here I am attending to my own affairs."

I liked him the better for his independence. I laughed, and nodded him good-morning.

"Your temper is not pretty," I said, as I walked off. "Indeed, I was thinking I should not care to occupy a house built by a person so profane."

He made two steps in my direction. His face paled in its circle of red hair.

"Do you mean anything?" he submitted hoarsely. There was an uneasy glitter in his eyes.

"Pooh!" I said. "I shall not cancel our agreement for a few 'damns.'"

His eyes still probed my face. My words had plainly relieved him. Yet I had a curious sense of something underlying that which appeared.

"When your six months are up, my friend," I soliloquised, "I shall exchange you for a steward of more prepossessing looks."

A month later I strolled down the same road. I stopped short at the gates of Simpkins' house—the gates which had had so sulphurous a baptism. On one was painted the name "EDENHOME." It stirred my sense of humour. Was it of Simpkins' giving? Lurked there beneath that red thatch of his a corner for sentiment? I decided otherwise. Simpkins and sentiment, though alliterative, were not compatible. The name was merely a lure for letting purposes.

I ran my eye over the house's front. Was it the same? Surely not. This was no house of only a few months' standing. I walked up the road and came back to it. This was the place, assuredly. I stood staring at it. What in the name of amazement had come to it? Where was the freshness that was to put its neighbours to the blush? The place had an air of ruin, as of a house unrepaired for half a century. It were as though a blight had fallen on it. The paint of the gates had dulled to a dirty drab, the hinge-end was discoloured by a rust-smear, which, like a blood-stain, had trickled from the iron sockets. Somebody had made it his business to scratch out the initial letter, so that the name stood "DENHOME."

The abridgment seemed to scowl. I opened the gate and went in. The same blight which had fallen on the house had fallen on the garden. The greater number of the shrubs had shrivelled and died. The walks were set with brown ghosts. The grass of the lawn had fallen in patches, giving an uncanny, piebald look. As I approached I perceived that blinds had been put to the windows—fresh, gay-looking blinds of a pink pattern. They only served to accentuate the gloom. Apparently the house was about to be occupied. I wondered how anybody could have been induced to take it. Coming closer, I found I had been betrayed into a singular error, for the paint was fresh and unpeeled, the structure in excellent condition. There was nothing to explain the impression I had had of ruin.

I started; for of a sudden at an upper window, from amid a daintiness of pink blind, a sinister face showed out. It was gone as soon as seen. But I knew the evil eye, I knew the Iscariot hair and beard, I knew the malign glance. Irritation succeeded. What business had Simpkins here? His duty was with my affairs a hundred miles away. I strode up the steps. The door stood ajar—I entered. Inside, the house was as sombre as without. Gloom and ill-omen possessed it like black-browed tenants. I mounted the stairs, my footsteps echoing hollowly and fleeing before me noisy and afraid, like sound running amuck in the empty upper spaces. Suddenly they seemed to turn, and came hustling back upon me—leaping, stumbling down the stairs as if in panic. A rumbling echo rolled like distant thunder. For a moment I thought the house about my ears—its premature decay had culminated in the falling of the roof. Then there was silence, the echoes slipping into quietude.

I went straight on, making for the room in which I had seen him. My temper was up. I determined to give Mr. Simpkins a piece of my mind. At the top of the stairs I halted. Not a sound stirred. The landing was broad and well lighted. Into it four doors opened. The construction was different from that I had expected. There was a broad blank passage wall where I had supposed the door of the front room—the principal bedroom—would be. It was a construction as singular as it was unsightly. It had been so obvious to place the door of that centre room in the centre of this wall.

Suddenly I felt faint. The passage was pervaded by a curious heavy odour, arising, I imagined, from the paint. My head throbbed.

I made for one of the rooms facing me. The air here was fresh. I threw up a window and leaned out. When I was quite myself I looked about the room. I was astonished to find it small. Holding my handkerchief to my nostrils I went down the passage and opened the other door, the only other door in the front wall. Another little room! And no Simpkins! Where could the fellow be? And where was the door of that room in which I had seen him?—a room which must take up nearly half the house front I went all over the house. Not a sign of him; yet he could not have escaped unperceived. And why should he escape? My head throbbed heavily from the curious fumes. It did not smell like paint. Nor was its effect like that of paint.

I threw up another window. Doing so I looked out. I was in the second small front room. To the left of me was the big bay-window at which I had seen Simpkins. I went to the end of the corridor. From the window of the other room the bay showed to my right. I felt maddened. Where was the entrance to that room in which, doubtless, Simpkins still was? Pacing the passage I heard a sound as though something dropped. I knocked angrily upon the wall.

"Simpkins," I shouted, "what is the meaning of this fool's play? Where and why are you hiding?"

The words came back to me like gibes, out of the hollows of the house. I shouted again, only to be answered in the same strain. I went downstairs, and out into the garden. I ran my eye over the house front. It was as though I were being mocked. For not only were the windows I had opened still thrown up, but the three sashes of the bay, which before had been closed, were now raised. Out there in the daylight I could not help suspecting myself of some stupidity. There must be a door leading from one of the smaller side-rooms to that centre room—a door I had missed. Yet I had carefully looked for such a door. Bah! my senses must have been fogged by that vapour. My head even now throbbed with it. A room without entrance were an absurdity!

I returned to the house. The door was shut fast. I rattled it. I threw my weight against it. It was fast locked. Yet I had left it ajar. Was I being fooled, or was I fooling myself? Had I indeed seen Simpkins? Was anything as it seemed to me that morning? I strode to the nearest telegraph office and wired him at Rossmore. In an hour a reply came: "Am here, at your lordship's service.—Simpkins." I took a course of Turkish baths and drank no wine for a week. If there be one thing I despise it is a man who cannot keep his head clear.

The villa of Simpkins faded from my mind, as did likewise, to some extent, my first impression of its builder. To say I ever liked him would mis-state the truth. But I could not help recognising his exceptional business gifts and the zeal wherewith he prosecuted my affairs. I began to re-consider my intention of parting with him.

One morning I received the following letter from a girl dismissed a year before from my employ for bungling some business whereon she had been set:—

"Honoured Lord,—Pardon my addressing you, for I know you think low of me since the Smithson case; but any girl would have been frightened when Smithson took the carving-knife to her. But even Smithson's, honoured lord, was not as bad as this place. Yet mistress and master is bride and bridegroom, and a nicer couple couldn't be. 'What is it?' you'd ask. It's the house, honoured lord. Yet it's a nice house, and the kitchen and pantries everything you could want for. But there's something about it. What that is, time, if I ever have the nerve to stop long enough, will show. It's called 'DENHOME' on the gate"—here I pricked up my ears— "but young mistress calls it 'EDENHOME,' which we lay to soft-heartedness. Honoured lord, the Lovells are not gentry; which when I found out I never thought to stop. But Mrs. Lovell's an angel, and there's no stint, them having come in to a fortune. I don't rightly know the facts, but as they taught us at the Institute not to leave out anything, I mention that the Lovells got their money curious. Someone else had it, an uncle of theirs—Mr. Sinkin his name is—"

"My good young woman," I here interjected, "you are disregarding one of my most stringent rules—that of getting names correctly."

"He'd had the money—two thousand a year they say it is—for nearly ten years, when it was proved it wasn't his, but Lovell's. He'd kept back a will or something, they say, but it couldn't be proved. So he had to turn out. He must be a kind man, because he's built them this house, and won't take any rent for it. He says it eases his conscience. And, of course, he can't help there being something horrible about the house. It's a nice view, and polished floors, but the strangest noises and feel about it. Mr. Sinkin comes sometime He isn't a nice-looking gentleman, being cross-eye and carroty, but he's wonderful kind, and keep telling master to look after his health, being delicate; and as Sinkin would get the money if master was to die, I call it kind. He's that careful of them nobody would expect—considering. The first time he came he was quite taken up because they didn't sleep in the best bedroom. 'It's a south aspic,' he said, quite angry, 'and a big atmosphery room. It was built special for you.' He quite stamped up and down the carpet, and mistress put her pretty white hand on his shoulder—though she's afraid of him—and she says, 'Uncle, we keep it for visitors. We keep it for you when you come. You've been so good to us.' He stared and looked quite queer. He was terrible vexed they didn't use the room he made for them.

"'Oh, you keep it for me, do you?' he says. Then he burst out laughing. He laughs rather hoarse, and young mistress, she got nearer to master and put her hand on her throat. I was setting the table for dinner, and I wasn't hurrying. Mr. Sinkin isn't good-looking, but he's nice-spoken, and though I only hung his great-coat up for him he gave me five shillings and says, 'you look after my nephew and niece. I'm fond of 'em.'

"It came up again at dinner. I had just handed him his pudding—mistress made it with her own hands—when he says again, shaking his fist playful at her, 'and don't let me hear any more of your not sleeping in the front bedroom—the room I built special,

so sunny and healthy for poor Ned. Ned's lungs want a south aspic.' Master laughs and says, 'Why, uncle, all the front rooms are
south.' Sinkin looked vexed. And I thought myself it was all they
could do to please him and not argue. He says, frowning, 'It's the
atmospheriness you want, Ned,' and he turned to mistress and says
something about cuba feet, and ends, 'so I look to you to see Ned
sleeps there. His mother died consumptive.' Mistress turned pale
and caught the master's hand. 'O Ned, dear,' she says. 'I've no
cough,' he answers, 'it's only uncle's over-kindness.'

"'Ought he to go abroad?' she says to Sinkin, almost sobbing.

"'He's best where he is,' he says short. 'The drains abroad are
shocking.'

"'Uncle,' she says, shivering, 'there's noises in the room—the
strangest noises. Could it be rats?'

"He looked hard at her and says slowly: 'Rats in a new house—
and a well-built house like this? Nonsense.' After a minute: 'There
aren't noises every night?' he asks.

"'No,' she says, 'only sometimes—horrid rumbling noises, and
I think the gas escapes. That's why I thought it must be rats. They
say rats eat the pipes.'

"I don't wonder he looked cross. It wasn't like mistress to argue
so. Master broke out laughing. 'Uncle will think we're very ungrate-
ful, Milly,' he says. 'And you can't be so silly as to think rats eat
gas-pipes.'

"'Will you sleep there to-night, uncle,' she says. 'I should feel
comfortable if somebody had slept there.'

"He finished picking out a walnut. Then, 'There's nothing I'd
like better,' he says. But after all he fell asleep in the library. I
found him there when I went to do it next morning. His boots and
coat was off, and he was on the couch covered with rugs almost as
if he'd meant to sleep there. He gave me half-a-crown. 'You needn't
say anything,' he says, 'but I was that tired I dropt asleep.' And he
took his coat and boots and slipped up to the spare room. Honoured
lord, it wasn't a week after when a young gent stopping here went
to bed in the spare room—mistress couldn't bring herself to sleep
there after all—as cheerful as might be, and in the morning he was

dead—poisoned the doctor said, with prussic acid. There he was, stretched out with his eyes staring horrible and his face blue, and the room like an essence-of-almonds bottle. Mr. Sinkin came down in an awful state. He got the papers to leave out the name of the house and paid us servants to keep it quiet.

"'And, for Heaven's sake, don't leave the house,' he says to master, 'or I shall never let it again!'

"Master promised faithful. He had to settle it after with mistress. She begged him to take her away. She'd heard the noises that very night. 'I've promised uncle,' he says. So you see, honoured lord, I'm right in calling it an awful house. You don't know what a feel there is about it."

I wrote her one question. She replied, "The middle front-room door opens in the passage just opposite the stairs. There's a smaller room at each end of the passage."

"Simpkins," I said, "I shall be in Suburbia this week. Can I leave a message for you at Edenhome?"

He finished the few lines of a letter he was writing. Then he looked up. What eyes he had!

"Pardon," he said, "I am anxious to catch this post. Now I am at your lordship's service."

"Well, you heard what I said."

He scanned me narrowly.

"My lord," he returned, "I fancied I could not have heard aright."

"Imagine you did."

"I have let Edenhome," he said evasively.

"To a nephew, I know. Can I leave a message for you?"

"Your lordship is pleased to jest. My nephew is not likely to be so favoured."

"So so. I must introduce myself."

"There is not likely," he said sneeringly, "to be anything in common between Ted Lovell, the draper's son—I do not pretend to be a person of family—and Your lordship."

"I am interested in people," I returned, observing him, "I have heard of the suicide. I am interested in that haunted front-room."

The watch-chain on his waistcoat lifted high. But he spread his hands with a deprecatory gesture.

"I regret to say somebody has been playing on your lordship's— I dare not say credulity."

"You have no message, then?"

He followed me across the room with his sinister, cat-like tread. The air about him bristled with violence.

"You are pleased to be interested in my affairs," he said, with a suspicion of menace.

"I am interested in the construction of a certain room in a house I saw you building. You remember I went over it once," I added, quickly. But I was not quick enough. His eyebrows lifted.

"I was not aware it had been so honoured." His manner changed. "As you are so kind," he said smoothly, "I will take the liberty of asking you to talk with Lovell. Since Rudderford's case, he has spoken morbidly of suicide. It is idiocy in a man so well placed."

"I will advise him to sleep in the large front-room," I said.

He turned as if I had struck him, and went back to his work.

Hopkins opened the door. Her lids dropped on a gleam of recognition. It was the first rule of my institution that wheresoever or whensoever I should appear I was not to be identified.

A pretty, fragile little creature in a tea-gown tripped into the drawing-room.

"I am pleased to know you," I said, taking her hand. "I am Lord Syfret. You will perhaps have heard of me: Mr. Simpkins is my agent."

She blushed and fluttered, smiling up at me.

"Uncle was good to speak of us, and your lordship is kinder to come and see us," she said prettily.

Lovell was a pale-faced, ill-grown Cockney, proud of his lately-acquired money, proud of all he had exchanged some of it for, and genuinely proud of his little wife.

"She's a jewel I wouldn't change for the 'ighest lady in the land," he confided to me. His watery eyes were full of tears. The statement was not likely to be put to the test; but I believe he honestly meant it.

"If you can put me up for the night I shall be infinitely obliged," I said. They would be greatly honoured. I hinted to be allowed to occupy the front large room.

"Why, I'd just persuaded Milly we'd sleep there to-night," he blurted.

Milly broke in—

"I will have a fire put there for his lordship, Ted," and tripped away.

We had finished dinner, and Milly had sung me her songs— sweet little ballads she sang in a sweet little unaffected way—when there came a knocking at the front door. After an interval Simpkins entered. His eyes were blood-shot, his air restless. As he came in he shot a look at Lovell. That look said plainly, "I got your wire." I received him coolly. I regarded his intrusion as an impertinence. With his entry a reserve fell upon us. Poor Mrs. Lovell lost all her confidence and smiling gaiety. She watched him with a fascinated terror. She stole near me as if for protection. Presently she made her apologies. She was not well and might she be excused? She was faint and trembling. I gave her my arm to the door. She sent one long, shuddering look back at him. Then she drew a little agitated hand across her brow.

"Oh, my lord," she moaned through her white lips, "I am so afraid of him."

I steadied her to a chair. Lovell came out. I returned to the drawing-room. Simpkins sat scowling there.

"Your lordship's and my visits were ill-timed," he said, with a coarse laugh. "This night, even, may make me a great-uncle."

After a few moments, professing anxiety about his niece, he left. Out in the hall an altercation sounded. I could hear his rough voice raised. I could hear the sob and pleading of a woman's voice and Lovell's Cockney drawl. Once she cried out: "O Ned, I cannot, cannot sleep there."

I went out.

"Is Mrs. Lovell better?" I inquired.

She came to me with pleading hands. "O Lord Syfret—" she began. Simpkins caught her by the arm.

"You are hysterical," he said roughly. "You must not bother his lordship."

I took her hand. "Remember, my dear, that I am to have the haunted room."

"Do you say it is haunted?" she asked, with wild eyes.

"You frighten her," Simpkins interposed, adding curtly, "I regret the room has not been prepared for you. It is Mr. and Mrs. Lovell's own room."

She turned on him helplessly. She caught her breath with a sob Lovell put his arm about her and persuaded her upstairs at the top of the staircase she turned and swept one last terrified look down at us. Then she was gone. That look has never left me. To my death I shall regret that I did not act upon it and save her. I turned on Simpkins, who also stood looking up. There was in his face a singular malignant exultation.

"Why the deuce did you interfere?"

He looked me insolently in the eyes.

"Your lordship does not act with his accustomed breeding when he forces himself on an employé's affairs and even dictates the room his host shall put him in."

He followed me to the drawing room. There was an aggressive triumph about him.

"I sleep in town," he said. "Good-night."

I bowed. At the door he turned back.

"My agreement with you ends next week," he intimated, airily.

In the middle of the night I was roused by a curious sound. It seemed to be a muffled rumbling close at hand. I threw on some clothes and slipped into the passage. In the dim light I could see a thin line of shadow sliding down the wall—almost as if the wall had been moving. From somewhere sounded a hollow ticking, like that of an immense clock. Strange how the night develops sound! I had not seen nor previously heard a clock.

I was returning to my room, all noise but the sonorous ticking having ceased, when I thought I heard a cry—a faint cry—in the same little voice that had sung me her ballads. It was followed by two deep groans. Heavens! What had happened? I stood listening with strained ears. But no other sound came, nothing but that ghostly ticking. I groped my way along the passage, feeling for a door. I missed it, but coming to the centre, where I had seen it some hours earlier, I laid my ear against the wall. I was struck by its curious chillness. The wall was of iron! I did not stop to wonder, for now I could plainly hear a deep-drawn breathing. It kept time intermittently with the clock. I knocked on the wall. It might be merely Lovell snoring. But I did not like the sound of it.

Suddenly I became aware of the same heavy odour I had before detected. It was no escape of gas. I remembered Hopkins' words about the bitter almonds. This was a smell of bitter almonds. Then I laughed at myself. I should be seeing Rudderford's ghost next! Yet so strongly were my senses worked upon that I grew presently faint with the overpowering odour. And it was unmistakably a smell of bitter almonds. Again I groped for the door handle. I drew my hand along and up and down the wall, going over the whole expanse between the rooms at either end. I could find neither handle nor panel nor jamb. The whole extent was one smooth, iron-cold surface. The clock clacked tick! tick! tick! with sonorous beat. By this the stertorous breath-sounds had ceased. On the other side was silence.

Groping once more and finding no door, I became alarmed. I ran back to my room—my head throbbing till I reeled—and lighted a candle. I dipped my handkerchief in water and bound it loosely across my mouth and nostrils. Then I carried my candle into the passage. It was as I had suspected. There was no door. As on that morning, so now, the space between the rooms at either end of the corridor was one smooth surface. Tapping and testing brought out the chill feel and hollow note of metal. An iron plate had been dropped over the door—barring egress and ingress. The horrible clock ticked on. For what purpose? Convinced of some catastrophe, I knocked and called. I pounded with my fists upon the iron plate. It sounded thunderously, reproducing in exaggeration the noise which had awakened me. But no other sound answered. I rushed upstairs and stood in the passage calling for help. I beat on one or two doors. Soon a man appeared—the single man-servant of the establishment. He thrust his head out sleepily.

"Come," I insisted, "something has happened."

As we descended, the same low, rumbling sound was audible. In the flickering light the wall was crossed again by a rapid line of shadow—a line which now ascended. Then all was silent. Even the clock stopped. By this the almond smell was overpowering. I made the man protect his mouth and nostrils. The first thing my light flashed on was the door of Lovell's room, the door of which a minute earlier there had been no trace. What devilry was here? And what the calamity? I knocked loudly on the panels. An ominous still-ness reigned. I knocked again. Then I turned the handle and went in.

They were dead. They lay quiet as in sleep, only a curious blue-ness of skin and glassiness of the widely staring eye-balls showed their sleep final. Her hand was in his; her head lay on his shoul-der. So they stared straight into eternity, a smile on their faces.

But this was not all. The pitifulness of it—the pitifulness! For at her side, curled up as if in slumber, lay a newborn babe—a tiny premature thing nestling a darkly-downy head against her arm.

Before it was day I had interviewed a magistrate and the po-lice. They pooh-poohed my version of the case, rejecting it as melo-drama; such things were not out of romances. The case was mani-festly one of concerted suicide. The sliding walls excited smiles. In the middle of the night, they said, one can be pardoned some fogginess of sense. They did not consider there was a tittle of evi-dence on which to arrest Simpkins.

I sent for a London detective. I set an expert to explore the wall. It was impossible, he said, to explain a singular construction without some preliminary and considerable damage, which pend-ing the inquest was not advisable. There were grooves in the door-jambs of the small rooms off the passage—there was space to con-tain such a sliding-wall as I had indicated.

That night I secreted in the house my detective, two police-officers, and a friend. I knew Simpkins would come, and he came, as I likewise expected with materials for a conflagration. Hopkins admitted him. He would remain the night, he said. He professed an overwhelming grief. He had already supped. He would go straight to that room where the dead lay.

Through a peep-hole punctured in the wall we watched him from one of the adjoining rooms. No sooner was the door shut than he dragged chairs, cushions, towel-rack, all else combustible, toward the door. He even tore the curtains from the bed. Then he saturated the whole with oil he had with him. He had lighted a fuse and was making for the door when suddenly he stopped.

Tick! tick! began the clock. Tick! tick! It startled us with its suddenness and nearness. In a panic he flung his fuse. It fell short and lay smouldering on the floor. But he heeded nothing. He was beating frenziedly upon the door. However, we had seen to that. Tick! tick! went the clock. He thundered with his fists and feet and shouted desperately.

A rumbling began. He flung himself upon the panels. But they held out bravely. Tick! tick! went the clock; rumble, rumble, rolled the descending wall. He sprang to the windows; but we had seen to those. Suddenly I realised what was about to happen. The devilry planned by himself was on his track, hastened, it might be, by the explorations of my expert.

"Quick, quick t" I urged. "Unlock the door; we must not take the law into our hands."

But we were too late. Outside, in the corridor, the sliding wall came down—the door was sealed.

The rumble ceased; but the clock ticked on, counting his minutes. The almond smell rose strong.

"From where do the fumes come?" I questioned.

The detective, with an impassive face, stepped aside from a peep-hole. I looked long enough to see that a soft spraying like tiny rain was falling in the room.

Already he lay on the floor with gasping breath and distended eyes. I left the peep-hole to more interested watchers. Tick! Tick!

went the clock, counting his moments. Tick! tick! tick! "He's dead," they said. Tick! Tick! went the clock.

We passed into the corridor. The wall slid presently up with its curious rumble. Then the clock stopped. We opened the door and went in. He was dead, truly. And death in his guise was not dignified. He had been caught in the trap of his own ingenuity—for the mechanism showed a devilish ingenuity. The clockwork regulating it—clockwork set by his own hand—had with a fine unerring justice timed away his life. I will wager clockwork has rarely done the world a greater service.

IN A TERRIBLE GRIP

I had taken a house at Dover. I avoid publicity, and a case I had been dipping into threatened to come to trial, in which event I should inevitably find my name figuring in the papers. Therefore I conveyed myself and my effects to the coast, and had my yacht in readiness in order that a wire from my lawyer should give me some sea-miles' start of the person charged with the serving of my subpœna. I slept at Dover, going down most days by the five o'clock express.

About half an hour out from town I observed a strange old tumble-down house standing a little distance from the railway, a house noticeable for being a curious graft of villa upon farmhouse. This house had impressed itself on the outer tablets of my consciousness for some days, perhaps, before it struck deep enough to focus my attention. I know this by the circumstance that one day it remained in my memory with the clear and sharp intensity of something I had been acquainted with for years. I even found that my outer consciousness had arrived at the conclusion that the house belonged to an artist.

There was a long low room built out from it, a room with complicated blinds and a large top-light—a studio to all appearance. Then I asked myself why had the house impressed me, and what was my impression? I have, as I have said, an instinct for a house with a history, but, unfortunately, imagination and this instinct occasionally become confused. This was a house calculated by its quaint construction to excite the fancy. Fancy alone might be at work.

As I neared it next morning I examined it attentively. Certainly
it was a charming old place, and the garden a tangle of perfume
and colour. A hurried glance as we rushed past showed me the interior of the studio. There were no pictures nor sign of artistic properties. Not even an easel. Indeed, the only thing in the room was
an immense chair, a chair which caught and held my attention. It
stood on a platform raised from the ground. It was fitted with levers
and flanges and screws of every conceivable form and shape. I put
my head out of the window, staring back at it. It looked like some
horrible instrument of mediaeval torture. Before it had passed from
view I burst out laughing. Truly, my imagination was at ferment.
The chair was an instrument of torture without question, but a
modern one. It was a dentist's chair! Not such a dentist's chair as
I had ever seen, but manifestly a dentist's chair. The annex was,
then, no artist's studio, but a dentist's surgery.

I decided in the evening that the dentist had retired, and had
preserved this relic of his stock-in-trade possibly from some sentiment of professional pride, for the house stood a mile at least
from other dwellings, and these were a mere score of squalid cottages. There could be no scope for professional practice.

A man stood out on the lawn as we passed. If he were the dentist, he was young to retire—young, and yet old. His hair was grey:
he was thin to emaciation. He stood scanning the train with a wild
gaze. He looked like a man who had sustained some mental shock.
This impression was increased by the fact that a sudden shriek from
our engine at the moment of passing set his face contorting. Then
he clapped his hands spasmodically over his ears, and turning, shot
into the house, his coat-tails flying.

"My good sir," I reflected, "before you chose a dwelling within
thirty yards of a railway you should have discovered that your
nerves were not equal to the shriek of a locomotive."

A day later I was interested to see that the dentist had a patient.
The torture-chair was occupied. I could not make out much of the
occupant, and strangely enough the dentist was not visible. Neither were there to be seen the table set with picks and files, nor

the drill, nor any of those other contrivances for anticipating the tortures of the lost, wherein the dental mind is so prolific. As we glided opposite I got a better view. The man lay back in the chair motionless and gagged, with such a look of horror in his starting eyes as was absolutely appalling. His face was livid, his hands purple and patched with white about the knuckles, as though he were straining every effort for composure. It was evident he was undergoing mental torture of the extremest kind. Yet he lay back motionless—the convulsions of his features being the only evidence of muscular activity about him. I wondered, rather contemptuously—for after all the tortures of dentistry are not more than a man may bear—I wondered, if he felt so mortally bad about it, why he did not get up and beat a retreat. We passed so close that I learned his reason. A curious writhe and shiver of his limbs made it plain that to retreat was out of his power. He was locked in. The levers and flanges and screws had him immovable in their grip. Heavens! an ordinary dental chair were bad enough, but this one—this which locked the limbs and gagged the mouth, and held a man as in a vice—was altogether fiendish. Again I was struck by the fact that the man was alone, and that none of the paraphernalia of dentistry were about. The dentist was a cool hand indeed to leave his patient thus to his imagination.

"I say! man in a fit," my opposite fellow-passenger broke in. He leaned out of the window. "Poor wretch! and nobody with him!"

He resumed his seat. "I don't think it was a fit after all," he said thoughtfully; his eyes were conscious.

The same man travelled with me in the evening. As we neared the house we instinctively strained our necks in its direction. Every blind was drawn. It was like a house which had dropped its lids on a secret. My companion made a gesture toward it.

"Dead, I suppose," he said, with a little shudder. "Poor beggar! I hope they found him while he was alive."

I had it on my tongue to tell him my view, but I refrained. After all, he might be right. For surely no man ever looked like that over a tooth.

Next day the blinds were up. The chair was empty. The dentist
sat in the garden. I had searched the papers vainly for a case of
sudden or mysterious death. Two evenings later the chair was again
occupied. Again a man alone, convulsed and livid, lay with his
gagged face turned to the window, his eyeballs starting. I could
make out but little of his face for the screw and flange of the gag.
But I noticed the wild grey hair of the man I had seen in the garden—the man I had taken for the dentist. I reverted to my first
view. It was no case of dentistry. The room was a studio, the man
an artist's model. The torture on his face was simulated—excel-
lently well simulated. He was posing for some impressionist picture. Where then was the artist? And where the picture? There was
neither easel, nor palette, nor even a mahl-stick. I could see every
corner of the room. There was nothing in it but the chair—nobody
in it but the man.

I had come to the end of my imaginative patience. I would guess
no longer.

Next morning I got out at the nearest station. Inquiring my way
to the house, I was aware of being an object of interest, if not of
suspicion. I congratulated myself. There was something to sift.

"You mean Massey's house," a woman answered to my queries.
"Ah! poor gentleman! Up the lane and past the Spotted Corcodile,
and round by Meakin's forge, and it'll be the first house you come
to."

"Why do you say 'poor gentleman'?"

She shut her lips and shook her head. She tapped her forehead.
Then she reeled off a string of mild invective, and darting across
the road, whipped a small son of hers out of the gutter, and applied a palm in forcible and rapid iteration to the side of his face. I
am sensitive to discordant sound. I hastened on, pondering how it
came about that a woman could have in the same moment sympathy
and to spare over a strange "poor gentleman," and not a grain of com-
miseration for a lonesome little chap of her own with a taste for mud-
pies. I gained the Spotted Crocodile and passed Meakin's forge,
where a man, who might have been Meakin, was shoeing a horse,
and so to the house. Its front was pretentious but commonplace.

One would not have looked twice at it. The rambling farmhouse forming the back was faced by the most ordinary of villas, a villa of a conventionality of aspect which to me is always nauseating. Every blind was drawn to an equal depth down every window. Such windows as were open were lifted to an equal height. The muslin curtains stretched immaculately prim on burnished rods. The steps and flags before the door were chalked to the whiteness of sepulchres. The knocker glittered till its lustre stabbed the eyes. Altogether I was unfavourably impressed. The house was like a man whose teeth are too white. I mentally rubbed my hands. I love a house with so smiling a front. It rarely fails me. The door was opened by a sly-looking dapper housemaid. I had an impression of her levelling those blinds and polishing that knocker the while she was laughing in her sleeve.

"Mr. Massey in?" I inquired.

"No, sir, he's just gone out," she answered glibly. "If you was to walk up the road and turn to the right you'd be sure and catch him up," she added, pointing her hand.

I know a lie when it is told me. I knew it then. I stepped over the spotless threshold into the immaculate hall.

"I will wait," I said.

Had I been less quick she would have shut the door on me. She stood observing me with eyes like knitting-needles.

"Master's not very well, and doesn't see anybody," she said, a little abashed.

"He will see me," I said confidently.

There is no situation in the world which cannot be carried by confidence. After a moment's hesitation she crossed the hall and flung a door open. I entered an old-fashioned parlour. I gave her my card. She seemed impressed.

"I will tell Mr. Smithson, my lord," she said, with a new-found civility.

"Now who the dickens is Smithson?" I reflected.

He was by my elbow while I did so. I had not heard him come, but there he was—a smooth-faced, restless-eyed fellow with a chronic smile, and a superfluity of teeth phenomenally white.

"Mr. Massey is not well this morning, my lord," he said obsequiously. "Can I take any message from your lordship?"

"He is not out then?"

Smithson shrugged his shoulders, and displayed his teeth as if to acquit himself of all responsibility in that particular lie.

"He will be sorry to miss you," he said.

"I will call again."

He made another deprecating gesture as if to imply that such labour on my part would be unrewarded.

"Your master is a dentist?" I remarked in the hall.

"Pardon me, my lord, I am not at liberty to talk of my master's affairs," he said suavely.

Just then a voice shouted hoarsely:

"Smithson, for God's sake let me out. I can't stand it any longer, I shall go mad."

The cry was repeated with groans and panting gasps. Smithson's eyes met mine.

"My master requires me," he said, speeding my departure.

"He seems in pain or some extremity. Go to him. I will open the door myself."

But he would not leave me.

"Oh! I am suffocating—suffocating!" the strangled voice expostulated.

Then the door was shut and locked. I caught the next train back to town. I had walked rapidly to the station. Not more than half-an-hour elapsed between my leaving the house by the front door and passing its rear in the train. I looked into the large room. The dentist's chair was occupied, and by the same grey-haired young man. His face was contorted, his eyeballs strained, his hands clutched the chair-arms with the same lividity of spasm.

The solution of the problem suggested itself. Massey was a lunatic, Smithson his keeper. The chair was a contrivance for restraining him in violent moods. The cries I had heard were thus explicable enough. My interest was now engaged. I set inquiries afoot but could learn little. Only, people shook ominous heads at the

mention of Smithson. I sent Massey a line. I should be in the neighbourhood shortly, and hoped for the pleasure of making his acquaintance. He replied that he would be honoured to see me.

Smithson eyed me with no favour.

"Are your master's violent fits liable to come on at any moment?" I inquired, as he preceded me across the hall. He turned
and stared.

"I think it must be some mistake," he answered, "my master is
not a lunatic." He still stared at me.

"He said he had not your lordship's acquaintance. You must be
mistaking him for somebody else."

"That I will settle with himself," I said. He still hesitated as if
doubtful about admitting me. I pushed on.

"Lord Syfret," he announced to the old-fashioned parlour. The
grey-haired young man came forward, stretching out both hands.

"You do me an honour," he said nervously. Smithson left us.
We plunged into conversation. He was a friendly fellow, and
seemed flattered by my visit. I apologised for the intrusion. I was
a person burdened with leisure and a bit of a busybody. I had remarked his house from the railway. Its quaint appearance interested me. Had it a story? Might I go into the garden? Might I see
his studio?

"My studio?" he questioned, fixing his prominent roving eyes
on mine.

"I take the large room with the top-light to be a studio?" He
seemed sobered.

"I do not paint," he said. He was a stockbroker, and had spent
the greater part of his life in America. He had no friends in England.

"You shall see the room if you wish it," he continued, a shade
reluctant.

I wished it. As I had gathered from passing glimpses, it was a
great bare room with nothing in it save the chair. I observed it sur-
reptitiously. I would not hurt his feelings by being seen to remark it.

It was the most complicated piece of mechanism I had ever
chanced upon. It bristled with clamps and devices.

We stood staring about the room. Somehow our eyes turned always on the chair. I could scarcely keep it off my lips.

"You have a pretty view," I said, still staring at it.

At length he broke out nervously:

"You are looking at the chair?"

I scanned him closely. The mention of it was calculated to excite him. But he was quiet enough. Only his expression sobered, his lips twitched.

"It looks like a dentist's chair," I said tritely.

"It is a dentist's chair." He added under his breath: "Don't ask me about it."

"Certainly not, if you do not wish it. Let us go into the garden." But he still stood there.

"You never saw a chair like that," he asserted jealously.

A new idea struck me.

"It is an invention of your own?"

He turned on me peevishly. "You said you would not ask!"

"Pardon; let us go into the garden."

But he did not move. Suddenly he broke out: "I invent it? No, thank Heaven, it wasn't so bad as that."

He was growing agitated.

"Let us go into the garden," I said a third time.

He stood irresolute. He passed a thin hand over his brow.

"No, it was bad enough," he muttered. "Heaven knows it was bad enough, but it wasn't as bad as that." He looked furtively about the room. "I have never told anybody," he demurred.

I waited.

After a pause. "That chair nearly cost me my life." From under his faded hair a sweat-drop rolled, and, gathering moisture as it travelled, trickled down over his forehead and fell on his hand. He took out a handkerchief and mopped his face. "It cost me my health and peace of mind," he muttered.

Suddenly he looked me in the face with a wild appeal.

"Do you think a man might go mad brooding over things?"

"I should think a man who recognised the possibility would not be such a fool as to brood over things," I said firmly.

"Oh, it's so easy to talk," he muttered, staring at the chair. He took a key from his pocket, and slipping it into a triangular opening, turned it.

With a whirring click a lever slid down slowly, the seat tilted, the flanges revolved. Then the chair flung wide its arms with the suggestion of a steel embrace. I thought of a certain metal "maiden," of Inquisition frame. He motioned me toward it.

"Will you try it?"

I declined with thanks—to his surprise. He stepped on to the platform with alacrity and seated himself.

"Lock it," he said, handing me the key.

I slipped it into the aperture and turned it.

Immediately the former process was reversed. The seat levelled, a series of plates jointed like armour closed down over his extended arms, a collar of iron gripped his throat, a steel thorax shut its two halves across his chest. He smiled me a pale smile from out of a vizor of iron.

"Isn't it marvellous?" he commented.

"Devilish," I replied.

"I cannot move hand nor foot. You might cut my throat and I couldn't lift a finger."

Suddenly his expression changed. His eyeballs started. His skin took on a greenish pallor. Though he could not stir, his hands purpled under the tension of his muscles. He was the man I had seen from the train.

"For Heaven's sake let me out!" he gasped. "For Heaven's sake!"

I turned the lock. The chair flung wide its iron chest and arms. With a bound he leapt out, vaulting to the other end of the room. If ever joy painted itself on a poor wretch's face, it painted itself on his. He shook me by the hand.

"Thank God!" he gasped. "It took me too soon. I must be losing my nerve."

"To tell the truth," I said bluntly. "You are a fool to play with your nerve in such a fashion."

In the garden he explained.

"The chair belonged to a friend of mine. Indeed, it was his invention. He spent years perfecting it. He was an American dentist, not very well off—an ingenious chap. He invented it so that he should not need an assistant in operating. The patient was absolutely controlled, and the operator unhindered. It was in America it all happened. He found it a great assistance to him, and was doing well. Indeed, he was doing too well. He was doing the work of three men.

"Having been awake one night with toothache I took my way to him next morning. He had just moved into a new house. He was on the point of marrying a girl he had been fond of for years, and was looking forward to happiness.

"As I went up the steps that morning I was surprised to meet him coming down. He had a travelling-bag in his hand.

"'Hallo!' he said.

"'Hallo!' I answered.

"'I'm just off to Newport for a week. The heat has been so terrific I'm dead beat. Doctor says another few days without a rest might do for me.'

"A man with a toothache is no Christian. 'For goodness' sake,' I begged him, 'turn back and relieve me of this aching fiend.'

"He was a good-hearted chap. 'Why, certainly,' he agreed, 'I can do it and yet catch my train. I'm well on time.'

"He unlocked the door, and we went back.

"'It's homicidal weather,' he said, 'and as I was going, I've given the servants a week off. There's not a soul in the place.'

"'Chair answering?' I asked, as I took my seat in it.

"He flushed proudly. 'I've taken out a patent. I showed it at the Dental Society's meeting last night. Congratulate me on a fortune.'

"He turned the key. For the first time I was locked in. It isn't altogether a pleasant sensation.—What do you want, Smithson? No, I did not call, but you can bring some wine."

He waited for the wine with strained, absent eyes. Then he went on with his story.

"Well, I was locked in. I lay back as if I had been in a vice, my mouth gagged open. I could not move a muscle. Would you not like to test it?"

I shook my head.

"You will never altogether realise what I felt.

"I heard him cross the room behind me. I heard him coming back. You know the sensation? I was aware he was hiding a demon of a forceps in the palm of his hand. I braced myself for the wrench. I wondered vindictively why teeth had not been otherwise planned.

"Just as I thought he was on me I heard a stumble, a thud, a groan. I thought he had tripped.

"'Hurt yourself, old boy?' I questioned.

"There was no answer. Only a deep, catchy breathing. He must have hurt himself a good deal, I thought.

"The breathing grew quieter. I repeated the question. Instinctively I tried to turn—an impossibility, of course.

"'I hope you are not badly hurt,' I said 'I can't go to you.'

"Still there was no answer. He must have seriously hurt himself. I mentally confounded the chair which held my head immovable. Then I spoke to him again. With no result. There was nothing to believe but that he had fainted. The breathing was now so quiet as to be almost inaudible. The necessity of freeing myself, so that I might go to his assistance, wrestled so urgently with my inability to do so that I was on the verge of strangulation. With an effort I controlled myself. There was nothing to be done. Of the two, though he were insensible, I was by far the more powerless, for I was dependent on his aid before I could lift a finger. There was nothing for me to do but to wait. I waited. With how little patience you may guess. A clock in the room struck ten. It had 'ting'-ed the half hour after nine as I entered. I fairly groaned with vexation. Poor Newby would lose his train. Why the deuce had I not let him take himself off? My tooth could have waited, or could have found another extractor. I grew serious as to how far he might have injured himself. Possibly even when he should recover consciousness he might not be in a condition to release me. He might in falling have broken, or at least have dislocated, a bone. A hundred harassing probabilities occurred to me. I fumed and fretted, straining my eyeballs vainly to this and that side trying to catch a glimpse of him. I could still hear him faintly breathing. The stretched muscles of my gagged jaw began to throb and ache. I tried to call, but the gag choked my voice. Moreover, I remembered that the house was empty. He had sent his servants away for a week. There was nothing for it but to wait. I waited. The clock on the table struck eleven. Half-a-dozen clocks outside reiterated the fact. It was eleven O'clock—eleven o'clock on a summer's morning. The world on the other side of the window was astir and busy. I could hear men's footsteps beat the pavement. They seemed to be leaving us behind. The rattle of cabs and clack of horses' hoofs mocked the empty quiet of the room. I stretched my ears for sounds of my poor friend's returning consciousness. I even dreaded that return lest it should prove him incapacitated. In that case what in the wide world were we to do? I put the thought away. Heaven knew I needed my wits to keep me from bruising myself in my iron bonds. I found myself cursing the evil genius of Newby's ingenuity with more intensity than reason.

"The clocks struck twelve. By this time the breath-sounds were scarcely audible. Heavens! Was he dying? Was he dying for the need of help? Dying with a strong, whole man, and that man his good friend, within a yard of him? For a whole half-hour I shouted at the top of my voice—shouted, indeed, till my voice was a mere rough thread in my rasped throat. The sounds of life outside went on with a brisk indifference which seemed brutality. Was there no power, no telepathy, of human sympathy, to communicate to those outside that within the room whose window stared at them a man lay, it might be, dying, while another, gagged and bound, strove with unspeakable torment to go to his aid. The hours wore on. The horrible dread of listening for them, and learning from their iron tongues that another sixty minutes had closed down like an inexorable door between the man I had been in the morning—the free man, with no worse trouble than an aching tooth—and the bound, helpless wretch I then was, became intolerable. Sound, thought, feeling, merged in confusion. My brain throbbed in my ears, my blood beat in my veins; I could hear it like waves on shingle. Out of the confusion I distinguished nothing. The steps outside, the faint breathing, the striking clocks—all were lost in a curious hustling dread. I must have fainted. I awoke to a sense of surprise. But the torture of my constrained position left me but shortly in doubt. My lips and cheeks seemed cracking under the stretch of the gag. Like some swollen horror my dry tongue filled my mouth. Behind me all was—silence—"

He stopped and looked me wildly in the face.

"Do you think I shall forget it if I live to be eighty?—the horror of that moment when I listened for his breathing, for his movement, and heard—nothing!"

He sat panting like one spent with running. I poured out and passed him a glass of wine.

"The sun was levelling, it shot in presently beneath the blind and stabbed my starting eyes. Its hot glare turned me sick. It seemed to be searching the room with a lurid inquisitiveness. Presently I thought it halted, resting stationary with a dull astonishment on something I could not see, something behind me that I could not see, but felt with a horrible intensity. Again I shouted as well as my stiff jaws and swollen tongue would let me. I sent cry after cry into space. My voice was strange and hoarse. It put me in a panic to hear another man's voice shouting out of my throat. But nobody heard. There was nobody to hear. Each man tramped over the pavement, bent on his own pursuits. Just while the sun illumined us, had anybody turned his head, he might have seen me through the wire blind—a man in torment.

"But nobody turned his head. Night came, and with it a measure of coolness. The dusk was grateful to my nerves and eyes, and I had a hope that when the passers-by had taken their clattering footsteps home, I might, by Heaven's kindness, make myself heard. But by the time the silence came I had no voice to make heard. It was as much as I could do to draw my breath between my swollen lips. The night silence brought out that other silence into which I listened for his breathing. If I could only have caught a glimpse of him! If I could only have seen the reality, rather than the horrible phantasies my mind began to conjure! I pictured him bruised and contorted; I pictured him weltering in blood; I pictured him lying, kneeling, sitting. I pictured him conscious and cunning, standing

above me with a whetted knife. It came to me that he was not really dead, but had gone suddenly mad. I could feel him crouching
close behind me waiting for the moment. I could hear him steal
about the room. I strained my eyes to see his head come suddenly
over my shoulder, his eyes glare into mine. I could feel his hot
breath on my cheek. It was a trap. It was the devilry of one with
homicidal mania. This was the motive of his horrible chair. This
was the object of his years of planning. How many men before me
had been victims? The room seemed peopled with them. They
stared from every corner. They laughed with ghastly laughter at
another dupe. I wondered if he would kill me outright, or leave me
to die in the chair. I called to him to cut my throat and end it. I
thought he chuckled!

"Again I was sure he was dead. And I was afraid of him—afraid
of the grisly thing that lay so still behind me. I had rather he lived
and stood by me with whetted knife. He was more fearsome dead
and girt with the horrors of violent death than he was fearsome as
an assassin, breathing, intelligible, and murderous.

"He seemed to me to lie there lifting clammy, hands with the
continuous impotent movement of corpse hands stirred by a tide.
I could hear them beat the carpet, rising and falling with a rhyth-
mic thud. Then I went back to the beginning. He was not dead, but
something had fallen on his face—something that his faintness
prevented him from removing yet left him conscious enough to
know that he was suffocating. I pictured the long, full breath he
would draw if I but turned and freed him. I drew that breath for
him, instinctively. I suffocated. I struggled in my bonds to turn
and free him I rasped my wrists and limbs till they were raw, trying to turn and free him. Then it was nose-bleeding—he had suffered sometimes from nose-bleeding. He was dying of that, dying
for need of the simplest aid. The room swam red. It streamed before me in crimson jets. Could any man's body hold so much blood?
It rose and rose and lapped my face. Again I heard him lift his body
dully in the dark. He came dragging himself round to look me in
the face, his chill hands swept my forehead, importuning me. My
hair lifted on my scalp. Why had I come between him and life?

Why had I robbed him of happiness? His spirit moaned about the room. I prayed for his knife at my throat. Only let it end! let it end! A thousand times he crossed the room as I had heard him cross it, to return with feet which at first were light, then dragged, then halted and passed into that sickening thud. He seemed to try so hard to reach me, returning again and again and starting afresh for my chair. A thousand times I held my breath, hoping, praying that he might reach me, when he tripped and fell—fell with that sickening thud.

"His children came, the children who might have been his, and looked at me with phantom eyes. I could not turn my face from them. Anything that liked to come might come and stare at me; I could not turn my face."

I interrupted him. The man was possessed. The veil between him and madness was stretched to cracking point.

"How did it end?" I demanded.

He started and stared.

"How did it end? I insisted.

"Let me tell it," he said peevishly. After some moments of childish petulance during which he weakly whimpered, "It went on three whole days and nights," he said, moistening his lips. "In lucid moments I knew he was dead. The odour of death and dissolution in that hot terrible room became intolerable. I was without food or drink. I could not sleep. I could not call. I could but think and feel—such thoughts, such feelings I only knew of that which lay and decomposed behind my chair. I am only thirty. But do you wonder my hair is grey? I had intervals of unconsciousness, thank Heaven—prostration and delirium. Hunger and faintness do that for a man.

"In the small hours of the fourth morning, while it was still dark, a noise at the window roused me. I wonder I was still alive; but men take a good deal of killing. At first I thought it fancy. I had had so many fancies. But I heard a sound as of bitten glass, then the hasp of the window flew back, the sash was raised. Between my swollen lids there came a glare of light. Black things flitted on the ceiling. I heard whispering. I thought they had come to kill me. The scalding water of my tears ran down my face as I thanked God they had come to kill me. It seemed hours they were stealing about the room, with hoarse whispers. I could only see their shadows on the ceiling. How many there were I could not say, but a hundred heads at least passed blackly over the ceiling.

"Then my tears ran cold. They were only shadows. It was only another phantasy. My imagination was at play again. I hurled wild imprecations at the shadow-heads. 'You are not, you are not!' I cried to them out of my voiceless throat. 'You do not deceive me. I know you are not.' Then a horrible face—a face half black, half white, leaned over me. A hoarse cry broke in my ears. Two horrible piebald faces leaned over me. A second cry came, a third, and they stood panting there. One touched the thing beside me with his foot.

"'Both dead,' he muttered, as one baulked of prey. I mustered all my strength and moaned. They made for the door. My desperation nerved me.

"'For God's sake, cut my throat!' I gasped. I heard them turn back. Then I knew nothing more till I found myself in hospital. I had been rescued by burglars, and three weeks mad.

"When I was well I knew the truth. Newby had died that morning of an apoplectic seizure. Nothing could have saved him, the doctors said."

"Why did you not have the chair destroyed?"

He turned on me angrily.

"It is my only comfort. I recompense myself for past misery by multiplying the joys of release. I have a man, a faithful fellow—the only person beside yourself who knows my story. I get him to lock me in, leave me, and then when I have worked myself to the limits of terror, believing myself deserted, he lets me out. The joy of release is the only joy left me. I need and allow myself no other indulgence."

I had been making up my mind.

"Are you a good sailor?"

He was. By superhuman eloquence I persuaded him to a voyage in my yacht. I was sailing next morning. I am no philanthropist, but a man's sanity is worth saving. An hour after I had left the house I went back to it. There was a look on Smithson's face when told to pack which had remained with me. I went by the side-door into the garden. As the annex came in view Smithson appeared at the window. He was smiling unpleasantly. The room was lighted. Massey was in the chair. (Was the fool worth saving?) Smithson turned presently into the room. I made my way to the window, and stood in the shadow of a shrub.

"I'll have the gag," I heard my king of idiots say. "I want to get up a real good sensation. It's the last I'll have for a time."

I heard the click of metal.

"Now go," Massey mumbled, "and keep me a long time to-night."

But Smithson went not. On the contrary, he turned and flicked his victim in the face.

"Not before we've arranged a bit of business," he said jauntily. "Now then, young man, I've put up with you a good many months, and you're a-going to send me adrift, are you?"

Inarticulate dissent from Massey.

"Oh! yes you are. Syfret's got hold of you. You've passed out of my hands. There'll be no more chair and gags for you, I can see plainly. But I am going to be paid for all my trouble. Fifty pound a year hasn't paid me, I can tell you. I shall loose your right hand for you to sign this. If you don't—well, you've been locked in before, and you know how you like it. There'll be no one in the house. Bess and me was married this morning, and we're off to America by the night boat. If you was to refuse to sign, I should lock all the doors and windows and put up the shutters. I've told everybody we're going a voyage. And you need not look for burglars this time. There's nothing in the house to take, Bess and me has seen to that. Now then, are you going to sign?"

Massey managed to query through the gag: "How much?"

"Only five thou'. You could spare ten easy. But I'll do with five."

Massey groaned. But of course he relented. What else could he have done?

I went in behind Smithson while he was busy with the lock. I set my knee against his back and threw him. He fell heavily, striking

his head. He was safe for some minutes. In those minutes I released Massey. Together we lifted the rascal into the chair and
turned the key. It was a capital contrivance for extracting truth.
We discovered the whereabouts of the plate and other things Mr.
and Mrs. Smithson had appropriated. With some of them she was
waiting in the kitchen. Then I let him out and bundled him into
the road.

When I went back, I discovered Massey with a pitchfork falling
manfully foul of the chair. He raised his weapon high. He brought
it down with violent invective. He banged and battered till the
clamps and flanges were a mangled mass; he ripped its velvet
cushionings, he broke its arms and legs. With a fell and final swoop
he hurled himself upon it, and smote the gag with such a blow that
it bounded across the room, and breaking a pane of glass, whirled
into the garden.

Anybody seeing him would have taken him for nothing less than
a homicidal maniac. Yet this murderous attack was about the first
symptom of sanity I had remarked in him.

PRINCE RANJICHATTERJEE'S VENGEANCE

I

Lord and Lady Wycombe had been dining with me. They were new friends, or, to speak quite accurately, new acquaintance, for I never regard as my friend a man I have not known ten years. I have calculated to a nicety that period as being needed for sufficient oxidation of the social polish to enable one to judge of what metal a man is made.

Lord Wycombe had no social polish whatsoever. In dealing with him you at no time saw yourself brilliantly or flatteringly reflected. He was not even nickel-plated, he was pewter right through—from the mugginess of his outer person to the inner recesses of that purely physiological contrivance which served him for heart. Indeed, I used to wonder by what manner of means its valves worked. Without doubt, they worked stiffly and occasionally "clicked."

The Wycombes were in my neighbourhood for the first time since their marriage, and for the first time since that Ceremony were dining with me. I had ceased long before this to speculate as to why women marry particular men, or why men marry particular women. When the Powers had fashioned our world, they detected in it the possibilities of an Eden. This being not at all their intention, they inspired man with the fatal expedient of marriage, whereby he should make the one act of his life into which he would inevitably crowd the greatest measure of folly—irrevocable, and Eden has since translated itself to some remote and inaccessible region of space. The Wycombes were a signal example of the human discord tethered fast and for all time with lawyer's tape.

After she had left us that evening we remained long over our wine. Or, rather, he did: for I, with marked intention, sat with an empty glass before me.

Suddenly he broke out brutally: "You wouldn't suspect that woman of being a common thief!" His face was flushed, his hand unsteady. Before we began dinner he had already taken his quantum of wine.

We had been speaking of his wife. I could not pretend ignorance of that he meant.

"Nobody would suspect Lady Wycombe of any more serious crime than that of breaking hearts," I answered tritely.

"Ah These lovely creatures have a dashed sight more original sin in 'em than most people give 'em credit for. But I'm no fool. Never was. Before I was twenty I could give you most women's price—and calculated fine at that, even to the farthings."

"I believe I could have done the same—though I will not answer for the farthings—at the same age," I said. "Ten years later I was not quite so sure of my arithmetic. Now I have given up the practice altogether. To find the unknown quantity one requires certain data, and the difficulty of finding the difference between these in different women makes the calculation altogether too fatiguing, especially as it is pretty sure to come out wrong in the end."

"Ah, you price 'em too high, I expect," he said knowingly. "Now I never suffered from that." He poured himself another glass of port. "Good wine," he commented.

"And so you wouldn't suspect her charming ladyship of being a common thief. Now you're fond of stories, I hear—"

I pushed my plate of nutshells noisily before me. The pallid misery of a beautiful face was beside me again as it had been during dinner. I thought of her sitting upstairs alone but for some grief that was sapping her life, while we men laid bare her sorrows over a bottle of port.

I rose. "Lady Wycombe is by herself," I said. "We must not leave her longer."

He stared. Then he filled his glass again. "By Your leave," he laughed, "we'll finish this excellent bottle."

I had no alternative but to sit down again.

"I don't tell everyone," he began, "though she thinks I do." (I remembered the haunting appeal her eyes had sent him over my shoulder as I held the door for her.) "You've got to keep the whip-hand of a woman—when she don't care about you. If it wasn't for that little slip of hers she'd be always on a pedestal and out of reach. And she'd never have been Lady Wycombe," he added, with an ugly look.

"Pooh!" I protested again; "if it is so long ago as that, let it rest. Don't rake up an old story. You would be sorry for it to-morrow."

He struck his fist on the table. It rattled with a pewter ring.

"Damn her!" he cried. "I'll take the airs out of her. She don't talk to me and look at me like she did with you to-night."

The brute was jealous. Heavens! And we had but been discussing some sanitary alterations she was planning for her cottagers, with a little hopeful eagerness.

"She was a Wells," he persisted, "a family of handsome girls with a gambling father. I was easy with him. He got more and more in my debt. I wanted her: she was the best-looking of 'em. But there was another man—some poor beggar of a diplomat—and she wouldn't look at me. I talked straight to Wells. I said, 'Look here, you know she's got to have me or—' Well, he was mortgaged up to the hilt, and I was mortgagee. 'Well,' I said, 'you must talk it over with her.' I was fond of her—I'm fond of her now," he interjected with bloodshot eyes. After a pause, during which he rolled my wine appreciatively on his tongue, he continued: "I knew how women sell their souls for diamonds. I sent her a magnificent necklace—a thing I'd picked up somewhere in the East"—he was silent for some minutes— "never seen such a thing," he resumed abruptly, "a rope of diamonds as big as beans, splendidly cut, and each set in the centre of four gold petals. It must have been worth at least ten thousand pounds. 'Put it round her neck,' I said, 'and take her to the glass, and tell her while she's admiring herself.' Well, I never saw the necklace after. Wells turned up next day with a long face, and the case; said he was deucedly sorry, but Miss Aline declined me at any price. Supposed things must take their course. I locked the case in my strong-room like a fool, without looking into it. I instructed my lawyers. Just then, as luck would have it, somebody left the Wells a fortune, and I was paid in full. Wells sent a cheque and mentioned incidentally that Aline was shortly to marry her beggar. Now I might never have opened the necklace-case from that day to this, because I was not at all set on marrying, and Aline had given me a dose, but three days before that fixed for her wedding, something made me go to the safe and open the case."

"Well?" I questioned eagerly.

He tossed down the last glass of port. He turned his hot eyes on me. "So you're interested?" he said.

I made an effort. I rose. "I think we have finished our wine. Let us go upstairs."

He put a purple hand on mine. "By Heaven," he cried, "you shall hear me out. When I opened the case—" he burst into a rough laugh. "What a fool I might have been: in two days she would have married the other man. When I opened the case—"

"There was nothing there?" I broke in, and could immediately have bitten out my tongue.

"Oh, she was not so fresh," he said. "There was a string of metal beads with a brass enamelled clasp—worth, I should say, some couple of shillings—but heavy enough and capable of rattling so that the fraud might have been long undetected."

"Of course, it occurred to you her father took them?"

"I cleared that up. He wasn't that kind of man. He was dumbfounded. There was no mistake about it. He was like a madman. Offered to sell all he had to keep it quiet. Aline had taken charge of them that night."

"Where did she put them?"

"Locked the case up, so she said, with her other things. Took it out next morning, and handed it to her father. She had guilt all over her when I confronted her. She didn't marry the beggar."

"Why did you marry her after such—"

"Oh, I had never supposed her an angel," he said coarsely, "and I wanted her."

II

I was calling on Lady Wycombe. I had been able to give her some hints as to the new plans. When that look of fixed misery slipped out of her face she was a lovely woman. As I was leaving, her manner changed. She hesitated. The hand in mine trembled. She raised a pair of appealing eyes.

"Lord Syfret," she said, "Henry has told me your kind—most chivalrous intention. I cannot thank you enough, but, believe me, the very greatest kindness you can do me is to let the matter rest. It is five years, and, Heaven knows, I have suffered enough."

"Lord Wycombe should not have mentioned it. I asked him particularly not to do so. Only if I discover the real culprit—"

She shrank before me. A hot flush rose in he: cheeks.

"You believe me innocent?

"The question needs no answer."

She dropped into a chair and covered her face with her hands. "For Heaven's sake, if you know what pity is, let the matter rest. Even should you clear me—" She broke off, abruptly. Her manner made it evident that she knew something.

"Even should you clear me—" I finished the sentence: "—you would inculpate someone dearer." I do not approve of scapegoats, howsoever willing. Let each man take the blame due to him. "Lady Wycombe," I objected, "you know my hobby. You must please permit me to ride it on this occasion. I give you my word that should I discover anything—a remote possibility—I will not move a step nor say a word without first consulting you."

"Thank you," she faltered, "but your greatest kindness would be to discover nothing."

"Have you the metal beads?"

She lifted her head out of her hands.

"I have never seen them," she said simply.

Then perceiving the significance of her admission, "Please, please," she entreated, "let the matter rest; I can bear the blame."

On the stairs I met Wycombe. He scowled under his shaggy brows. He was jealous of any man who lifted hat to her.

"By-the-by," I said coolly, "do you happen to have those metal beads you spoke of?"

"What the deuce should I keep such rubbish for?" he blurted bluntly. "I flung them out of the window."

"You acted like a fool," I said as bluntly; "they were the chief clue to the thief."

Two days later I opened my *Times* with interest. I turned to the advertisement sheet. "I hope it has a prominent place," I reflected.

It had, and read as follows: "*A Thousand Pounds Reward.—* Anybody giving information which shall lead to the recovery of a certain diamond necklace of unique pattern, consisting of thirty-four large diamonds—each set in the centre of four beautifully-wrought gold petals, shall receive the above reward. Apply, &c."

And below this, another: "*Ten Pounds Reward.—*Any person who picked up, or has knowledge that will lead to the recovery of a string of metal beads lost outside a house in Eaton Square on or about the 10th of April 1883, shall receive, on proving it to be the same, the above sum. Apply, &c."

"Now for bogus applicants," I mused, when I had found the advertisement duly published in the half-dozen papers to which I had ordered it to be sent. Then, "Good heavens!" I ejaculated. For immediately below my second advertisement I found the following: "*Four Thousands Pound Rewards* shall be given to any mans informing news to discover a diamond necklace composing of thirty-eight beautifully-cut diamond dews dropped in richly embossed golden tulip-flowers with four leaved. To be communicated with Somers, Grand Hotel, between ten and four."

Below this still another: "*Four Thousands Pound Rewards* shall be given to any mans informing news to discover a string of thirty-eight large beads in bluish-greys metal with octagonal clasp of gold enamel. To be communicated with Somers, Grand Hotel, between ten and four."

These advertisements I found in four of the papers wherein mine appeared. I further learned that both had appeared every morning for the preceding week.

"So," I remonstrated with Wycombe on meeting him later at the club, "you have taken that matter of the diamonds out of my hands?"

He stared. "I am a little curious to know why you did not put your advertisement into intelligible English. Or were you the victim of an unlettered printer?"

"Perhaps you will explain what you are talking about," he said.

I took him to the reading-room. I showed him the advertisements.

"Good Lord!" he broke out; "why, it is my necklace. The description is exact."

He assured me he had nothing to do with the advertisements. He had come to his conclusions long before. I thought he looked perturbed. He begged me to let the matter drop. But the chase had grown exciting. I took my hat. I jumped into a hansom, and was soon at the Grand Hotel. It was within seven minutes of four as I drove up.

"Is Mr. Somers in?" I inquired of the porter.

"Is it the advertisement, sir?"

"Yes."

"Ah, that's Prince Ranjichatterjee."

A little man with long white beard and Hebrew features slipped something out of his eager dirty fingers into those of the porter.

"Remember I wash firsht," he whispered. The coin was small. I cast a calculating eye over the shabby Jew. Sixpence I decided. I put a half-crown into the porter's other hand.

The Prince was in, I believed, giving him my card.

"This gentleman was first, my lord," the man responded firmly and passed the dirty Hebrew on to a page-boy.

"I am afraid your lordship is too late for His Highness," he added civilly. "He sees nobody after four; and to-day's the last day. There's been about three hundred people to see him already."

He tested between his teeth the coin the Jew had given him. It was a half-sovereign. I anathematised myself for a fool; Jews are not stingy when four thousand pounds are in the running.

At that moment the Jew came hurrying back. His face was crestfallen. The boy behind him grinned wide-mouthed. The Jew darted at the porter.

"Gif me back my 'alf-soferings. The Prince not see me," he shrieked.

The porter gazed benignly and unconsciously upon him from a height of six feet two.

"No, sir," he said indulgently. "No ole cloes to-day."

The clock marked three minutes to the hour. "Take me to the Prince," I insisted.

There was some demur at the door. Then my card was sent in, and after a minute I was admitted to a room which had been Orientalised so far as were possible to a room in a London hotel. Divans and couches draped with magnificent rugs and luxuriously cushioned, took the place of chairs. Hanging lanterns, curiously wrought, and with panels of rich glass, shed a dim light. There was a heavy aromatic odour on the air.

In the middle of the room, with a table before him, sat a lithe, eager-looking man—a Hindoo. His eyes flashed toward me like two lamps. He returned my bow without rising, and waited for me to speak.

Behind his chair four men stood like sombre shadows. "I have the pleasure to address his Highness Prince Ranjichatterjee?" I began. He bowed again.

"You advertised I believe—"

The Prince extended a finger with a curious gliding stealth. Not a muscle of his face moved. I heard the distant "ting" of a bell. Immediately four other shadows seemed to start up from the floor, noiselessly and like inanimate things. Two of them took up their stations at opposite doors of the room, at the same time folding the heavy wadded *portières* well over these. I felt two steal up close behind me. Instinctively I had ceased speaking.

"I advertised—" the Prince suggested with a sinuous bend of his dark head.

"You advertised with regard to a diamond necklace. I also am seeking a diamond necklace—"

"You have lost a diamond necklace?" the Prince insinuated. I nodded. It was sufficient for his purpose.

His eyes emitted light. "The necklace I have seeking," he said softly, "is uniquitous. It do be consisting of thirty-eight diamonds."

"Ah!" I said, "the one I mean had only thirty-four."

He seemed taken aback.

Then a wily look stole into his face.

"It is not difficult to subtract four diamonds from thirty-eight."

"So then," I said, "you lost it first?"

He fixed his eyes expressionlessly on me. I felt the steamy breath of the men behind me unpleasantly hot on my neck.

Then the Prince observed suavely:

"In a world where the lady is half people, there is many necklaces."

"That is true, of course," I admitted, "but your necklace was composed of diamonds set in the centre of golden tulips, golden tulips with four leaves?"

"Tulips has five," he said simply. "It be a mistake. The jeweller was his head chop off." There was quite a sweet smile on his face as at the recollection of something delectable.

"Good gracious! is that how you do things?"

"We do things so there is no more talk," he purred.

"Well, sir," I went on, "I should think there is not much doubt about it that your necklace and my necklace are one and the same. The four-leaved tulip settles it. There would not be two necklaces of so curious a pattern."

His face paled. His eyes seemed to go out.

"No," he said, almost inaudibly, "it was my idea. She was the lovely dew-drop, the petals of my heart to enfold her."

"How did you lose it?" I questioned.

His eyes lit up again. His face got colour, he made a little motion with his hand.

"That you will tell me," he said blandly.

Before I knew where I was I found myself gagged, upon my knees, with four men standing over me, and round my throat by some mysterious means, a bowstring drawn sufficiently tight to be somewhat more than an unpleasant hint.

III

It sounds like a bit from the "Arabian Nights." At the moment, even above the consciousness that my life was not worth a minute's purchase—for there was no mistaking the grim sincerity of the Prince's face, nor the strictly business intention of the men about me—even at that moment I was conscious of a sense of the ludicrous. But there is an ugly feel about a bowstring, and the irrelevancy between it and my Bond Street collar soon ceased to amuse.

The Prince rose and came toward me noiselessly across the richly-carpeted floor. He spat before me. He struck me with a womanish feeble spitefulness on either cheek. Then he rubbed his long dark hands exultantly

"So I be found you at last!" he said, with an evil chuckle. "I be found you at last, you robber of women."

His mood changed. He flung himself prone on the floor. He moaned, and writhed, and beat his clenched fists against the carpet. He struck his brows.

"She is gone," he cried passionately, "my dew-drop, my pearl, my Moon of the Heavens. She is gone, and only it be with me to vengeance."

He continued in the same strain for some minutes, but the remainder of his lament was Hindi and unintelligible. He sobbed and gasped as though he had been a fractious child.

A woman stole in through a lifted curtain—a woman like a tawny tiger-lily, with wide full eyes deep-fringed and liquid, and a mouth like a scarlet flower. She glanced contemptuously at his groveling figure, then moved toward it with the undulance of flowing water. She laid an ivory hand on either of his shoulders, and spoke to him in a foreign tongue. He rose with an abashed look; then, his eyes lighting on me, he made as if to renew his childish assault. But she withheld him, motioning him with a flash from her tropical eyes to his seat at the table. She took up her place beside him, and for the first time, so far as I had seen, though I was aware she was conscious all the while of my presence, her dark glance fell on me. It was a long, penetrating glance, and seemed to search my very soul. Then she stooped and whispered the Prince. He made a motion of his hand. The gag was removed from my mouth at the same time that one of the fellows beside me gave a warning tug to the string about my throat.

After a moment the Prince demanded in a voice of concentrated fury:

"Was it from her you got the necklace?"

I shook my head.

"The necklace has never been in my possession," I said. "You are making a mistake."

"Yet you have confessed you lost it," he insisted furiously.

"I have never seen it. I am seeking it for a friend who lost it five years since."

He scrutinised me fiercely.

"Have you been once in Calcutta?"

"Never."

"Do you swear?"

"I swear."

The woman touched him questioningly on the shoulder. He evidently interpreted my words to her, for she scanned me narrowly. Then she stretched her hand toward the table. A bell rang. Immediately a swarthy negro entered. She directed his attention to me. He shook his head violently, mumbling something. He came toward me and carefully examined my face. Then he spread his hands with an emphatic repudiation, shook his head, and mumbled again. A question being put to him, again he shook his head The Prince dismissed him. Then turning on me he demanded with sullen balked anger, "Who is your friend?"

"That," I said, feeling my tongue somewhat dry in my mouth, "I am not at liberty to tell."

A minute later I did, however. And let any man feel his brain full and throbbing fit to burst with black blood, and his eyeballs force themselves between his lids like peas out of a pod, and I imagine he would have done the same. After all, I was not bound to take on myself Wycombe's responsibilities, supposing him to have incurred any in the affair, a suspicion I had no reason for entertaining. Certainly I did not suspect him of stealing diamonds; and in any case he need not be fool enough to put his head into such a noose as I had done. They slackened the string and dashed water on my face. After a time I got breath and told what I knew of the matter. I was compelled to point out Wycombe's name in a *Peerage* which they laid before me. The Prince put an ominous angry-looking cross in red ink against it.

"And the lady?" he said.

He made a gesture of inquiry toward the face of the woman beside him.

"No," I said; "she is an Englishwoman. She has never been to India. My friend had the necklace before he knew her—"

"Among the women of his house is there a lady of my race?"

I could hardly remain serious. The notion of Lady Wycombe harbouring such a rival beneath her roof was so preposterous.

"My friend bought the necklace," I insisted. "A man of his wealth and position does not steal diamonds."

"Nor women?" he questioned, with an evil look.

I shrugged my shoulders. "Lord Wycombe assures me he bought the jewels in Calcutta. I have no doubt he will give you the name of the man from whom he bought them."

He motioned one of the men behind him. "Bring Lord Weekam here," he said imperiously. The man moved to the door.

"Prince Ranjichatterjee," I said, "you are, maybe, a powerful prince in your own country, and one accustomed to be obeyed. But in England men do not go hither and thither at another man's word. I warn you Lord Wycombe will not come."

He started up with clenched hands. "I shall make him!" he cried shrilly.

The woman cast some contemptuous epithet at him. With a spasm of uncontrollable rage he motioned one of the guards toward her. The man took two steps forward. She laid her scarlet lips back over her gleaming teeth, and pointed him with a scornful finger to his place again. Then she spoke low in the Prince's ear.

"Will you send a letter to your friend, asking he comes?" he demanded petulantly.

"No," I replied, "I do not like your way of treating your guests."

Livid with rage, he interpreted my answer to her. I thought she glanced toward me with the suspicion of a smile. She addressed me, but her words were unintelligible. I bowed and shook my head.

"What will you do?" the Prince interpreted.

"I will do what I can to bring my friend here tomorrow," I replied.

"Do you swear by your God?"

"If you insist on it," I said. "I cannot be sure he will come, but I will do my best."

"And the lady?" he questioned, with flaring eyes.

"No," I said, "not the lady; she has nothing to do with it."

He lost his temper again. He could not tolerate the slightest check. Again the woman soothed him. I was sworn by half-a-dozen oaths to secrecy as to that which had occurred. I was put upon my honour. Then the bowstring was slipped up over my chin, with permission to retire.

As I took my way down the hotel steps, where the Jew stood expostulating still with the blandly dissenting porter, I congratulated myself on an adventure the recollection whereof would preserve me from boredom for many a long day, though all round my neck was a girdle of raw skin which my collar unpleasantly rasped.

IV

"Ranjichatterjee!—the devil!" Wycombe ejaculated, with a curious change of expression.

"A near relative, assuredly," I acquiesced.

Why did his lips blench? He lost his accustomed bluster. There was a strange, sudden stiffness about him, as of a man meeting his fate.

He saw my eyes on him. "I hate these Hindoo fellows," he blurted, drawing in his breath.

"You need only give him the name of the jeweller," I said.

"Oh! the name of the jeweller," he echoed stupidly. His mind was elsewhere.

He broke out suddenly: "Why the devil did you ever go into the thing at all? See what you've done, with your confounded meddling."

"Plainly," I said, "the necklace had a history before it came into Lady Wycombe's hands."

"I did as much for her as anybody would have done," he cried. "I didn't want her wretched necklace. I told her to take it with her."

"The jeweller's name is by no means all the information you will be able to give his Highness," I said, drily.

"His Highness will whistle a cursed time," he retorted with that same stillness about him, "before he makes my acquaintance."

"Who was she?" I inquired.

"Oh, you can have the whole story. She was one of his—wives. The harem garden overlooked mine. She was a soft little creature, with eyes like moons and a little red mouth no good for anything but kissing—the kind a man gets tired of in a week. Of course, I got tired of her—dead, dead sick of her. But what could I do? She crept in one night with her hands running blood. He'd found out something, and, in a rage had her wretched little thumbs cut off. Of course, I had to take her in. There was a tremendous hue-and-cry, he is a great man out there, and she was his favourite wife. I kept her hidden as long as I was in Calcutta, and brought her as far as Bombay when I left. I couldn't bring her to England—"

"What did you do with her?"

"I didn't do anything. I gave her money."

"She couldn't work without thumbs, poor creature."

"Oh, she couldn't work," he said. "Women like that don't work. I gave her money. She was pretty."

"And the necklace?"

For a time he would not speak. Then he said suddenly: "Oh, have the whole story if you like. She was a little fool. The night before I left she found she wasn't coming. She crept in and kissed my feet and hands and cried, and bent her head before me—the women there have different ways from our women, goodness knows—and next day I found she'd left her confounded necklace round my throat. I tried to trace her."

"Did she take the money?"

He got up blustering: "What the deuce does it matter. She would have if she'd had a grain of sense."

"Well," I said, "I don't think I should have mixed up a necklace with a history like that, in a love affair of any importance."

Later he came to me with it sick face. "I'm off to Paris to-night. There's a beast of an Indian been following me about all day. These fellows stick at nothing. My life was attempted in Madras. Why the deuce did you rake up the affair?"

"Why the deuce," I answered, "did you not tell me the truth in the beginning? Then I should have known there was excellent reason for letting it rest."

I called next morning at the Grand.

"No, thank you," I responded to the porter's invitation to walk upstairs; "I will see his Highness in the public drawing-room."

I adjusted my shirt collar. That galled furrow round my throat rode on the edge of it as martyrs are said to have ridden on plough-shares. I chose a recess wherein we might talk unobserved. The Prince came in presently, glancing about him with a haughty intolerance as though he expected the several occupants of the room to salaam, and abjectly retire.

"So your friend—he sail away," he began maliciously.

"My friend had business which deprived him of the pleasure of meeting you this morning," I returned, with an uncomfortable sense that Wycombe had by no means got out of the wood when he booked for Paris.

"What he do with her?" he demanded feverishly.

I declined to say anything. I had no personal knowledge of the affair.

"I make him tell," he said with evil eyes.

I warned him that should anything happen to Wycombe, suspicion would fall on him.

"Pooh " he said, "you have to prove. I no fool."

"By-the-bye," I urged, "I see you advertise for a string of metal beads, and oddly enough offer as large a reward for these as you do for the diamonds. What do you know about the metal beads?"

He scanned me curiously. Then he said with a significant smile: "Weekam, he shall tell you."

For the first time I felt a suspicion of Wycombe's good faith in the matter. Next morning I received a note from Lady Wycombe:

> DEAR LORD SYFRET,—I shall be glad of your advice. Lord Wycombe is away. For the last few days the house has been watched and I have been followed by some curious-looking foreigners. As I left the carriage two evenings since, one put his face close up to mine, examining me as if for some purpose, and my maid last night found my bedroom door locked. She ran downstairs for help, and on returning she and some of the men found my jewels lying about the room. Nothing had been stolen—I suppose the thieves were frightened and left hurriedly.

I drove at once to Piccadilly. The house was in the hands of the police. Lady Wycombe looked very much alarmed. She held an open letter in her hand. "It is strange," she said, "but they write from the Towers (the Wycombes' country house) that similar dark foreigners have been haunting the place, Peering inquisitively, into the women-servants' faces and asking questions in the village."

"Heavens!" thought I, "I have indeed brought a hornet's nest about my friends."

I reassured her, at the same time keeping my own counsel. I knew well enough no danger threatened her. They were but seeking the Hindoo woman and the necklace. I called again next morning. I was shown into Wycombe's library. "I will tell her ladyship," the footman said. Then he blurted an apology, for her ladyship was already there—her ladyship confronting a tall distinguished-looking man, who stood over her with angry eyes.

"And you dismissed me on so pitiful a lie!" I heard him say as the door opened.

I had met the man some evenings earlier at a reception given by one of the Embassies. He had but lately returned from abroad. In a moment I made up my mind that this was the "beggarly diplomat" Lady Wycombe had been within three days of marrying.

We exchanged bows. "Lord Syfret," he said at once, "I hear from Lady Wycombe that you are moving in the matter of a certain diamond necklace. I shall be infinitely obliged if you will transfer the affair to me. I have good right, indeed, for it appears I am under suspicion of having stolen it."

She made a gesture of protest.

"Oh, how cruel you are!" she cried, under her breath. "I have never said a word."

"It should give you some pleasure," I said formally, "to take the suspicion on yourself. Lady Wycombe has borne it long enough."

"Lady Wycombe," he echoed. "Aline, has anybody dared—"

She burst out in tears.

He bent above her prone head. "That, then," he said tenderly, "is the reason of your miserable face?"

"No, no," she whispered. "I could have borne that if—if I could have kept my faith in you."

"And that was a woman's faith," he said bitterly, "to take the man she was within a few hours of marrying for a common thief—to dismiss him without a chance of clearing himself, and to marry another man within six weeks."

"What could I do?" she faltered. "You were with me that evening. You unclasped the necklace with your own hands and put it in the case. The case was returned to Lord Wycombe next day. Father himself returned it. When Lord Wycombe opened it there was nothing but a string of beads. He threatened proceedings. I knew you were poor. Forgive me—Oh, forgive me—I thought it would be discovered, and I—I married him."

"It was a trick on his part—" he began.

"I think not," I said. "Wycombe was certainly sincere about it. He believes honestly to this day that Lady Wycombe stole the jewels. The mystery goes deeper than that."

I took him aside. I told him all the circumstances.

"Why did Ranjichatterjee advertise for a string of metal beads in connection with the diamonds?" I inquired.

"We will find out from himself," he said.

But the Prince had only a tissue of Oriental lies to tell us.

"The diamonds, they was charmed," he said, turning his wily looks from one to the other of us. "On the throat of the disloyal wife the dew-drops be lose their crystal lustre and become as mere dross till they be charmed again. The *yogi* jeweller I threaten him with death if he make me not such a necklace, so I keep my women's hearts my own. Seven times the charm it worked, and seven times I rid the world of the disloyal wives."

"He is only laughing at us with his *yogi* rubbish," Redvers said indignantly.

"Your friend, Lord Wycombe, be he well?" Ranjichatterjee queried guilelessly, as we departed.

But it appeared our friend, Lord Wycombe, was not well, for Lady Wycombe met us with a telegram.

"Henry is very ill," she said. "I am starting immediately for Paris."

I travelled with her, leaving Ranjichatterjee to Redvers.

But we were too late: Lord Wycombe had been found dead in his room that morning, from what cause was never discovered. There was evidence neither of violence nor of poison. Redvers and I kept our suspicions to ourselves, for Ranjichatterjee disappeared within ten minutes of our leaving him.

V

It will be remembered that in advertising I offered a reward for a certain string of metal beads which could be proven to have been picked up in Eaton Square on or about a certain date—the date whereon Wycombe had furiously flung it from his window. I had continued to doubt his good faith in the matter, when one morning there was ushered into my room the little old Jew I had previously encountered at the Grand Hotel. I recognised him in a moment.

"There wash ten guineas offered in reward for a shtring of beads?" he began.

"Ten pounds."

"Oh, shay ten guineas for a poor ole man," he insinuated, with a detestable leer.

"Not a penny more than I have said. Why did you not come before?"

"The rewardsh was not enough to pay a toiler for ish trouble," he retorted, slyly.

"You thought the fool who offered a reward so large for a thing so worthless must require it badly, and would offer more?" I said.

He grinned. I was evidently a person of intelligence. "Oh, they are very good beadsh," he said heartily. "My little grandschild—my dear little grandschild—pick them up in Eaton Shquare. I take great care of them since."

"I suppose round the grandchild's neck," I said.

"What it matter?" he replied, distinctly abashed. "It do no harm if she wears them shjust a little. She very careful."

"Where are they?"

He produced cautiously from the shabbiest of leathern bags a paper parcel, which, unfolded, proved to contain a string of blue-grey beads of a curious metallic lustre. I counted them. There were thirty four. I thought them strangely heavy.

"Of what are they made?" I inquired.

"Foreign metal," he said; "very good foreign metal. I do not know."

"You will have to prove your grand-daughter picked them up in Eaton Square on or about the date specified."

"Yes, I shee her," he said glibly, "and my wife she shee her."

"Ah," I said, "I shall want some other evidence than that."

He burst into tears. He protested that his word was as the Gospel. I had been mechanically slipping the beads from one hand to the other. Suddenly I dropped them into my pocket. I took ten pounds from my desk. "Well," I said, "I will take your word for it. I believe these are the beads." I put the note into his dirty hands.

He looked up cunningly into my face. "You very glad," he said; "your hand shake bad—your voice change. Gif poor man some more—a little more because he take such very good care of that you prize so much."

"Not a cent," I protested, controlling my voice; "but if you send your grandchild here to-morrow I will give her a five-pound note for herself."

Lady Wycombe and Redvers were to be married the following day. Her year of conventional mourning was up.

"Let me present you with a second wedding-present," I said nonchalantly, calling on her that evening. Redvers was on the point of bidding her good-night.

"What trick or double-dyed generosity is this?" he questioned. He was looking well pleased into her lovely eyes. Then—

"Good Heavens, Syfret why don't you let that story drop? One is weary of the name of metal beads."

"Permit me," I said. I clasped them round her throat. In doing so I pressed a spring in the enamelled clasp.

Instantly there was a dazzle of light. The soft electric lamps sent sudden challenging and interchanging gleams across the room to where a focus of prismatic radiance played in parti-coloured flame about her. For her throat was strung by a string of four-leaved golden tulips, and from the yellow cup of each a magnificent diamond blazed.

Ranjichatterjee's *yogi*-jeweller had practised a slight deception on his princely master.

A BEAUTIFUL VAMPIRE

I

There was a flutter indeed in the little town of Argles, when it became known that Dr. Andrew had made an attempt upon the life of Lady Deverish. Andrew was a youngish, good-looking fellow, junior partner in the firm of Byrne & Andrew, the principal doctors in the place. Everybody liked him. He was as clever as he was kind. He would take equal pains to pull the ninth child of a navvy through a croup seizure as he would have done had it been heir to an earldom. Some people thought this mistaken kindness on the doctor's part—the navvy's ninth could well have been spared, especially as the navvy drank, and in any case was unable to provide properly for eight. Some went so far even as to assert that Andrew was flying in the face of Providence—to say nothing of the ratepayers—when he brought this superfluous ninth triumphantly through its fifth attack of croup. Otherwise, he was as popular as a man may be in a world wherein flaws and scandal lend to tea and bread-and-butter a stimulating quality denied to blamelessness and good repute.

"The butler says he heard raised voices," it was whispered over dainty cups, "and then Lady Deverish shrieked for help, and he ran in and found the doctor clutching her round the throat."

"And only just in time. Her face was perfectly black!"

"Isn't it awful? Such a kind man as he has always seemed. Is there any madness in the family?"

"It is not certain. They say his mother was peculiar. Wrote books, and did other extraordinary things. Always wore very large hats with black feathers. Quite out of fashion, Mrs. Byass tells me. She knew her."

"What have they done with him?"

"That is the strangest part of it. She wouldn't charge him—said it was all a mistake. So he just got into his carriage, and continued his rounds."

"Gracious! Strangling everybody?"

"Oh, I believe not."

"Her throat was bruised black and blue. Old Dr. Byrne went at once and saw to her. He got a new nurse down from London. They say it was a nurse they quarrelled about, you know."

"Well, they won't get anyone to believe that, my dear."

"No, because she was as plain as could be. And Lady Deverish's groom told cook that Dr. Andrew scarcely looked at her."

"And I never heard that he admired Lady Deverish."

"Ah! well, most men do."

"I don't see what she wants a nurse at all for. She's the picture of health."

"She says she suffers from nerves."

"If all of us who suffer from 'nerves' were to have trained nurses looking after us, there wouldn't be enough trained nurses to go round."

"No, but all of us are not widows with the incomes of two rich dear departeds at our bankers, my dear."

Now, knowing both her charming ladyship and Andrew, I was naturally interested as to why he had put hands about her beautiful throat in anything other than loving kindness. Therefore, I made a point of drinking tea with a number of amiable and gracious persons of my acquaintance during the week following this most notable attempt. All the information I got for my pains has been condensed into the foregoing gossip, and since it was insufficient for my purposes I set about seeking more. I called early at the Manor. I did not entirely credit rumour's whisper concerning the victim's mangled throat, but I knew Andrew's muscular lean hands, if he had been in earnest, would, to say the least of it, have rendered prudent her retirement for the space of some days, so that I did not expect to see anybody but her companion, Mrs. Lyall.

"Gracious, how ill you look!" I could not help exclaiming, as she entered.

I had known her some months earlier as a buxom matron. Now she was a haggard old woman. Her features worked and twisted. She slid into a chair, her hands and members shaking like those of one with palsy. For several minutes she could not speak.

"You must have been sadly troubled," I said.

She was a mild and somewhat flaccid person, one of those plump anaemic women who give one the impression that their veins run milk. But as I spoke her face became contorted. She struggled up and brandished a trembling, clenched hand.

"If he had only done it!" she cried passionately, "if by some mercy of Providence he had only done it!"

She was transformed—distorted. It was as though some mild and milky Alderney had suddenly developed claws. She slid trembling again into her chair.

"My dear Mrs. Lyall," I remonstrated, "if he had only done it, the world would have lost a beautiful and accomplished member of your sex—and poor Andrew's career would have come to a summary and lamentable end."

"No jury would have convicted him," she protested, "*not when they knew.*" She dropped her voice and searched the room with apprehensive eyes. Then she whispered, "She is a devil."

Now I was aware that some plain and very good women are in the habit of regarding every comely member of their sex as allied in one or another way with the Father of Evil, but it was clear that some sentiment stronger than general principles was moving Mrs. Lyall.

My interest was roused. But she had come to the end of her remarks. She glanced round timorously.

"For Heaven's sake, Lord Syfret, do not mention a word of this," she stammered. "I am sadly unnerved. I scarcely know what I say. Poor Lady Deverish has been rather trying." She shut her weak lips obstinately. I assured her of my discretion. I expressed sympathy, and went my way.

Byrne had nothing to tell. "Andrew will not say a word," he said. "He was over-taxed. Been up several nights. She must have exasperated him somehow. Shouldn't have thought he had it in him. He has always been the kindest of fellows."

"What does she say?"

"Laughs it off, though she don't seem amiable. Looks as if she don't want things to come out."

"You don't mean—?"

"My dear fellow, whatsoever I mean, I do not say."

It has always been my habit in life to take the bull by the horns whensoever circumstances have rendered this feat at the same time possible and prudent. I determined to attempt it now. Andrew, after all, was a very mild and tractable bull, despite his recent outbreak.

"I will not disguise the object of my visit," I informed him. "You know my weakness. Anything you tell me will go no further. The ball of Argles' scandal will get no push from me. But I like to probe human motive; and you must admit the situation is suggestive."

He smiled—a nervous smile. I had never seen him so careworn. He shook his head. "She has tied my hands," he said. "If they had let me I would have strangled her."

"I do not wonder you are hard hit," I adventured, watching him. "She is certainly a siren of the first water."

He burst out laughing. "Great Scott!" he said. "Is that what they say? Do they think I am aspiring to the Deverish's hand and acres? No, no; I am not altogether a fool."

At this moment somebody ran up the stairs, and after a preliminary knock, burst into the room. "Please, doctor, come quick," a page-boy blurted. "There's Lady Deverish's nurse has fallen down in the road, and they says she's dying."

The same change came over Andrew that had come over Mrs. Lyall. His face became contorted. He held a clenched fist in the air. "Damn her!" he cried, and rushed out.

Now this ejaculation had every appearance of applying to her ladyship's nurse, and would point to an amount of callousness on

Andrew's part—considering the moribund condition of that unfortunate young person—whereof I am sure he was incapable. I hasten, therefore, to inform the reader that it was intended solely and absolutely for her ladyship's bewitching self. It was as fervid and whole-souled a fulmination as I remember to have heard. It left no doubt in my mind whatsoever as to the fact of her ladyship owing her life to that timely advent of her butler. My interest was not abated. I followed Andrew out. In the next street a knot of curious persons were assembled.

"Stand back," the doctor called as we went up. "Give her air."

The circle widened, disclosing the figure of a young woman in nursing dress, lying senseless on the pavement. Her upturned face was curiously pinched though the conformation was young, and her hair fallen loose about her cheek hung in girlish rings.

"She does not look strong enough for nursing," I remarked to Byrne, who came up at the moment.

"Strong enough," he echoed testily. "A week ago she was sturdy and robust. The Deverish takes care of that. Can't stand sickliness about her." He added half to himself, "Must be something wrong with the house. Ventilation bad or something. One after another they've gone off like this." The girl now began to show signs of consciousness. She opened her eyes, and seeing Andrew, smiled faintly. Presently she sat up.

"When you feel equal to it, my dear," Dr. Byrne said, "we will help you to my carriage, and you can drive straight back."

"Back," she repeated wildly, "where?"

"Why, to the Manor. You must—"

She interrupted him he caught his hand. "No, no," she gasped, "not there, never there. I cannot stand another hour of it."

"The beautiful Deverish must be something of a vixen," I reflected, seeing the expression in the girl's face.

Andrew was helping her to her feet. "Don't be afraid," he said quietly, "I will see that you do not go back."

She looked into his face. "What is it?" she whispered, with white lips. "Do you know?"

"Yes, I know," he answered, meeting her look.

I had an inspiration. Among my clientele I numbered several trained nurses. I called at the post-office on my way home and wired for one. In less than two hours she was with me. I despatched her to the Manor. "Say you have been sent from Heaven or Buckingham Palace, or any other probable and impressive source, and keep your eyes and ears open," I enjoined her, with that utter disregard for truth and scrupulousness which I have found the greatest of all aids to me in my researches.

She returned in an hour. There was anger in her eyes. The gauze veil streaming from her bonnet fluttered manelike to the offended toss of her head.

"You did not stay long," I said.

"My lord," she returned, "I did not have the opportunity. Lady Devilish—I believe you called her Devilish—just came into the room and gave a little cry, and turned her back on me as if I'd been an ogre. 'Oh, you would never suit,' she said, 'I must have someone young'—my lord, I am twenty-six— 'and plump'—I weigh ten stone— 'and healthy'—I have never had a day's illness. 'Send some-one young, and plump, and healthy,' and she marched out."

"I suppose that would not be difficult?" I commented.

"Not at all," she said resolutely, "a little padding, a touch of rouge, and some minor details are all that are needed."

"You mean to go yourself, then?"

"Yes, I mean to go," she returned. "If there is anything to find out she may be sorry she wasn't more civil," she added meditatively.

"Would she not recognise you?"

I admire grit. I admired the uncompromising and superior disdain with which she met my question. She turned and left without condescending a word. In fifteen minutes she came back, or, rather, somebody did whose voice was all I recognised. Her disguise was perfect. Before, she had certainly looked neither youthful (despite her assurance as to twenty-six), nor plump (despite her boasted avoirdupois), nor healthy. Now she was plump, and young, and rosy. She had been dark; now a profusion of rich red hair rippled from her brows. I wondered why she did not always go about disguised. She explained.

"In most houses, my lord," she said, "there are sons, and brothers, and husbands. A woman who has her living to get by nursing can only afford to sport cherry cheeks under exceptional circumstances."

When she had gone I dipped my pen in coloured ink and entered her name in my diary. Whether or not she succeeded with Lady "Devilish," she was a capable person. And capable persons are red-letter persons in a world where incompetency rules seven days out of most weeks.

II

NURSE MARIAN'S STORY

She received me with open arms. "You are just what I want," she said effusively. "I loathe sickliness. There was a gaunt, haggard creature here an hour ago. Ugh!" she shuddered, "I would not have employed her for worlds."

I may be prejudiced, but after her first remark I confess to feeling somewhat antipathetic to her ladyship. She has a curious way of staring. I suspect her of being short-sighted and shirking glasses for the sake of her looks. Certainly I have never seen anybody so brilliantly beautiful.

Upstairs I was introduced to her companion, Mrs. Lyall. She did not strike me as being altogether sane. She has rather a grim smile.

"You'll soon lose those fine cheeks," she said the moment she saw me.

"I trust not," I returned, with some amount of confidence. (I had only just opened a new packet.) "Is Lady Devilish rather a trying patient, then?" I asked.

She broke into a laugh. "What did you call her?"

"I understood her name to be Devilish," I said.

"No, it's her nature," she retorted, looking furtively about. "Her name has an 'r' instead of an 'l.'"

Her ladyship was plainly no favourite of Mrs. Lyall. Indeed, everybody in the house seemed to be in mortal terror of her. The servants would not, if they could help it, enter a room where she was.

From the unhealthy faces of the household I came to the conclusion that the house was thoroughly unsanitary. I determined to investigate the drains. Whatsoever there might be that was unwholesome it did not affect the mistress. Her energy was marvelous. She never tired. When after a long day picnicking or a late ball, everybody looked as white as paper, she was as fresh and blooming and gay-spirited as possible. It seemed a mere farce for her to employ a nurse. But she had a fad about massage, and insisted on being "massed" morning and night.

"You don't look tired," she remarked in a puzzled way, at the end of my first night's operations. She was staring curiously at my rouged cheeks. Strangely enough I was feeling actually faint. Strong-nerved as I am, I fairly reeled.

"Whatsoever I look," I answered her, a little irritably, "I certainly feel more tired than I ever remember feeling."

I thought she seemed pleased. Certainly I had said nothing to please her. No doubt she was thinking her own thoughts.

Her engagement to be married again was announced the day after my arrival. She had been already married twice. The young man—the Earl of Arlington—was, with a number of other persons, stopping in the house. He was handsome and pleasant-looking. I was told he had thrown over a girl he had cared for and who had cared for him for years in order to propose to Lady Deverish. He did not look capable of it. But, to all appearance, he was head over ears in love. He could not keep his eyes from her. He sat like a man bewitched, and neither ate nor rested.

"Poor young gentleman He'll go the way of the others," Mrs. Plimmer, the housekeeper, confided to me.

"You don't suspect Lady Deverish of poisoning her husbands?" I returned.

"It isn't my place to suspect my betters, Nurse," she said with dignity. "All I say is there's something terrible mysterious. Why does everybody who comes to the Manor fail in health?"

"Drains," I suggested.

She tossed her ample chin. "Why did her two young husbands, as likely men as might be, sicken from the day she married them, and die consumptive? Was that drains, can you tell me?"

I thought it might have been, but having no evidence, did not commit myself.

Mrs. Plimmer tossed her ample chin again, this time triumphantly. "And why," she proceeded, "did Dr. Andrew, as kind a gentleman as walks, try to strangle her?"

I braved her scorn and ventured "jealousy."

She eyed me witheringly. "The doctor's no lady's man," she said, "and besides if he was, its no reason for strangling them."

I was unable to find any fault with the drains. I began to grow interested. I myself felt strangely out of sorts—a new experience for me.

Lord Arlington's infatuation amounted to possession. He sat staring at her in it kind of ecstasy of fascination. He was pale and moody and obviously unhappy. I was told he had lost health and spirits markedly since his engagement. Probably his conscience troubled him about the other woman. At breakfast one morning he unwrapped a little packet which had come by post for him, without, it is to be supposed, observing the handwriting As he undid it mechanically there dropped from the wrappings a ring, a knot of ribbon, and a bundle of letters. He seemed stunned. Without a word he gathered them together and quitted the room. I met him later pacing the garden like a madman.

Poor man! His love-affair was short-lived.

A week later I was involuntary witness to a curious scene. I was sitting late one evening in the garden. Lady Deverish would not need me until bed-time, when her massage was due. Suddenly he and she, talking excitedly, came round the shrubbery.

"I have been mad," he exclaimed, in a hoarse, passionate voice. "For God's sake let me go free. They say her heart is broken."

She put her two hands on his shoulders, and lifted her face to his.

"I will never let you go," she said, with a curious ring as of metal in her voice. She wound her arms about his neck and kissed his throat. "And you love me too much," she added.

"Heaven only knows if it is love," he answered. "It seems to me like madness. I had loved her faithfully for years."

"And now you love me, and there is no way out of it," she whispered. She leaned up again and kissed him. Then with a little cooing laugh she left him.

He remained looking after her. "Yes, there is one way out of it," I heard him say slowly.

That night he shot himself.

Now, although I had known her but a fortnight, I had known her long enough to believe her superior to the weakness of being very deeply in love. Yet the night he died I was inclined to alter my opinion. He had bidden her a hasty good-bye, saying he was summoned to town. He took the last train up.

During the night I was called to her. I found her sitting up in bed, her face ashen pale, her eyes distended, her hands clasped to her head. She was gasping for breath. She seemed like one stricken; her features were picked out by deep grey lines. She didn't speak, but pointed with an insistent finger to her right temple. I put my hand upon it. Then I called quickly for a light; for my fingers slipped along that which seemed to be a moist and clammy aperture, moist with a horrible, unmistakable clamminess. But when the light was brought there was neither blood nor aperture, only a curious blanched spot, chill to the touch.

I gave her brandy, and put hot bottles in her bed. She was shaking as with ague. She clutched my hands, holding them against that ice-spot in her temple till I was sick and faint. Soon she seemed better. Some colour returned to her.

"My God, he is dead!" she said, through chattering teeth. Then she crouched down in the bed, a shuddering heap.

Next morning the news came. In that same hour he had put a bullet through his right temple. She was ill all that day, nerveless and almost pulseless. She looked ten years older. I never saw so singular a change. I sent for Dr. Byrne, who attributed it to the shock of bad news. Why it developed some hours before the news arrived he did not explain. He only said, "Tut, tut, Nurse, life is full of coincidences;" and prescribed ammonia.

Next day she was better, and suggested getting up, but changed her mind after having seen a mirror. "Gracious!" she said, with a shudder, "I look like all old woman." She broke into feeble weeping. "He ought to have thought of me," she cried angrily.

She demanded wine and meat-juices, taking them with a curious solicitude, and carefully looking into her mirror for their effect. But she saw little there to comfort her.

"Do you think it might be my death-blow?" she questioned once through quivering lips. I shook my head. "Ah, you don't know all," she muttered.

In the afternoon she asked that the gardener's child should be brought to her. He was a chubby, rosy little fellow, whom everybody petted. "I must something to liven me," she said. I had never supposed her fond of children. But she held her arms hungrily for him, and strained him to her breast. Her spirits rose. Her eyes brightened: she got colour. Soon she was laughing and chatting in her accustomed manner. The child had fallen asleep, but she would not part with him. When at last she let him go, I was horrified to find him cold and pallid. He was breathing heavily, and quite unconscious. I concluded the poor little chap was sickening for something. Later, I was surprised to receive a note from Dr. Andrew, whom I did not know. I dismissed him as I had done Mrs. Lyall, and probably Mrs. Plimmer, as not altogether sane. "I have been called in to attend Willy Daniels," the note ran. "For Heaven's sake, do not let her get hold of any more children."

Next day she was better. She seemed to have forgotten Arlington and talked only of her health. She asked again for the boy. I told her he was ill. She broke into a curious laugh which seemed uncalled for. "Thank goodness, I haven't lost my power," she said a minute later. But she did not explain the saying.

She was in high spirits all the morning, talking and singing and trying on new laces and bonnets. She still complained of pain in the right temple. After her massage she turned peevish, protesting that it did her no good. "If you hadn't such a colour I should not believe you healthy," she said crossly.

She had the parson's children in to tea. It would amuse her, she said, to see them eat their strawberries. They seemed afraid of her, and eyed her from a distance. When she attempted to take the little one, it clung to me and shrieked. But she persisted, and it soon fell asleep in her arms. On presently taking it from her, I found it chilled and breathing stertorously and quite unconscious. I thought of Dr. Andrew's injunction. Heavens! what had she done? Was she a secret poisoner? I dismissed the notion forthwith. I had not left the room a moment during the time the child was with her, nor had it taken anything to eat or to drink.

"What is the matter?" I demanded.

Her eye avoided mine. She answered nonchalantly: "What does one expect? Children are everlastingly teething or over-feeding or having measles."

Next morning I was called up at daybreak. Dr. Andrew was waiting to see me. I threw on my things and went down. He was stalking up and down the drawing-room. He stared.

"You seem to have resisted her," he muttered, looking at my checks. I have a long memory, and had not forgotten my rouge. He told me a wild and incredible story. He wound up by handing me a small bottle.

"Give her that dose so soon as she wakes," he said. The man was probably a better doctor than he was an actor. His manner paraded the nature of the dose. I took out the cork and smelt it. It was as I suspected. I walked across the room and emptied its contents out of the window. "Pardon me," I said, "but you are exceeding your duty."

"Is she to be allowed to go on murdering people?" he protested. "Do you know I have been up all night with that unfortunate baby? Do you know Willy Daniels is not yet out of danger? Good Heavens! if I am willing to take the consequences, how can one who knows the circumstances hesitate?"

"I have a safer and more justifiable plan," I said. "If what you say is true the remedy is simple, and poison is uncalled for. After all, Dr. Andrew, your story would sound lame enough in a law-court. By my plan you run no risks."

I laid it before him. He seemed interested. But he would not, after the manner of men in their dealings with women, permit me to take too much credit to myself.

"It might work," he said lukewarmly, "and as you say it would certainly be safer."

I went to my room and opened a further packet of rouge. I applied it lavishly. I began to see that the health tint on my cheeks had an important bearing on the situation. I put vermilion on my lips. Then I carried my patient her breakfast.

She seemed restored and lay in her rose-pink bed, a smiling Venus. She fairly glowed with beautiful health. I thought of that poor little sick bed.

"Goodness!" I said with a start, "how ill you look!" She ceased from smiling. She leapt across the floor, her draperies clinging round her pink flushed toes. She fled to the glass. She turned on me peevishly. "Why did you tell me?" she protested. "I should have thought I looked well."

I went and stood beside her. "Compare yourself with me."

She was pale enough indeed by the time she had done so. "Am I losing my power after all?" she muttered. "Heavens! shall I grow old like other people?"

Suddenly she flung herself upon me. She pressed her lips and cheeks against my throat and face.

"Give *me* some of it," she cried ravenously. "You have so much vitality. Let me drain some of that rich health and colour."

I nearly fell. It seemed as if she were actually sucking out my life. I reeled and sickened. Then with a tremendous effort I pushed her away and stumbled from the room. Was Andrew's story indeed true? Was she a monster or merely a monomaniac?

Years ago he had said she was dying of consumption. So far as physical signs could be trusted, she had not a week to live. Suddenly she began to recover. She made flesh rapidly, gained health, and came back to life from the very jaws of death. Meanwhile, her sister, a school-girl, whom she insisted on having always with her, sickened and died.

Then a brother died, then her mother. By this time she had grown quite strong. Since then she had lived on the vital forces of those surrounding her. "The law of life," he said, "makes creatures inter-dependent. Physical vitality is subject to physical laws of diffusion and equalisation. One person below par absorbs the nerve and life sources of healthier persons with them. Many old, debilitated subjects live on the animal forces of the cat they keep persistently in their chair, and die when it dies. Wives and husbands, sisters and brothers, friends and acquaintances: there is a constant interchange of vital force. Lady Deverish has to my knowledge been the actual cause of death of a dozen persons. Besides these she has drained the health of everybody associated with her. And in her case—a rare and extreme one—the faculty is conscious and voluntary. She was living on Arlington. The man was powerless. She paralysed his will, his mind, his energies. She robbed him of strength to resist her. The sequel is interesting, psychologically. She being for the time charged with his vitality, his sudden death, by some curious sympathy, affected her in the way you have described. She was all at once and violently bereft of the source whence she was drawing energy. But she will soon, if she be allowed, find some other to prey on. For some years I have studied her closely. She is the arch-type of a class of persons I have long had under observation. I find such power depends largely on force of will and concentration. If she can maintain these there is no reason why she should not live to be a hundred. There will always be persons of less assertive selfishness to serve as reservoirs of vital strength to her. At present her confidence is shaken, her power—therefore her life trembles in the balance. In the interests of humanity and justice she must not be allowed to regain her confidence. She lives by wholesale murder."

III

I drank a glass of port and went back to my patient. She lay panting on her bed.

"Fie!" I said; "that was a bit of hysteria. Come now, take your breakfast."

She looked me in the face. A terror of death stood in beads on her skin. "I have heard of transfusion," she said faintly; "if you will let me have some of the rich red blood run out of your veins into mine I will settle £500 a year on you."

I shook my head.

"A thousand," she said. "Fifteen hundred."

"I should be cheating you," I insisted, "even were I willing. The operation has never been really successful."

She broke into raving and tears.

"I cannot die," she said; "I love life. I love being beautiful and rich; I love admiration. I must have admiration! I love my beautiful, beautiful body and the joy of life! I cannot, cannot die!"

"What nonsense!" I said. "You are not going to die."

"If I could only get it," she raved, "I would drink blood out of living bodies rather than I would die."

An hour later she summoned the housekeeper. She had been cogitating with a fold between her brows; her teeth set like pearls in the red of her lower lip.

"Plimmer," she said, "give all the servants a month's wages and an hour's notice to quit. I cannot endure their sickly faces. Get in a staff of decently healthy people. These cadaverous wretches are killing me."

Plimmer left the room without a word. At the door she cast one look toward me and threw her hands up, as one who says: "The Lord have mercy on us!"

I followed, and bade her stay her hand. Whether Andrew's theories were true, or whether my lady were but a person with a mania, there was no doubt but that her convictions played an important part in the case.

I threw on my things and expended a half-sovereign at the chemist's. I came back the possessor of sundry packets. These I distributed among the household with explicit directions. Her ladyship was not well; her whim must be humoured.

It is surprising what a little rouge will do. In a few minutes the servants' hall was a scene Arcadian. Even the elderly butler reverted to blooming youth. Then I said to her cheerfully:

"You are making a mistake about the servants. For my part I am struck with their healthy looks."

"Since I have been ill?" she faltered.

She lay quiet, breathing hard through her dilated nostrils. "Send some of them in," she said presently.

By the time they had gone she was as white as paper. "Good Heavens!" I heard her mutter, "I have lost my power. I am a dead woman."

Then she flung out her arms and wept. "Get me healthy children," she cried; "I must have health about me."

Dr Byrne, who was attending her, assented in all innocence. "Why, of course," he said; "it will be cheerful for you. Get in some cherry-cheeked children to amuse her ladyship, Nurse."

I nodded—in token that I was not deaf—not at all in acquiescence. Food and wine I supplied in plenty, but neither children nor adults. I isolated her *in toto*. I allowed her maids only to come near her long enough to dust and arrange the room. I have seen her fix them with a basilisk stare, straining her will. She had undoubtedly some baleful hypnotic power which set them trembling and stumbling about in curious, aimless fashion. They would seem drawn, as by some spell, to stand motionless and dazed beside her bed, Then I would turn them face about and parading their roseate tints, scold them for idleness and dismiss them. She would stare after them in a despair which, under other circumstances, would have been pitiful. The sense that her power was gone robbed her actually of power. She raved and cursed her self-murdered lover for involving her in his death.

Whether Dr. Andrew and I were justified in that we did I sometimes wonder now. Then I had no room for doubt. In face of the horrible facts it did not occur to me to question it. If that she believed were true, we were assuredly justified; if not, that we did could not affect results.

Andrew's theory of those results is that she had lived so long on human energy that food in the crude state stood her in little stead. Certainly, though she was fed unremittingly on the choicest and most nourishing of diets, she was an aged and haggard woman in a week. Nobody would have recognised her. She shrivelled and shrank like one cholera-stricken. One day her dog stole into the room. She put out her hand and clutched it voraciously. I took it an hour later from her. It was dead and stiff.

How I myself, and a nurse I had called in to help me, kept life in us I cannot say. I had been an abstainer. Now I drank wine like water. All round her bed was an atmosphere as of a vault, though outside it was sunny June.

She raged like one possessed. "You are murdering, murdering me," she cried incessantly.

Dr Byrne thought her mind wandering. I knew it centred with a monstrous, selfish sanity. He sent for one of the first London consultants. After a lengthy investigation the great man pronounced her suffering from some obscure nervous disease. "Nothing to be done," he said. "I give her three days: most interesting case. Hope you will succeed in getting a *postmortem*."

Once she fixed me with her baleful eyes, how baleful was seen now that their fine lustre and the bloom beneath them were gone.

"I have had ten years more of life and pleasure than my due," she chuckled in her shrivelled throat— the throat now of an old, old woman.

Then she broke into dry-eyed crying. "I thought I could have lived another ten." She begged once for a mirror. I thank Heaven that with all my heat of indignation against her, I was not guilty of that cruelty.

Dr Andrew called daily for my bulletin. Everything science afforded in the way of food and stimulant, he scrupulously got down from London.

"We must give her every chance," he said, "every justifiable chance, that is."

After a few days I was again single-handed. My nurse-colleague succumbed. I felt my powers failing. I could scarcely drag about. I prayed Providence for strength to last so long as she should. Even in the moment of dissolution, such was her frenzied greed of life, that I believed should some non-resistant person take my place, she would struggle back to health.

Once when I arranged her pillows, she seized my hand, and before I could withdraw it she had carried it to her mouth and bitten into it. I felt her suck the blood voraciously. She cried out and struck at me as I wrenched it away.

She died in the third week of her isolation. I saw the death change come into her shrivelled face. Then in the moment wherein life left her she made one supremest effort.

It seemed as though my heart stopped. My head took on my chest, my hands dropped at my side. Then I swayed and fell headlong across her bed. They found me later lying on her corpse. I am convinced that had she been a moment earlier, had she nerved her powers the instant before, rather than on the instant life was leaving her, she would be alive to this day, and I— As it was, I did not leave my bed for a month."

"If I were to write that story in the *Lancet*," Dr. Andrew said, "I should be the laughing-stock of the profession. Yet it is the very key-note of human health and human disease, this interchange of vital force which goes on continually between individuals. Such rapacity and greed as the Deverish's are, fortunately, rare; but there are a score such vampires in this very town, vampires in lesser degree. When A. talks with me ten minutes I feel ten years older. It takes me an hour to bring my nerve-power up to par again. People call him a bore. In reality he is a rapacious egotist hungrily absorbing the life-force of anyone with whom he comes into relation— in other words, a human vampire."

AN EXPIATION

Only in exceptional cases do I trouble to put the law on the track of murder, though in the course of their activities on my behalf, my agents witness the commission of such a crime. For my part, I prefer the delinquent to escape, that I may find, as I do find, penalty closing in on him as an indirect consequence of his action, rather than that it shall take the clumsy form we dignify by the title of justice. Far crueller, subtler, and a hundredfold more fitting to a particular crime are the methods whereby time, character, and circumstance enmesh the criminal. Expedient it may be to rid ourselves of the confessedly vicious. But the Powers which are moulding us to ends our finite minds have so far failed to grasp are neither assisted in their ultimate objects nor appeased in their far-reaching wrath—so to put it—by our crude expedients. The long arm of development which encompasses the human family, and places effect in the unerring train of cause, will find the murderer, many years it may be after we have done with him, but find him it will as inevitably as the impulse given to pool by pebble laps the shore.

How can it reach him after death? you ask. Death is but change of identity. Entities in the school of evolution pass through myriad lives in training for eternity, and the ill acts of one existence may not find expiation until a later one. A theory, you say! A theory, I admit. But I ask you for another which shall equally explain the inexplicabilities of human life.

I have a story illustrative of my theory. Read into it any other interpretation that you will, and judge if it apply as mine does.

In a cottage on one of my estates a gamekeeper lived, some ten years since, with his young and pretty wife. He was middle-aged and morose, considering, as does many another, that the one cardinal virtue he practised—in his case that of honesty—absolved him from the obligation of practising any of the minor amenities and amiabilities of life. Nobody could imagine by what sorcery or fortuitous concomitance of accidents he had persuaded pretty Polly Penrose to mate with him. He had saved a certain sum of money, for to other unlovable qualities he added that of screw. Polly had swains better circumstanced than he, however, so that this offered no solution of the problem. The village wondered, chattered, and finally decided that "you could nivver calculate on what gells do, for they're chock full o' whimsies;" and so they let the matter drop. Cooper was but one of Polly's whimsies.

It is probable I should never have concerned myself with Polly's affairs had I not one day come upon her crying her eyes out in a wood. On seeing me, she blushed and stole away. Matters just then were dull. I had no other case on hand; and, without anticipating much result, idly determined to trace the cause of Polly's tears. I had, among my agents, a girl of about her age and temperament, who soon made Polly's acquaintance. It came out then that Polly had married for pique. There was a certain stalwart sweetheart of hers—another of my keepers—of whom she was fond, but he rousing her jealousy, in a fit of temper she accepted Cooper. To make a long story short—for this is but a preface—Polly and her lover made it up again too late, for Polly was then Mrs. Cooper.

Polly was a good girl, and I do not believe Cooper had any substantial reason for complaint, as she saw Dell but rarely. But she grew pallid and depressed. Occasionally she was seen with Dell. The circumstances reaching Cooper's ears, with doubtless some embellishment, there was trouble in the cottage. Cooper even went so far as to strike her. In her fear and agitation—the poor girl was soon to be a mother—she fled to Dell.

Cooper, following, found her in a shed near the latter's cottage. From words the men passed to blows, and eventually Dell struck Cooper over the head with the butt-end of his gun. Whether he meant murder or not, who can say? but a long acquaintance with the poor fellow makes me confident the impulse was momentary and uncontrollable. But murder it turned out. Cooper's skull was fractured and he died in a few hours.

Dell made no effort to escape. His one fear seems to have been for Polly. He remained with her in the cottage, soothing and reassuring her till he was handcuffed and taken to gaol. I did all I could on his behalf. I even had the gaol-lock tampered with. I had an instinct of what would happen should his case come to trial, and hanging was the last death for the fine young fellow he was.

I was a magistrate, and could easily have contrived his escape. But the blockhead would not take his liberty. He could not now marry Polly, he said, and he did not care for life.

A thick-skulled jury, directed by a judge who on the Bench was as keen a stickler for the proprieties as off the Bench he was obtuse about them, put the worst—and, I believe, the false—construction on Dell's and Polly's fondness. He was convicted of murder, and sentenced to death. Under the circumstances it was a monstrous sentence. There had been assuredly no premeditation, and his provocation was great. We petitioned the Home Secretary; we petitioned Parliament. We might have spared our signatures and ink. When Dell's time came he was hanged. And now comes the gist of my story.

I filled up the places left vacant by Dell and his victim, putting in two keepers from a distance. There was a strong local feeling against the occupation of either of the cottages. For it was rumoured that the shed wherein the murder had occurred was haunted. But the new keepers, unaffected by the tragedy which to them was merely hear-say, pooh-poohed the rumour.

Curiously enough, the wife of one turned out to be a distant cousin of Dell's. She was a buxom person, strong nerved, and braced with common sense. She scoffed at ghost-talk.

"Depend on it, your lordship," she said once to me, "there's a deal more to be afeart on in the livin' than the dead; and as long as it's noboddy comin' to meddle wi' Johnson's belongins, why, let the poor things, if things there be, come an' go as it pleases 'em."

I mention this to free my story from an implication to which it may presently seem open. Mrs. Johnson was as unimpressionable a woman as could be, and was as little affected by the talk of ghosts as she would have been by their apparition.

Now the ghost which was said to walk and to have been seen by more than one person, was not, as I have gathered is the way of ghosts, the shade of the murdered man, but that of his murderer. All who had caught the fleeting glimpse which is as much as the ghost-seer generally permits himself, agreed that the apparition haunting the wood-shed was Dell's. Round and round in a re-stricted circle, skirting the space whereon a ghastly form had stretched, the ghost was seen to pass. Its head was bent, its face leaned down. Its eyes stared, frozen with horror. Moans and sighs of the direst distress were heard to issue from the shed. But the man from whom I had a description, a tramp who, unwitting of its reputation had stolen there one rainy evening for the purpose of a night's lodging, described the thing he saw as mute and noiseless, making a dumb and ceaseless circuit of the floor. To him the cir-cuit taken by the apparition was but a stretch of dusty boards, but the stark horror in the shadow's eyes told of some ghastly visibility.

The man was green with fright. He had lain there staring nearly all night, afraid to move, afraid almost to breathe, lest he should turn the horror of the eyes upon himself. He painted in the vivid speech of panic the curious effect of morning: how as the light grew, it left less and still less of the apparition visible, how from being something luminous against the darkness it passed into a thin translucent shade against the light: how the outlines slowly faded and the form was lost, yet he could see it whirling like a grey smoke round and round six feet of floor. When the sun came up it slipped away as mist slips into air. In the morning when the man was brought to me he was piebald. The hair and beard of one side had gone white in the night.

A time came when the ghost was seen no more. The sighs and moanings ceased. Still the shed lost no whit of its evil reputation.

A year after the Johnsons' advent to the cottage, a child was born to them. They had already several children—buxom, cherry-cheeked youngsters, after the type of their mother. This child was different. The difference did not show at first. The infant was as other infants—a mere homogeneous mass of red-pink flesh, with the slate-grey eyes of its kind; eyes which deluded mothers call dark or light according to their fancy, for the rest of the world perceives that not until long after seeing the light do babies' eyes take on the shade they eventually keep. But this infant, though like enough to others, differed from them in one particular—it had a large blood-red spot in the palm of its right hand. The doctor pronounced the spot accidental and ephemeral; it would disappear before the week was out. Subsequently, he modified his opinion. It was a variety of naevus, but he considered that it did not call for operation. The child would outgrow it. But the doctor was wrong. As the palm grew the blood-spot grew, and its colour did not wane. Presently, when the child assumed with age the waxen whiteness afterwards characterising it, the spot had a curious effect of focussing all the blood in its body.

As the babe slowly evolved an individuality out of its pink homogeneousness, it was seen to differ singularly from the rest of the Johnson children. In the place of their fair chubbiness, it was pallid and dark. Its brows were strongly and sombrely marked, and its eyes gathered slowly a weird look of horror. It cried rarely or never. Nor did it smile. It sat staring before it with a fixed expression and a blood-red palm upturned.

A child is born with its hands knotted into fists, fists which for weeks are opened with difficulty. It is an instinctive action of grasping the life before it. A man or woman dies with the palms extended. The life has been wrought and is rendered up. The Johnson baby never curled its fists as normal babies do. It held its palms limply open with the blood-red spot for all to see. The villagers talked as villagers talk of something out of the common. They drew conclusions—the short-sighted conclusions of their kind. They pronounced the child's uncanniness a judgment on the mother for her scoffing.

"It don't do to make light o' they things," they croaked. They predicted the baby's early death. The child attracted my attention from the first. I got a curious impression about it. Its face had a familiar look. The horror in its eyes reminded me of something. It was not until later that I knew of what.

I had a vacant cottage near. In it I installed an elderly woman of observant faculty. She made friends with the mother, and having leisure took the infant frequently off her hands. By her means I am able to relate that which happened. So soon as it showed signs of intelligence—signs such as those used to children interpret, while to others they are still meaningless—the Johnson baby developed interest in the haunted shed—now, it must be remembered, no longer haunted.

The moment it was taken out of doors its eyes turned in the direction of the building, which stood but a short distance from the cottage. It was restless and wayward out of sight of it, and would weary and fret with inarticulate demands until carried whence it could see it. So soon as it was able, it would drag itself along the floor and out at the door to sit there with its hands on its tiny knees, staring with fascinated looks.

Before it was ten months old it was found, having crept across the patch of ground between the house and shed, tired with its efforts, lying extended on the grass, its waxen face turned solemnly upon the building. Later it managed to escape attention long enough to reach the shed, shuffling along as infants do on hands and knees. It was discovered huddling at the open door, its head dropt till its chin rested almost in its lap, its pupils wide upon some portion of the floor. An illness followed. For some weeks the child's life was in danger. It had taken a chill, the doctor said. Even then, though weakened with fever, the poor little creature, left for a moment, would struggle feebly to the foot of the bed, whence through the window a corner of the shed was visible. There it would be found staring with wide, frightened eyes.

When strong enough to be up again it made always for the window, to stand there with its face pressed close against the glass. The doctor diagnosed the child as weak-minded, but I cannot say the term at all described the terrible intelligence looking out of its eyes. The women shook their heads.

"It knows too much, poor little dear," they said. "There isn't nothing that's said it don't know. If anybody could find out what it's always askin' in its eyes, per'aps it ud be able to die quiet, for anybody can see it isn't long for this world."

Mrs. Johnson paid but little heed to the talk.

"I don't see anything much different in the child from other children," she said impatiently, "only it don't thrive. I expect it'll be stronger on its legs when it's got its teeth and can take a bit o' meat wi' the rest of us."

But the child grew no stronger on its legs, nor did it grow the least bit less unlike the chubby-cheeked Johnson brood. It seemed to have no wish to walk. It was a patient little thing, and when planted by a chair would stand there; but so soon as attention was drawn from it, it would drop to its hands and knees again, and creep to the door.

Johnson made a little fence, to keep it from straying; but it developed a weird sagacity for evading this, wriggling through or clambering over, or escaping by a back door. Then, if not intercepted, it would work its way across the ground till it reached the doorway of the shed. There it would sit for hours together, straining its eyes upon some portion of the floor—always the same portion. Rain, snow, or wind, it minded not. Frequently it was found squatted in the entrance, wet to the skin, with a heavy rain beating on it, to all appearance conscious of its wet and chilled condition—its gaze and powers magnetised. It took but little food, and was a puny, miserable morsel. Such food as it took, it took mechanically and in obedience to its mother. It never seemed hungry, or interested, as babies are interested, in the sweet and edible.

It did not play, nor did it seem to have a notion of the use of toys. A doll or painted ball it would turn seriously over in its fingers, then lay aside with a quaint solemnity as though it had weightier matters on hand. Its only comfort was its thumb, which it sucked gravely, and with a thoughtful sobriety as of an old man smoking a pipe. It had no fear of darkness. It has been found in the shed at midnight, having scrambled from its cot, down the cottage stairs, and out at the door. Sometimes it sat at a distance, gazing spell-bound. Generally its time was spent in shuffling round and round a certain area of floor, dragging itself laboriously on hands and knees, as one doing penance.

The villagers grew scared, and whispered that it had the evil eye. They would turn back to avoid passing it in the road. I have had boys thrashed for stoning it. Even its matter-of-fact mother came to have a horror of it, with its weird ways and terrible eyes. Yet it was patient, and gave no trouble, so long as it were permitted to be in the shed. Its limbs, they told me, were raw and red, from the continuous rub of the boards against its baby skin. And the nails of toes and fingers were worn to the quick with ceaseless clambering.

That the child suffered mentally, I cannot say. Possibly not. It seemed to gather satisfaction from its treadmill labours, though there was always that dread in its eyes.

"Perhaps your lordship would be pleased to come and see it," my agent suggested one day, when I chanced to pass the Johnson cottage. "Mrs. Johnson has gone into the village. The baby was shut in, but it has got out somehow and crept to the shed."

I followed her. We went quietly; but I doubt if the child would have heard in any case, so absorbed was it. We watched it through the window. Its frock and feet were stained with the soil over which it had dragged itself. The day was damp, and mud clung about its hands. But it minded nothing. In the half-sitting, half-kneeling posture of creeping children it dragged itself sideways round and round a circle encompassing some six feet of floor—six feet in length, and from three to four in breadth. Dust lay thick on the boards, so that its circuit was clearly traced. It went always over the same ground, marking a curious zigzagged shape. Round and round, now up, now down, tracing the same inexplicable course it plodded, a thick dust rising on either side to the infantile flop of its skirts.

Its face was bent toward the centre of the trail it followed, its eyes rivetted. Sweat stood moist on its skin, and in the moisture dust clung, giving it a dark, unearthly look. It sighed and panted at its task. Every now and again it would cease from utter weariness, and, sitting up, would lift a dusty frock and wipe its lips. After a minute it resumed that treadmill round. I went in. It lifted its awed and grimy countenance and looked at me with its terrible intelligence. Then it resumed its dusty way.

I took it up and sat it on a pile of wood. It whined and fretted, stretching its arms to the shape on the floor. I crossed the shed, and stood looking down upon the figure traced. I could make nothing of it. It was an irregular oblong of indefinite form, wider to one end, narrowing to the other. A grim thought struck me that it resembled a coffin. I was interested. What was the meaning of it? What, if anything, did those weird eyes see? I bade the woman bring some cake or sweets. She came back with an orange.

"He'll do anything for an orange," she said.

I made her take the child and set him on the floor to one side of the figure. I placed myself on the other. The oblong was between us at its widest part. I held the orange up, and beckoned him.

"Go, get it!" the woman urged.

He gazed at me questioningly, as though probing my intention. His eyes rested on the orange; then something which in another child would have been a smile floated over his face. He set out, creeping toward me. I watched him intently. Would he cross that circle? He came on, shuffling slowly, raising a cloud of dust. But when he reached the further limit of the oblong, he stopped short. He turned his face down, and bent his looks on something he seemed to see within the circle—something about the level of his eyes.

I stamped my foot and called to him. He looked up curiously, but did not move. I held the orange toward him. He stretched a hand out, raising it carefully as though to prevent it coming into contact with the something there.

"Come," I said.

His eyes again levelled. They travelled slowly over that I could not see. Then he looked up, dully reproachful.

"Come," I called again, tossing the orange.

He shook his head with a grave, old-man solemnity. I stamped my foot once more.

"Come," I insisted.

His lips quivered feebly. Tears came into his eyes. Suddenly his features quickened with a new sagacity. He swerved aside and came creeping to me round the outer edge of the figure, bending his looks with an awed avoidance upon that he saw there. I tried a dozen times. But he would not cross the line. He scanned me plaintively. Why did I so torment him?

I took him in my arms. I carried him toward the charmed circle. Looking back, I can see that the act was a brutal one, such a brutal one as the curiosity we dignify by the term intellectual or scientific is frequently guilty of. But the woman stopped me. She caught him out of my arms.

"For Heaven's sake, don't, my lord," she gasped; "I did it once. I thought he would have died."

I looked into his face. Poor little wretch! There was all the dumb agony of a ripe intelligence frozen there. He clung to me strenuously, turning his rigid looks from that over which we stood. I gave him to her.

"Take him away. Get the poor little wretch out into the air. Give him the orange. Give him anything—only drive that look from his face." She took him out. He turned a shuddering head over her shoulder, seeking that spot. It was the spot where Cooper had lain. I knew it now. He had lain there full length, and over him Dell had stood with stricken eyes. Heavens! Why had the child those eyes? And why had it been cursed with this terrible vision? Had re-birth come so soon? Were the retributive forces of murder expiating in a little child?

I stood looking down at the figure traced in dust. I thrust my stick into it. Did I really feel a dull resistance? I lowered my hand to within some inches of the floor. Was the air truly chill? Pshaw! The babe had infected me. It was but a draught from the door. As I stood my stick slipped from my hold, and sliding, stopped between the curves composing the lower end of the oblong. The branch of a tree, stirred by a wind, shot its shadow through the doorway immediately across the tracery. In a moment, as a few strokes put to outlines which had had no meaning gather the lines into life, so now the unmeaning tracery took shape. The stick formed a line of demarcation between extended legs, a limb of the shadow tree lay like an outstretched arm and hand. Even for a moment convulsing features were given to a curve which might have been a face, as a flicker of twigs and fluttering leaves hurried like vanishing pencil-marks across the outline. In that moment the murdered body of Cooper was reproduced as I had seen it. I am sufficiently strong-nerved. Yet I admit I turned sick. I picked up my stick and went out.

I knew now that what had been momentarily visible to me was ever before the doomed baby, that to its eyes the murdered man was always there. I felt my hair lift as though an ice-wind swept under my hat.

I had the shed pulled down. I had the ground sown with flowers. But the spot kept its old fascination for the poor little creature. He could not now drag round it, the way being barred. But he sat for hours tracing with a waxen finger something that for him lay there, something which to us was but space between flower-stalks.

I sent him to the sea, a hundred miles away. In three days his life was despaired of. His impulse in living was gone. He fell into a state of stupor. When brought back he revived. He dragged himself out to the flower-bed, and sat there crooning with a kind of plaintive content, tracing that outline with his pallid hands.

One morning they found him dead there. He had crept from his cot at some time during the night, and had scrambled in the darkness—he never learned to walk—to the old spot. Rain was falling, and he lay on his back with face upturned and wet, his fair hair limp about him. His brows were unbent and tranquil, through his half-closed lids peace at last looked. The flowers stood round him like gentle sentinels, their flower cups full of rain as eyes with tears. For the first time in his life the smile of a child lay over his lips. And the blood-spot in his palm was white as wool.

Coachwhip Publications

CoachwhipBooks.com

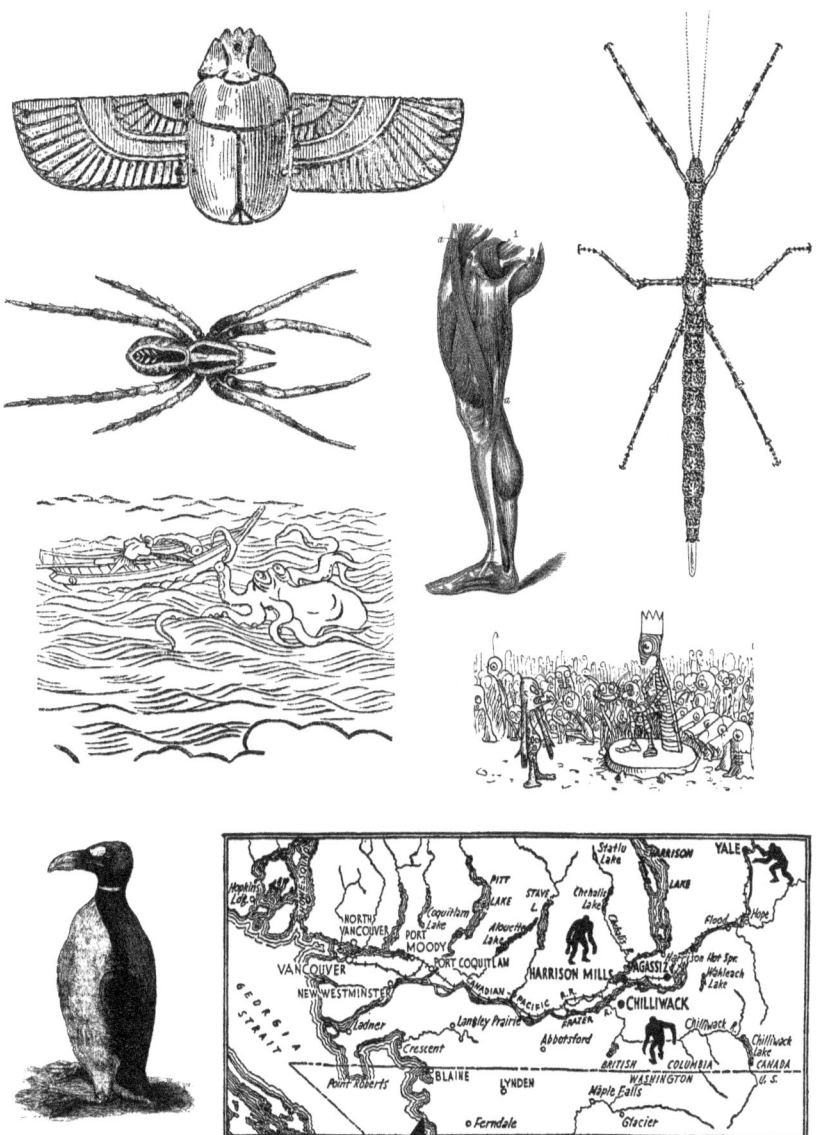

COACHWHIP PUBLICATIONS

ALSO AVAILABLE

Supernatural Detectives 1:
Carnacki / John Bell
ISBN 1-61646-086-5

COACHWHIP PUBLICATIONS

ALSO AVAILABLE

Supernatural Detectives 2:
Aylmer Vance / Morris Klaw
ISBN 1-61646-086-5

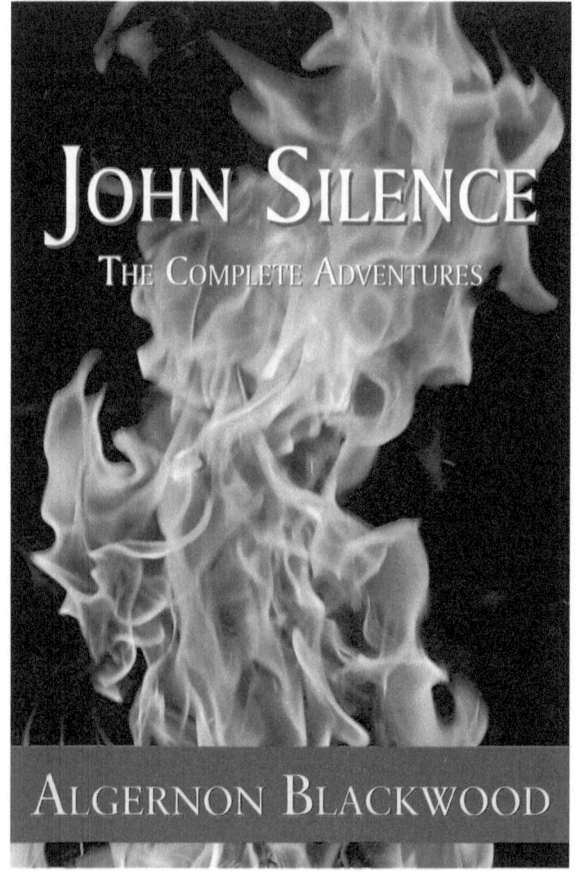

COACHWHIP PUBLICATIONS

ALSO AVAILABLE

Ancient Haunts
ISBN 1-61646-005-9

2 Detectives:
Average Jones / Dr. Furnivall
ISBN 1-61646-098-9